PRAISE FOR BETHANY TURNER

"The winsome charm Turner creates in the small mountain town of Adelaide Springs will have you researching vacation rentals long before the book's end! It's the best written small town I've read in decades. Sparky, fun, and offbeat in all the right ways."

—NICOLE DEESE, AWARD-WINNING AUTHOR OF *BEFORE I CALLED YOU MINE*, FOR *BRYNN AND SEBASTIAN HATE EACH OTHER*

"Set in a charming small town and populated by well-developed, believable characters, *Brynn and Sebastian Hate Each Other* is a thoughtful and often tender exploration of two wounded souls seeking redemption and learning to trust again. I couldn't get enough of Bethany Turner's witty banter or the loyal found-family and sweet nostalgia threaded throughout this delightful story. A must-read for lovers of romantic comedy with healthy doses of pop-culture, humor, and depth . . ."

—JULIE CHRISTIANSON, AUTHOR OF *THE MOSTLY REAL MCCOY* AND *THAT TIME I KISSED THE GROOMSMAN GRUMP*

"From the moment I heard the title and saw the cover, I knew I NEEDED to read this book. And if you are someone who loves quirky small town settings, enemies to lovers, and crisp, delightful prose, you do too! You'll be rooting for Brynn and Sebastian, not just as a couple, but as two people in need of a little redemption and maybe a life reset. This is a romcom that brings some real depth and development, but will also leave you smiling. Longtime fans of Bethany Turner and new readers alike will love this one!"

—EMMA ST. CLAIR, *USA TODAY* BESTSELLING AUTHOR

"Bethany Turner has a magical, effortless way with words, and *Brynn and Sebastian Hate Each Other* showcases this perfectly! You also get an adorable small town, enemies to lovers vibes, and all the feels you expect when two protagonists figure out themselves as they figure out each other. Add in a cast of unique and delightful secondary characters, and you get a feel-good story sure to delight and entertain."

—JENNY PROCTOR, AUTHOR OF *HOW TO KISS YOUR BEST FRIEND*

"Readers who haven't yet discovered the savvy, comedic rom-coms of award-winning author Bethany Turner are in for a treat with her latest second chance romance, *The Do-Over* . . . While romantic comedy may not be the genre for every reader, many will enjoy this light-hearted escape, especially anyone looking to drift away with a well-paced, feel-good story."

—*NEW YORK JOURNAL OF BOOKS*

"Pitch-perfect comedic timing, a relatable heroine, and a refreshing sweetness elevate this novel above the sea of modern rom-coms. The rare author who can make me laugh out loud, *The Do-Over* is Bethany Turner at her best."

—LAUREN LAYNE, *NEW YORK TIMES* BESTSELLING AUTHOR

"For anyone who's ever questioned the path they've chosen, Bethany Turner's *The Do-Over* offers a heart-warming look at what happens when life goes off-script. She takes that old saying 'People plan and God laughs' and runs with it in the most entertaining and endearing fashion. A sweet and satisfying read."

—MELONIE JOHNSON, *USA TODAY* BESTSELLING AUTHOR

"A charming and delightful story of what-ifs, second chances, and discovering what you really want. *The Do-Over* pulled me right in from the get-go and had me grinning all the way to happily ever after."

—KATE BROMLEY, AUTHOR OF *TALK BOOKISH TO ME*

"Bethany Turner has crafted a delightful, witty story with zippy dialogue, warmly relatable characters, and hilariously apt pop-culture references. I found myself sneaking off to read just one more chapter. I'm still smiling thinking about this book. Reading *The Do-Over* felt like eating a big bowl of Lucky Charms mixed with Fruity Pebbles. A colorful explosion of happy. ;)"

—RACHEL LINDEN, BESTSELLING AUTHOR
OF *THE ENLIGHTENMENT OF BEES*

"Turner crafts an entertaining rom-com that spans ten years and keeps the reader guessing who will claim the heroine's heart . . . As the slow-burn romantic mystery of who Olivia will end up with builds to an amusing and satisfying conclusion, Olivia's witty narration will hold readers' attention. This is a treat."

—*PUBLISHERS WEEKLY*, FOR *PLOT TWIST*

"Turner's humorous latest has an enjoyable New Adult vibe . . . There is a happily ever after, but not the one most readers will be expecting."

—*LIBRARY JOURNAL*, FOR *PLOT TWIST*

"*Plot Twist* gave my rom-com loving heart everything it could hope for: pop-culture references, frequent laugh-out-loud lines, an enduring friendship, a determined heroine to root for, and (of course) a love story with plenty of twists and turns. A sweet, funny read about the many kinds of love in our lives, perfect for anyone who loves love or dreams about meeting George Clooney."

—KERRY WINFREY, AUTHOR OF *WAITING FOR TOM HANKS*

"With a decade-long span of pop-culture fun, playful romantic possibilities, and the soul-deep friendships that push us to be real, *Plot Twist* is everything a reader has come to adore from Bethany Turner . . . plus so much more!"

—NICOLE DEESE, AWARD-WINNING AUTHOR
OF *BEFORE I CALLED YOU MINE*

"Funny, clever, and sweet, *Plot Twist* reminds us that sometimes love doesn't look just like the movies—and that it can be so, so much better than we ever dreamed."

—MELISSA FERGUSON, BESTSELLING AUTHOR OF *THE CUL-DE-SAC WAR*

"Bethany Turner just keeps getting better! *Plot Twist* is like experiencing the best parts of all my favorite rom-coms, tied together with Turner's pitch-perfect comedic timing, an achingly sweet 'will they or won't they?' romance, and the BFF relationship most girls dream of. Add in some Gen-X nostalgia, and you have a book you'll want to wrap yourself up in and never leave."

—CARLA LAUREANO, RITA AWARD–WINNING AUTHOR OF
THE SATURDAY NIGHT SUPPER CLUB AND *PROVENANCE*

"With a sassy Hallmark-on-speed hook and a winning leading lady, Turner loans her fresh, inimitable voice to her strongest offering yet: a treatise on how love (and the hope for love) paints across a canvas of fate and happenstance, and how life undercuts our expectations only to give us the biggest romantic adventures."

—RACHEL McMILLAN, AUTHOR OF *THE LONDON
RESTORATION*, FOR *PLOT TWIST*

BRYNN AND SEBASTIAN HATE EACH OTHER

BRYNN AND SEBASTIAN HATE EACH OTHER: A LOVE STORY

BETHANY TURNER

THOMAS NELSON
Since 1798

This one goes out to my dad, who has insisted for years that I would achieve instant superstardom if I wrote about a dog. I created Murrow just to (lovingly and respectfully) shut him up, but ultimately Murrow was the key to understanding Sebastian. So . . . thanks, Dad. (Disclaimer: Dedication is contingent upon superstardom status. The author reserves the right to retroactively bestow this dedication upon Paul Rudd.)

Brynn and Sebastian Hate Each Other

Published in Nashville, Tennessee, by Thomas Nelson. Thomas Nelson is a registered trademark of HarperCollins Christian Publishing, Inc.

Thomas Nelson titles may be purchased in bulk for educational, business, fundraising, or sales promotional use. For information, please email SpecialMarkets@ThomasNelson.com.

Publisher's Note: This novel is a work of fiction. Names, characters, places, and incidents are either products of the author's imagination or used fictitiously. All characters are fictional, and any similarity to people living or dead is purely coincidental.

Library of Congress Cataloging-in-Publication Data

Names: Turner, Bethany, 1979- author.
Title: Brynn and Sebastian hate each other / Bethany Turner.
Description: Nashville, Tennessee: Thomas Nelson, [2023] | Summary: "Beloved author Bethany Turner returns with a hilarious enemies-to-lovers rom-com, packed with snappy pop-culture references, earnest small-town politicians, and enough heart to make anyone want to go back for seconds"—Provided by publisher.
Identifiers: LCCN 2023005698 (print) | LCCN 2023005699 (ebook) | ISBN 9780840706874 (TP) | ISBN 9780840706881 (epub) | ISBN 9780840706898 (audio download)
Subjects: LCGFT: Romance fiction. | Christian fiction. | Novels.
Classification: LCC PS3620.U76 B79 2023 (print) | LCC PS3620.U76 (ebook) | DDC 813/.6—dc23/eng/20230210
LC record available at https://lccn.loc.gov/2023005698
LC ebook record available at https://lccn.loc.gov/2023005699

Printed in the United States of America

23 24 25 26 27 LBC 5 4 3 2 1

CHAPTER 1

BRYNN

FRIDAY, MARCH 18
8:45 a.m. Eastern Daylight Time

"Coming up in the third hour of *Sunup*, Elena and Hayley are going to sit down with a few of the heroic women and men who were on the ground fighting last month's tragic wildfires in the Sierra Nevadas. So many amazing stories, Mark."

"There really are, Brynn. So many unsung triumphs among the heartbreaking devastation."

"And later, Lance will be joined in the kitchen by one of the queens of the Hallmark channel, Lacey Chabert. I hear they'll be cooking up a batch of Lance's perennial game-day favorites—sweet-and-spicy fried plantains. Yum! I may just have to stick around for hour three today, Mark. How about you?"

"If not for the plantains, then for the inside scoop on the first round of NCAA March Madness, courtesy of ASN's Ellis Haywood. Have you been keeping up with ASN's behind-the-scenes coverage on Facebook, Brynn? It's really been a lot of fun."

"Well, no, I haven't, Mark. But I *have* been keeping up on TikTok."

Mark laughed . . . just as the teleprompter told him to. "Oh, I get it. I see how we're playing this today. Subtle, Brynn. Very subtle."

I feigned innocence. "Whatever do you mean?"

The crew in the studio laughed, just loud enough to be heard perfectly on-air in the background. They didn't have to be told when to laugh. After years in the business, they could sense the exact moment to make their off-camera presence known, to help our viewers believe we really were just a big, happy family they invited into their living rooms each morning.

"It's no secret I'm the elder statesman around here." Mark threw his hands in front of him in surrender. "Guilty as charged!"

"I'm not giving up until I get you on TikTok." I strategically faced the camera. "Don't you want to see Mark Irvine on TikTok, America?" Mark laughed and shook his head as I read my next lines. "You would *crush* some of those dances, Mark. I just know it!"

It was probably as clear to all of America as it was to me that our producers were gearing up for some megalaunch onto TikTok for Mark. Probably during sweeps. And indeed, America was going to love it. Was Mark truly going to crush it? That was much less certain. In fact, they would probably play up his elder statesman persona and allow him—nay, force him—to humiliate himself for the amusement of millions.

I'd been making bets with myself over which long-obsolete trends they would subject the poor man to first. Would it be that bottle-flipping thing that had been so popular with teenaged boys forever ago? Nah . . . that was too lame, even for Mark Irvine. Besides, as much as he professed obsession with March Madness coverage, I'd witnessed the effort he had to put forth in sports segments. The effort he had to put forth for anything that required more hand-eye coordination than it took to avoid jabbing a microphone into his own eye, really. Bottle flipping would not go well for him.

They'd probably make him film something like the first-name challenge or one of the other trends that had been popular among middle-aged adults whose teenagers fled TikTok the moment their parents set up an account. Yeah . . . that was probably the low-impact effect they would go for. He'd "surprise" his wife by calling her by her name (Lulabelle, I think?) instead of "Bunny"—the name *Sunup* audiences had been hearing him refer to her as for fifteen years. They'd eat it up. Mark Irvine had turned his hokey-dad personality into an art form, despite the fact that at—what? forty-seven?—he was only about a decade older than me. Yet here I was, cast in the role of the young, trendy ingenue.

Morning audiences were great about accepting whatever twenty-first-century version of a Norman Rockwell painting you threw at them. And you wouldn't hear the thirty-six-year-old trendy ingenue complaining.

Mark's charming, self-effacing monologue came to an end on the teleprompter, and I refocused my eyes on the words that began next to my name.

"I know what trend would be perfect for you, Mark. *The Rockafeller Skank*!!"

I hadn't been listening or following along with whatever Mark had been saying, but it didn't matter. I didn't have any trouble faking the enthusiasm the two exclamation points were intended to help me feign. Yes. *The Rockafeller Skank* was absolutely the only-trendy-among-TikTok-users-with-a-handsome-401k trend they would make him start with. Ballroom dancing to an annoying, repetitive dance beat from a few years before Billie Eilish was born? What's not hip about that? Yeah, it had Mark Irvine written all over it.

Mark's featurelessly handsome face morphed into an expression of good-natured horror. "Rockafeller . . . what?" He continued to play his part perfectly, and I couldn't help but wonder if it was possibly not just an act. Perhaps he had done what no one else on earth had been able to accomplish: he'd somehow lived nearly fifty years on this planet free of both TikTok and Fatboy Slim.

I laughed sweetly at his "scripted" cluelessness and patted him on the arm. "Don't worry about it, Mark. I have a very, *very* strong suspicion this will all make sense to you very soon." I patronizingly patted again, and the crew laughed to perfection.

"I'll trust you on that, Brynn." He shrugged for the benefit of the camera and then carried on with his lines. "Now, before we hand things off to Elena, Hayley, and Lance, I want to say, on behalf of all of us—on behalf of the entire *Sunup* fam, tuning in all across the nation—what a joy it has been to finally have you seated next to me on this couch. It's been a long time coming."

"Has it? For me, the last ten years have flown by," I responded. Because that's what the teleprompter told me to say. Never mind that I could have told stories for days about being passed over for the "fresh face" or "up-and-comer." About the "good old boy" guys from the network's club of safe, boring, demographic-approved men like Mark filling the rotating vacant seat on the couch while I kept working hard and paying my dues and smiling sweetly when network executives dangled the "your day is coming" carrot in front of me to keep me happy. "I feel like every seat I've been blessed enough to sit in here at *Sunup*, no matter the hour and no matter the role, has been as cozy as it could possibly be. And I loved every single minute of my time in the third hour."

Mark nodded. "I know that Elena and Lance are going to miss you dearly."

Well, now, that simply wasn't true at all. It was one thing to serve one's time. To earn one's keep and prove one's worth. To invest the time and effort it took to become an invaluable asset.

It was another thing entirely to spend five years on a couch with Elena Delgado, pretending to be besties while the cameras were rolling and skillfully avoiding every attempt she made to sabotage my career when they weren't.

And Lance . . . Well, he had just never liked *anyone*.

But the lies came so easily once you knew how to play the game.

I clasped my hands over my heart and squished up my face like I was watching a baby bunny rabbit eating a carrot. Then I spoke into the camera. "You guys! Thank you. For everything." I knew this was what they all wanted from me. What the public wanted to believe. They wanted to believe—they *did* believe—that Elena and Lance were watching from the studio next door with tears in their eyes, cheering me on and making plans for our Sunday brunch together. "I love my fam, so much." I curled my fingers in front of me and made a heart. "And of course that fam just got bigger and better, with the addition of Hayley Oswell to the *Sunup3* couch. Isn't Hayley just a stellar addition to the fam, Mark?"

Convincing viewers I loved the *Sunup* fam was the job. I would continue to do it each and every morning and every single time I spoke to the press, forever and ever, without complaint. But I had just about reached my limit on concealing the disdain I felt every time they made me say the word *fam*. One time—*one time!*—two years ago I had read what was on the prompter, not realizing they had abbreviated what they actually intended for me to say: "Happy holidays from our *family* to yours." Ever since, #SunupFam had been our official hashtag, sunupfam.com was our website, the *Sunup* Fam Reunion was the name of our annual fan gathering in Washington Square Park, and you could purchase *One Big Happy Fam* shirts in the network store.

Fine. But did we really have to work it into every sentence?

"She really is, Brynn. And I speak for all of us—our little fam here and the entire extended *Sunup* fam—when I say we're so glad Hayley made her way to *Sunup3* and that you've made your way to hours one and two."

"Aww, thanks. I certainly have big shoes to fill." Considering my predecessor, Shauna Magwell-Moray, seemed to give birth every ten months, it seemed likely that was a physiological fact. Though, from what I heard, it wasn't her ever-swollen ankles that had caused her to be replaced so much as the fact that she and Mark had the on-screen chemistry of a piece of chalk and a marshmallow.

"We'll certainly miss Shauna around here, but our loss is Trevor and the kids' gain. Shauna texted me just this morning to say how nice it was to join Trevor in the school drop-offs all week."

Okay, yeah. Sure she had. Former Miss America Shauna Magwell-Moray had texted Mark Irvine, with whom she had worked unhappily for all of six months, to tell him she and her NHL goalie husband—who, I was pretty sure, lived on the road this time of year—were running their kids to school together every morning.

There was just a certain suspension of disbelief that accompanied being a devoted *Sunup* viewer.

"That's so nice for them, Mark."

I glanced at the clock in the corner of the screen next to Orly at camera one. Six minutes? We still had six minutes left? How much more schmaltzy tripe were they going to make us subject America to on a Friday morning?

Mark shifted toward me and camera three. "We have a surprise for you, Brynn. This won't be on newsstands until next week, but the verdict is in." He held up an advance copy of *People* magazine. "'America's Ray of Sunshine: Shining Brighter Than Ever,'" he said, reading the title superimposed above my photo.

Ugh. "America's Ray of Sunshine." There was nothing in life that I simultaneously treasured and loathed as much as that designation. It's not like it was clever or original in any way, shape, or form. But for whatever reason, it had stuck. It was how I'd been introduced at the White House Correspondents' Dinner, it was the title of a memoir I'd been paid six figures to write (of which I had yet to write a single word, incidentally), and it would probably be the epitaph on my headstone. America loved me and felt like they knew me. *Fantastic.* If there was anyone left who *didn't* love me, surely reminding them over and over that I was just a happier version of them—*People* magazine, White House Correspondents' Dinner, and six-figure book deal aside, of course—would do the trick. Right?

"Would you look at that?" I pretended to humbly marvel at the "surprise" magazine cover that I had posed for. "Thanks, *People* magazine. And thank you, Mark. I have to admit, after some of the rustier bits this week, I thought you might want to cart me off to a less public hour of *Sunup.* I really think we're missing out on a key middle-of-the-night demographic, come to think of it. Don't you think I would *kill* as the host of *Sunup2am?*"

There it was. *That* was what made me "America's Ray of Sunshine" in the minds of the network suits. The gleeful, good-humored self-deprecation that made everyone believe I was just happy to be there. That was my trademark. As if I ever had the opportunity to say a single word that wasn't written for me. As long as they *scripted* me as self-deprecating, that's who I was. No matter that, as a result, I never got to draw attention to my own accomplishments and instead had to act embarrassed whenever someone else pointed them out. No matter that *Sunup* seemed to have perfected a business model that had apparently been crafted while June Cleaver was cleaning the house in heels. It worked. Viewers across all mediums were insisting on diversity. They were rallying around strong, independent women. But here at *Sunup,* our favorite pastime was choosing not to care how Little Ricky was conceived from two separate twin beds.

"You're being too hard on yourself!" Mark replied with a laugh. "As for the 'rustier bits,' some of those names are really difficult to pronounce."

My eyes caught the monitor, which was currently focused in on the death glare I had received from Turkish president Recep Tayyip Erdogan when I'd pronounced his name with all the enunciation skills of a drive-thru window.

Of course. They were going to wrap up my first week as the cohost of the number one morning show in the world with a blooper reel. Why not? What could be better than humiliating me for the sake of uniting three and a half million live viewers—not to mention another ten million or so later online—in laughter? Laughter that they no doubt believed would further endear me to America but that I suspected would inch me ever closer to the role of lovable-but-inconsequential morning dingbat.

Mark adjusted his position on the couch next to me so he could offer me a good-humored sideways glance. "It is true, though, that it hasn't *all* been smooth sailing this week."

In response I covered my eyes with both hands and shook my head dramatically. I also laughed, of course. I had no choice but to laugh.

"Oh no," I groaned and then took a moment to silently rehearse the next two words from the teleprompter before saying them aloud. "Chiwetel Ejiofor has forgiven me, Mark." *Nailed it.* "Don't you think the noble thing would be for *you* to let me off the hook as well?"

"Noble, yes," Mark replied. "But not nearly as fun."

The red light on the camera directly in front of us shut off as a monitor began rolling footage of the multitude of blunders I had made in five short days.

"Don't worry," Mark whispered to me and straightened his tie once we were no longer being filmed. "Audiences eat this stuff up.

Your mistakes make them see you as human. And once they see you as human, they can decide whether or not they trust you and want to spend time with you."

"That's what I'm afraid of," I muttered.

"You've just got to be a good sport."

I looked down at the hemline of my skirt and made a small adjustment. Just enough to keep my eyes concealed while I rolled them into the back of my head.

"Oh, I think I've got the good-sport thing down. No worries there."

"*There* it is." Mark chuckled as the clip of me stepping into a mountain of elephant dung at the Central Park Zoo flashed across the screen. "That's my favorite."

At least Chiwetel Ejiofor had laughed and charmingly insisted I continue to call him Chai-WET-ul for the remainder of the interview. My Jimmy Choos and I had yet to make amends.

"Fifteen seconds," the new production assistant shadowing Carl at camera two called out. Carl whacked the production assistant on the shoulder and pointed to the clock, causing him to yell out, "Five seconds! Sorry!"

"Colton!" Mark called out to our director with an impatient groan, and we each sat up a little straighter and perfected the angle at which his gray-slacked knees and my pantyhose-encased ones faced each other.

Colton raised his hands in acknowledgment before shouting, "Carl!" in the second before the red light illuminated once more. Poor Carl. It wasn't his fault the new guy under his skilled tutelage kept looking at the wrong clock. Even I had to admit the main stage of studio 2-A was a confusing place to be, timewise. Sunday night, before my first episode, I'd dreamt that all the different digital clocks—ticking down until we were live, ticking up until commercials ended, and in some cases communicating something only Colton seemed to understand about local affiliates versus the network—were accompanied by the theme music from *24*. When my 3:30 a.m. alarm clock went off, I woke up in a panic, certain I had prevented Jack Bauer from saving the world because I couldn't remember my employee code for the Xerox machine before the day ran out.

"I think everyone will agree, Brynn, that you didn't take long to make a mark here on *Sunup*." Mark carried on as Carl indecipherably lectured the protege who got him yelled at.

"Do you mean *me* or the footprints I left behind after we got back in the van at the zoo?"

"Both!"

We laughed together in that way only two coworkers who barely know each other but are trying to convince America they are the nearest and dearest of friends can.

"Well, regardless," I resumed, reading the continuation of our "spontaneous" witty banter. "This week has been one I'll never forget. I'm grateful to you, Mark, for being so welcoming. You've shared this couch with so many legendary cohosts through the years, and I know that each one of them no doubt felt as I do now—honored and more than a little bit awestruck to be sitting here next to you."

Oh, give me a break. Awestruck? Mark is a nice enough guy, but have we forgotten that his storied career was launched by "Pet Disasters with Mark-Paul Irvine" on a public television station in Cleveland? Or, for that matter, that he was Mark-Paul Irvine until Zack Morris from Saved by the Bell *beat him to stardom?*

"And to you, the viewers . . . I can't tell you what it means to this homespun, small-town girl to know you've put out the welcome mat." *Not this again.* "Growing up in the precious, rural community I call home, I just never dreamed that one day I'd get to become friends with all of you. People from every walk of life, all across this great nation of ours. I couldn't be more grateful."

"And we're grateful for *you*, Brynn. And speaking of dynamic duos—"

Were we, though?

New Guy scrolled the lines in front of us. And scrolled. I'm not sure where Mark's line had come from, but it was gone in a flash. And then *all* of it was gone in a flash, leaving a black screen in front of us.

Mark froze.

Oh, poor New Guy. The next time I saw him he would be Unemployed Guy, I suspected. Maybe Zamboni Driver at Madison Square Garden Guy.

In less than two seconds of awkward dead-air time, Colton whisper-yelled at Carl and Carl shoved New Guy out of the way, leaving camera two unmanned so he could take over at the teleprompter, while I heard an urgent "Brynn! Get us to break!" in my earpiece.

And yet, no one seemed to have any concerns about the fact that our cagey veteran, the senior man on the morning news-entertainment team at the highest-rated network in the country, was sitting there speechless and shuffling next to me, completely undone by the lack of a script and a hiccup in production.

Before we'd hit the three-second mark on any of those clocks, I smiled at the red light on camera four. "Dynamic duos besides us, you mean?" Camera four was awkward at the angle we were sitting, but Orly at camera one was geared up and ready to go to Maria at the news desk, and everyone else was caught up in the complete meltdown of broadcasting professionals in the middle of the room. Seriously, how many people did it take to make sure Mark Irvine knew how to say goodbye? The world's oldest-living triplets were probably still in the building after our interview with them. Maybe we could call them in too.

"That other dynamic duo, Elena and Hayley, are making their

way to *their* couch, so it's almost time for us to hop back in the *Sunup*mobile and head back to the *Sunup*cave." I patted Mark on the shoulder and nudged him to turn to our right and focus on camera four with me. "But we'll see everyone again soon, right, Mark? Same *Sunup* time . . ."

Mark nodded at the camera and grinned. "Too right. We'll be back to wrap up right after this from your local station."

Same Sunup *channel. Same* Sunup *channel! How much more perfectly could I have possibly lobbed that pitch to him?*

The light on camera four went off, and I exhaled and relaxed against the back of the couch. "Yikes," I muttered to Mark. "Who needs coffee with adrenaline bursts like that?"

He stood up in a huff and shouted to the ever-growing huddle. "Colton!"

I glanced at Colton, who responded to Mark's bellowing with a forced smile for his star. "I know, Mark. Sorry about that. We're working on it."

Greta hurried over to me with powder for my nose. I felt the trickles of sweat running down my back, undoubtedly ruining a perfectly-gorgeous-five-minutes-ago Jason Wu silk blouse, and I had no doubt my face was showing the perspiration just as much.

"Eddie had the bad luck of antiquated equipment taking its last breath in one of the first moments he had actual responsibility," Greta informed me quietly with a pained expression on her face.

"Who's Eddie?" Mark asked as Deb touched up his face. Without makeup, the man had the complexion of Dr. Bunsen Honeydew.

"Eddie," I stated calmly. "The new production assistant."

No, I hadn't known New Guy's name either, but if you weren't even capable of using context clues, you deserved to be shown up in front of the crew, at least a little bit.

Not that Mark was only shown up a little *bit today.*

Greta fluffed my hair and winked at me before backing away. I smiled back at her, as humbly as I could, straightened my skirt, and prepared for one final sign-off segment.

"So I bet you're actually from Philadelphia or somewhere, aren't you?"

I did a double take toward Mark. "I'm sorry?"

He looked down at the lapel of his suit jacket and picked off a minuscule piece of lint. "You're always talking about your small town, rural roots—"

"I do seem to do that a lot, don't I?" I grimaced.

"I get it. It works. I just think you could stand to tone it down a bit. It was cute when you were third hour, but we cover serious news here." He looked over at me and grinned, and I resisted the temptation to remind him we'd built a snowman with the Biebers on Tuesday.

"You know as well as I do, Mark, that Colton decides what the audience should know about me. If the down-home thing is what viewers respond to, that's what they're going to have me talk about."

He tsked and tightened the knot of his tie. "Rookie mistake. Yes, you read the lines they give you, but when the camera stops rolling, you must lay down the law. If they want you to be 'down-home' and you refuse, they'll change tack."

He made it sound so simple, but I knew it wasn't. If they wanted me to be "down-home" and I refused, what was to stop them from hiring one of the million other women who wanted my job and didn't mind saying "Aww, shucks" on occasion?

More than anything I wanted to ask Mark what he had refused to be that had caused them to change tack toward Snoozeville. Hip? Cool? Had Mark Irvine stood up in front of the network honchos and blatantly refused to let them exploit him as *interesting*?

But he wasn't trying to be unkind, so I didn't need to be either. He was patronizing, sure, but I perfectly understood the expression on his face and the sentiment behind it. I'd experienced it countless times throughout my career. He was *helping* me. Imparting wisdom. Taking me under his wing. I would never receive any kudos or straight-out gratitude for saving his butt on-air—today or in any of the inevitable days to come—but in his chauvinistic, out-of-date, out-of-touch way, *this* was him saying "Thank you."

And I was expected to say "Thank you" in return.

Colton came running over to us, huffing and puffing like a man wearing Ferragamo loafers and sporting a pocket square was never supposed to. "Great work, you two."

Two?

"I was just telling Brynn she's been going a little over the top with the country-girl routine, but for her first week . . . not too bad. I'll work with her to—"

I accidentally scoffed, interrupting him. I attempted to turn it into a clearing of my throat, but their eyes were already on me.

I patted my chest and coughed as believably as I could without producing phlegm. "Pardon me." I looked over my shoulder and called out, "Greta, could you please get me a lozenge?"

Colton eyed me with concern. "We're back from affiliates in ninety, and then you hand it over to Elena. Can you tough it out for a little longer?"

Oh, forget that. Greta reached into our midst with a tin of lozenges, but I ignored her hand. "I'm fine." My lips tightened into an expression that I hoped could be described as easygoing—but really, I would have settled for anything this side of homicidal. "Do we have a prompter or—"

"Just wing it," the dummy next to me answered before I could offer to break out my amateur ventriloquism skills. "Which camera?"

A voice from the control room boomed over the speakers. "Colton, we've almost got the feed back to the eastern affiliates. Should we key up the other—"

"No!" Colton threw his hands up in the air and spun on his heel. "When did we lose the feed?!" He turned back to us but began backing away toward the increasingly urgent chorus of his name being cried out from every corner of the room. He put the index finger of one hand to his ear and gave us a thumbs-up with the other hand. "Stick with four."

I readjusted my position toward camera four. At least this time I had a little bit of warning and I wouldn't have to twist around into a television broadcasting pose best described as the Linda Blair *Exorcist* Maneuver.

"That was a perfect example. You should have stood up for yourself." Mark was bestowing wisdom upon me once more. "I took your credit. You should have taken it back."

I tilted my head and studied him. What do you know? Maybe Mark Irvine wasn't as clueless as he seemed.

"Yeah, well . . ." I tucked my ankles and knees together and folded my legs into the ladylike position Kate Middleton had taught me when I first met her at Wimbledon. (In return, I had taught her how to use apple cider vinegar as deodorant in a pinch.) "You catch more flies with honey . . . That sort of thing."

He snickered. "Not anymore."

"What do you mean?"

"Honey works—*sometimes*—when you're climbing. I'll give you that. But you've reached the top. You're not climbing anymore. Now it's your job to fight off everyone else who's climbing and clawing for your spot." He adjusted the knot of his tie and then lowered his hands back into their precise position of staged nonchalance. "Viewers might love the farm girl, but people in the business will walk all over her."

He was right, of course. Mostly. Except that I wasn't done climbing. I hadn't even reached the top of the *Sunup* couch yet . . . although it wasn't surprising that in his eyes I had gone as high as

I possibly could. But nothing in me would ever be content peaking as Mark Irvine's happy little sidekick.

I wasn't Robin in our dynamic duo. Someday that would click for him. But not yet. Not today.

"Why *are* they so obsessed with making sure I'm beloved in the heartland?" I asked, meeting him halfway in the mentor/mentee partnership he needed to believe in. "Seriously, they act like I'm from a two-cow town in Oklahoma where Pa tilled the soil and Ma baked apple pie, all day every day."

Everything from the dusty-rose eyeshadow that had tested well with mid-America viewers to the baby animal videos they made me pretend to be obsessed with to the way they made me talk in the early years of *Sunup3* (because seventeen years in the Rocky Mountains followed by four years at the University of Southern California will *totally* lend themselves to developing a southern lilt) had been about making me into who they—they, they, *they*—wanted me to be.

Mark laughed. "Was I right? Philadelphia?"

"Thirty seconds!" a voice called out, and Mark and I focused on camera four.

I shook my head gently, careful not to mess up the cascading waves Greta had perfectly sculpted over my shoulders. "I'm from a little mountain town in Colorado called Adelaide Springs."

"I've never heard of it."

"No one has. It's a tiny, insignificant blip on the map, made up of a few hundred people with about twelve brain cells and forty-two bucks among them."

"Ouch!"

"I'm sorry, but it's true!" I giggled but didn't move my face out of the camera-ready smile. "They're obsessed with colonial times—" I felt his eyes snap to me for just a second before looking back to camera four, and the corner of my mouth twitched in satisfaction. Mark Irvine was interested in me, even if just for the length of a story about my crazy hometown. It was only week one, but I was pretty sure he already found me more interesting than he'd ever found Shauna Magwell-Moray. "Yes. American colonial times. In Colorado. It's so stupid." I rolled my eyes. "My hometown's the worst. I got out the very first chance I had, and I've never looked back. So let the viewers believe I'm from Iowa or Philadelphia or whatever. Anywhere except that pathetic little town with its pathetic little people. As long as it's all being sold by America's freaking Ray of Sunshine, I'm sure they'll keep buying it."

"Cut the feed! Cut the feed!" Colton yelled from the back of the room, but his voice got closer quickly. "Go straight to the *Sunup3* buffer and tell Elena she'll need to cover the seven extra seconds."

I didn't want to pull my eyes away from camera four, but I also instinctively knew the red light wasn't going to come on.

"Colton, what's—"

He pointed at me to silence me. It worked like a charm. "Don't talk," he muttered, and then he yelled, "No one talk!" We all stared at him, not breathing, I'm pretty sure, as he raised his finger to his ear and closed his eyes. He took a deep breath, and then another, and then said softly, "Nicely done, Elena. I owe you one." His eyes rose slowly until they met mine. "Some people owe you more than that."

"Um . . . Colton?" the previously booming voice from the control room whimpered. "Bob wants to see you in his office."

Colton sighed in response to his summons from the network president. "Yeah. On my way."

Everything was moving in slow motion as the pieces finally began clicking into place. *Cut the feed?* There had been a feed? We had been . . . *live*?

The breath I had been holding released in a gust of words and angst and trembling. "But the light never came on. You told us to stick with four, and we were looking at four the whole time. You . . . *someone* . . . said thirty seconds, and there's no way that was—"

Colton's head was hanging, and then it began shaking from side to side in that horrible "I'm not mad, I'm just disappointed" way that is so much worse than being yelled at. "The whole day was a wreck. I told the control room to stick with four. As in the New York affiliate link—NY4. And thirty seconds was for Elena and Hayley. That's when we went live. It wasn't . . ." He sighed again. "*That part* wasn't your fault. The day was a wreck."

He turned away from us and faced the crew. "That's on me, everyone. We'll, um . . ." He cleared his throat. "We'll sort it out. The wreck's on me." He began walking toward the door but stopped just short of it. He spun on the heels of those Ferragamos one more time, but his entire demeanor had changed. Now he just looked like a dejected teenaged boy trying to fit into his dad's fancy suit for prom. "Brynn?"

"Yeah?"

"I need you to wait for me in my office."

I nodded. "Okay."

My eyes followed Colton until the studio doors closed behind him, and then I turned to seek a little bit of consolation from the other half of the dynamic duo, but he was already off the stage and heading toward his dressing room. And there wasn't a single set of eyes in the room that would meet mine.

Wham, bam, thanks for nothing, fam.

CHAPTER 2

BRYNN

FRIDAY, MARCH 18
10:18 a.m. Eastern Daylight Time

The obnoxiously large grandfather clock in the corner of Colton's office seemed to be losing time. It wasn't, the reasonable side of me knew, but it sure seemed to be. The seconds were ticking on, slower and slower. I'd taken as long as I could getting unmic'd, changing my clothes, and cleaning my face, and still I'd been sitting, waiting, dreading, and absolutely losing my mind for thirty-five minutes.

You'd have thought my phone call with my agent would have killed more time, but it had basically consisted of Robyn saying, "Fix it!" over and over again in a voice vaguely reminiscent of a coyote yipping at a freight train, until she finally hung up with an emphatic "It'll be fine."

I still didn't understand what had happened. Oh, I understood that I'd stepped into a pile of poo bigger than the one Mark had been teasing me about just over an hour earlier, but I was having a difficult time understanding *how* it had happened. One moment

I'd been having a shallow-but-promising bonding moment with my cohost and had been at the top of my game. *So* near the pinnacle of my industry. And the next, the security guard outside the studio was avoiding my eyes as he held the door for me.

"Hey, Brynn." Colton greeted me wearily as he walked through the door of his office. "Sorry that took so long." Before closing the door, he called out to his assistant, "Please hold my calls, Claudia."

I'd startled when he entered, and my cell phone fell out of my shaky hands. I'd been holding it loosely, trying to muster up the courage to google myself and ultimately being too much of a coward.

"That's fine." *Fine.* Robyn probably hadn't believed in the word when she used it any more than I did now. I reached down and grabbed my phone from the floor and stuffed it into my jeans pocket as I stood from the leather couch.

He sat on the other end and left plenty of room for me to sit back down and join him if I so chose. I did. I wasn't sure how long my knees would last standing.

"Colton, I'm so sorry. I didn't know we were live." I rolled my eyes at myself. *Yeah, I think that much was obvious.* "I mean, I really thought you told us to stick with camera four . . . Not that I'm blaming you. I'm not. I just hope you know I never would have said what I said . . ." *Again, obvious.*

What *wasn't* obvious, at least to me, was how much of what I said had made it to air. The only thing more frightening than what people were saying about me was what *I* had actually said. For about half a second I had comforted myself with the possibility that only the tail end had been broadcast before Colton cut the feed, but then I remembered that the tail end was the part where I essentially called our viewers gullible dimwits for believing I was a good person. There was no bright side here.

I cleared my throat. "Colton . . . how much of what I said—"

"From Elena and Hayley's thirty-second cue on."

I was pretty sure I was already sitting down, so why did it feel like I was falling?

"So when I said that stuff about twelve brain cells and forty bucks . . ."

"It was forty-*two* bucks, but yeah. Clear as a bell."

In an instant, my legs catapulted me up from the couch just as my throat seized and the air I was attempting to breathe got caught somewhere between my throat and my lungs. I released a very undignified honking sound from my mouth—maybe from my nose . . . who could say?—and my eyes flew open in terror and panic. Maybe because I couldn't breathe. Maybe because I'd just perfected the mating call of the Canada goose. Or maybe, just maybe, because I'd known it was bad. Now I knew how nice just "bad" would have been.

"Hey, hey, hey." Colton jumped up and flew over to me. He wrapped one arm around my shoulders and squeezed my arm. "Breathe. Come on. Nice and slow. In and out." He began demonstrating, and I was grateful. Turns out I'd forgotten how that was supposed to work. "In and out. That's good. Keep going. In . . ." Deep breath in. "And out . . ." Deep breath out.

He repeated the process several more times for me, and I tried to focus on a framed photo of his family on the table in front of us as he patted my back gently. They were at Disney World. Colton's wife and their three daughters, who looked to be preteens at the time, laughing at Colton, who was wearing one of those Goofy hats with the ears hanging low and two buckteeth protruding from the cap. The Epcot ball glistened behind them, but nothing else was happening in the picture.

Those laughs. That ridiculous smile on my boss's face. It was all fueled by the five of them being together.

"I bet you're a really good dad." My voice was raspy and my

breath ragged, but I felt like I was in control once again. Of breathing, anyway.

He followed my eyes and then smiled as he patted me on the back one final time and pulled away. He guided me back to my spot on the couch and said, "I hope so."

"How old are your daughters now?"

He sighed. "Skye is twenty-four, Roma is twenty-two, and Lizzie's nineteen. She's finishing up her first year at University of Southern California."

I looked at him in surprise. Maybe because I hadn't known— I'd certainly never bothered to ask—where his daughter was going to school. Maybe because I never would have suspected that a simple thing like the name of my alma mater would stabilize me and give me something to grab on to. "I went to USC." My voice sounded deceptively normal once again.

"I know." He chuckled. "And believe me, Lizzie *certainly* knows."

My eyebrow quirked. "Why's that?"

"She wants to *be* you. The only thing that has made me cool to her over the course of the past couple years is the fact that I work with you."

"Are you saying she's going to USC *because* I went there?"

He shrugged. "Let's just say it gave her one more in a compelling list of reasons to move to the complete other side of the country rather than go to NYU or Columbia, as her mother and I would have preferred." He grinned, and I was surprised to discover I didn't detect any sadness in it. "She wants to be in television news, God help her. Paige and I couldn't argue with the quality of the broadcast journalism program there, even if we wanted to."

He crossed to the small refrigerator behind his desk and walked back with two bottles of water. He leaned forward and pushed one toward me on the table as he sat back down. I grabbed the bottle and began greedily gulping as I stared at the photo of Colton's family. Lizzie Passik, whom I'd never met in my life, wanted to emulate my career path. Or at least she *had*, as of when her dad left for work that morning. Hoda Kotb had gone to Virginia Tech. Maybe they were still accepting enrollments there.

"What do I do now, Colton?"

He sighed and leaned forward, resting his elbows on his knees. "I'm not exactly sure. I think I've got Bob convinced, at least for now, that we can't fire you."

My eyes widened. "Bob wanted to fire me?"

He tilted his head and released a humorless chuckle. "Did you seriously not realize that would have to be an option on the table?"

Droplets clung to my lashes as I lowered my gaze and focused my eyes on my clenched hands, squeezing my knees. "I guess I hadn't gotten that far yet."

Fired. I'd never been fired in my life. In fact, I'd never left a single job I'd ever had for any reason other than to move onward and upward to a better opportunity. But there wasn't a better opportunity in the entire industry for someone who got fired for cause from *Sunup*.

I sniffed. "Thanks for talking him out of it."

"Trust me, it would be easier if we *did* fire you." He released a heavy sigh. "But we've got too much invested."

He didn't have to explain what he meant by that. The last two months had been an endless barrage of photo shoots, interviews, appearances, and hype. Hype, hype, hype. The stars of every show on the network had recorded promos welcoming me to *Sunup*. Fashion designers from all over the world sent original creations in my size, vying to get me to wear their clothes on-air. And Ben & Jerry's had launched Sunup Sundae just the day before. My face was on a gazillion pints of ice cream. Yeah . . . a lot had been invested.

I implored him again. "Tell me what to do."

"Bob recommended I get Hayley to fill in for you for a while. Until we sort it all out."

I liked Hayley Oswell. She had certainly always been nicer to me than Elena had been. Hayley was smart and personable and terrifically charismatic on-screen, and from what I had seen, she'd never used the fact that her daddy was the network president to get her out of the hard work. I had no doubt her day on the main couch would come. I'd imagined she'd sit there with me someday, once I replaced Mark in the top seat, and she and I would make up the first all-female seven o'clock couch in *Sunup* history. But it wasn't her turn yet. And I couldn't take a chance of getting lost in the fray during a particularly intense game of morning television leapfrog.

I cleared my throat and sat up straight. I didn't even take time to wipe away any stray tears on my face. There was no more time to be wasted on any of that stuff.

"I'll make it right, Colton. I'll apologize. We'll explain that the prompter was malfunctioning. That we were short-staffed and the wrong cue got piped into 2-A." I nodded and took a final swig of my water before setting it on the table and standing up. Energy was suddenly coursing through my veins. Hope-fueled energy. "I mean, I know it was bad, but that was a lot to go wrong all at once. People will understand. Don't you think?"

I nodded again, answering my own question as I lifted my thumb to my mouth and began chewing on my fingernail for the first time in twenty years or so. "Yeah. They'll understand. I'm only human, after all. Who hasn't said something they shouldn't? Sure, I did it on a much grander scale, but—"

"They won't trust you. Don't you see? *That's* the problem. Now, whatever you say, they'll just think it's an act."

I shook my head. "No, they won't."

"They *will*, Brynn. Because you just told them it was."

Tears sprang to my eyes again, but I refused to let them fall this time. I blinked rapidly and turned away from him so I could fan my face with my hands. He was right, of course. He was absolutely right. No matter how insincere viewers now believed me to be, it was going to be nearly impossible to convince them that I had been anything less than completely truthful in that accidental moment. That moment when I told them I *didn't* have the natural personality, warmth, and glow of a thousand suns (and that they were all stupid for ever believing that I did).

"Okay, then . . ." I turned back to face him. "There's a way to make lemonade out of this situation. We can talk about the pressures placed on successful women of my generation. On all women. Of *any* generation. Maybe I go away for a little while. Get some rest . . . do some work on myself . . ."

"What are you suggesting? That we send you to rehab?"

"Sure! I'm good with rehab!"

Colton chuckled again, and this time there did actually seem to be a bit of humor behind it. Yeah. This was all *hilarious.*

He pulled his phone from his pocket and quickly clicked around before reading aloud. "'Does anyone else feel like they woke up this morning to discover what big teeth their granny has? At least the wolf was already in Granny's house when Little Red Riding Hood got there. I guess we viewers are pathetic, like she said. We invited the wolf in. #firebrynncornell. There are thousands upon thousands of posts just like that. Or worse." He sighed. "Brynn, if there's a quick and easy fix here, I'm not seeing it. And I'm sure you understand that I can't let you sit on that couch until this dies down. *If* this dies down."

I looked down at my toes and muttered under my breath as the sting of tears and the pressure of keeping them from falling began to shoot bursts of pain through my head.

Colton leaned forward. "I'm sorry, what?"

I cleared my throat and tried to ignore the single tear that had just landed on my canary-yellow Saint Laurent pumps. "I never said the viewers were pathetic."

Just my hometown.

And there it was. The problem. The solution. All wrapped up in 0.925 square miles of beautiful middle-of-nowhere. Adelaide Springs, Colorado—0.925 square miles I hadn't stepped foot into for nearly twenty years; 0.925 square miles I'd sworn to never return to.

Resolve and refusal fought against each other as they each pulsated through my body, warming me and making me queasy, all at the same time. Warmth and queasiness. Yep. That was the dichotomy of home everyone hoped for.

"Do you mind if I . . . ?" Colton asked, a rectangular box in his hands and fatherly concern in his eyes, if I wasn't mistaken. It was similar to the depth that had been evident in his eyes as he talked about his daughters. It was unlike anything I had ever seen in the eyes of adults in the home I grew up in. And in that moment, when my thoughts were stuck in memories void of parental love and kindness, it confused me.

"If you what? What's that?"

"They're called tissues, Brynn. Kleenex." He pulled one from the top and held it out in front of him as he threw the box on the couch. "They're really good for wiping tears. Blowing noses. Squashing the occasional spider. That sort of thing." The left corner of his mouth rose as he dabbed the tissue on my cheek. "It's just that right now you resemble a really creepy goth clown." He pulled back the tissue to show me, and sure enough it had turned black—Tom Ford Ultra Raven, to be exact.

At least I was a creepy clown with impeccable taste in cosmetics. And I was a creepy clown with a plan that I *knew* would work.

"Send me to my hometown, Colton."

He was halfway to the trash bin with the mascara-smeared tissue when he stopped in his tracks. He looked back over his shoulder at me. "What are you talking about?"

"You're right. No one's going to trust me. Those people—the ones saying I should be fired and that they never should have let me into their living rooms every morning—nothing I say will change their minds. But if they see that the people I insulted the most have forgiven me . . ."

He dropped the tissue into the trash and walked back to me. "But *will* they forgive you? The people in your hometown. Surely they won't be super happy to see you after all this. Do you even know anyone there anymore? How long's it been since you've been home?"

How many people could name every single person in their high school graduating class? Their middle names. The names of their parents. What they wanted to be when they grew up. Their favorite song. Their best subjects in school. Whether or not they'd had braces. What they liked on their pizza.

I could.

My senior class was made up of Addie Atwater, Laila Olivet, Wes Hobbes, Cole Kimball, and me. That was it. For the first seventeen years of my life, I'd known everything about each one of them. Laila and Cole had been best friends since birth, Addie and Wes had been in love nearly as long, and I was the fifth wheel. Except I wasn't. We were a well-tuned five-wheeled machine, each wheel dependent on the others. They were my family. The only family I'd ever had, really.

And I hadn't told a single one of them that I was leaving Adelaide Springs and never coming back. I hadn't spoken to a single one of them since.

Now, I didn't know anything. I didn't know if they still lived there, if they were married, if they had kids of their own. And statistics would lead us to believe at least one of them had to be gluten-free or lactose intolerant, right? Did they even eat pizza anymore?

"It's been a lifetime since I've been there. A literal lifetime. I don't know who's there now."

They'd all had plans to get out and go on to bigger and better things, but that town had a way of sinking its teeth into you if you let it. It was like there was a window of opportunity, and if you didn't leave when the window was open, you'd die there. The majority of people—the older generations—seemed perfectly fine with that. Why would they ever want to live or die anywhere else? The five of us had always wondered if the older people were different from us or if they'd just missed their window and somewhere along the line forgotten they'd ever had different dreams. Was that what would become of us if we stuck around?

When my chance to get out came along, I hadn't even turned back long enough to see if the window had closed behind me.

Colton took a deep breath and fell back onto the sofa. "I can't deny it would make for good television, so I don't think I'd have any trouble selling it to Bob. But it would be risky, Brynn. For you, I mean. If it didn't work . . . If viewers didn't buy it . . ."

I nodded. "I know. That would be it."

My mother—the woman who raised me, if that's what you could call it—had predicted I would never amount to anything. That's what she'd said, right? Over and over she'd drilled that into me. She'd been dead for a decade now, but there could be little doubt that her impact and reminders of a life I'd worked hard to forget would still linger there. In that town. In those people.

But she didn't get the last word. She didn't get to whisper "I told you so" or "I knew it" from beyond the grave.

I looked up and met his eyes, already making a mental list of all I needed to do to prepare. At the very top was swinging by the Tom Ford store on Madison Avenue to see if Ultra Raven came in waterproof.

"Set it up, Colton. If I have to go back there in order to escape that town, once and for all, that's what I'm going to do."

CHAPTER 3

SEBASTIAN

FRIDAY, MARCH 18
8:45 a.m. Mountain Daylight Time

Sebastian Sudworth rolled out on his mechanic's dolly from underneath Andi's Dodge pickup truck with flourish, pushing his heel off the cement at the last second to add in a 360-degree spin.

"You sure *look* like you know what you're doing. That should count for something," Andi teased.

"It really should," Sebastian agreed. He stayed on his back and used his motor oil–covered hand as a visor as he squinted up at her, standing directly between him and the early-morning sun. "Having said that, I'd strongly recommend you have Roland swing by and double-check my handiwork."

"Aww, Seb. Don't worry." She threw a towel at him as he stood. "I always do."

He chuckled and wiped off his hands. Truth be told, he thought he was beginning to get the hang of the simple things—changing out fluids and filters, tightening gears, that sort of thing. Roland Cross was a good teacher. Andi Franklin was possibly an even better one, if only because she let her student get his hands dirty.

Adelaide Springs, Colorado, didn't have any Uber or Lyft drivers, but it had Valet Forge, the car fleet Andi had taken over when her husband died of cancer a few years prior. Well, it was generous to call a 2013 Jeep Wrangler, a 2016 Chevy Silverado, and a hideous orange-and-white 1974 Ford Bronco a fleet. Most of their passengers were tourists passing through, staying there just for the night and afraid to drive on the icy mountain roads after dark. Valet Forge employed one full-time driver: Fenton Norris. No one seemed to know exactly how old Fenton was, but Sebastian had noticed he could be counted on for a "When I was your age . . ." story no matter who he was talking to—from seven-year-old regional spelling bee champ Olive Morissey to seventy-something-year-old mayor Doc Atwater.

Neil Pinkton, fresh out of high school, manned the dispatch. Neil was saving up money for college, or maybe just to move to Denver and give city life a try, but Andi would love having him there for as long as it lasted. Before he went the way of the other few Adelaide Springs residents of his generation.

Sebastian picked up shifts a couple times a week—sometimes because Fenton was scheduled to have the night off and sometimes because Fenton forgot he was scheduled to work until after he'd had a couple of beers. Sebastian usually jumped at the chance. He enjoyed chatting with tourists, and it was fun to drive that ugly old Bronco. It was a classic, of course, and getting it out on the mountain roads was Sebastian's go-to trick for experiencing adrenaline and comfort, all at once.

The pickup truck was Andi's personal vehicle, and that morning was the first time she'd allowed Sebastian to try out his developing mechanic skills on it. He felt good about it. He'd feel even better when Andi made it safely home that night—in other words, when she *didn't* go careening into an elk herd because Sebastian had unknowingly cut her brake line or something.

Yeah . . . it would be good for Roland to swing by. Just in case.

"What's on your agenda for today?" Andi asked him as he took a second to stretch his arms over his head and rotate his shoulders. "Heading back to the Bean? Coffee's on me."

The Bean Franklin. Andi's other Revolutionary pun-inspired enterprise.

"I can't. Council meeting."

He hadn't meant to roll his eyes at the mention of that morning's city council meeting, scheduled to begin at nine, but he hadn't fought very hard to prevent it either. Andi's laughter indicated his disdain had slipped through.

"Ah yes. Today's the big vote. How could I have forgotten?"

"Ha! *Vote.* As if the outcome isn't already decided."

"It's going to be good for the town, Seb." The laughter was still in her eyes, but there was a slight hint of lecture in her voice. "There are only a few weeks left of ski season, and Jo's only had a guest or two at the inn every night. At most. What's it going to look like once the season's over? At least bringing back Township Days will get some tourists passing through again."

Township Days. Sebastian didn't understand how anyone in Adelaide Springs kept a straight face when they talked about Township Days. It was the stupidest thing he'd ever heard of in his life.

Apparently, in 1975 an advertisement had run in whatever the 1975 equivalent of *AARP* magazine was, promoting the big upcoming celebration happening in Adelaide Springs, Colorado. The big upcoming four-day celebration with Revolutionary War reenactments on Adelaide Battlefield—where Patriot militia had infamously been defeated by the British after failing to bring the gunpowder in out of the rain, of course. (It was early in the war. They got better.) It was worth celebrating, in 1975 and beyond, because the Massacre at Adelaide Battlefield availed the surviving members of the Fourth New Hampshire Regiment to provide their assistance at the Battle of Bunker Hill. You know . . . any excuse for a parade and a carnival.

The problem, of course, was that the Massacre at Adelaide Battlefield had taken place in Adelaide Township, New Hampshire. Not in Adelaide Springs, Colorado. Obviously. Since Meriwether Lewis and William Clark would have still been toddling around in their colonial nappies at the time.

But when a tour bus of senior citizens back in 1975 showed up to check out the historically inaccurate absurdity, some particularly industrious citizens of Adelaide Springs—suffering from the economic impact of the worst drought in thirty years—made the most of it. It was a ridiculous farce, but they sold it with aplomb for the length of an afternoon.

By the time the country was celebrating the bicentennial the following year, word had spread about the kitschy battle reenactments and butter-churning expertise worthy of Mount Vernon happening in the Centennial State—so nicknamed because of its statehood that didn't come along until one hundred years after the Declaration of Independence.

"But see, Andi, these aren't the types of tourists we want."

She crossed her arms and leaned her shoulder against the wall of the Valet Forge garage. "Why? Do these types of tourists not have money?"

Ah. That old chestnut.

It was the same argument that everyone in town threw at him when he voiced his objections. It was the argument that was going to result in the rest of the city council overruling him three-to-one in today's vote.

He grinned and made his way to the sink beside her to wash his hands. And his arms. His neck, maybe? Good grief. Had he gotten any oil into the truck?

"Yes, they have money. And I know there's something to be said for an immediate influx of cash. I'm not downplaying that. Really." He pumped a handful of the powder soap that always reminded him of elementary school and began scrubbing. "But that won't last long. They'll be here a day. Maybe two."

"It's a four-day festival, Seb."

"Fine. They'll be here four days. And then they'll go home—"

"And tell their friends about this adorable little mountain town that's only forty-five miles from Telluride—"

"Oh, come on! That's as the crow flies, and you know it. It takes four hours to drive to Telluride."

"And they'll tell their friends that this little town had the best mountain views they've ever seen, and the best hospitality, and it would be a delightful scenic detour on a trip to Denver or Vegas or LA—"

"See, that's the thing. That's *not* how it will get communicated." He finished rinsing and grabbed a clean towel from the utility shelf. "They'll tell their friends about all the times they got lost because the signs off the highway were outdated and unclear. They'll talk about how they got stuck in the snow or mud or dust storm or elk migration, and by the time they got to Adelaide Springs, late at night, the two restaurants in town were closed. There was an inn, but by the time they got there, all the rooms were full."

Andi guffawed. "Jo has nine rooms, you know. I'm pretty sure she's *never* sold out." She thought for a moment and then asked in earnest, "You really think the inn will be full?"

Still drying, he turned to face her and rested his hip against the sink. "I don't know, Andi. And that's sort of the point. We don't know what to expect, and we don't know if we're prepared for it, and everyone wants to rush into this thing for September. It just makes no sense. We can't act out of desperation and expect anything better than a mess to clean up on the other side."

She eyed him warily and appeared deep in thought, and he began to feel hopeful that maybe he'd helped one person apply some logic to the situation.

After a few more seconds of silent staring, she shrugged. "If the inn is full, they can just drive on to the next town—"

"Where they have fewer rooms than we do."

"—or to Alamosa. They have plenty of chain hotels in Alamosa. And it's an easy drive since it's interstate almost the whole way."

Why did no one ever realize that when they were arguing these same points with him, over and over, they were actually helping him prove *his* point?

"First of all, it's more than forty miles of interstate, after driving on twenty miles of back roads just to get there. An hour out of the way is a big deal at the end of a long day. But more than that, is that really the first impression we want to give? If our answer for them is going to be to head to Alamosa, why didn't we just encourage them to make reservations there in the first place?"

There was more he wanted to say. More that he *had* said, so many times.

His fellow city councilors—Doc Atwater, Josephine Stoddard, and William Kimball—hadn't given much credence to any of his arguments. Of course he was pretty sure Old Man Kimball had a filter on his hearing aid that made the voices of anyone under sixty indecipherable, so there was no real way to tell what he really thought. Sebastian was convinced he just voted with the majority on every issue so he could get home sooner.

The young guy on the council, at forty, and certainly the new guy, at only a year and a half into his service as opposed to the rest of the council's collective decades, Sebastian always felt like they were just humoring him by even letting him attend meetings. When the citizens of Adelaide Springs had unanimously elected him to fill the council seat vacated by Mabel Morris on the occasion of her eighty-sixth birthday, he'd taken it as a vote of confidence and a desire to embrace progressive leadership. It didn't take him long, however, to realize he'd unknowingly been campaigning for the Ignorance Is Bliss Party, unopposed by any staunch Better You Than Me Party candidates.

Maybe they hadn't realized just how stubborn he could be. Of all the things Sebastian Sudworth could be accused of, he knew that "yes-man" would never be among them. He'd become quite accustomed to sharing his viewpoint—about Township Days or anything else this town got stuck in a rut about—with anyone who would listen. Before, during, and after votes were cast.

They'd called him a hipster for trying to convince Jo Stoddard to start using an online reservation system—which, he feared, was going to be about as likely as convincing the Kardashians to live the rest of their lives off the grid. (He would never stop advocating for both of those things.) They called him a worrywart for insisting that before they even considered bringing back Township Days, they needed to figure out how—and if—they could pay for it. And he was pretty sure Old Man Kimball had called him a communist for suggesting it would be beneficial to conduct studies of the demographics of tourists they hoped to bring to Adelaide Springs rather than casting out the wide net based on niche hospitality data from the bicentennial. (Bill Kimball was also known to call Pat Sajak a communist when there were no vowels left in the puzzle, so he didn't take that particular insult too personally.)

"Okay, then . . . tell me." Andi walked past him and grabbed his down puffer jacket from the hooks on the wall and tossed it to him, then pulled on her own similarly styled coat—in orange as opposed to Sebastian's green. "Who's the ideal tourist in your mind? Since apparently money's not enough."

He was grateful for the follow-up question. He rarely got that far in council meetings.

"We need tourists who would appreciate the beauty and the serenity. There are people out there who are seeking the solitude we can offer. People who will find joy in the opportunity to disconnect and maybe even get lost for a few days. Stressed-out businesspeople seeking inspiration. Families wanting to put down their devices for a day or two. And I know we need money coming into the town soon. Probably sooner than we can get new highway signs and better Wi-Fi in place. I get that. But we've got to find a way to let people know we exist—everything Adelaide Springs *already* has going for it, just as it is. We shouldn't become something we're not to attract people we don't really want. The last thing we should want is to be a joke to people."

"Hey." She raised her hand in protest. "I remember Township Days from when I was a kid. Yes, it was a ridiculous fluke that started it, but it really turned into something special. It *did* attract families. It was a tradition for a lot of people. Everyone took part, doing reenactments, giving presentations, supporting local businesses—"

"Andi, I'm not meaning to be insensitive about it. I'm not." No matter how insensitive he was in the privacy of his own thoughts. "But what was the population then? A thousand? Fourteen hundred?"

"Something like that."

"And now it's 317. There are all of eight local businesses, and the same three or four families own them all. Who's going to do all the work? Is Bill Kimball going to be out there with a musket? I would legitimately fear for our lives. Are Maxine and Mabel going to throw caution and rheumatoid arthritis to the wind and climb ten-foot ladders to hang up banners?"

With a chuckle Andi switched off the lights in the garage and motioned for him to exit through the overhead door. Once he had, she elbowed the control on the wall and followed out after him as the door slowly lowered. They turned left and headed toward downtown.

"I hear you. I do. And there are people who agree with you."

"Like who?"

She zipped up to her neck and then adjusted back down to her collarbone. "You know . . . Laila. Cole, certainly. Jake and Lucinda, I would guess. Me, sort of. Depending on the day. Um . . . Neil, probably."

That was what he figured. His viewpoint had the complacent support of the few adult citizens of Adelaide Springs who'd been born after the Cuban Missile Crisis.

Sebastian sighed. "Well, I guess it doesn't matter. Not as it pertains to today's vote, anyway."

"Maybe they'll surprise you." She laughed at the skepticism on his face and amended her statement. "Maybe *Doc* will surprise you. Common sense tends to ultimately rule the day with Doc."

There was truth—and hope—in that, if nothing else.

He hadn't zipped up as they exited the garage, and a whip of frigid wind rushing up Main Street reminded him of his negligence. "Maybe."

He glanced down at his watch. Eight fifty-four. The city council meeting was to begin in six minutes, but considering that he could look a few feet down the sidewalk and see both Jo's old Range Rover and Doc's '76 Chevy—affectionately named Beulah—still parked in front of the Bean Franklin, he knew he didn't have to rush. They kept walking side by side at a leisurely pace. *Leisurely.* The official speed of Adelaide Springs. There were moments when he almost felt like he had acclimated to it.

"I love this town, Andi. This town . . ." How could he even begin to sum up his feelings for the town and the people in it?

"I know," she responded lightly with a compassionate smile.

"How can . . ." He cleared his throat, hoping his voice would then come out stronger. It didn't work. "How can I stand by and do nothing as the wrong decisions are made? Everyone's too busy living in the past or, at best, living in today. We need to be preparing for the future—making sure there *is* a future."

"No one could ever accuse you of standing by and doing nothing. Waxing philosophical a little too often . . ." She smirked at him with affection. "Now that's a fair accusation."

Andi's smile and Sebastian's eyebrows, peeking up over the collar that had become his barricade against the persistent wind, communicated the same things. Humor. Understanding. Gratitude.

There was a tap from the other side of the picture window of the Bean Franklin, just as they arrived in front of it, and Andi and Sebastian both turned to see Laila motioning for them to come inside.

The Bean was a reliable hub for early-morning activity. You would consistently find seven or eight tables of two to four people each, and Laila or Andi took care of them all just as quickly as they could, but most of the patrons wouldn't have noticed if they were ignored altogether. When they needed a refill, they'd step behind the counter and get it. If they needed another pastry, they'd grab it from the display and jot it down in the black-and-white composition notebook Andi used to track inventory. And of course whenever they got up for more coffee or more food, the conversations continued. They'd cross the creaky wood floor, calling over their shoulders to their breakfast companions—and, really, the room at large—sometimes asking if anyone needed anything while they were up, but mostly just carrying on with whatever they'd been saying while they were sitting.

It looked a little different in there this morning. Doc Atwater was standing against the far wall with a phone to his ear, and everyone else was huddled around the nineteen-inch television on the Bean's counter. Sebastian could have been staring at an artist's rendering. Apart from Laila motioning with urgency, life had become so still. With their huddled backs to him, he couldn't see what had grabbed their attention, but he instinctively knew it was something that mattered.

Peter Parker had his Spidey-Sense and Haley Joel Osment saw dead people, but Sebastian Sudworth's sixth sense was an awareness of news in the making.

Andi sighed, blissfully oblivious to the change in the air. "Coffeepot's probably acting up again." She stepped onto the landing and opened the door. "Sure you won't come in for a minute? Looks like the rest of the council's still here."

"Nah. I'm going to head on over. I need a few minutes to brush up on recipes with ham hock and molasses . . . or whatever colonists ate. Presumably we'll have some venison food trucks set up?"

She rolled her eyes and laughed, and he smiled and waved goodbye. Then he used the three-block walk to the school to remind himself it was okay that he wasn't the first to know. It was okay to wait a few minutes to find out what was happening in the world. It was okay that he still had to chew on his lip and ball up his fists and rail against his instincts to be at the center of whatever was causing the huddled mass. He'd made progress. *This* was progress. A few more minutes of waiting wouldn't kill him. It would be good for him, in fact. That wasn't his life anymore.

And maybe, someday, his blood pressure wouldn't spike and his pulse wouldn't quicken in contradiction to that fact.

CHAPTER 4

SEBASTIAN

FRIDAY, MARCH 18
9:09 a.m. Mountain Daylight Time

Nine minutes. Sebastian had been alone at the table in the school library for nine minutes, and all his mature self-talk was growing less effective with every second that passed. He jumped up from the table for easily the fifteenth time and glanced at his watch for at least the thirtieth.

Finally he heard footsteps in the distance. There weren't classes on Fridays, so he knew it was them. And if there *had* been any doubt, it went away as the rhythm of Old Man Kimball's walking stick, tapping against the terrazzo flooring, got closer. As their elevated voices grew louder. Particularly Jo's. He hadn't met her until years after her retirement from teaching, but in some ways, once a teacher always a teacher. Jo still had her authoritative, booming teacher voice when needed, that was for sure.

Sebastian hurried to the doorway to meet them. Self-control had won the day. He hadn't looked at the newsfeed on his phone once. He hadn't even taken a single one of the flirty women of a certain grandmotherly generation who lived at Spruce House, right

41

next door to the school, up on their long-standing offers that he should stop by anytime for tea and crumpets, just so he could take a look at their television. (Mainly because he had so often been offered "crumpets" since moving to town that he was suspicious it was a code word of sorts among the senior citizens of Adelaide Springs. He lived in fear of accidentally breaking the code.) So . . . yippee. He'd shown restraint and kept a level head and proven once again that he was now in a healthy and emotionally stable place. His therapist would be so proud.

Now, for all that was good and holy in the world, could someone please tell him what was happening?

"What's going on?" he asked as soon as they appeared around the corner.

"Good morning to you too." Jo patted him on the arm and slid past him into the room. She sat in an adult-sized orange plastic chair at the round table and sighed.

"Doc?" he asked softly and directly to the town's unofficial patriarch as he entered the room just behind Bill Kimball, who had grunted his standard greeting.

Doc responded with a heavy sigh and then placed a firm grip on Sebastian's shoulder. "Come on over and we'll get into it."

There was comfort to be found in Doc's presence. In six years he'd come to look up to the older man as a father figure. Not that Sebastian would ever tell him that. That wasn't the sort of emotional confession Sebastian felt equipped to handle, or that he'd ever seen Doc open the door to. And it wasn't that he was lacking an actual father. Martin Sudworth was the single biggest influence in his entire life. With the possible exceptions of Bob Woodward and Carl Bernstein.

Okay, that wasn't entirely accurate. It sure made him sound smarter when he named Woodward and Bernstein as his earliest role models, but the truth was he had aspired to be Robert Redford and Dustin Hoffman in their *portrayals* of the two men scooping the Watergate story in *All the President's Men*. Back in the day, when he used to wear ties to work, you could almost always find him with his sleeves rolled up and his collar unbuttoned, because a film from years before he was born had instilled in him the belief that that was how serious newsmen dressed.

His dad's influence on his life went even deeper. Martin had worked in the Office of Administration during the Carter presidency, and then worked with the next administration to help form the Office of Presidential Correspondence—which definitely entailed a whole lot more than responding to requests for a signed photo from Ronald Reagan. When he worked in that White House—or next door in the OEOB, to be precise—the elder Sudworth's value was soon recognized. Before the end of that first term, he had become an advisor to the president. A nonpartisan one who had gone on to advise, in some form or other, every president of the United States to follow, right up through the present day.

That was what had been instilled in Sebastian throughout his life. That the United States may have needed men and women who chose political sides and ran for office to advocate for the beliefs of the people, but the *world* needed solid men and women who *didn't* pick sides to contribute calm, order, clarity, and hopefully an ample serving of wisdom to the conversation. And while his father traveled the world as an unknown-to-the-public, indispensable-to-the-president asset, Sebastian spent his formative years watching the news every single evening, hoping for a glimpse of his dad.

When he finally got tired of playing I Spy alone night after night—never once spying his dad with his little eye—he shifted his obsession to *All the President's Men*. The fictionalized portrayals of Woodward and Bernstein caused him to grow his hair out past his collar (no matter how much his parents hated it), wear corduroy jackets, and vow to one day make his dad (and Jason Robards as Ben Bradlee) proud.

His relationship with Doc Atwater was something else entirely. Sebastian sought his approval—the need to earn the respect of those he respected was a character flaw he had no desire to rid himself of—but he also knew Doc wouldn't turn his back on him because his story had holes or because he showed weakness.

That had taken some getting used to.

They all sat around the table, and Sebastian braced himself. "So what is it? Tell me."

They all looked to Doc, and he spoke with quiet measure. "Brynn Cornell just saw fit to . . . how should we say it? To make clear her feelings about Adelaide Springs."

Sebastian did a double take. "Um . . . okay." The National Guard wasn't going to get called in for that one. "But I mean, what was everyone huddled around watching at the Bean?"

Jo crossed her arms and leaned back in the chair. "That. *Her.* Doc is being his normal diplomatic self, of course, but don't be fooled. That ungrateful little girl smeared the good name of our town on national television, and did all but cuss us each out by name in the process."

"Well . . . it wasn't quite as severe as all of that." Doc turned to Sebastian. "I didn't get the impression it was intentional."

"Oh, she meant it, alright," Bill grumbled.

"Well, yes, Bill," Doc said. "She probably meant it. But she didn't mean for us to hear it."

Sebastian sat up as straight as he could in his awful chair, which must have been designed in the eighties to address that nagging good-posture outbreak among America's youth. "Hang on. Brynn Cornell? As in local-girl-made-good?" You couldn't spend a day in Adelaide Springs without hearing someone talk about how they had once worked with her or gone to school with her or once had to call her because she had an overdue library book. "You're saying she said something *on-air*? On *Sunup*?"

Sebastian had been picturing a deranged gunman in a stand-off with police. A new pandemic. An old-fashioned dramatic car chase. Maybe the death of a world leader. It had never occurred to him that the news would be something quite so personal to the people of Adelaide Springs. He didn't know what she had said or how she'd said it, but it didn't take refined journalistic senses to put the pieces together. And Sebastian *did* have refined journalistic senses. He could put that thousand-piece puzzle together in his sleep.

She'd probably already been fired—not that they'd call it that. On second thought, they might not even fire her. The way her face was plastered across every single magazine short of *Birds & Blooms* and the way her network seemed adamant that she was the future of all that was good in the world, they wouldn't want to let her go over a slipup. They'd invested too much. They'd probably go the "pressures of stardom" route. She'd be sent to a spa and out of the spotlight for the appropriate amount of time, which would be determined by the court of public opinion, of course, then she'd carry out her penance by getting caught by TMZ serving meals at a Bronx soup kitchen, where *of course* she'd been helping out for years.

Would she be a Winona Ryder who needed to step away long enough to usher in a new generation? Coming back as the comfortingly, excitingly familiar but clearly more mature mom in *Stranger Things*? Or on *Dateline*, which was probably the news equivalent? Or would she fall into the "We don't want to go on a road trip with you, but we'll keep paying at the box office" category, like a Tom Cruise? Surely her outburst hadn't instituted the rules of Amanda Bynes martial law, had it? It couldn't have been that bad.

"What did she say, exactly?" Sebastian asked, his pulse finally returning to normal. This wasn't news. This was *entertainment* news. In the grand scheme of things, it really didn't matter. Not to the world, anyway. To his friends, it understandably mattered very much. He was interested. He was just interested in a lower gear.

Doc cleared his throat. "I don't think it's worth rehashing—"

"She called Adelaide Springs a tiny, insignificant blip." Jo leaned forward onto her elbows. "She said we're stupid—"

"And poor," came the assertive contribution from Old Man Kimball.

"That's right," Jo continued. "Stupid and poor. She called us pathetic, Seb. Pathetic! Can you believe that? I tell ya . . . I've never seen someone grow up to be such a spoiled, ungrateful—"

"You didn't tell him about the part where she insulted our greatest tradition."

Bill Kimball claimed he hadn't heard Sebastian when he made a motion to allocate some town funds for a recycling initiative, he mistook his yays for nays more often than not, and half the time he seemed to think his name was Sercastian. As if that were a real name. But doggone it if he hadn't heard and committed to memory every word out of Brynn Cornell's mouth.

"What tradition is that?" As soon as he asked, he unfortunately knew the answer.

A deep, guttural, preparing-to-shoot-fire-through-her-nose laugh erupted from Jo. "Township Days, of course! She didn't say it specifically, but it was very clearly implied. She said something about how we're obsessed with colonial days. Obsessed. Can you believe that? We haven't celebrated Township Days since the late nineties. And she knows better. She was here in those golden days. For her to be so demeaning . . . so dismissive . . ."

Choose your words wisely, Sebastian.

"That's not cool," he muttered. And it wasn't. Even if, at this particular moment, he and Brynn Cornell seemed to be the only two people on the planet who saw how absurd their "greatest tradition" was. But insulting it in front of the biggest morning-television audience in the world was not cool at all.

Doc remained silent, nearly motionless, apart from the thumb and forefinger of his right hand spinning the simple gold band around the ring finger on his left hand. His eyes seemed focused on the shelf of reference books across the room.

Sebastian sighed. "Well, I'm sorry this happened. I know it has to feel like a pretty major betrayal." As always, there were lots of things he wanted to say. *Can we please take "Birthplace of America's Ray of Sunshine" off the city's welcome sign now? Should we consider suing her, at least for enough money to expand the "zoo" beyond the various bugs that entomologist left behind when his grant money ran out and the fat, lazy prairie dogs the school lunch workers feed leftover french fries to?* And, of course, *No matter how wrong of her it was to say it, shouldn't we reevaluate the desire to bring back Township Days, now that it's been made fun of on a national stage?*

He'd get to all those things, he figured. But as Doc Atwater's eyes rose slowly and met Sebastian's, he realized he hadn't heard the whole story yet. Jo had released a deep breath and collapsed back into her chair, seemingly exhausted from the retelling, and Bill was scanning the pages of the *Denver Post* as if none of it had ever happened, so he was pretty sure they hadn't either.

"There's something else?" he asked.

Doc's eyes passed slowly across his three fellow council members. "I think it would do us all some good to remember this is one of our kids."

Jo scoffed. "I don't know about that, Doc. She just made it pretty clear that she's disowned us."

"Fine. But that doesn't mean we disown her." He pushed back from the table enough that he could cross his boot up onto his knee. "You taught her, Jo. Bill, you created a job for her cleaning up the back room at the bar so you could keep an eye on her when Elaine went off the deep end."

Old Man Kimball glared over the newspaper at Doc. "I did no such thing. I hired her to do a job that needed to be done, plain and simple. She wasn't even any good at it. Should've fired her right off the bat."

"Okay, Bill. Whatever you say." Doc looked down at the still-twirling ring and nodded. And, if Sebastian wasn't mistaken, smiled. The smile slowly faded over the next several seconds before he looked up again. "I know none of us were crazy about the way she left, but I still remember when she and Laila would come over for sleepovers with Addie. In my head I can still see those three girls sitting around dreaming and conspiring about all the things they wanted do with their lives. All the things they were going to become. So maybe we don't like who it seems she's become. That doesn't mean we turn our backs on her."

Jo grumbled under her breath, and that was good enough for Doc, it seemed.

He returned his boot to the ground. "Let's officially call this meeting to order." Doc waited as Jo pulled her yellow legal pad from her canvas shopping bag and then dove right in. "I have a new item for discussion. Sorry, Jo . . . I didn't have time to get it on the agenda. I got a phone call from New York, right before Brynn's on-air mishap, warning me it was about to happen—"

"It was a setup?!" Bill crumpled up the center of his newspaper and looked over it, enraged.

"Time zones, Bill. Time zones." Doc remained calm and quiet as he carried on. "Of course, they didn't give me *much* of a heads-up. I think you guys were seeing it happen before it even registered who I was talking to."

Time-zone confusions were a running theme in the history of Adelaide Springs, Sebastian had discovered. Back after the 1960 presidential election, when the tiny little community of Dixville Notch, New Hampshire, gained recognition for being the first in the country to cast their votes by gathering the entire populace (all four of them) at midnight, Adelaide Springs had wanted to prove they were every bit as patriotic. So, obviously, they started casting their votes at the exact same time as Dixville Notch, which was 10:00 p.m. the night before. From what Sebastian could tell, no one in Adelaide Springs cast a valid vote again until 1988.

"Who *were* you talking to?" Sebastian asked.

"A man named Passik."

"Colton Passik?" Sebastian hadn't intended to let any knowledge of anything slip in, but once it was out there, all eyes were on him.

"That's the one," Doc confirmed. "You know him?"

"I know of him." And he'd known him, in a different life. "He's sort of a bigwig. They must really be scrambling if he's making the calls himself." All eyes were still on him, as if they were waiting for him to reveal more. But this wasn't about him, and he'd prefer to keep it that way.

"Rather than call and warn us, why didn't they just edit that out for all the other time zones? We don't get anything live in Mountain time zone anyway."

Jo raised a reasonable point, but the answer was obvious. At least to Sebastian. "It would still be out there," he told her. "Social media and YouTube and the like. And then *Sunup* would have a much bigger issue to deal with than their star going off the rails. Everyone west of Georgia would start wondering what was being kept from them every morning."

It should have clicked for him sooner that something was happening that involved Adelaide Springs directly. He'd seen Doc leaning against the wall at the Bean, talking on a cell phone.

Doc didn't own a cell phone.

Adelaide Springs didn't have a town hall. There was no one manning the phones or greeting visitors in some outdated office with neglected houseplants. Jo kept a filing cabinet in her office at the inn, and the historical archives were kept in boxes in the vault at the closest branch of the Mineral County Community Bank, just one town over. A year ago Sebastian offered to add another cell phone to his service plan, but before that if anyone needed to contact the local government, their best bet was to head to the Bean Franklin or, later in the day, Cassidy's, the bar and grill owned by Bill Kimball. Once you walked into either of those locations, you could just talk to whichever city councilor you spotted first. Otherwise, you could call the city's official landline, which it shared with sheriff dispatch, the library, and the historical society.

Now the council members passed the official town line around in a rotation each month. Well, Doc, Jo, and Sebastian passed it around. Bill had feigned lack of understanding of how to answer a call on a "newfangled" refurbished iPhone 8 long enough that the other three had given up on the hope of stretching the rotation to once in four months instead of three. It was March, and Doc was up.

"I'm guessing Passik didn't call with a friendly warning out of the goodness of his heart?"

Of course the network was worried the town would sue. If they played their cards right, maybe they could get a lot more than a few fish tanks and some reinforced fencing for Mr. Ripley, the Olivets' retired steer.

Doc chuckled. "He seemed like a nice enough guy, but no. There was a bit more to it than that. He said Brynn's mortified by what happened. Life pressures, the increased spotlight, exhaustion . . ." Doc looked pointedly at Sebastian. "You know the drill."

Sebastian scoffed and then added in a cough or two to try to cover the reaction. Brynn Cornell's cushy celebrity drill was very different from the drill Sebastian knew, as Doc was fully aware. He and Doc could discuss that later. He'd never been more grateful for the avoidance allowed by doctor-patient confidentiality.

"But she couldn't even be bothered to call us herself to say all of that?" Jo tsked and shook her head. "What has happened to that girl?"

"That's what the call was about. She wants to come out here next week and apologize in person." Doc sat back and let them all process that in their own ways. Jo was speechless, Bill was Clint Eastwood in *Gran Torino*, and Sebastian returned to his thousand-piece puzzle.

If the town wanted to file a lawsuit, there was probably a case there. But it wouldn't get that far. If Adelaide Springs so much as made a call to Denver to chat with a lawyer, the network would offer to settle, and that would be the end of it. How much would they have to take out of Brynn Cornell's wardrobe budget to offer more money than the tiny little town would know what to do with? Would she have to wear the same dress to the Emmys *and* the People's Choice Awards? No . . . they wouldn't go that far. But she might have to wear something off the rack.

They weren't worried about protecting their money. They were worried about protecting their golden child. Their biggest asset, as they saw her. Sebastian was willing to bet all the eggs had been placed in her basket. She *was* the future of *Sunup*. It had never occurred to them to come up with plan B. Why would it? Until this morning, she'd been a bulletproof angel.

"What sort of crew are they wanting to bring?" Sebastian asked. "And for how long?"

Doc shrugged. "Small. Not sure what that means, exactly. For the week."

"Footage of her making nice?"

"Yep. And a live broadcast from here on Friday."

Jo threw her hands up in the air. "Can someone please tell me what in tarnation you're talking about? I neglected to bring my secret message decoder ring with me today."

Doc gestured for Sebastian to go ahead.

"*Sunup* wants to film her here . . . on location in her hometown. I'm sure they're desperate for her to get back in America's good graces, so if they show her being charming and delightful and contrite—"

"And forgiven," Doc added.

Sebastian pointed at him. "Yes. Forgiven. That's what it's all about."

Jo nodded. "I see. If we can forgive her, she must not be so bad after all."

"Exactly." Doc cleared his throat and started spinning his wedding band again. "So it's up to us. No one in town outside of this room knows that this is on the table. The *Sunup* people can't take over the town and film here without our permission. So we need to decide."

"I vote no," Bill blurted and then smoothed out his crumpled paper and began reading again.

"Don't check out yet, Bill," Jo said. "Robert's Rules of Order still have to mean something around this place, and we don't have a motion yet."

"Fine. I make a motion that the answer is no."

Jo sighed and laced her fingers behind her head. "Look, Doc, can I be honest?"

Doc grinned. "Josephine Stoddard, in more than sixty years, I've never known you to be anything but."

She lowered her hands to the table and picked up her pen. "She's already humiliated us in name, from afar. I'd just as soon not be humiliated on camera, in person."

Doc nodded. "That's fair. Any other thoughts?"

Bill picked up his newspaper again and began folding it. "Seems like a no-brainer to me."

"Yeah, I agree with Bill." Jo tapped the tip of her pen against the table, lightly but with a regular tempo. "I was hurt when she left. You know, just like everyone else. But that hasn't stopped me from cheering her on as she became a big star. I was . . ." She trailed off.

Doc reached over and patted her hand on the table. "You were proud of her. I think we all were."

Jo cleared her throat sharply. "But that's that. She made it clear how she feels about us. I don't wish her any ill will, but I don't think we owe her anything either. I feel like we gave her plenty in the first seventeen years of her life."

After one final pat, Doc pulled his hand back and sat up straighter. "Okay, so I think we're all in agreement. Jo, call for the motion, and I'll let this Passik guy know. Then we can get back to the business at hand."

"Township Days!" Jo practically squealed. "I was talking to Lucinda Morissey, and she's pretty sure she has her great-grandma's recipe for apple tansey." She turned to Sebastian. "I don't know if you've ever heard of apple tansey, but it's—"

"Yeah, I've had it," Seb interjected. He refrained from adding that he'd eaten apple tansey as a kid, with his mom and brothers, visiting Colonial Williamsburg. Where apple tansey made sense.

"Well, anyway, like Doc said, let's wrap up all this Brynn Cornell unpleasantness first. Can I get a motion that Adelaide Springs will not allow a crew from *Sunup* to film here next week?"

"So moved," Bill stated.

"I'll second it," Jo said as she scribbled in the minutes. "All in favor?"

Silence.

Jo's eyes darted between Sebastian and Doc. "Did I miss you guys saying 'aye' while I was writing?"

Sebastian looked at Doc, who was looking right back at him. "What is it?" the older man asked.

"I'm just not sure . . ."

Bill threw his paper on the table and then threw his body back into the chair. "He always does this!"

"I always do *what*?"

"You just have to vote different. Push back. No matter what we want to do, you go the other way."

"That's not true, Bill," Jo defended. "Seb just represents a different generation. A more worldly view." She looked at Sebastian and smiled, but the smile faded quickly. "Having said that, since you don't know her, and none of this really affects you at all, I'd think you might want to go with us on this one."

"I know." The metal feet of Sebastian's chair scraped against the floor as he pushed back from the table. "Except . . ." He bent over and buried his head in his hands to shield his eyes from the fluorescent lighting that wasn't making it any easier to think. "Look, I'm not trying to be difficult. I promise. Can you guys just give me a minute? Sorry."

They kept talking among themselves—they probably even kept talking to Sebastian—but he allowed himself a moment to tune them out. It wasn't difficult to understand how Bill could see him the way he did. The fact was, he *did* usually vote differently than the rest of them. Three-to-One could have been the Adelaide Springs City Council's boy-band name. But he was never obstinate for the sake of obstinance. Never. He voted in line with his principles and what he believed was best for the town. Township Days would not be good for the town. Was it possible that a visit from Brynn Cornell would be?

His gut said no. Without even seeing it for himself yet, he could picture how that morning's meltdown probably looked. He'd seen it before. For whatever reason, people who were paid obscene amounts of money to smile and be likable seemed to eventually find that too taxing. He had no patience for celebrities, and he wanted nothing to do with anyone who could treat his friends the way she had.

But when he brushed his personal feelings to the side, it was difficult to deny that this whole thing could potentially help the town in ways he hadn't even dreamt of. This wouldn't be some kitschy, doomed-to-fail Hail Mary. If they went forward with Township Days, they wouldn't even have the marketing budget to spread the word via the midnight ride of Paul Revere. They would have to rely on blogs and editorial pieces, all of which would be making fun of them—if they managed to get anyone's attention at all.

They were being handed *Sunup*. Millions of loyal viewers would be tuning in just like they did every morning, not to mention the millions more who would be rubbernecking the Brynn Cornell debacle. He didn't trust her, he didn't trust *Sunup*, and he didn't trust the industry as a whole. But if anything was certain, it was that in their eagerness to get their star off the hook, they would paint Adelaide Springs in the most positive light possible. They would show off its beauty. Its solitude. What it was and what it strived to be. What it *could* be.

"Nay." He raised his head from his hands. "Sorry."

Doc spoke over Jo's gasp and Bill's mutterings to ask, "Can you tell us why?"

Sebastian met Doc's kind, searching eyes and spoke quietly. "I don't want her to come. I know it would be difficult for all of you. For anyone who knew her." Under his breath he added, "It won't be super fun for those of us who didn't know her either." He sighed. "But this is the sort of publicity usually reserved for the Olympics and the Super Bowl. How can I vote against exactly what I've been saying we need . . . only about a trillion times bigger and better?"

They all stared at him with varying degrees of what he interpreted as disappointment and confusion in their eyes. "It's not like my vote even matters. But still . . . there it is." The boy band would remain intact. As would his conscience.

"Okay," Doc said, looking to Jo. "I vote nay too."

"What?!" Bill exclaimed. "So it's a tie?"

Jo continued to look at Doc and Sebastian in surprise—though she couldn't have been half as surprised as Sebastian himself. "No. That's it. She can come. In the event of a tie, the mayor has the deciding vote."

Sebastian opened his mouth, but nothing came out. That wasn't the way that was supposed to go. He'd finally gotten through, *finally* won a vote, and it was *this* one?

One small step for integrity. One giant leap backward for Sebastian Sudworth's popularity.

"But . . ." He cowered under the glare of Old Man Kimball. "This is going to be a disaster. Doc . . . why . . ."

"You made good points."

Sebastian scoffed. "Well, thanks, but I always make good points. That's never mattered before. And I might be wrong, you know."

Doc shrugged. "Could be."

"They're going to try to take advantage of us." Sebastian took off his ball cap and ran his fingers through his hair. "These television people . . . They're going to come in here and make it seem like they're doing us a favor by gracing us with their presence, and they're going to stir up all sorts of problems. Before we know it, it's going to be, 'Hey, hope you don't mind. That hundred-year-old aspen was throwing off the white balance on the shot, so it had to go.'"

"We can't let that happen," Doc said.

"No, we can't." Sebastian put his hat back on.

Doc nodded, his mind made up. "If they try anything like that, we're counting on you to keep things under control."

"Um . . ." Seb looked from Doc to Jo, whose sly grin was beginning to overtake her face, and then back to Doc. "It shouldn't be me. You guys know her. I've never met her in my life."

"That's a good point." Doc stood from his chair and squeezed Sebastian's shoulder. "I hadn't even thought of that, but that's more reason why you should do it. She's already insulted me on national television. Lucky you, you weren't really included in that." He squeezed again. "I hereby move that Sebastian Sudworth act as the town's representative for the purposes of Brynn Cornell's visit to Adelaide Springs."

"Second." Jo and Bill said it in unison, and Jo recorded it all on her yellow legal pad.

"I vote nay!" Seb looked around at them in horror. "I most *adamantly* vote nay!"

"Hey, Jo, make sure Sebastian's adamant objection is reflected in the minutes."

She nodded, and even though her face was mostly concealed, it was easy to tell her expression bordered on gleeful. "Sure thing, Doc."

"Alright, then." Doc pushed his chair in, and Bill copied his action. "Thanks, everyone. I'll make a motion to adjourn."

Sebastian finally shook off the stupor enough to stand up, run to the door after them, and call out his objections to adjournment, but it was too late. Three-to-One was back to singing their greatest hit.

CHAPTER 5

BRYNN

"You're not afraid of flying, are you, Orly?"

While it was undeniable that I had been lost in my own thoughts for much of our endless day of travel—from JFK to Denver on a real plane, and then from Denver to Telluride on a twelve-seat commuter—I certainly hadn't noticed anything amiss with my traveling companion. But now, as we made our descent into the county's municipal airport on a craft I was fairly convinced was typically used for crop dusting, Orly was shaking. And not just from our rickety transportation.

"Uh, not typically, no," Orly called out to me in a loud voice. *Almost* loud enough to overpower the frightening soundtrack of our flight—something akin to water erupting from a whale's blowhole during the countdown to a NASA rocket launch. His eyes were squeezed closed, and his knuckles were literally white.

I couldn't claim to always be the most observant about other people, but I did know that Orly Hill had been a Black man as long as I'd known him, so that didn't seem quite right.

I took a quick look out the window. No imminent danger in sight . . . I mean, provided the pilot saw that fourteen-thousand-foot peak directly in front of us. He'd managed to dodge them all so far, so I took the risk, unbuckled my seat belt, and hurried across the aisle to sit next to Orly. As soon as I sat down, his eyes flew open to see what was happening. He seemed to regret that instantly, in light of the sharp angle we took just then to avoid the aforementioned mountain.

I latched my belt and then placed my hand on his arm. "It's okay, Orly. This is totally normal."

"It shouldn't be."

I couldn't argue with that. I could remember three flights into Adelaide Springs in my life, prior to this one. They'd all been terrifying.

"When I was eleven, I flew on a plane for the first time. It was a plane a lot like this one." I dared not share with my trembling cameraman the thought that passed through my mind—that there was a very good chance that flight all those years ago had been on *exactly* this plane. "My friend Addie's mom had died, and her dad had to go up to Denver to deal with the will and stuff. I got to tag along to keep Addie company. And it was awful. *Much* worse than this. You know how we kind of had to go between the mountains out of Telluride and gain a lot of elevation really fast to get over the peaks?"

Orly peeked at me with one eye, as the other remained closed. *You're not helping, Brynn.* "I'm just saying, it used to be worse. The runway was shorter . . ." *Still not helping.* "But as awful as it is, it's totally normal. And it's almost over."

I leaned over him enough to peer downward. The sun was already starting to set, and no matter how much I was dreading touching down, I couldn't deny that the orange of the sky glistening on the snow of the valley was a sight to behold.

"Hey . . ." I nudged Orly with my elbow. "If you can stand it, I think it's worth taking a look."

He opened his eyes and looked at me first, and I used my chin to motion his eyes toward the window. In an instant his fear was replaced by wonder. "It looks like a postcard."

I chuckled. "Yeah. Enjoy the view. This is the town's best vantage point."

Orly spent another moment soaking in his view of the snow-capped mountains and the ever-closer aspens and spruce trees, all saturated by the dazzling orange and blue sky that Coloradoans liked to use as evidence that God was a Denver Broncos fan, and then shifted in his seat to face me. There were no more mountain passes to avoid between us and the runway, so it was beginning to feel—finally, just as we prepared to land—like we might not die on this flight after all.

"So tell me. What's so awful about this place?"

He had asked the question softly enough that it was tempting to pretend I hadn't heard him. But I figured he would just ask again. Besides, I needed him to be my ally for the week. I'd been in the business long enough to know the camera was capable of forgiving a multitude of sins—and therefore never allowing viewers to see them at all—if you had the right crew on your side.

Orly probably didn't want to be here any more than I did, but Colton said he had the most on-location experience of the entire crew, and Bob Oswell had insisted one cameraman was enough. He may have been coming at it from a budgetary standpoint—and quite possibly even an "If she crashes and burns, at least my daughter is ready to step in" standpoint—but I was still inclined to agree with him. I wanted my week in Adelaide Springs to have a grassroots feel to it. It needed to feel cozy. Homey. It needed to *feel* like a postcard.

"Where did you grow up, Orly?"

"Baltimore."

I chuckled. "Okay. Well, I daresay growing up in Adelaide Springs was a little different from growing up in Baltimore. Small towns are like foreign countries. There's almost a separate language, you know? Different currency. Different laws. Different rules of engagement. I don't know how to explain it exactly."

The pilot called to us over his shoulder. Something about landing and making sure we had our seat belts on. As if we would have dared to sit there without them as the wings wobbled in a way that resembled Annette Funicello dancing on a surfboard.

"I bet you don't remember every time a new family moved to Baltimore when you were growing up, but I could name every person who moved to Adelaide Springs from the time I was five until I graduated from high school."

I opened my mouth to add some sort of joke—"Both of them," maybe—but my brain had begun doing exactly what I knew I couldn't allow it to do. It was getting a little too real a little too fast. I was thinking of those people who had moved in and out of town—the rich, retired snowbirds who used to spend summers there and winters in Tucson; the ski bums who wanted to be close to the slopes but couldn't afford to live *too* close to the slopes; the guilt-ridden parents determined to get their kids away from crime and drugs and peer pressure, but who ultimately realized they still wanted to be near a McDonald's PlayPlace—and before I knew it I was thinking of the men who came to town in pursuit of my mother. She'd meet them in bars all across the western slope of Colorado, and each of them was the love of *her* life just long enough to wreak havoc on mine.

I cleared my throat and pulled my eyes away from the trees just below our elevation, right outside the window, and forced a smile onto my face as I focused on Orly again. "Some places are nicer to visit than to live in. There aren't a lot of postcards highlighting droughts and dried-up economies and limited opportunities and zero romantic options and not being able to escape the people who make your life a living hell." The smile was still plastered on my face, but Orly was studying me a bit too intensely, trying to see what was underneath it, I was pretty sure. *Too real too fast, Brynn. Better keep it on Ray of Sunshine terms.* "But it really is *such* a gorgeous area. On a clear day when the sun is out and the mountains are still covered in snow . . . I'm serious, Orly, you never knew a sky could be so blue."

The weather is beautiful. Wish I wasn't here.

After we came to a rocky, screeching halt on the runway, we unbuckled our belts and began grabbing our things. Orly first made the sign of the cross and then carefully tucked the rosary he'd been holding on to for dear life into his backpack.

"I didn't know you were Catholic," I said, and then felt immediately uncomfortable. "Not that it matters. Sorry." Religion, politics, sex. Those were the issues you only discussed with someone if you were interviewing them. And usually only if you were interviewing someone running for office.

"Nah, it's okay." He threaded his arms through the straps of the bag and hoisted it onto his back. "I don't mind talking about it. My faith's important to me." He leaned his elbows on the headrest of the seat in front of him while we waited for the pilot to open the door. "I won't be ostracized in Adelaide Springs for being Catholic, will I?" There was a smile on his face, but I seriously considered the question.

"No. I mean, you'll probably be the only one in town. We're very Protestant up in here." I rolled my eyes. Not at Protestants but at the pronoun that had grouped me in with the locals. "But you won't be ostracized for it." The door opened, and I led the way toward the front, adding over my shoulder, "You'll just be ostracized for being 'city folk.'"

We were almost to the steps—it wasn't much of a journey—

when I halted so abruptly that Orly ran into me. I turned around to face him.

"Look, Orly, this is probably going to be weird. Okay?" I'd spent forty-eight hours trying to convince myself it was just another assignment. I would get in, do my job, and get out, and then I'd get my life back. It would be like those twenty-three seconds on Friday morning never even happened. But the truth was, I had no idea what to expect. Would I have to pretend to care about people I hadn't thought about in twenty years? Would I even recognize anyone? Would they be happy to see me? Colton had said the mayor told him it was a split decision by city council as to whether I could even come for the week and film around town, and that was surprising on a lot of levels, because when I left town the mayor had been a yellow-bellied marmot named Lady Xanadu. "The truth is, I don't know what to expect."

"Have you been in touch with anyone? Since Friday, I mean."

I shook my head. "No. Not since Friday."

"But there are people here you're on good terms with?"

I leaned back and tried to look out the open door, but I couldn't angle my neck enough to see anything. "I'm really not on any terms with anyone."

He shrugged. "Okay, so you've lost touch. That happens when we leave home. Don't sweat it. I've seen you charm the uncharmable more than once. This is your turf, Brynn. You just take control of this thing from the get-go, and you'll be fine."

Yep. There it was. That was the reminder I needed. My teeth released my bottom lip, and I let out the breath I'd been holding.

Just another assignment.

"Thanks, Orly."

I prepared to take the final two or three steps, but Orly tapped me on the shoulder. "Do you want me to get my camera out now? Do you think we should start filming right away?"

Hmm. I took one more step forward and crouched over to see the entrance to the little shed-sized building that served as a makeshift airport. When I was a kid, it had also been where Addie, Laila, and I came in the summer to buy snow cones with these gift certificates we always had. I couldn't remember where they came from, but I could remember us signing our names and having access to all the snow cones we could possibly eat.

"Might not be a bad idea."

"It would probably be good to capture your initial reaction to being back home and such."

I turned back to him and nodded as he took his camera bag from his left shoulder, set it on a seat, and began getting his equipment ready. "Exactly what I was thinking."

Except I hadn't been thinking that at all.

I'd been thinking about the first time I had signed my name *B-R-Y-N-N*. I'd been in California for about eight weeks when Adelaide Springs tracked me down for the first time. More specifically, Addie Atwater tracked me down. I still didn't know how she had found me. I'd had three paying jobs at the time (well, if you added them all up, I *almost* got paid a living wage), but Addie managed to find me at *Good Day LA*, where I was just an intern picking up dry cleaning and taking coffee orders.

I saw Mike, another intern, heading my way with mail in his hands, and I knew. Somehow I just knew that someone had tracked me down. He wasn't walking toward me in his usual "Jillian needs a protein shake" way. I'd never been so happy to be unknown. To matter so little. Because when he said, "You got mail from someplace called 'Adelaide Springs, Colorado.' I've never heard of it. Is that even a real place?" I was able to cover my name badge with my hair, hand the envelope with Addie's familiar handwriting back to him, and say, "No idea. That's not even my name." And though he was a little confused, he didn't know or care enough to argue. I turned my back on him, walked to the intern director's office, and changed all my paperwork from *B-R-E-N* to *B-R-Y-N-N*.

So many years later, it was difficult to remember why I had thought that was enough of a change. Why hadn't I become Penelope? Or Genevieve? Why hadn't I thought to change my last name and break off that familial tie to the woman I had taken a bus nine hundred miles to get away from? I really don't know. It seems so silly to have been so satisfied. But for whatever reason, I was. Everything changed that day.

"Ready when you are," Orly said from behind me.

My reaction to being back home. I was guessing that handing the pilot my credit card and begging him to take me as far away as he could wasn't the reaction Orly was hoping to capture. That's what *B-R-E-N* wanted to do. I just had to remind myself that wasn't even my name.

"Zip up your coat, Orly. It's a different sort of cold out here."

I took a deep breath, and Orly must have attempted to fill his lungs at the same time.

"Holy cow! Where'd the oxygen go?"

I turned to face him again with a smile. "Have you ever been in the mountains before?" My smile faded quickly at the sight of his paling face.

He shook his head. "My wife, Jenni, and I went to Vegas for our twentieth anniversary."

Um . . . "Okay. Vegas has an elevation of about two thousand feet."

"Lots of travel for work in the old days. Spent some time in Berlin," he panted. "How high is that?"

I just ignored that question and chose not to tell him there were spruce trees right outside the windows of the plane taller than Berlin.

The temps were hovering right around freezing as the sun

set, and dropping fast, but sweat was dripping from Orly's brow. I looked up toward the cockpit, such as it was, to see if the pilot was available in case altitude sickness kicked in too strongly, but he'd left us alone on the plane. I was no aviation expert, but I was pretty sure that went against regulation.

I was feeling a little bit of the burn, but my lungs were already beginning to acclimate. I supposed growing up in Adelaide Springs and a few trips in recent years to cover the Telluride Film Festival for *Sunup*, not to mention being twenty years Orly's junior, worked in my favor. A probably long-ago trip to Caesars Palace might not have provided Orly with the recommended amount of endurance training.

"We're a lot higher than Las Vegas here."

"How much higher?"

He didn't need to know all the details just yet. "About a mile." *And then another Vegas or so . . .* "Do you need to sit? Here . . ." I tried to guide him back to his seat, but he shook off my assistance.

"It's okay." His breaths grew deeper, and I became less worried that we'd need the pilot to drop the oxygen masks. (As if this plane had oxygen masks. Yet another thing I didn't need to mention to Orly.) But he still looked as clammy as I'd ever seen anyone look, and I'd once attended a traditional New England clambake on a beach in Maine where Elena dressed as Elvis and Lance dressed as an actual clam to celebrate the fiftieth anniversary of the film *Clambake*.

"What's the holdup?" I heard steps come up the stairs at the front of the plane.

Sure. *Now* the pilot bothered to check on things. "Wow . . . *Really* appreciate your help." I whipped around to face him. "Everything seems to be okay *now*, no thanks to you."

He tilted his head. "Excuse me?"

"First you made the poor man fear for his life in this crap

bucket you call a plane, and then you don't even stick around to make sure everyone survived the Flight of Terror?"

He folded his arms across his chest and smiled. *Smiled!* "For the record, I wasn't the one who decided to call this a plane. I'm not quite sure whom you need to file your complaint with on that. The engineer? The dictionary, maybe? Leonardo da Vinci or Orville and Wilbur may have some responsibility in this. But I do not."

"Hey, Brynn . . ."

"Not now, Orly!" I snapped. I wasn't done chewing out the infuriating pilot for the rude and inconsiderate way he had treated my cameraman. "And another thing—"

"Okay, stop talking now," the pilot said as he put his hand up and looked around me. "Orly?"

Oh no. Had he passed out? I was going to lose some of my righteous ground if he swooped in and played the hero now. I looked behind me—determined to finish this once we got Orly hooked up to an IV or something—but he was fine. He was just standing there, no longer sweaty, squinting at the pilot.

"I thought that was you!" Orly took a step forward and looked around me in the narrow aisle, just as the ball-capped pilot was doing. "Nah! Can't be." He started laughing and took another step toward him. Basically *through* me. "What in the world are you doing here, man?" He extended his right hand past me, and I was forced into the nearest seat row as the pilot did the same and matched Orly in an enthusiastic handshake.

"I was going to ask you the same thing . . ." His voice trailed off, and the smile fell from his lips. "Oh." He turned his head and examined me. Not in a look-me-up-and-down sort of way, though. No. He just looked straight into my eyes a little longer than was polite or comfortable and then back to Orly. The smile returned. "What'd you do to get stuck with *this* assignment?"

"It's not a bad gig. Rickety planes and thin air aside." Orly laughed again and glanced at me, the humor still evident. Something in my expression must have squashed it. He cleared his throat. "I don't suppose you've met Brynn Cor—"

"That's not necessary." I picked my bag back up from the seat where it had landed during the handshake rigmarole and hoisted it back onto my shoulder. I turned to the pilot. "Look, no offense. Any friend of Orly's is a friend of mine, but the truth is, it's been a long day and some of us take our jobs seriously enough to want to put our best foot forward. So let's just forget about the subpar service and the blatant rudeness from a few moments ago." I stepped back into the aisle, toe to toe with the stranger. "I just want to get off this plane—"

"I thought we were going with 'crap bucket.'"

"Alright. That's enough. Where are you based?"

"Where am I *based*?" He squinted his eyes at me, and his smirk grew.

"Yes, where are you based? Telluride? Denver? Grand Junction?" I hoisted my bag higher and took another step forward. I wasn't going to be intimidated by some crop duster who wanted to believe he was Han Solo piloting the *Millennium Falcon*.

Rather than step back or move out of my way, something in him seemed determined to double down. He leaned over and placed his elbows on the headrests on each side of the aisle. "I'm based here."

Admittedly, that was a bit of a surprise. "Here? In Adelaide Springs?" He looked to be about my age. Maybe a few years older, but definitely of the same generation. When I was growing up here, there had never been any local pilots. Small charters like the one we were on flew in as needed, if the exorbitant price was right. Was it possible there was actually enough business to merit having someone based in town?

Hopefully none of that interfered with the booming snow-cone trade.

"Well, then, please tell me whom you report to."

"Whom I *what*?"

Orly tapped my shoulder. "Okay, seriously, Brynn."

I ignored him, of course. It was almost certainly going to be a week of unpleasant reminders that I was once again in the middle of nowhere. It was going to be a week of trying to keep my cool and playing nice and not letting things get to me. But Han here did not get to start on me before I even stepped off the plane. "Whom you report to. I realize you may not know who I am—"

He spoke over me. "If only someone had tried to introduce us."

"There are people waiting for me. People I need to impress. And I need everything—*everything*—to go perfectly for the next few days."

"And you don't think this is meeting that standard?" He stood up straight again and smiled as he looked down at me. "Don't sell yourself short. I think you're doing great."

What is with this guy?!

"Let's go, Orly," I stated in my most authoritative New Yorker voice, mastered in the early days of my career on *Sunup3*, when we still hailed cabs rather than ordering them on an app. I didn't show an ounce of intimidation as I stepped forward. "You need to move now."

"Yes, ma'am," he responded as he tipped his hat and stepped aside. As he did, I read the emblem. Manchester United. Okay, yeah. Some jerk of a pilot who supported a European soccer team was going to last about a minute in Adelaide Springs.

I stepped in front of him and finally turned to head down the stairs and off the plane but was blocked by another man in a different baseball cap. Bass Pro Shops. Now *that* was the Adelaide Springs style.

"You're still here?" the man asked, most unnecessarily. "I have to refuel and get back to Telluride. No offense, but can we move it along a little?"

I snapped my head back to look at the other guy. After witnessing the smug expression on his face, I began noticing the differences between the two men. I turned and faced the one I now understood to be the actual pilot and noticed the short gray hair peeking out from under his hat. The clean-shaven face. The other guy had stubble. Dark, matching the slightly longer, seemingly shaggy locks. Those characteristics combined with the Smashing Pumpkins concert tee evident under his jacket made me really glad that Mr. Bass Pro Shops had been the one responsible for our safety.

"Sorry about that," I said to him. "We're going now."

He sat down in the pilot's seat, and I walked past him and exited, followed by Orly and then the other guy.

"Thanks, Steve. Have a safe flight back."

"Will do. See ya, Seb."

Our other bags were waiting for us on the ground, having been unloaded from the cargo area. I looked around. It all looked the exact same as it always had. Mountains. Nothing but mountains. The airport still essentially looked like a to-scale Snoopy Sno-Cone Machine made of dilapidated pine and a green metal roof. There were two vehicles parked near the building—an ugly red pickup truck and an even uglier orange-and-white-striped thing that looked like it belonged on safari. Apart from the color. The color wouldn't blend in with anything, with the possible exception of the Nerf gun you carried to protect you from stampeding lions.

"Should I keep filming?" Orly asked quietly, shivering in his boots.

Okay. It's go time. Orly wanted to film my reaction to being back here. And what *was* my reaction? *No, Brynn. That's the wrong question.* What did my reaction *need* to be?

I turned and faced Orly, a *Sunup*-worthy smile painted on my face. "The feel of stepping off a plane onto this ground . . . It's crazy how little that's changed. I remember the second time I ever flew on a plane was over Christmas break my junior year of high school." I forced myself to think of the memories in a positive light. I knew I needed Orly to film me waxing nostalgic about my beloved hometown. And truth be told, I didn't have to work all that hard to focus on the good memories of that trip. "These four friends of mine and I saved up as much money as we could, for months, to go on this ski trip to Telluride. There were closer slopes, certainly, but we skied those all the time. And we could have driven there, but it's a five-hour trip. None of us wanted to waste that much time." I blocked the ever-lower sun from my eyes with my hand and looked around the flat valley surrounding us. A little bit in the distance, to the east, I could just make out the grand Adelaide Springs skyline: some aspen trees, a few redbrick buildings, and a radio tower that was the tallest man-made structure in town, though it wasn't quite as high as Berlin. "That trip was special. Just like I know this one will be."

I pulled my sunglasses down from the top of my head and covered my eyes. "Okay, that's enough for now, Orly."

I heard a slow clap behind me. "Wow. You really can just flip the switch like *that*." He snapped his fingers. "It's impressive."

"I'm sorry, *who* are you?" I whipped around to face him. "Don't get me wrong, I've really enjoyed this little tête-à-tête thing we've got going on, but I don't know that I'm super comfortable being followed around by a complete stranger any longer."

He chuckled. "Fair enough. I mean, you didn't pay enough attention to the man transporting you at four hundred miles an hour to know I wasn't him, but no . . . Makes sense." He zipped up his jacket and walked into the wind, toward me, with his arm outstretched. "Sebastian Sudworth."

I glanced at Orly and confirmed he had his camera put away before crossing my arms. "Great. But I'll ask again: *Who are you?*"

His arm remained in front of him, and the grin on his face widened as he looked down at my closed-off stance. "Oh, you really are America's Ray of Sunshine, aren't you?"

Orly spoke up sheepishly. "Brynn, I'm not sure if you know, but Sebastian is—"

"A big fan of yours," he interjected. He winked at Orly and turned back to me. I rolled my eyes, then I remembered I still had my sunglasses on. What a waste of a good eye roll. "Yeah. Guilty as charged. I've always loved the fake emotions and the tears on cue, and the way you are *everyone's* biggest fan. From George Clooney to Boy George. Tony Blair to Tony Danza. That's really some great stuff. But then, as if that wasn't enough, you went and humiliated the town I love on national television. The *people* I love." He threw his hands up in the air. "I mean, after that I just had to rush out and buy a Brynn Cornell poster to hang on my wall."

I grabbed the hinge of my sunglasses between my thumb and forefinger and pulled them off. "Okay, I see what this is. You're a protester or something. A troll." A nagging voice in my head tried to remind me that this troll somehow knew Orly, but my righteous anger was seeing to it that that got pushed to the background. "Well done. You managed to get on my plane. That's impressive and certainly shows more dedication than the usual hater who gives up after trying to slip into my DMs." *That's also scary, come to think of it. Except the pilot knew him by name . . . Nope. Righteous anger now. Sort out the facts later.* "But this ends now!" I yelled at him, my anger reaching its boiling point. "I'm here to do a job—"

"Oh yeah? And what is that job, exactly?" He was cool as a cucumber. And that just made me mad.

"Convincing the people in this stupid little town that I'm

America's freaking sweetheart, so the rest of the world can know they should still love me!"

"Well, may I just say you're off to a *fantastic* start."

He chewed on his twitching bottom lip and barely suppressed a smug smile as he pulled his sunglasses from his jacket pocket. He opened them up and put them on, patted Orly on the shoulder, and then bent over and picked up my suitcase in one hand, Orly's in the other, and began walking toward the ugly orange-and-white thing.

I stood there, flabbergasted, as Orly followed him.

"He's okay, Brynn. Come on," Orly instructed.

"Not until he tells me who he really is!"

Sebastian spun on his heel. "I'm the lucky city councilor of this 'stupid little town' who gets to babysit you all week. So if you don't mind, would America's freaking sweetheart please move her freaking feet and get in the freaking vehicle?" He turned back around and kept walking, but I heard him mutter, "America and I would appreciate it ever so much."

CHAPTER 6

SEBASTIAN

SUNDAY, MARCH 20
4:56 p.m. Mountain Daylight Time

He wasn't going to survive the week. That's all there was to it. She'd somehow, on first sight, robbed him of his ability to be civil. Not friendly or kind. Just civil. That was all he'd needed to achieve. He was the son of a man with diplomacy running through his veins. Civility should not have been too much to ask.

At first, as he loaded the bags into the back of the Bronco, he'd told himself it was Orly's presence that had thrown him off. And it was true. Seeing a familiar face had rocked his equilibrium a bit. In the six years he'd called Adelaide Springs home, he hadn't welcomed a single visitor. Hadn't experienced a single tourist staring at his eyes in the rearview mirror of the Bronco, trying to figure out where they knew him from.

For a long time, he'd expected it. Not just from the tourists but from the locals too. It was just a matter of time, right? It wasn't like he'd been a low-profile personality in his former life. Surely, sooner or later, someone was bound to ask, "Hey, aren't you that news guy? I thought you were dead or something." But no one ever did. And eventually he'd relaxed into the anonymity. Whether it was because he looked like a completely different person than he had when he was clean-shaven and professional, or because he'd aged about twenty years since the last time he was on camera six years ago, or maybe just because no one really cared who he was as long as he minded his own business and stayed out of their way. Whatever the reason, he'd clearly begun taking for granted that no one was ever going to say, "Sebastian Sudworth? What in the world are you doing here?"

So, yeah . . . Orly saying pretty much exactly that had been a shock to his system.

Truth be told, he'd somewhat been bracing himself for Brynn Cornell to recognize him. She was, after all, employed by the same news division of the same network he had spent most of his career with. It had never made sense to him that the morning entertainment shows were under the news division, but so it was. Had she never heard his name? Had the history of his existence in that world been consigned to oblivion? Or was it just that if you'd never appeared on a red carpet with Zendaya, Ms. Cornell didn't bother to take note?

Regardless, he couldn't even use any of that as justification for his lack of decorum. He'd been rude to her beginning with the very first words out of his mouth, before he even saw Orly. Before she had a chance to prove she was exactly the delightful little ray of sunshine he'd suspected her to be.

"Hey, Orly?" Sebastian motioned for him to step aside for a second as his other passenger pushed the front bucket seat forward and hoisted herself into the back of the vehicle. As she attempted to, anyway. Twice her foot got caught in the seat belt, and twice the seat rocketed back onto her hip as she moved to get in, causing her to fall back onto her freestanding leg, which was just barely able to reach the ground.

His natural instincts had never been to deride people. He'd never been a bully. But this week was going to be tough.

"Yeah, man, what's up?" Orly's back was to the symphony of motion that was Brynn Cornell climbing into a Ford Bronco.

Sebastian sighed and held up his finger. "Be right back." He took the three steps over to the Bronco, pushed the bucket seat toward the front, and hoisted up Brynn's bottom using his shoulder. She fell back onto the bench seat, mouth agape and eyes ablaze as he reached down, pulled her aqua shoe with easily a three-inch heel off her foot so she could free it from the tangled seat belt, and handed it to her. Then he took a little too much delight in slamming the door shut.

The outraged expression on her face through the backseat window assured him he had done the right thing—for enjoyment if not civility.

"It's really good to see you, Orly," he said as he walked back over. "It's been . . . what? Seven years?"

Orly looked over his shoulder at a fuming Brynn, still staring at them, and then back to Sebastian. "You're not doing yourself any favors there." Orly was just managing to keep the smile off his face. "She's really not so bad, you know. Admittedly, she didn't show you her best side back there."

Laughter erupted from Sebastian. First because he initially thought Orly was referencing the graceful climb into the Bronco. He quickly realized Orly was talking about their time on the plane, but not before he had to acknowledge to himself that the side he'd hoisted into the vehicle with his shoulder was far from her worst.

"Not so bad, huh?" Sebastian glanced at her again. Little Miss Thang was growing impatient in the back seat, and she began tapping against the window with her fingernail. "If you say so."

Orly smiled and shrugged. "She's always been nice enough to me."

"Sure. You're the one who makes sure her warts don't show."

"Yeah. Well, we all kind of let her down in that department on Friday." He looked down at his feet and then seemed to catch himself from looking back at her again. That was probably a good move, since she was still throwing eye daggers in their direction. Ahem . . . Sebastian's direction. "It really wasn't her fault. The whole day was a disaster. She had every reason to believe she wasn't on camera."

Why did anyone believe that was justification to make it all okay? The public backlash and the pain the citizens of Adelaide Springs were facing didn't stem from disappointment that she wasn't as good at the job as they had thought. They were disappointed that she wasn't the person they'd thought she was. Truth be told, based on the stories he'd heard through the years, he didn't understand why they'd carried around such faith and pride in her to begin with. Maybe it just hurt less that way. It seemed to Sebastian that her entire career had existed between the bookends of being disloyal and disrespectful to every person in the world he counted as a friend.

"If you say so," he repeated with a smile. They might have to agree to disagree on Brynn's culpability, but in that moment it wasn't *her* notoriety he was particularly concerned about. Sebastian looked around unnecessarily to verify no one else was within earshot. Roland Cross's truck was still parked beside the Bronco, but he probably wasn't going anywhere soon. Not when the airport had a satellite dish, and he could catch the WWE Royal Rumble without any interruptions from his wife and four kids.

"Look, Orly, I don't really mention my past around here. There are only a few people I've ever talked with about my old job. Even fewer who know why I left." Doc. Only Doc. "It's just not part of my life anymore. You know?"

As he stood with Orly, who had been a camera operator in the nightly news studio at the time, he was surprised by how much his mouth dried out and how all that moisture made its way to his palms, even all these years later. It had been a long time since he'd spoken to anyone who had their own firsthand knowledge of his previous life. Who'd ever worked with him. Who understood that Sebastian had been at the top of his game one day and essentially persona non grata the next. Even if Orly didn't have any knowledge of what had caused the change, it was unrealistic to believe he didn't experience the network whiplash that must have taken place in the aftermath.

"They certainly won't hear anything from me. Truth be told"— Orly shrugged—"I don't know why you left either."

Sebastian felt his shoulders relax. Nondisclosure agreements were one thing. Knowing they had seemingly been honored was another. "It was just time to get out."

"But the people around here know who you are, right?"

Sebastian chuckled. "I really don't know. If they know, they sure don't seem to care." And that was what had helped turn Adelaide Springs from a refuge into a home.

Orly nodded. "Got it." He dared to turn his head enough to glance back at Brynn, who at that moment was wiping away the fog her breath had left on the window as she gawked out of it. "Pretty sure she doesn't know."

"And that's probably for the best. I'm stuck being the chaperone for the week, but I think if I can stay low-key—"

"And off camera," Orly completed. "Not a problem."

The passenger-side door of the Bronco creaked open as Brynn leaned forward and her head popped out. "I don't want to be rude, but are you two almost done gabbing? It's freezing and I'm starving, and I'm just not sure how interested my viewers are going to be in a week's worth of footage from an airport with two flights a month."

Sebastian knew he had tortured her as much as he could for the moment. Not that torture had been his intent. Just an added bonus. Now, he suspected, it was time for his torture to begin.

Five minutes later Sebastian was thinking of all those people in Adelaide Springs who made up that group of "every person in the world he counted as a friend" and contemplating the cost of a little disloyalty and disrespect of his own.

Doc would eventually forgive me if I dropped her off on his porch.

Andi might, if I bribed her with free manual labor.

Cole already has his grandfather to contend with. No one deserves to be saddled with Old Man Kimball and Brynn Cornell.

"Oh my goodness, would you look at that?" Brynn gasped and leaned up between the two front bucket seats where Sebastian and Orly sat. "Orly, are you getting this?"

Orly lifted his head from the headrest and opened his eyes to look at her. "You mean . . . with my camera? Should I grab it from the back?"

Brynn laughed loudly. Obnoxiously close to Sebastian's ear. "Oh, sorry. I thought you had it. You should probably keep it with you all the time from here on."

"Of course. Sorry about that." Orly turned and attempted to look out the window at whatever had caused Brynn to gasp. "We can come back later and get some footage. What was it?"

She sighed. "Nothing, really. Just memories."

Jo might not forgive me, but we're not all that close anyway.

Sebastian slowed down as he steered the Bronco onto Main Street. Slowing down was the last thing he wanted to do, but the main quarter-mile thoroughfare through town was pretty much the only stretch where you actually had to watch for people.

Everywhere else you had to be alert for deer. Elk. Even the occasional bighorn sheep or cougar—and he wasn't just referring to Maxine Brogan, who sashayed like Blanche from *The Golden Girls* toward his pancake line to show him her latest cross-stitched quote every Saturday when he served breakfast at the senior center.

"So tell me more about you, Sebastian," Brynn ordered as she relaxed back into her seat. "What do you do? What brought you to our beautiful little mountain oasis?"

She was insufferable. Completely intolerable. Since the moment he and Orly had climbed into the vehicle, she had been dripping with sickly sweet fake adoration of her hometown. She couldn't help herself from being overtaken by "waves of emotion" with every building, tree, and mile marker they passed. *Waves of emotion.* Surfing enthusiasts waited their entire lives to encounter the quality and quantity of waves she had supposedly been overcome by in the last five minutes. Everything was "cute" or "charming," and not even Gollum overused the word *precious* as much as she did.

And while he certainly didn't want to talk about himself, he knew he'd be a fool not to step in and rid the air of her grating effusions, at least for a few seconds.

"I do lots of things. City council, of course. Sometimes I'm a driver. A bartender. I'm trying to get the local paper started up again—"

Another gasp. "The church is still there! With that precious little prayer garden in the back!"

Sebastian muttered under his breath. "On weekends I run our local house of ill repute, and of course there's that black-market trading ring that's really starting to take off."

Orly chuckled. Brynn was oblivious.

"So where are we heading? Are there any big happenings tonight?"

He looked up and caught her gaze in the rearview mirror. "What sort of big happenings?"

"Town gatherings? Parties? Maybe a bonfire somewhere?" She shrugged. "I don't know. I just want to be where the action is. I'm so excited to see everyone. To reunite." Her gaze broke away and returned to the side window. Sebastian's eyes probably should have been on the road, but he was driving so slowly as he approached the inn that he was able to catch the nearly indiscernible moment when she began chewing on her bottom lip. "That's the moment I've been waiting for." Those seven words were quiet. Her enthusiasm was muted. There hadn't been a "precious" or a perky grin in sight.

CHAPTER 7

BRYNN

SUNDAY, MARCH 20
5:21 p.m. Mountain Daylight Time

The vehicle rolled to a stop in front of an old brick house that I hadn't thought of in twenty years but that I certainly would have recognized at any time, in any context. Apart from the Atwater home, where Laila and I had most often joined Addie for sleepovers, I had probably spent more time in that old brick house than I had anywhere else in town. Including my own home, if I could help it.

Clarence and Hazel Olivet, Laila's grandparents, had let us turn their attic into a clubhouse, and it had instantly become *the* cool place for the stylish elementary set of Adelaide Springs to hang out. Andi Gardner, who was a few years older, would get paid a buck or two to supervise when we were really young. She'd bring her little sister, Wray, who was a couple years younger than us, and as long as we were nice to Wray, we could get away with pretty much anything.

Not that we ever tried anything too scandalous. We'd make prank phone calls sometimes. On occasion we'd sneak one of Hazel's romance novels up there with us—and truth be told, I guess those were sort of scandalous. But we'd usually grow too shy and scared of getting caught to get engrossed in the really juicy parts. We'd send Wray downstairs to fetch us snacks, and in exchange we'd let her try on our dress-up clothes.

Things had become slightly less innocent as we got older, but we never outgrew our fear of getting caught, so there were limits. We'd sneak Wes and Cole up there when Clarence and Hazel weren't around, which was a big no-no—not that they had any cause for concern. At least not in middle school. In middle school the only off-limits thing we ever did with the boys was steal homework answers. And let's face it: by that time we'd all become quite skilled at cheating off each other. We didn't need to hide away in an attic to commit that particular misdeed. We were just as likely to do it right under Mrs. Stoddard's nose in class.

We tried playing spin the bottle once, but only Addie and Wes were comfortable kissing each other, so that hadn't lasted long. And the one time Cole and I tried to make out, in high school, it had been sitting under the eaves, with only the moonlight cascading through the dormer window. It was the perfect setting for a first kiss, but the moment our lips touched, we dissolved into a fit of childish giggles, thus ending the only realistic prospect of a grade-level romance that existed for either of us.

I was startled out of my nostalgia by the grating creak of the driver's side door opening.

"What are we doing here?"

Sebastian didn't wait around to answer my question before slamming the door shut. Orly opened his and began climbing out just as the tailgate opened. I turned around and sat on my knees to face Sebastian.

"Do the Olivets still live here? Am I staying with them?"

Hadn't they been ancient then? Was it wise for them still to be navigating all those steps?

He looked up at me as he pulled out the bags. "Larry's place is over on Elm."

I shook my head. "No, not Larry. Clarence and Hazel. Larry's parents." Although it was interesting to know that Laila's parents still lived on Elm after all these years.

I received no further information. Only old metal slamming practically in my face.

"You coming, Brynn?" Orly asked.

I looked at him over my left shoulder. He had pulled the front seat forward and, unlike our driver, was leaving the door open for me like a gentleman.

"I'll be right there. I just need a minute."

It all felt like such a whirlwind. It had only been . . . what? One hundred and fifty-five hours ago? Last Monday morning had been the beginning of everything I had worked toward, and by Friday it was all falling apart.

I folded my arms on the back of the seat and rested my forehead against them. "You can do this."

Okay, so I'd screwed up. Yes, yes . . . I'd been through all of that over and over again in my mind. There were other people who screwed up worse than I did, but I was the only one America *saw* screwing up. Fine. I couldn't undo it—I just had to fix it.

I probably hadn't made it easier to fix by mistaking the city councilor for the pilot. Or, more accurately, by once again revealing my true feelings about Adelaide Springs in front of a city councilor who seemed to hate me even before I gave him some pretty good reasons to.

Strike two.

But since then hadn't I been rather delightful? Sure, we'd had that whole awkward climbing-in-the-vehicle debacle, but that was on him.

Except it wasn't. Not entirely. Yes, he'd been the one to make it awkward, and he had definitely handled it much worse than I had, but I needed to do better. I'd grown up in these mountains. I knew how to fish and hunt and camp and fend off bear attacks. And sure, it had been a while since fishing entailed anything more than ordering the omakase sashimi from Sushi Yasuda on Forty-Third Street, but I *had* to do better. There wasn't any margin left for stupid mistakes. From that moment on, I would be exactly who they wanted me to be.

And who is that, exactly?

"I'm leaving now," Sebastian said from the open passenger side door. "Would you like to get out before I do, or are you planning on sleeping in the back of the Bronco and taking your chances with hypothermia tonight?"

I raised my head, looked out the back window, and took one more deep breath. I just needed a little more fuel before I plastered on the smile yet again.

"You're leaving so soon?" I asked, turning around—smile firmly in place—and then climbing out. "So if the Olivets don't live here, why are we . . ." My voice trailed off as the wooden sign in front of the familiar old house answered my question. That's not to say there weren't many more to follow.

The Inn Between.

"Oh . . . I didn't know this was an inn now. That's just . . ."

"Precious?" he asked.

I stood in front of him as he glared at me, and I heard my nervous, bubbly voice from the ride over play back to me.

We'd call that strike two and a half. I wouldn't give him the opportunity to finish me off.

"Look, Mr. Sudworth, I think we got off on the wrong foot. Can we start again?"

I smiled at him as genuinely as I could. It wasn't that I didn't think he was worthy of a genuine smile so much as, at that particular moment, I didn't know if I was capable of one. My face felt tight. Maybe because I was so tired. Maybe because the wind that suddenly whipped past off the mountains made it feel like I'd just received a Botox injection. Or maybe just because I was having a really difficult time figuring out what exactly I should be smiling about.

He sighed. "I guess that depends."

"On?"

"Is there a point in it?"

I tilted my head. "What do you mean?"

"Is anything actually going to be different?" He looked behind him at the door and then back at me. "You don't want to be here."

"That's not true!" My voice had gotten a little too squeaky, but I thought that had *mostly* been believable. "I'm really excited to reunite with—"

"Who?"

"What?"

He stuffed his hands in the pockets of his jacket. "Who are you really excited to reunite with? Who have you stayed in touch with? Who have you *attempted* to stay in touch with?" He took a step toward me and lowered his voice. "Do you even know who lives here?"

"*Now*? Well, no." Heat rose to my cheeks, probably from frustration with this guy who didn't know anything about me but who was taking terrible liberties. Nonetheless, I found myself almost grateful for the increased blood. Whatever had been causing the freeze in my face, a thaw was imminent. "But I can hardly be held responsible for not knowing that an old couple's house was converted to an inn at some point over the course of the past twenty years."

"Yeah, I don't mean in the house. Do you know who lives in

this *town*? I'm just so curious about these anticipated reunions of yours."

I admit, he got me a little on that one. "I, um . . ." The truth? *I sort of just assumed I'm the only person who ever left.* "Look, I don't know why you've already decided you don't like me—"

"Really?!" His laughter filled the air. "How do you not understand? I mean, is it possible? Are you seriously so out of touch with, oh, I don't know, any actual human emotions that you don't understand how deeply you hurt the people of this town on Friday?"

"I didn't know that we'd come out of the commercial break." *Dang it.* I hadn't meant to say that. I knew how weak that was. I knew, as I'd just been reminding myself, that ultimately those facts didn't matter. I opened my mouth to do better, but he beat me to the punch.

"Yes. Obviously. And you didn't know that I wasn't the pilot. I get it. And if you hadn't been caught, no harm would have been done. If I *had* been the pilot rather than a city councilor, it would have been fine that you were rude and demeaning. Right?" Once again I opened my mouth to respond, but this time I was glad I didn't get the chance. The words didn't seem to be there. "But you *were* caught. And there isn't a single person in Adelaide Springs who didn't hear every single word you said about them."

"It wasn't really about *them*—"

"Oh, *that* I believe. It's hard to imagine that you ever have a moment in your life that isn't one hundred percent all about *you*."

The heat in my cheeks was suddenly flooding my entire body. "Alright, that's it! I tried to be nice. I tried to start over. But I've had it with you." The smirk that spread across his face just added fuel to my fire. "You were a jerk to me too. Before I gave you any reason to be."

"I shouldn't have been a jerk. I do apologize for that. But you say I didn't have a reason? My reason, Ms. Cornell, was that I know who you are."

"You don't know me. You don't know anything about me."

"Are you kidding? I know all I need to know."

"Oh yeah? Well, tell me. What do you know?"

"You mean *apart* from the fact that the only honest, authentic words that ever come out of your mouth are the ones you don't mean for anyone to hear?"

"Yes! Apart from that!" *Hang on.* "I mean . . ."

He crossed his arms and laughed, so pleased with himself. *Who is this guy?*

I pointed my finger in his face. "No, listen. That's not fair. That's not what I meant. I'm not saying you're right."

"I know that it all came too easy to you."

"What did?"

"Success. Fame."

I scoffed. "Nothing came easy. *Nothing.* But by all means, *please* feel free to speak as the authority on my life story. And remind me . . . What was it you said you do for a living?"

"Maybe if you had stopped talking for ten seconds—"

"Oh no." I shook my head. "I heard you. City councilor. Driver. Bartender. House of ill repute." His smirk mellowed. *That's right. I'm not the self-absorbed dingbat you think I am.* "But it's the newspaper thing that's probably the key here. You're a journalist, right? Because you're resurrecting a little town newspaper that was only ever good for town gossip and articles stolen from *real* newspapers? Great. Good for you. I'm sure, in your mind, that qualifies you to look down your nose at me with your journalistic integrity and your 'fourth estate' self-righteousness because you would *never* make the same mistake I made. Am I close?"

He glowered at me for a couple of seconds and then turned away from me, muttering to himself as he did. *Interesting.* I'd touched on something finally.

"Is that it? Are you hoping to get some story on me for a nice little column in your nice little paper? Is bringing out the worst in me supposed to lead to your big break?"

"Now you're just embarrassing yourself. As if you haven't done that enough already." He stormed back over to me. "Listen, I don't know what you expected, but there's no big welcome wagon waiting for you. I think that if you hope to save yourself from further embarrassment, it's important you understand that. No one is looking forward to seeing you. No one wanted you to come. That's the truth."

I think I'd known that. At least I'd suspected. That didn't keep it from stinging a little, but that didn't matter. Not really. I wasn't here to deal with the skeletons of my past or make sure we all got back on each other's Christmas card lists. I just needed to put on a good performance. To create some good television. And once that happened, none of us had to be in the same room ever again.

"Besides," he continued, "I wouldn't run that piece if my only options were an in-depth exposé on *you* or the raccoon that keeps turning over garbage cans on Banyon."

"Oh, you're hilarious. Well, let me give you a little advice, journalist to journalist—"

A scornful expression overtook his face. "You're no journalist."

"But you are, I suppose?"

He opened his mouth, but no words came out. I crossed my arms and raised my eyebrows, anxiously awaiting whatever gem was about to fill the air between us, but he disappointed me.

"I'll be back at eight tomorrow morning." I nodded, feeling a bit of whiplash from the sudden pivot to logistics. But disdain was back, lickety-split. "If you're going to have breakfast, you need to do it before then. I'll drive you and Orly around, but I'm not your tour guide and I'm not your den mother. I'm not here to *serve* you. I'm here to keep you in check. I'm running this. Not you."

Without another word, not even so much as a cordial "Get out of my way," he walked past me and slammed the passenger-side door closed. Then he circumnavigated the vehicle, climbed in the driver's seat, and screeched back onto Main Street.

It remained to be seen whether or not I would reunite with old friends, but it was pretty evident I would not be making any new ones.

I grumbled to myself as I watched his taillights fade into the night. Finally, I was thinking of comebacks. Of all the things I should have said. Too little, too late—but there was always tomorrow.

I looked up at the familiar old house and sighed. Adrenaline subsided and blood resumed its normal flow, and once again I felt the wind and realized how cold it was. That was reason enough to go in, even if everything else in me would have just as soon headed to the highway, stuck out my thumb, and hopped in with the first non-axe-murdery-looking person to come along.

Wouldn't have been the first time.

I walked up the wooden steps and peeked in as much as I could through the frosted glass window in the door. I could see shapes and light, but nothing to give me any indication as to whether I would be greeted on the other side by friend or foe.

"Here goes nothing," I muttered.

I turned the knob and walked inside and, thankfully, saw Orly first thing. Oh yeah. I *did* have a friend here. Or at least one person who maybe didn't absolutely hate me. He was sitting on a leather couch in front of a fireplace that I didn't remember being there in the past. No one else was around.

"Everything okay?" he asked, craning his neck over his shoulder.

I looked around the room and tried to reconcile the old memories with the new observations. It didn't look all that different, actually. Yes, the fireplace was new, and there was a reservation desk by the door where Laila's grandparents had housed their china hutch, but it wasn't so different that I couldn't still see Addie playfully hiding in the corner behind the coatrack when Doc came to pick her up, or Wes and Cole politely hanging out in the foyer, acting like they *weren't* over here all the time when Clarence and Hazel were away.

"How do you know that Sebastian guy?" I asked Orly as I plopped down in the armchair next to the couch where he sat.

A yawn escaped from him before he lowered his feet from the ottoman in front of him and turned to face me. "We worked together."

I did a double take. Small-town city councilman, driver, bartender, black-market trader, and self-proclaimed journalist. I didn't know much about Orly's background, but one of those careers seemed like a more probable meeting point for the two of them than the others. Still, Orly was obviously significantly older. And if he'd been working at the network level long enough to be a favorite of Brokaw or Jennings or Rather or whichever of them I'd heard through the grapevine had considered Orly the one they depended on, it was unlikely he and Sebastian had ever inhabited a local affiliate studio together.

"Did you used to moonlight at a bar or something? Were you and Sebastian some Tom Cruise and Bryan Brown–type *Cocktail* duo?" I smiled. "'Hippy Hippy Shake' and all that?"

It was his turn to do a double take. And then he just kept staring at me, his jaw slack and his eyes wide.

"What?" I finally asked with a shrug. "I'm kidding, obviously."

He looked around the empty room and then turned back to me and whispered, "He's Sebastian Sudworth."

What was it going to take for me to get the two of them to understand those words meant nothing to me? "Okay . . ."

"Oh, wow." He began laughing as he pushed himself up from the couch. "I'm heading to bed. See you in the morning."

"Hang on!" I jumped up and hurried after him as he walked past the registration desk toward the staircase. My mind was suddenly full of questions, but first things first. "Where are you going? Where am *I* supposed to go?" I looked around the room as he had a moment earlier, not that there was much point. We were alone. "Is anyone going to get us checked in?"

He pointed toward my suitcase and overnight bag by the desk. On top of them sat a key on a big, vintage-looking key chain with the number *9* on it in gold lettering. "The innkeeper was here and got me checked in, and then she excused herself to her room. She said we're the only guests, so just make ourselves at home. There are some cold cuts in the fridge if you're hungry."

"Oh. Okay." Only two visitors passing through town at any given time. Some things hadn't changed at all.

"Good night," he said as he yawned once again and began walking up the stairs.

"Good night, Orly." I glanced down at my watch and then studied it, trying to make sense of what I was seeing. Was it really only 8:00 p.m.? I would have sworn it was much later. But then again, both Orly and I operated on the *Sunup* schedule, which began each day long before the sun was actually up.

I turned around and faced the front door to make sure I had shut it behind me when I came in and was surprised to see there was still as much sunlight as moonlight reflecting off the snow plowed on the side of the road. *Oh, good grief.* I looked down at my Apple Watch again and fidgeted around to turn off Airplane Mode. The time instantly changed to 6:01 p.m., and I was somehow more exhausted than I had been when I was still operating on Eastern time.

I moseyed into the kitchen and discovered that apart from an island that had been added and some updated appliances, it looked pretty much the same as it had twenty years prior. Muscle memory kicked in, and I felt my hand reaching for the cabinet with the plates; my other hand reaching to pull out the utensil drawer. I knew I would find bread in the bread box next to the toaster and a cutting board in the cabinet next to the sink.

The familiarity seemed to chase away my appetite.

I reached into the refrigerator and grabbed a slice of cheddar cheese from the prepared tray of cold cuts, folded it over, and stuffed it into my mouth. I picked up another slice for good measure before closing the fridge and pocketed an apple from the fruit bowl on the counter before heading back to the entryway. I picked up the key Orly had left on my luggage and turned the key chain over in my hand.

THE INN BETWEEN
Adelaide Springs, Colorado
Josephine Stoddard, Proprietor

A lump formed in my throat at the sight of her name, and I was suddenly grateful that my aggravating time with Sebastian had kept me outside until Mrs. Stoddard excused herself for the night. I wondered if I could manage to leave before she got up and get in after she went to bed for the entire week.

Talk about someone I was pretty sure had already been ancient when I was a child . . .

Mrs. Stoddard had been our teacher in second grade and again in fifth when they were still bussing us to the elementary school in the next county. By high school, when the district no longer had the funds to transport us the thirty-something miles to Del Norte every day, and Adelaide Springs reopened its own school for the first time in a couple of generations, Mrs. Stoddard pretty much taught us everything. She'd been the principal in addition to teaching every math class through all four years, and she also stepped in as the most frequent substitute in every subject across every grade.

She'd also served as our de facto guidance counselor and, to steal Sebastian's term, den mother. Sometimes she'd been closer to an *actual* mother. Addie lost hers in fifth grade, but she still had Doc. When Wes lost his mom senior year, he didn't have anyone. And, of course, I might as well not have had a mother. Most days, I wished I didn't.

Mrs. Stoddard stepped in for all of us.

I looked down at my watch one more time—6:04 p.m. I stuffed the second piece of cheese into my mouth and then carried my bags up the stairs and peered down the hall. There were five doors with numbers on them, and none of them were mine. With dread but also a sense of inevitability, I looked up the next flight of stairs. Of course room 9 was the clubhouse. Of course Mrs. Stoddard had put me in the room where I would, undoubtedly, be assaulted by memories across every square foot.

A little touch of hypothermia in the back of Sebastian's Bronco was starting to sound pretty appealing.

CHAPTER 8

SEBASTIAN

SUNDAY, MARCH 20
6:04 p.m. Mountain Daylight Time

"Hey, pal." Sebastian greeted Murrow after turning the key in the knob of his front door and walking inside. "Where've you been all day?" He threw his keys on the table by the door and then bent over and picked up his ever-faithful and desperately-in-need-of-a-haircut eight-pound Havanese. He responded to Murrow's yaps with a quick chin rub before grabbing his leash from the same table where his keys now sat and clipping it on his collar. "Okay, come on. You must be about to burst."

He set Murrow down and watched his tiny little legs scamper under him for a moment, reminiscent of the Road Runner preparing to take off in an old Looney Tunes cartoon. Rather than go back out the front door he had just come through, he allowed Murrow to lead him to the sliding glass door across the room—which was also on the complete other side of the house.

He loved his strange little cabin sitting on two acres. Well, it wasn't his yet. It was one of several rental properties owned by the Olivets, all of which had been available when he moved into town.

He'd certainly picked the ugliest of them all. Part prefab modular, part stick built, part log cabin, part log sided . . . Various owners and tenants through the years had made well-meaning attempts to turn it into something. Sebastian was determined to finally finish the job before he took Larry up on his offer to let him buy it. He knew Larry would sell it to him for a dime, but he wanted to make it actually worth something and then give Larry the chance to get a better price for it, if he would.

He was pretty sure Larry still wouldn't let him pay what he was owed, but Sebastian would cross that generosity bridge when he came to it.

For the first couple of years he'd lived in Adelaide Springs, the idea of purchasing property and putting down long-term stakes would have sent him running for the hills. It was all supposed to be temporary. Temporary was all he'd ever known, after all.

Adelaide Springs was meant to help get him back on his feet. A little time of rest and self-reflection. A little time of healing.

He'd chosen his patchwork cabin *because* it was the sort of place no one would ever want to settle down in. But it hadn't taken long to figure out that the place offered so much more than Larry had been able to communicate on the flyer he'd picked up off the counter at the Bean Franklin that first time he went in for coffee, after the first night he spent at the inn.

His isolated piece of land, less than three miles from Main Street, had allowed him to discover the stars again. He'd never seen them very much, growing up in an early-nineteenth-century Georgetown row house. He'd fallen in love with them, years later, when he traveled to Afghanistan and Darfur and Ukraine, but somewhere along the line he'd stopped remembering to look up. Realizing, when he arrived in Adelaide Springs, that they were all still there, and seemingly pleased to see him again—they must have been, because he couldn't remember them ever putting on such an elaborate show for him before—had been the first time he'd felt like he was home. It may have been the first time in his entire life.

"Would you please go pee already, Murrow?"

It wasn't that Sebastian was in a hurry to get back inside. Not at all. He'd have gladly stayed out there until the wind turned his fingers numb. But he'd promised Cole he would help out at Cassidy's. He wasn't due for almost an hour yet, but he was more anxious than usual to get there.

Truth be told, he'd come to love the evenings tending bar while Cole ran the kitchen and Laila waited tables. Most Sunday evenings, they were the only ones on duty. It was usually the most fun he had his entire week—apart from the weeks when he also got to attend city council meetings with Cole's grandfather, of course. What a party that was.

But Sunday evenings at Cassidy's were borderline joyous. After 7:00 p.m., when his shift started, hardly anyone came in for dinner. If tourists were passing through, they were sure to be there. There wasn't anywhere else to be, really. But otherwise, it was just the same group of regular locals who drifted in and out—some of them to grab a drink, some of them to see what gossip they could pick up while others drank.

Tonight, he was hoping no one came in. He could hardly wait to talk to Cole and Laila and see what insight they could impart to try to help him understand the town's vain, fake, and obnoxious visitor before he had to be in her presence again in just over thirteen hours.

"There he is!" Laila called out when the door swung open at Cassidy's. She had a tray tucked underneath her arm and was wiping down tables. The place was empty except for Roland Cross sitting with his wife and their two youngest kids at a table, finishing up dinner, and Fenton Norris, sitting at the bar, downing a beer and reading the captions from ESPN on the muted television on the wall.

"Hey, Laila, can I get another one, please?" Fenton asked over his shoulder, holding up his freshly emptied mug. "Hey, Seb."

"I've got it," Sebastian said to Laila in greeting as he passed her and ducked behind the bar. "Can you give me a minute to get my coat off and wash my hands, Fenton? Or is the need a bit more urgent than that tonight?"

The old man smiled at him. "Depends on how good you want your tip to be."

Sebastian laughed and unzipped his jacket—slowly and deliberately—before walking back over to the door and hanging it on one of the hooks. Then he made a point to very noisily excuse himself to the kitchen to wash his hands.

Fenton Norris had never tipped in his life.

"Hey, man," Cole greeted him from the fryer, where he had just dropped some onion rings, by the look of it. "How goes it?"

"Pretty good." Sebastian turned on the water in the sink and began scrubbing his hands like he was prepping for surgery. He would have wanted to be sanitary regardless, of course, but Cole Kimball ran a tight ship. At least once a week they all got told that just because Cassidy's was a little hole in the wall in the middle of nowhere, that was no excuse to slack off in their pursuit of excellence. "How's it been around here? Much of a dinner rush?"

"Eh. Typical Sunday."

The fact was, Cassidy's was a great little restaurant. It didn't look like much, and the building was in desperate need of renovation, but the more Old Man Kimball had backed out of the day-to-day over the years, the more his grandson had been free to turn it into something that deserved more attention than it got.

Every ingredient was fresh, Cole's take on dishes was trendy and delicious, and the customer service was top notch. Especially when Laila was on duty. Pretty much every person who ever walked through the door knew each other, but they probably would have been made to feel that way even if it wasn't the truth.

Cole slung a perfectly juicy burger from the grill and attractively plated it with all the fixings before adding the onion rings. "Order up!"

"Is that mine?" Fenton asked through the serving window as he stepped behind the bar.

"Fenton, sit down," Laila called. "I've got it."

"Okay," Fenton agreed before stepping around the doorway into the kitchen and adding, "I'll get the ketchup."

"It's already on there." Cole crossed his arms and smirked at Fenton. "What? Do you think I suddenly forgot after preparing the exact same dinner for you at least once a week ever since I was nineteen years old?"

Fenton shrugged. "You forgot last time."

"I did not forget last time. You just want something to complain about."

Fenton grumbled, and Sebastian thought he heard him mutter, "What's wrong with that?"

"Is it going to snow more tonight, Fenton?" Laila asked. Fenton loved being asked about the weather.

"Higher up. Not here. And then we're in for a few days of the unseasonably warm stuff before the next storm blows in."

"Another storm, huh?" Laila indulged him.

"Hopefully they'll get the mudslides on 285 cleaned up before it hits. Otherwise they're gonna be shut down awhile. When I was your age, we didn't even have highways. But kids today don't know how to get anywhere unless it's fast."

"Come on, let's get that beer." Sebastian ushered him back to his seat and then returned to the tap. Fenton reached out for the new icy mug he filled, but Sebastian backed up, out of reach. "Andi's on call for Valet Forge, right? I've got to be here tonight, so I can't cover for you." That wasn't even entirely true. He could probably drive a stranded tourist from one side of the county to the other before anyone who wasn't comfortable serving themselves walked through the door, but someone had to keep Fenton in check.

"You know I don't work when the Broncos are playing."

It was strange to realize it, but yes, he was aware of that fact. Fenton didn't do anything but sit right there at that bar when the Broncos were playing football, the Rockies were playing baseball, the Nuggets were playing basketball, or the Avalanche were playing hockey. But the NFL season had ended more than a month ago. Sebastian glanced over his shoulder at the television just in time to see Rod Smith catch an eighty-yard pass and run it into the end zone at Super Bowl XXXIII.

"Oh, come on," Sebastian said, handing Fenton the mug with a laugh. "Your work schedule now takes into account replays of games from 1999?"

"I didn't appreciate Elway enough when he was on the field. It's a gift to be able to relive the golden days. Andi understands that." Fenton took a sip and turned his eyes back to the excitement of a game that would hold no surprises—apart from how far the world had come from being a society that once thought to team up Stevie Wonder, Gloria Estefan, and Big Bad Voodoo Daddy for a Super Bowl halftime show.

"Hey, Seb, can you take an extra shift Tuesday night?" Cole leaned through the serving window. "The PTA group is coming over at five thirty."

"Ooh, they like when *you're* behind the bar," Laila said to him as she returned her tray to its spot. "I don't get *nearly* the tips you do from them."

Sebastian knew that was probably true. The PTA ladies were a usually laced-up group of moms who behaved respectably when you met them on the street. But once a month they got together at Cassidy's for "a glass of wine." A glass of wine begat a daiquiri, and a daiquiri begat tequila shots, and before the night was over there were usually at least a couple of them downing Fireball and stone-cold stingers.

PTA Night was also a successful enterprise for Valet Forge. By 10:00 p.m. it was all hands on deck.

Those ladies may have been respectable when you met them on the street most days, but if you happened to meet them the day following the PTA gathering, they were also wearing sunglasses and refusing to make eye contact with anyone.

"Sure, I should be available . . ." His voice trailed off. *Well, shoot.* Maybe, maybe not. Either way, he couldn't have asked for a better segue. "Well, I think so, anyway. I can't imagine there would be anything happening that late. You know, I'm chaperoning this week." He rolled his eyes for effect. But also because having to babysit Brynn Cornell was eye-roll worthy.

Laila's eyes flew open. "I didn't want to ask, but since you brought it up . . . How'd it go? How is she?"

How'd it go? How is she? Such simple questions, at least in theory.

Cole had nonchalantly mentioned Brynn once or twice through the years, and he seemed weighed down by neither resentment nor nostalgia. Cole was a pretty matter-of-fact guy. Kind, generous, and really funny . . . but levelheaded. Sensible.

Laila was all those things, too, but she did seem to wear her heart on her sleeve more than Cole. Cole liked to tease her about how easily she cried at movies, but even Sebastian wept while watching President Whitmore's speech in *Independence Day* and pretty much every single time James Earl Jones said the word *baseball* in

Field of Dreams. And how could anyone's eyes stay dry when *All the President's Men*'s Ben Bradlee risked his career and reputation by saying he was going to "stand by the boys" and let Woodward and Bernstein run with their story? Sure, maybe that one meant a little more to Sebastian than most, but he still believed the only people who didn't cry were cold, unfeeling robots whose hearts and tear ducts had been replaced by microchips and cynicism.

Sebastian had never really talked to either one of them about Brynn, but he knew enough to know they'd all been friends once upon a time. He had no idea how they felt about her now—in response to Brynn's twenty years away or her hot-mic reentry into their lives. He would need to be careful and proceed with tact, sensitivity, and careful consideration.

"She's just the worst," he blurted out before listening to any of his own good advice about decorum. *Well, okay, then.* "Sorry. I shouldn't be so quick to characterize her that way. I don't really know her." Although he certainly knew all he ever cared to know. "I'm sure deep down she's . . ." What? How was he intending to finish that sentence? *I'm sure deep down she's every bit as artificial and annoying as she is on the surface?* No, that wouldn't do. ". . . maybe *not* the worst?" That was the absolute best he could come up with, and if he'd been hooked up to a lie detector test, he still would have failed.

Cole responded with a sigh from the service window. "I was afraid that was the case. How do you go on national television and say all the things she said if you're not basically the worst?"

Laila echoed Cole's sigh, though hers was heavier. Sadder. "I just don't want to believe that. I want to believe there's some sort of explanation. You know? I mean, an explanation *apart* from her being the worst." She and Cole shared a sad smile, and then Cole turned his attention back to his kitchen.

"I'm assuming she hasn't *always* been the worst?" Sebastian asked. If he was going to survive the next few days, he was going to need some help believing that she was more of a misunderstood villain than a purely evil one. He could suffer through a few days of Severus Snape or Inspector Javert. He'd just have to be careful not to turn his back or steal a loaf of bread. But if she was a Hannibal Lecter, he might need to track down one of those caged mask things.

The downcast smile was still on Laila's lips. "No, not at all."

"Her mom was, though," Fenton volunteered.

Laila nodded. "That's true. All in all, I guess it's sort of a miracle she turned out as well as she did."

"What was so awful about her mother?"

"You name it, really." Fenton continued watching the TV and chewing on onion rings as he answered the question.

"She was horrible to her." Laila spoke quietly. Sadly. "She blamed Brynn for ruining her life."

"How?"

Laila shrugged. "By being born. She'd done some modeling when she was younger—not runway or anything, but department stores and stuff. Then she had Brynn, and that was the end of that. Either because she didn't have the same figure or no one wanted to hire a single mom back then. Maybe just because her look went out of style. Who knows? Regardless, it was all Brynn's fault as far as Elaine was concerned."

"But Elaine wasn't even the worst part," Fenton contributed with a full mouth.

Laila began studying her fingers as she drummed them on the counter. "It was so awful for her, Seb." She sniffed and looked up at him. Apparently it was awful enough that the memories and compassion for her former friend brought tears to her eyes all these years later. "Elaine seemed to think each new guy was the solution to all her problems. You know? And Brynn was expected to just welcome each of them into her life." She shook her head, as if trying to shake away the ancient details in her mind. "They were usually just passing through. The somewhat decent ones got scared off by Elaine being obsessed with them, but trust me . . . there weren't very many decent ones."

Cole walked up behind Laila, wiping his hands on a towel hanging from his waist, and then slung his arm over her shoulder. She leaned into him. "She never talked about it very much, even to us," he said. "But we all knew."

Laila nodded. "For the most part, we just did what we could to keep Brynn away from home. Away from home, she was safe."

Sebastian couldn't say for certain yet if Brynn Cornell was misunderstood, but he was beginning to lean a little more toward her being a villain of the Half-Blood Prince variety rather than the sort who enjoyed fava beans and Chianti.

The bell over the door jingled, and Laila, Cole, and Sebastian all turned to greet whoever was entering with a welcoming smile, which they had each quickly adopted. The gravity of the subject they'd been discussing had to take a temporary back seat to the Cassidy's customer service Cole demanded.

"Hey, Doc," they all said in unison. Fenton kept his eyes glued to the TV and his mouth full of burger but raised one hand in greeting.

Laila headed back out to check on Roland and his family.

"Good evening," Doc called out to the room at large, since Roland and his wife, Paula, had said hello as well.

Laila didn't bother offering him a table. At least a couple nights a week, he came in for dinner alone and sat at the bar to chat with Sebastian, Cole, or whoever else was working that night. And almost always Fenton, of course.

Cole reached out and shook Doc's hand. "What can I get you tonight?" Unlike Fenton and a lot of the regulars, Doc was usually one to mix it up.

Doc looked over at Fenton's plate. "That burger looks good, but you know . . . I'm really craving a steak."

"You want the sirloin off the menu, or do you want me to surprise you? I've been playing around with some flavors—"

A wide smile spread across Doc's face as he raised his hand to silence the chef. "Cole Kimball, you've known me your entire life. Do I really have to answer that question?"

Cole laughed. "No, sir. On it." He headed back into his kitchen.

"Anything to drink?" Sebastian asked.

"Just a decaf coffee, thanks."

Well, that was going to require a bit of teasing.

"Decaf, huh?" Sebastian asked as he poured and then glanced at his watch. "I've always sort of imagined you kept an IV drip of dark roast going all night so you didn't get decaffeinated while you slept."

"I'm grateful for women, Seb. I am. Their hearts and their instincts and their wisdom. The way they care." Doc took a sip of the decaf and then scrunched up his nose at it and returned for another round. "But right now, women are ganging up on me and trying to tell me they know what's best. I don't take too kindly to that."

Sebastian set the orange-rimmed coffeepot back on the burner. "Jo?"

Doc nodded. "Of course. And Addie, long distance." He exhaled. "Mostly Jo."

Sebastian rested his hip on the counter and crossed his arms. "You don't take too kindly to it, and yet you're forcing down decaf."

"Well, like I said . . . I'm grateful for women. Certainly for the women in my life. And sometimes you have to be willing to take one for the team to make sure they feel appreciated." He grinned, and Sebastian laughed.

"So tell me." Doc forced down another gulp. "How's the new lady in *your* life doing?"

Laughter exploded from Cole in the kitchen, and Sebastian flashed a glare over his shoulder.

"Oh, great. She's just . . . swell." Sebastian gave two thumbs up in front of him.

"Can I take it she doesn't come across much better in person than she does on television?"

Sebastian gave that some serious consideration. Truth be told, she came across so much worse in person. Last Friday aside, of course. On TV it was at least possible to see what people saw in her. Why she was so well liked. He himself had never partaken of the Brynn Cornell Kool-Aid, needless to say, but he didn't hold everyone else to his own discerning standard of journalism. He'd never been a regular viewer of any of the morning shows, but he probably respected *Sunup* least of all. For one thing, he'd known Mark Irvine for a lot of years, and each of those years had pre-sented increased evidence that Irvine possessed all the personality and individuality of a water molecule. In contrast to him, and so many of the institutional figures like him, Brynn Cornell was a breath of fresh air. Or at least he could understand how viewers might regard her that way.

It was easy enough to judge her for not actually being what he considered a journalist, but in fairness, he knew that wasn't what she was hired to be. No, he couldn't imagine her in a war zone or even in a yellow slicker trying not to be blown away by rain and hurricane-force winds, but there were other people out doing that. She was paid most likely a great deal of money to be the woman who men wanted to go out with and other women wanted to be friends with. Who college students would aspire to be and who parents would dream of their sons marrying. Who put celebrities at ease and who made "normal" people believe that if only they had the good fortune of running into Brynn Cornell on the street, she'd walk away actually remembering their name.

106

But in real life? In real life, Brynn Cornell boasted all the three-dimensional authenticity of a coloring book. The Mark Irvines of the world were almost better. They were the same dreadful drips in person as they were on the air. They didn't go about deceiving their audience so much as deceiving themselves into believing they were brimming with talent and charisma. In reality, people liked them because they were human ranch dressing. You wouldn't want a bowl of them by themselves, but they went with everything.

Brynn Cornell was no ranch dressing. She was matcha, or some other bitter ingredient that the world had somehow been tricked into believing should be added to everything. All it actually did was ruin the taste and occasionally upset your stomach.

But she was also a victim of her upbringing, from the sound of it. He didn't have to like her, but Sebastian had to admit that learning a little about her past made him at least want to give her the benefit of the doubt a little while longer.

"She's fine, Doc. Today was a little rough, but maybe tomorrow will be better."

Heaven knows it couldn't be any worse.

CHAPTER 9

BRYNN

MONDAY, MARCH 21
7:49 a.m. Mountain Daylight Time

Well, shoot. I'd meant to be out of there a whole lot earlier. Not that I could have gone far. I had to wait for Orly and our Bronco-driving host with the most. But I could have scavenged around the kitchen for a granola bar or something and then enjoyed it while hiding under the back porch with only raccoons and mountain lions to fear and avoid. But I was too late. There were delicious smells wafting up the stairs. That part was nice. But there were also voices.

I stood at the top of the second flight of stairs and took a series of deep breaths. *You can do this, Brynn.* I could. Of course I could. And I *would.* A good night's sleep had helped my perspective tremendously, and the only reason I wasn't out of the inn by the time I wanted to be was that I'd spent my morning figuring it all out. All I'd been missing was a plan.

When I'd told Colton to send me to my hometown, it had been all about action. Sometimes you didn't have the luxury of taking time to think things through. You couldn't always sit down and write out a pros and cons list. Sometimes you had to make a move when an opportunity arose and then, a little later, figure out how to deal with the consequences of the move you made. That was how I'd escaped Adelaide Springs, it was how I'd gotten my first on-air segment at *Good Day LA*, and it was how I ended up sharing a beach house in the Hamptons with half the original cast of *Hamilton* over Thanksgiving weekend. It was also how I'd ended up on a blind date at Chipotle with a Borat impersonator, so obviously my "Act now, deal with the consequences later" approach to life came with risks. But the times it had failed me had been few and far between.

I knew I could count on Orly to do what he did best. He would capture the right shots and make sure I stood in the best light. He'd been in the business a lot longer than I had, and he understood what we were going for here every bit as well as I did. I didn't have to worry about Orly's details. I just needed to worry about mine. It was time for me to kick into gear and do what *I* did best—and that was charm the snot out of people.

The only problem, I'd quickly surmised as I'd spent the morning thinking about the move I'd made, was that Sebastian Sudworth was uncharmable. So now the plan was to somehow ditch him. It should be easy enough.

After all, he had nothing to do with any of this. Kudos to him for sticking around. For making some impact. For breathing some new life into the town. I wasn't sure how long he'd lived here, but obviously he didn't enter until after I had exited. At the absolute maximum of things, maybe he'd been here close to twenty years. Great. Again, kudos. To get voted into city council with any less than the deed to some property that had been obtained under the Homestead Act of 1862 was quite the accomplishment.

But I had a history with these people. For better or worse, I *was* a descendant of one of those pioneer bloodlines. My mother had squandered the money and the land deeds and the mineral rights left to her by her parents long before I was old enough to vote, much less run for local office, and when an attorney tracked me down after her death ten years ago, all I was bequeathed was debt that Elaine had fraudulently associated with my name. *Brynn.* Not the name she had given me. No, she used a name she had never once known me by—which made sense, I figured. *B-R-Y-N-N* was successful, even ten years ago. *B-R-Y-N-N* was considered pretty and talented, and was on the verge of being famous. *B-R-Y-N-N* had value.

My legacy in this town was not a proud one, but deep down they still considered me one of them. They had to. For one week, I *needed* them to think of me as one of them. And Sebastian Sudworth just wasn't going to get the job done.

I took one more deep breath and looked down at myself to make sure I was ready. Admittedly, I looked a little too much like a tourist, with my skinny jeans tucked into boots that were a little too pristine and a light blue cable-knit sweater that reached midway down my thighs, but I'd done the best I could with the time I had. Did we even have a Cabela's in Manhattan? How would I have gone about finding an Adelaide Springs wardrobe without time to shop online?

Panic began rising in my chest, though I wasn't entirely sure if it was due to the fear of being outed as a fraud or the sudden realization that it would take a miracle to simultaneously fit in like a local and avoid ruining my new Prada knee-high boots.

The voices and the smells got stronger as I approached the second-floor landing. Before descending onto the next flight of stairs, I peeked my head around the wall to see if I could figure out who was down there. I listened intently and was able to quickly pick out Orly. There was another male voice that I thought was probably Sebastian's, but it sounded so different when it wasn't berating me that I couldn't be entirely sure. That mystery was quickly solved as a third voice, that of a woman, spoke up.

"Now, Seb, how long are you going to hold that one over my head?"

Laughter from the entire group followed, and I pulled myself back to a normal standing position. Normal . . . except a little straighter.

Twenty years had done nothing to erase Mrs. Stoddard's voice from my head.

"Girls, if you don't stop giggling, I'll never get through this."

That was the reprimand I'd heard from her more than any other. The "this" that she was trying to get through had changed over the years—math equations, homework instructions, graduation rehearsal—but no matter what grade we were in, when we got together, Addie, Laila, and I had been gigglers.

I momentarily contemplated looking around for a fire alarm to pull as a distraction so I could run down the stairs, out the door, and into Sebastian's ugly orange-and-white thing, but thanks to Cole I'd long ago learned how grumpy that little fire-alarm trick made Mrs. Stoddard. It wasn't worth it.

It was possible to sneak out the window at the end of the hall, then shimmy across the trellis and down the tree. Cole had taught me *many* important lessons during my formative years, it seemed. But the way my luck had been going lately, there would probably be a paparazzo there to capture the moment when I inevitably got my hair tangled in the branches and came out looking like Treebeard from *Lord of the Rings.*

Grow up, Brynn, I lectured myself. *Last Wednesday you macraméd plant hangers with Sophie, Countess of Wessex and Forfar. This is not beyond you.*

My shoulders rose as I took in one last steeling breath and began descending the final flight of stairs. All the laughter and chatter instantly subsided as I approached. Either they had been talking about me or my very presence sucked all the joy out of a room. Admittedly, that seemed *more* likely, although the countess had said I was a gem.

Either way, I had a job to do. Last night had been a fluke. *Sebastian* had been a fluke. He didn't like me. So what? Colton hadn't sent Orly and me here to charm badly dressed newbie vagabonds with mysterious pasts.

Shoot!

That's what I'd forgotten. I'd intended to text Orly for more background on how he and Sebastian knew each other.

All three of them were looking at me, probably waiting for me to say something, but first I needed to get a better look at Sebastian, now that we were together in good lighting for the first time. *"He's Sebastian Sudworth,"* Orly had said to me, as if that explained everything, but he didn't look any more familiar to me with fresh eyes and brain.

He appeared to be wearing the exact same thing he'd had on the day before. No, wait. Yesterday had been Smashing Pumpkins. Now the Stone Temple Pilots graced the concert tee du jour. He wasn't bad looking, truth be told. He had nice cheekbones and a good build and kind of a cute, grungy-nerd thing going for him that would have made him quite the catch at Comic-Con, or maybe in Portland. He was wearing glasses today, and the black frames accentuated his moss-green eyes nicely, and if it weren't for a few isolated gray whiskers in the stubble on his cheeks and chin, I might have questioned whether he was old enough to be driving Orly and me around. Well, okay, that was an exaggeration, but seriously . . . If Kenneth Edmonds hadn't already claimed the name, this guy would have been deserving.

Stop it, Brynn. This is no time to be making Babyface pop-culture-geek references in your head. Focus.

In any other place, under any other circumstances, I wouldn't have spent nearly as much time studying his features in such detail. I probably wouldn't have even noticed him. But I'd stuck in there just a little too long already—his eyebrows were beginning to rise, making it clear there was nothing subtle about my observation skills. I was locked in on him like he was my one hope of not puking my guts out on the Gravitron ride at the carnival. I was spinning faster and faster, and the centrifugal force was kicking in . . . and if I turned my head, everyone on the ride with me would be subject to a little trauma at 3 g's.

Of course, true to form, it was just a matter of time before Mrs. Stoddard forced me to snap back to attention. *"Eyes on the board, girls."*

"Yes, yes. We all know Sebastian's very handsome, but you can stare at him later. Breakfast is getting cold."

Orly chuckled, and Sebastian muttered, "Oh, good grief," under his breath, and I was thirteen again, being called out by Mrs. Stoddard for being—in her words—boy crazy. The truth was, I hadn't *meant* to end up on the boys' bus after the all-district field trip to the Underground Mining Museum. I'd just been talking to Cole and Wes, and the next thing I knew, the bus was moving. That hadn't stopped Mrs. Stoddard from flagging down the bus, climbing on, and telling me, "My oversight is safety, not hormones," in front of every boy my age within a sixty-mile radius.

I cleared my throat and gave my cheeks a little lecture. *You will not turn pink. You will not turn pink.* "Good morning, Mrs. Stoddard."

"You haven't changed a bit, Brenda Cornell."

"Brenda?" Orly and Sebastian asked in incredulous and amused unison. Well, Orly was incredulous. The smirk on Sebastian's face made it very clear he was going with amused.

"Um, it's 'Brynn' now, Mrs. Stoddard." *As you very well know.*

I began studying her almost as intently as I had Sebastian. *Wow.* I was pretty sure she had not been complimenting me when she said I hadn't changed, but I wasn't sure how to wrap my head around *her* after twenty years. It was really weird. Mind blowing, actually. In my head, I'd been imagining her how she'd always looked. At least, how I *remembered* her looking. And then, of course, I'd expected to need to add on a couple decades. The reality in front of me just didn't make sense.

It was like when the *Sex and the City* reboot came out, and everyone realized that Carrie, Miranda, and Charlotte were all roughly the same ages Rose, Blanche, and Dorothy had been on *The Golden Girls*. It's really difficult to make sense of it in your brain. That's how I felt looking at Mrs. Stoddard. I would have sworn she was a Cloris Leachman or Angela Lansbury or something when she was teaching me in high school. Realistically, she had probably been in her fifties, which meant she was in her seventies now. But she was in her seventies in a Sigourney Weaver or Jane Seymour in their seventies sort of way. You know—in a way that defies logic and the laws of nature.

"You look really great," I said aloud, though I certainly hadn't meant to. I hated that that was my comeback to something she had said with likely intent to demean me. To put me in my place. But I just couldn't get over it. I tried to reconcile the woman in front of me with the memories in my mind, to see if it was just a lifetime away playing tricks on me. And sure, maybe there was a little of that. But some of it was undeniable and unmistakable. She looked fresher and more active and happier than I had ever seen her. "I mean . . . you look so *alive.*"

She tilted her head. "What did you expect, hon? D'you think we all just shriveled up and died after you left?"

"No. I didn't mean that." I shook my head and looked to Sebastian for assistance. I don't know why I thought he would be there for me. His head was bowed, looking at his feet—probably in discomfort. He certainly wouldn't be the first person to cower in Mrs. Stoddard's presence. I turned my gaze to Orly, and he just shrugged. *A lot of help you are.*

"I'm sorry, Mrs. Stoddard. I just . . ." I dug my fingernails into my palms. *This begins now, Brynn. If you can't gain the support of the closest thing you ever had to a mother, what hope is there of getting anyone else to welcome you back with open arms?* With a forced smile that I really hoped would pass for natural, I said, "Can we please start again? I just meant to say how nice it is to see you. And you do look really great. That's just fact."

How long was she going to keep staring at me, hand on her hip, eyebrow raised? It was 1999, and I was waiting for her to grade my oral presentation on King Ptolemy I and his role in the Hellenistic period. Would my public-speaking skills be enough to earn me a passing grade, or would she expertly cut through my proficiency and determine I had no idea what I was talking about? The silence was agony, and so familiar.

"Come on, Jo." Sebastian spoke to her under his breath and nudged her with his elbow. "Cut her some slack."

My eyes snapped back to him. In surprise, sure, but also in fascination. Confusion. New guy wasn't cowering? New guy was issuing instructions? New guy called her "Jo"? He lifted his eyes and peered over his glasses at me and then back at his shoes.

Mrs. Stoddard released a deep, heavy sigh. "I hope your room was comfortable for you last night. Were you able to get some rest?"

Mrs. Stoddard listens to the new guy?

"Um . . . yeah. It was great. I slept like a baby. Thanks."

She nodded, slid off the stool she was sitting on, and headed back toward the kitchen. "We have breakfast burrito fixings if you're hungry."

I glanced at my watch and then at Sebastian, who was doing the same. It was eight on the nose, and I knew I was running the risk of having my carriage turn back into a pumpkin, but my apple and slices of cheese had long ago worn off. The smell of bacon and green chile in the air was too powerful to resist.

"Did you eat, Orly?"

His eyes began practically rolling back into his head, and I was pretty sure I heard him slurp some drool back in. "Best breakfast I've ever had."

"Well, how could I say no, then?" I smiled at Sebastian, he smiled back, and I began to walk past him into the kitchen. But I had clearly been mistaken when I interpreted his smile as indulgent permission.

"See you later, Jo. Thanks for breakfast." He hopped off his own stool, grabbed his jacket from the back of the couch, and walked to the door.

"Where are you going?" I asked him in the same moment that Mrs. Stoddard handed me a plate with a giant, warm flour tortilla on it, just begging to be filled, wrapped, and devoured.

"You ready, Orly?" he asked.

Poor Orly. He looked like the little kid in *Kramer vs. Kramer* when he's asked which of his parents he wants to live with. On second thought, I don't know if that's an actual scene in the movie, but it might as well have been. Just to see if they could make it a little more depressing.

"Okay." Orly stood up and looked back at me while picking his equipment bags up from the floor.

"Well, wait just a minute!" I stormed at Sebastian, plate in hand. "I know you said you were leaving at eight, but . . ."

"But what?"

"But . . . I'm hungry."

He shrugged. "Orly understood the schedule. Didn't you, Orly?"

Panic filled Orly's eyes again. *Your Honor, can't I live with Meryl Streep and Dustin Hoffman?* "Okay."

"I think I might have some beef jerky in the car if you want it."

I erupted at him. "You *just* told Mrs. Stoddard to cut me some slack! Why can't you practice what you preach?"

The tip of his tongue licked the corner of his lips as a smile spread across them. "I thought she should cut you some slack for just being *you*. But there is no slack when you break the rules."

A growl bubbled up in me. *Today. You'll get rid of him today.* "Fine."

My face clenched up tight and I huffed and puffed air—maybe fire?—out of my nose as I spun on my heel and marched back into the kitchen. I set the plate down on the counter and unballed my fist before I slapped the flour tortilla onto my flat palm and added a small amount of bacon, eggs, hash browns, green chile, salsa, and sour cream. Then, rather than take the time to create anything resembling a burrito, I pulled the tortilla up around the contents like I'd packed them into a drawstring gift bag, tore a paper towel from the nearby roll, and stomped toward the door. "Get in the car, Orly!"

CHAPTER 10

SEBASTIAN

MONDAY, MARCH 21

8:03 a.m. Mountain Daylight Time

He'd had every intention of being nicer today.

And you have been, Sebastian reassured himself. *It's not your fault she doesn't know how to manage her time.*

All the same, he almost felt bad as he looked at her in his rearview mirror, still silently fuming as she tried to eat. It wasn't going well for her, it appeared. She was grappling to hang on to all the components as they fell onto her paper towel—and occasionally her lap, from the looks of it. Most of it had fallen apart before she even buckled her seat belt, as climbing into the back of the Bronco required practice and precision she did not possess. Orly had tried to get her to take the front seat, but of course there was no way on earth she was going to sit next to the man who had ruined her morning.

Sebastian watched her nibble on her southwestern breakfast, which now resembled an assembly line reject bao bun more than a burrito, and his pity momentarily took control away from his scorn.

"Hey . . . Sorry I was so militant about the time."

She looked up and met his eyes in the mirror, and Sebastian had to choke down a chuckle at the fury she communicated in her expression.

"Where are we going, anyway? What's on your itinerary that's so urgent?"

"I have to make a quick stop, but then I'll take you to the coffeehouse for some long-awaited reunions."

She rolled her eyes, and both of her fellow passengers caught it. Sebastian shook his head and pulled his eyes away from the mirror, while Orly took a more direct approach in communicating his displeasure to her.

"That *is* the reason we're here, Brynn."

"I know! I wasn't rolling my eyes at reunions. I was rolling my eyes at him! He was just saying that to aggravate me because last night . . ." Her voice had been getting whinier and higher pitched as she went, but she seemed to suddenly decide it wasn't worth it. She sighed. "Never mind. Sorry. Thanks."

"Happy to help," Sebastian replied. He wasn't happy to help, of course, but considering he had, in fact, set out to aggravate her, and his success had led to that admonishment from Orly, he figured he owed her that small concession.

Sebastian risked another glance in the mirror. She was looking out the side window, chewing on her lip again. At least for a moment. And then she was chewing on a torn strip of tortilla.

He'd been too closed off the day before to really look at her, but in the light of the morning—and maybe in light of the sympathy Cole and Laila had made him feel for her—he couldn't help but notice how beautiful she was. Right then, in that moment, when she was staring into space and not worrying about whether anyone was looking at her . . . he couldn't help but *want* to look at her.

Lucinda Morissey honked her horn at him as she passed by in her minivan to drop her kids off at school, and he waved. When he darted his eyes back to the mirror, Brynn had morphed into the version of herself that Sebastian wasn't nearly as interested in staring at. He didn't have any trouble keeping his eyes on the road when she had that fake grin on her lips and the manufactured *Sunup* sparkle in her eyes.

"Who was that?" she asked. "Anyone I know?"

"Lucinda Morissey." *And how am I supposed to know who you know?*

"Morissey . . . Morissey . . ." She held some bacon between her thumb and forefinger and nibbled on it. "Any relation to Peter and . . . What was his wife's name? Laney?"

"Lacey. Yeah. Lucinda's married to their son—"

"Jake?" Her voice showed genuine interest as she turned around to look out the back, trying to catch sight of the minivan that was surely all the way to the parent drop-off at the public school by now. "Jake Morissey is married? I babysat him when he was barely walking." She turned back around and that plastered-on smile momentarily fell. "Wow. That makes me feel ancient."

There was such a fine line between making friendly conversation and torturing someone you didn't like. It was nice when opportunities arose to kill two birds with one stone. "Jake and Lucinda have a couple kids of their own. Twin girls. I think they're in first grade. Maybe second or third. Or are they in fourth?"

They were in first grade. Sebastian was certain. But it was just too fun watching her eyes grow bigger and bigger until he couldn't help but wonder if they were just going to pop right out of her head.

"Wow," she repeated softly.

Her attention wandered to the passing landscape outside the window, and Sebastian's view of her softened again. When she didn't know anyone was watching, she looked so . . . human. Fragile, almost, but not in a weak way. Quite the opposite, actually.

Like the only reason she seemed fragile was because she had clearly already been broken so many times. But how was she put back together and standing at all unless she was stronger than she appeared?

He couldn't interpret her thoughts just then. Was that forlorn expression because she felt old? He doubted it. All he knew for sure was that what he perceived as her introspection made him unexpectedly sad.

"Hey, Orly," he diverted. "You have kids, right?"

Orly nodded. "Yes, sir. A son and a daughter. And three grandkids now, if you can believe that."

Sebastian whistled through his teeth. "See, Brynn? You don't have anything to worry about. *Orly's* the old one."

Orly laughed good-naturedly, and in response Brynn looked back up and plastered on her performance-ready grin again.

"How about you, Sebastian? Married? Kids?"

He probably would have answered with a simple and truthful "No" and been done with it, if not for the fact that Orly had adjusted in his seat to give him his full attention. The cameraman was probably genuinely interested in the answer. He'd probably been wondering about the current status of the man he'd once known. Sebastian knew there was a chasm between his past life and his current one, connected by details he wasn't willing to talk about. But he knew Orly deserved a little more than a curt two-letter answer.

"No kids. And not married." He glanced quickly at Orly and then shifted his attention back to his driving as he turned down the county road toward his house. "Not anymore."

"Sorry to hear that, man," Orly responded.

Sebastian shook his head. "No, it's okay."

And truthfully, it was. He'd loved Erin—there would never be any doubt about that—and he was pretty sure that once upon a time, she'd loved him. But he'd been a terrible husband. He'd always regret hurting her, and he'd probably always feel just a little bit like a failure for not being able to pull it all together to save it in the end, but he'd moved on. Not to other women. Goodness, no. He hadn't quite gotten to the point of trusting himself not to screw up again.

It wasn't that there weren't single women in Adelaide Springs. There were. Not many, but they were there. And a few of them were even within an appropriate age span for him to date. There was Andi, for instance, who was one of his favorite people on earth. She was widowed and only a year or two older, and she and Sebastian could have been great together. That is, if either of them had had even one iota of interest in the other before they passed into that magical, distant land some people are never fortunate enough to visit in their lifetimes—the village of Like Family to Me, just on the outskirts of The Friend Zone.

Then there was Laila Olivet—the only woman in Adelaide Springs whom Sebastian had even briefly contemplated asking out. She was fun and intelligent, with an artsy bohemian vibe, and had never met a stranger, and Sebastian had always admired how she laughed and cried freely and never apologized for any of it. Laila had been a good friend to him, but they weren't particularly close as an entity on their own. In fact, they were rarely ever in a room together unless Cole was there too.

And *there* was the reason Sebastian had never seriously considered allowing his affection for Laila to progress beyond friendship. Cole and Laila were their own thing. Longtime occupants of The Friend Zone who seemed to have taken the express train through Like Family to Me Village before setting up permanent residence in a kingdom that heretofore Sebastian had thought was only the stuff of legend: Soulmate City. (Where they diligently maintained the dual citizenship granted them by the Platonic Principality.)

So yes, in the end, Erin had been the one to leave. Quite possibly when he needed her most. But by that time, Sebastian had spent years not being there for her. Not giving her a reason to stay. Without her, he'd finally been forced to do the hard work on himself. And ultimately, he'd accepted that he'd done it *for* himself.

He'd always be grateful to Erin for that.

As attuned to the emotional atmosphere as ever, Brynn chose that moment to ask, with a chuckle, "Where are we? This is a sad little property you've brought us to."

He wasn't offended, of course. Just in awe of her once again. He'd never known anyone to stick their foot in their mouth quite as often as she did.

"This is my house. Glad you like it."

He shifted into Park and contemplated just how nice he was willing to be. It would have been the easiest thing in the world to tell her he'd had all those same thoughts about how sad—downright pathetic, even—the property was, every single day. But it was one thing to show her a touch of kindness and understanding. It was another thing entirely to make it seem like she wasn't as rude and thoughtless as she actually was.

She bent over to get a better view through the front windshield. "It does have a lot of personality, doesn't it?"

Sebastian unbuckled his seat belt, opened his door, and stepped out. But he just couldn't leave well enough alone. So he leaned back in and looked at her. "You could have just said, 'Oh, sorry. That was rude of me.' Why do you have to do that?"

She stared at him, and if she was feeling any regret or conviction whatsoever, it sure didn't show on her face. "Do what?"

"'Do what,'" he muttered. "Do you even *know* you do it?"

She looked to Orly as if to say, "What's he going on about?" What appeared to be genuine confusion etched across her brow.

Alright. That's it. No more talking to her. There's no point.

"I'll be right back." He faced Orly. "I have to drop off my dog."

Orly nodded, and as far as Sebastian was concerned, that was the end of it. But Brynn leaned up between the seats with a panicked expression on her face.

"No, you can't. I'm allergic to dogs." She looked at Orly and then back to Sebastian with enough genuine concern that he couldn't even give her a hard time about this one. "Can't someone else drop off your dog, wherever you need to take it?"

"I think you'll be fine."

"No, seriously, Sebastian. I won't be. I'm really not trying to be difficult. I know you don't like me very much, but please don't—"

"Hang on." What sort of Disney princess life did this woman lead? "You think that not liking you very much would be reason enough for me to intentionally send you into anaphylactic shock?"

Her face was red—not in anger or embarrassment, he was pretty sure, but in sincere panic that he would do exactly that. *Wow. And I thought I had trust issues.*

She spoke softly. "Well, it's not *that* bad. But I get really itchy . . ."

He laughed. "And are you itchy now?"

She studied him. "No. Why would I be?"

Sebastian shut the door, went to the back of the Bronco, and opened the gate. Brynn's eyes followed him every step of the way until she'd turned completely around in her seat, just as she had the night before. And there was Murrow, curled up in his bed, which was pretty much always in the back of the Bronco. As soon as he became aware of his human's presence, he jumped up, put his front paws on Sebastian's chest, and began dishing out some excessive love and excitement.

Brynn, of course, jumped back in surprise and, he supposed, mortal fear of getting really itchy. Orly, meanwhile, undid his seat belt, jumped out of the vehicle, and ran to the back in about four seconds flat to pet the dog.

"He's a Havanese. It's a hypoallergenic breed," Sebastian clarified as Murrow took *less* than four seconds flat to sniff and size up Orly and decide he, too, was worthy of his love.

Brynn had backed up as far as she could, between the two front bucket seats. "See, that's a myth. There are no truly hypoallergenic dogs."

"And yet . . . you're still not itchy?"

She scratched at her neck. "I'm a *little* itchy."

Sebastian tilted his head and smirked at her. "He's leaving. Don't worry." He swooped Murrow up in his left arm and began closing the gate with his right. He stopped at the last minute and bent over to look in at her. "Should I bring you some calamine lotion or something? An EpiPen, maybe?"

Brynn squinted at him, and Sebastian *almost* felt guilty. Once the idea of being itchy was planted in someone's head, it was nearly impossible not to feel the itch. That was legit.

Of course the guilt he felt wasn't enough to keep him from adding, "Better not scratch too much. That will just make it worse."

As she turned to face front and covertly scratched at her collarbone, he only felt guilty about having so little guilt.

Sebastian patted Orly on the shoulder as the older man gave the tiny dog one last rub under the chin. He took a quick peek at his watch. Eight eleven. As if it mattered. As he'd told Brynn last night, he was running this show. "Be right back."

Pulling his key from his pocket, he stepped up onto the front porch and set Murrow down as he crossed the threshold. He looked around his living room, which was also his dining room and makeshift office, and thought how it probably would have been nice to invite them in. But he didn't intend to be there very long. And he wasn't sure he was in the mood to hear whatever superficial remarks Brynn would make about his home.

Murrow picked up his favorite squeaker toy and began wrestling with it as Sebastian surveyed the room. It wasn't that the place was a mess, that was for sure. There wasn't enough stuff in there to make a mess. A little table by the door, a couch and recliner, a coffee table, a bigger table for eating, and a couple of dining room chairs . . . What more did a person need? There was a television, of course, but he rarely even turned it on anymore. Most of his viewing took place on his phone or his laptop when the internet signal was strong enough. And he read a lot.

When he first started living on his own, after Erin left, he'd tried playing the role of messy, carefree bachelor. Messy had only lasted a couple weeks. It just wasn't who he was. Even when everything in him—everything in his heart, mind, and soul—was in complete and utter chaos, he just couldn't see any reason not to put his socks in the hamper at night. And, of course, carefree had been just a fleeting aspiration. He was pretty sure he didn't have a truly carefree bone in his body.

"But we've come a long way, haven't we, boy?"

Sebastian plopped down on the couch next to Murrow, who had settled in with his little squirrel friend—a gift from Doc. He pulled his phone out of his pocket in response to the buzz he had felt. He'd been waiting for a text from Andi, and there it was.

> Yeah, feel free to bring her by the Bean whenever you want. The usual suspects are here.

He smiled as he typed his reply.

> Might as well get it out of the way. Can't wait to share her with you all.

The smile slipped from his face as he stared at the words he had just typed, and then with a groan he deleted them rather than sending them. He looked at Murrow for guidance.

"That's not very nice, is it? Do I need to be nice?" Murrow diligently chewed on the latex squirrel's tail, but Sebastian read the look in his uplifted eyes as scorn, judgment, and urging his human to be better. "Yeah . . . I should be nice."

I'm hopeful there can be some healing to come from people seeing her again. Maybe you can encourage everyone to be on their best behavior?

He chewed on the inside of his cheek while he contemplated the new words. He replaced "hopeful" with "hoping"—he wanted to be nice, not tell bald-faced lies—and then hit Send.

Andi sent back a thumbs-up emoji, and he let out a deep breath. Now if only he could somehow compel Brynn to be on *her* best behavior.

Leaning back until the vehicle was visible through the curtain covering the window behind him, Sebastian saw that Orly had climbed back in, and he and Brynn seemed to be engaged in conversation. She was leaning back, doing most of the talking, from the looks of it. That wasn't surprising. Sebastian imagined that a great deal of Brynn's life was probably spent trying to talk her way out of whatever foot-in-mouth thing she had most recently said by mistake.

He knew he should get back out there and share the burden with poor Orly, but he wasn't quite ready to sacrifice his moment of peace just yet. Even for the sake of poor Orly.

"Murrow, come here," he said softly, and the little guy abandoned his squirrel and all projected hints of contempt and hurried over to Sebastian. "We're doing okay, aren't we, pal?" He lifted

Murrow up onto his lap and combed his fingers through the silky tan fur on his ears as the dog curled up and settled in. And for just that little bit of attention, Sebastian was rewarded with all the love a dog could communicate in those chocolate, almond-shaped eyes.

If you'd told him anytime prior to Murrow's arrival in his life that he would ever be the kind of guy who would sit around his empty house alone talking to a dog—a tiny dog that he had to be careful not to lose in the snowbanks and who couldn't go outside untethered owing to the very real risk that he would get carried off by a hawk—he'd have thought you were crazy. His dad had never allowed the Sudworth boys to have dogs growing up. They would have even settled for cats (though he shuddered at the thought now), but they, too, were deemed troublesome, dirty, and unnecessary. Besides, his dad reasoned, people tended to form bonds with those types of animals—heaven forbid—and when they died, all you'd done was invite in unnecessary heartache.

His middle brother, Xavier, had once argued that if that was the case, they probably shouldn't have allowed Sebastian into the family. Someone was bound to get attached to him eventually. It had been a joke, and everyone had laughed—including Sebastian, since Sudworths were trained to have extremely thick skin—but he couldn't deny that it had all impacted the emotional attachments he allowed and didn't allow himself to make through the years.

Wasn't it funny how the most insignificant words could make the biggest impact?

It had taken a whole lot of counseling, self-help books, and prayer—not to mention dabbling in a few things that didn't help at all—for him to be able to put a lot of words and actions from his past into perspective. His and those of others. And it had taken Doc Atwater talking on the phone with his former therapist in London and deciding to prescribe him a *dog*, of all things, for Sebastian to open himself up to an emotional connection for the first time in longer than he cared to admit.

So, yeah . . . he talked to his dog. In some ways, he felt he owed his dog his life. At the very least, he owed him for his quality of life. He owed him for making Sebastian see that he and Lorenzo—the large, blue three-spot gourami fish that far outlived his life expectancy and had to move to Chicago with Sebastian when he started college—had not truly reached the pinnacle of pet-human relations. And he owed him for the peace, joy, and contentment he felt.

He and Murrow both jumped as they were startled out of that contentment by three sharp honks of the Bronco's horn.

"What's taking so long?!"

He peeked out the window again and saw that Brynn had climbed halfway into the driver's seat and was stretching her neck out the open window. Poor Orly was just sitting there with his head buried in his hand.

"That's Brynn Cornell," he said to Murrow with a sigh as he lifted him off his lap and set him back down on the couch. "Now do you understand why 'nice' wasn't my first instinct? She's just a delight, let me tell you." He stood from his seat, and Murrow's little legs took the leap off the couch and followed him. He swooped Murrow up before opening the door, then leaned out and yelled, "Hold your horses, Brenda!"

Her eyes and mouth flew open, but she remained silent as Sebastian shut the door again and set Murrow down. He pulled out his phone and typed up another quick text to Andi.

> I got the impression from Jo that Brynn's real name is Brenda? Everyone should call her that. I think it will make her feel more at home. Be there in ten.

He looked down at Murrow and shrugged. "I tried." He grabbed the leash from the table by the door and clipped it onto Murrow's collar as he began chuckling to himself. They walked to the back door. "Come on, boy. I'd better let you use the bathroom so I can resume thy ladyship's bidding."

CHAPTER 11

BRYNN

"I'll be right back," I heard Sebastian tell Orly, and then Orly climbed back into his seat.

I was still facing the back, but I turned around and sat as Orly mused, "Golly, that's a cute dog. Reminds me of this terrier we had when my kids were little. 'Blueberry,' they named him." He tilted his head to look at me. "You know . . . since our name's 'Hill.'" He shrugged and faced front again and locked his seat belt back into place. "Have you always been allergic?"

"Yeah." I scooted over and situated myself so I could see my reflection in the rearview mirror. I pulled back my jacket and lowered my sweater collar a little. My neck was red, alright, but I was pretty sure that was just from all the scratching. How warm I had gotten from all the activity and concern didn't help.

I yanked my jacket off, but that wasn't enough. "Do you mind if I roll this down?" I pointed to the driver's side window.

"I got it." Orly undid his seat belt again and leaned over. "Thanks."

There was a feeling that I'd never experienced anywhere else that accompanied certain winter and early spring days in the mountains of Colorado. At night, you'd freeze. Not figuratively. You'd literally freeze. Sometimes the temperature would drop down to single digits, with a windchill of negative eighty-four—or so it seemed. But once the sun came up, it felt like summer. I'd kind of forgotten that, but I certainly remembered it now.

"I didn't pack properly," I muttered, pushing up my sleeves as some cool air finally began to hit me.

Orly chuckled and rolled his window down some too. "Yeah, this is weird."

There's a reason the unofficial uniform of Colorado mountain-town youth is a hoodie, shorts, and a pair of Birkenstocks. As you get older, the more mature uniform can be described in one word: *layers*.

We sat in silence until Orly asked, "Did you manage to finish off some breakfast?"

I nodded. "Yeah. No thanks to our chauffeur, of course."

"I think that was the first time I ever had a real breakfast burrito. Life changing, man. Life changing."

"Life changing, huh?" I settled into the corner of the back seat and stretched my legs across the midway point. "Aren't tortillas and meat and eggs and all that pretty much the same the world over?"

His head snapped toward me. "Are you kidding me right now, Cornell? You mean to tell me you've found a place to get a breakfast burrito like that in the Garment District and you've been keeping it to yourself?"

I laughed. "Okay, maybe not." I thought about the flavors. "It's the green chile. It's like salt out here. It's in absolutely everything."

"No complaints here." Orly turned back around. "No, ma'am. You will not hear me complaining." He released a sigh . . . probably still thinking about the burrito. "Jo seems like a great lady."

My eyes widened. "*You* call her Jo?"

"Should I not? She told me to."

"I'm sure it's fine. Just . . . odd. Odd to hear, I mean. She was my teacher for a lot of years, so I'm not sure I'll ever be able to call her anything but Mrs. Stoddard."

My phone chimed from my pocket, and I lifted my hips a bit to be able to slide my hand in to pull it out. They'd been skinny jeans to begin with. Starting the morning with more carbs than I usually consumed in the course of three days hadn't helped, that was for sure.

I read the text. From Colton. To both of us.

"The boss texted," I informed Orly, and he dug out his own phone from the inside pocket of his coat.

How's it going? Getting some good stuff? Have you won them over yet?

"How should we reply to that one?" Orly asked with a laugh. "I can never interpret the tone in texts. I mean, we've only been here a few hours. He's kidding, right?"

Was he? It seemed ludicrous now, of course, to think of having made any significant dent in what we were here to do. Especially considering the only person I'd encountered from my previous life was Mrs. Stoddard, who had made it very clear from moment one that she wasn't at all happy to see me. And based on the reception I'd received from my only new acquaintance, it seemed pretty safe to assume Adelaide Springs wasn't planning to roll out the red carpet and give me the key to the city.

But was Colton joking? I really had no idea. I think I'd

imagined it would all progress better than it was. I would have sworn—in fact, maybe I *did* swear to him?—that it wouldn't take me any time at all to get back into their good graces. Once again, jumping into action without adequately considering the consequences could sometimes be a risk.

Then again, how much of the lack of progress was completely out of my control? All of it, probably. If I'd had the opportunity to interact with some people last night rather than being unceremoniously dumped at the inn. Or if the dog could have been squared away *before* the day began . . .

Yeah, it was pretty clear who was standing in the way of progress.

It was one thing for him not to help me along. For him to be rude and to make his feelings and disapproval known. It was one thing for him to be completely insignificant, as I believed him to be when the day began. But since then? I couldn't get a good read on him. I hadn't been able to shake the way Mrs. Stoddard looked to him. The way she course-corrected based on his guidance.

Oh, and then let's not forget the casual way he shared information about little Jake Morissey and his wife. Their kids. He talked like a local who actually knew the people in this town. He talked like he was one of them.

But when it came right down to it, none of that mattered. What mattered was that he was once again standing in the way of what I had come there to do. There was no reason whatsoever why Orly and I should be stuck roasting in an ugly metal heap on the most unappealing plot of land on the entire Colorado Western Slope when we could have been filming irresistible footage of me winning them all over.

I pulled up my knees and bolted through the space between the seats and pushed on the horn three times. "What's taking so long?"

I called out to Sebastian—maybe just to the whole disappointing world in general—through the open window.

"Brynn!" Orly looked around to see if anyone was around, which of course they weren't. Sebastian's property made the middle of nowhere feel like the epicenter of somewhere. All the same, he was embarrassed of me, if the way he covered his face and sank down in his seat was any indication.

"What? He's making my already difficult job impossible, and I've just about had it with him."

Finally, the front door of his house opened. "Hold your horses, Brenda!" Sebastian shouted from the doorway, still holding that blasted dog.

Oh no, he did not.

He shut the door and went back inside, leaving me to gape after him in shock. Of all the self-righteous, rude, insufferable people I had met in my life—and yes, I'm looking at you, Julie Andrews—Sebastian Sudworth topped the list.

"That's it." I huffed as I sat back in the seat again. "I'm done with this guy." I pulled up Colton's message on my phone again and began typing, saying the words aloud to Orly as I did.

> We got stuck with this impossible tour guide who is out to sabotage the whole thing. Prepared to handle it myself, of course, but am thinking it might be best if you made a call. We'll never get anywhere with this guy. Tried to make it work, but he's crossed the line.

"Um, I don't know that I'd send that if I were you." Orly's words seemed laced in urgency, so I tried to see his side of it.

"Fine." I began typing onto the end of the message, still reading aloud.

Probably best if they don't know I said anything.

"No, Brynn!" Orly laughed nervously and adjusted his body toward me again. "You can't send that. I know you don't like him, but trust me, you don't want to—"

With defiance I raised my phone for him to see and hit Send. "Done."

"Oh, Brynn." He shook his head and lowered it. "Are you *ever* going to stop self-sabotaging your career?"

"*Excuse* me?"

Our phones dinged again, and we both looked down.

Sorry to hear that. Orly, what are your thoughts?

Orly grimaced. I, meanwhile, felt like the air had been knocked out of me. No offense to Orly. I really liked Orly. But what did Orly's opinion on this matter have to do with anything?

"Great. Now look at the position you've put *me* in. What am I supposed to say to that?"

I threw my hands up in the air. "Whatever you want. Clearly I'm at fault here, though I don't have the foggiest idea why, so say what you want. I really don't care." I lowered my hands and crossed my arms as I reclined in the seat again. My posture was the perfect epitome of not caring. I could not *possibly* have cared less. *See? See how much I don't care?* "You and Colton work it out. I don't care." Nope. Didn't care one bit.

He studied me for a few seconds and then shook his head. "Fine." He began typing, but he didn't give me the courtesy I had given him of narrating as a heads-up.

And he texted soooo slowly. Seriously. I was tempted to honk the horn again just to get *him* to hurry things along. And maybe I would have, if not for the fear of being called Brenda again.

Hey, Colton. This is Orly. I agree that these two haven't exactly been hitting it off. But you should know that the "tour guide" is Sebastian Sudworth. I'm not sure it would be a good idea to cause a ruckus. That's just my opinion, and I will respect your decision.

"I'm sorry I had to disagree with you like that to Colton."

Orly's voice sounded pained, but I hadn't yet managed to look up to see if the expression matched the tone. I was too busy trying to make sense of it all in my mind. Unable to vocalize the questions and confusion in my head, and fascinated by the reply that had popped up immediately on Colton's end.

ARE YOU KIDDING ME???

I barely had time to read the brief—but incredibly emphatic—response before my phone rang. I looked up at Orly, whose big, surprised eyes mirrored mine, held it up for him to see it was Colton calling, and then put the phone to my ear.

"Hello?"

"Sebastian Sudworth. As in *Sebastian Sudworth*? Brynn. Please tell me Sudworth is a common name in your hometown—I don't know, like Jones or Smith. Please tell me this is not the Sebastian Sudworth I'm thinking it is."

I must admit . . . above all else, in that moment, I felt really stupid for spending my morning making mental lists of people in Adelaide Springs who might be willing to escort me around town instead of Sebastian Sudworth when I really should have been figuring out who the heck Sebastian Sudworth was.

"Well, Colton, to be honest, I know you and Orly seem to know who this guy is, but I—"

"Is Orly with you?"

"Yes. We're in a car outside of—"

"Put me on speaker."

I quickly did as he instructed and held the phone between Orly and me. "Okay, you're on speaker."

"Orly, this is who I'm thinking of, right?" He sounded calm, but an eye-of-the-storm sort of calm. Not any sort of calm that instilled confidence it was safe to remove the boards I had nailed up over my windows.

"Yes, sir, it is."

I could hear Colton inhaling and exhaling on the other end of the call. I took the opportunity to tap Orly on the arm and mouth the words, "Who is Sebastian Sudworth?" but before he could attempt to silently reply, Colton had apparently gathered himself enough to speak again.

"We're not even going to talk, for the time being, about how genuinely disturbed I am that the woman we just put in the second chair on *Sunup*—*ostensibly* a news program—has never heard of one of the most widely respected journalists of a generation. Although, honestly, Brynn, I am in awe of you sometimes. But be that as it may, here's what you need to know: Sebastian Sudworth has two Pulitzers in International Reporting. It's generally agreed upon that he was cheated out of five or six others. He has a handful of Peabodys. I'm not sure how many Emmys the man won. Probably more than me, although *that* seems difficult to imagine, doesn't it . . . considering the crack team of journalists I lead? He was on the ground in Afghanistan. Syria. Sudan. The network wanted him in the anchor spot, but he wouldn't take it. *Every* network wanted him, but he wouldn't leave the field. And then the guy just disappeared. He left the business and hasn't been heard from since. Now, I guess, we know. He's been holed up in your hometown. *Of course* he has." Colton laughed humorlessly and muttered, "Apparently Adelaide Springs, Colorado, is the Island of Misfit Broadcasters."

Yeah . . . okay. He probably would have shown up on Google if I had thought to look.

Even I, who according to the world-renowned journalist in the Stone Temple Pilots shirt had a gift for putting my foot in my mouth, knew not to say aloud the thoughts running through my head right then. Thoughts about how it wasn't really my fault that I'd never heard of the guy. Okay, sure, maybe he was a big deal in the international reporting game, but first and foremost, I was in the entertainment business. I interviewed politicians and dignitaries, and I reported on the events of the day, but I also once spent a week in Ibiza with Paris Hilton, testing different brands of sunscreen. What did he want from me?

Afghanistan. Syria. Sudan.

I'd covered the Olympics a couple times. I'd had lunch with the First Lady in Germany while the G7 Summit was happening. And I had been on location at Macy's on Black Friday more times than I could count, so you couldn't say I'd never been sent into a war zone.

I gasped. "Do you think he's doing a story on me? Some investigative piece?" That had to be it. Didn't it?

I heard Colton click his tongue against his teeth. "I don't know. I wouldn't think so." I opened my mouth, prepared to insist that *had* to be it, but Colton cut me off. "I'm not sure you're the sort of subject he would be interested in. What do you think, Orly? Any theories?"

Orly shifted position as much as he could in his confined space of the front seat and looked back toward Sebastian's front door. The coast was still clear. "Whatever it is, I don't think it's that."

Why in the world was Sebastian Sudworth in Adelaide Springs? I'd had plenty of questions before, of course, and that was just when he was a relatively young, relatively attractive guy who seemed to have laid down roots in a place that had never had the right climate to grow new trees. But if he was—or had been—all the things Colton said, why in the world would he be here?

"So what do you mean he disappeared? What happened?"

Orly looked at me, I think, imploringly. "Look, Sebastian's a good guy. I don't think we need to do anything to—"

"I agree, Orly," Colton chimed in.

Seriously, what did they think of me? "I wasn't suggesting we should use it against him. Give me a little credit, guys." *Except, whatever happened that caused him to walk away from such an illustrious career . . . Was there something there that I could use? Not to make his life worse, just to make mine better? No. Stop it. Don't be the awful person they think you are.* "I'm just trying to get caught up."

Colton sighed. "No one knows, really. There were NDAs and contract buyouts to the point that there was really nothing left but rumors."

"Like what sorts of rumors?"

Orly's face was overtaken by a fatherly, disapproving frown. I shrugged and continued with a squeakier, more defensive voice than I had begun with. "Shouldn't I know what I'm working with here, if I'm going to be stuck with the guy?"

"I'm not sure you *should* be stuck with the guy, now that I know who the guy is."

"Oh, Colton." I scoffed. "There's no need to rock the boat." I caught myself, right there in that moment, doing something I didn't understand. Why was I arguing against what I had wanted to begin with? I was on the verge of getting my way. Of getting rid of him. Was it just because I didn't like being told what to do? Or because Sebastian Sudworth had suddenly become a lot more interesting? "I don't like him very much—truthfully he's been a real pill from the moment we got here—but I'm sure we can make it work."

Or was it *that*? Did someone suspecting I wasn't up to a task make it imperative that I be given the chance to prove I was? To prove I could make it work, no matter what "it" was? "I mean, he dresses like a second-string pizza delivery guy, and it seems like he's done everything he can to get in the way of the story Orly and I are wanting to tell, but—"

"Is that true, Orly?"

"No, sir. I really don't think so." Orly mouthed, "Sorry," and shrugged, then diverted his eyes away from mine. "I think . . . Well, if I'm being honest, I don't think Sebastian necessarily has a lot of respect for Brynn, or at least not for the type of news—"

Colton's laughter drowned out the rest of Orly's sentence— not that anyone would have struggled to interpret what he was saying. "No, I wouldn't think so. Sudworth always was a bit of a journalism snob."

"But I don't get the impression he's trying to sabotage anything," Orly concluded.

Colton sighed. "All the same, I think it's best we just bring you home, Brynn. We'll figure out another way to—"

"What?!" I shouted into the phone and pulled it closer. "No way. If I leave now, nothing has changed. If I leave now . . ." I may not have had my wits about me enough to do a deep dive into Sebastian Sudworth research, but I *had* taken the time to do a search for #firebrynncornell, which, as of seven thirty that morning, had still been trending. "I'm not quitting. No. Forget it."

"Hey, I wasn't saying—"

"But I have to *fix* this. You *have* to give me a chance to fix this." *You just have to.*

Orly leaned over to get close to the phone again. "I'm with Brynn on this, Colton. I don't think there's any reason to leave. Not yet. If you don't mind my saying so, I think we just need to let her do the job she came to do."

I placed my hand on Orly's jacket-clad forearm and squeezed.

He winked in response and mouthed, "I got you." As I looked at Orly, my eyes beginning to mist, I caught some motion and pointed behind him. There was the two-time Pulitzer winner, locking up his house and carrying a bag of dog poop to his garbage can.

Orly cleared his throat, returned to his normal position, and rebuckled his seat belt while I pulled the phone back with me and lowered my voice.

"He's heading our way, Colton. What should I do?" *Why did I ask? Why didn't I tell him what I would do?* Maybe because I had no idea? All I knew was we couldn't leave. We couldn't give up. If I wanted to return to the *Sunup* couch, the only chance I had was to convince the world that the Brynn Cornell they'd witnessed insulting her hometown last Friday was not the real Brynn Cornell. And the only way to convince the world of that was to convince Adelaide Springs of that. And maybe the only way to convince Adelaide Springs of that . . .

Colton and I arrived at the same impossible directive at the same time.

"Brynn, what do you think are the chances you can turn Sebastian Sudworth into your biggest fan?"

Orly did a wide-eyed double take to the back seat and then tried to look normal again as Sebastian dropped the lid of the trash receptacle and began walking toward us.

Throughout our conversation with Colton, I'd been thinking back on all the interactions Sebastian and I'd had so far, trying to piece together all the reasons he hated me. Because I'd insulted the people and the town he apparently loved? Sure. That went without saying. Because he didn't think I was authentic? Fine. I'd be authentic. What else? He'd said something about journalistic integrity. Or maybe I'd said that? Oh yeah. That was when I was insulting his little town newspaper. True, I hadn't known about the

Peabody-sized upgrade he'd apparently given the *Adelaide Gazette*. I knew I'd hit on something there. I may not have known anything about him, but my gut had done a pretty good job pointing me in the right direction, all things considered.

"You're no journalist." Wasn't that what he'd said? So the journalism snob looked down on the woman who'd gone swimming with sea lions and Hugh Jackman. No surprise there. But now I knew what I was working with, and I could avoid stumbling into any more of those easy-to-attack situations. I could win him over. I would. Because, if nothing else, I'd already been completely authentic about one thing I'd told him.

Nothing in my life had come easy. *Nothing.* And if he thought I didn't have it in me to go toe-to-toe with him, he knew even less about me than I knew about him.

"Consider it done." I clicked the red button to end the call just in time to smile and greet my soon-to-be biggest fan.

CHAPTER 12

SEBASTIAN

It wasn't going to work. That was all there was to it. He was going to drive Orly and Brynn to the Bean, divert his eyes while the citizens of Adelaide Springs unleashed their wrath on her, and then beg the most kindhearted person in sight to relieve him of his duties. Well, the most kindhearted person who wasn't Laila. She was *too* kindhearted. He couldn't do that to her.

Spending a little time with Murrow had had the effect it always did. The very effect Murrow had been trained to deliver, in fact. But the fact that Sebastian had been thinking of Murrow that way again—as a psychiatric service dog rather than just a pet—was unsettling. It had been a while. He'd come too far and made too much progress to ignore the signs and triggers when he saw them in front of him.

Brynn Cornell was nothing more to him than a five-foot-eight walking, talking trigger in impractical boots.

And now, for some strange reason, that trigger was smiling at him and waving. That was new.

144

"Sorry I took so long," Sebastian offered as he climbed back into the vehicle. And he even sort of meant it.

"That's no problem at all." Brynn beamed at him in the rear-view mirror. A different smile than before. Still strange. Still fake, he assumed. But not quite as obviously, obnoxiously so. "Is everything okay with . . . Oh, I'm sorry . . . What did you say your dog's name is again?"

"Murrow. And everything's fine. Thanks."

"Murrow! That's a great name. After Edward R. Murrow, I presume?" She settled into the center seat of the bench and buckled the lap belt. A little more softly she added, "'And that's the way it is.'"

Seriously. The woman would have found a way to ruin journalism even if her sole responsibility was reporting on the Goofus and Gallant comic in *Highlights* magazine.

Sebastian cleared his throat and then backed out of his driveway and onto the county road toward Main Street. "'And that's the way it is' was Walter Cronkite. Murrow's sign-off was, 'Good night, and good luck.'"

Orly had said it in unison with him, both of them adopting their best low, gravelly Murrow voice, which caused them to look at each other in surprise and chuckle.

Brynn sighed in the back seat, and Sebastian glanced in the mirror again. What was it going to be this time? Annoyance that they were wasting time when they should have been talking about her? Disgust that they had left her out of their little inside joke? Or that other reaction? The one he actually sort of liked, even if that meant he was a horrible person—because when she seemed sad, she seemed real.

"That's right." Her voice was quiet, but she wasn't pouty. *Surprising.* "I should have known that. I loved the George Clooney movie. And before you say something about how *of course* I only know Edward R. Murrow because George Clooney made a movie about him . . . Well, I can't really deny it. I was in college when that came out." She stared out the window as she had so much already that morning, but this introspection took on a totally different temperament. It seemed every bit as real, but if there was any sadness there, Sebastian couldn't spot it. "I was an art history major—not because I was particularly into art . . . or history. But it just seemed like a classy, respectable thing to get a degree in."

She tilted her eyes upward at the mirror and offered Sebastian what he interpreted as a humble and self-aware smile. Again, surprising. "Then some friends and I went to see that movie. And yes, I was only interested because I had a crush on George Clooney, and if I'd had any idea it was such a 'brainy movie,' as my friend called it, I probably never would have gone. But that 'brainy movie' unlocked something in me. It made me care, I guess. Not about Murrow, necessarily. No offense to your dog." She caught his eyes again and winked. "And not about McCarthyism, specifically. Although . . . yeah. But mostly just about the power of television. The power of *words*, I guess, and what the right words could do when combined with a little bit of courage."

The space in the Bronco had completely transformed under her power. Sebastian was acutely aware of it at once, and boy oh boy, was it fascinating. It was sort of like elephant snot, or whatever that stuff kids liked to make explode in YouTube videos was called. You took simple ingredients—hydrogen peroxide and yeast or something. Ingredients you thought you knew and understood and that really didn't have any surprises left in them. And then you added salt or canola oil. Something. (Who could keep up with all the viral science experiments these days?) And those dull household ingredients that you thought you understood did this crazy thing and invaded the space all around them. And sure, it made a mess. But you'd deal with the mess later. For the moment, all you could do was enjoy being surrounded by this totally new thing that didn't resemble peroxide, yeast, or candle wax at all.

No . . . it wasn't candle wax.

Sebastian turned onto Main Street and slowed down to a snail's crawl. The illustrious quarter mile that was downtown Adelaide Springs was the most bustling few blocks for many miles around. Regardless of the weather, you could count on seeing citizens milling around on foot and dogs being walked. Depending on the temperature outside and Maxine Brogan's relationship with reality on any given day, there was even a chance of seeing a bearded dragon named Prince Charlemagne on a leash. This day was no exception. It was too cold for Prince Charlemagne, but everything else about Main Street was living up to its reputation. And Sebastian fully expected the sight of people and places and the anticipation of the interactions to come to send the Brynn Cornell of the last couple minutes back into her fortress.

But apparently her household components weren't done interacting with the magnesium citrate. (He was going to have to look up that third ingredient later or it was really going to nag at him.)

"I know that probably sounds really stupid." She sat up straighter, and she was definitely taking in the view outside the window. But her voice remained calm. The subdued smile stayed in place. "Choosing a career path because of a movie, I mean."

"For me it was *All the President's Men*," Sebastian said without thinking. He had never intended to broach the subject of his past career. Orly knew, of course, and Brynn probably did, somewhere deep down, at least. Even with all the humility and self-deprecation he felt most of the time, he knew that outside of small-town America and outside of his own brain, he had been a pretty famous guy. But still. The last thing he wanted to do—with *anyone*—was invite in prying eyes and inquiring minds.

He waved at Clint Boyd and waited for him to back his Lincoln out of the angled parking space so he could pull into it, and he tried to think of a way to surreptitiously change the subject. But Orly—intentionally or not—took that bullet for him.

"*Rear Window.*" Brynn and Sebastian both turned to look at him in confusion, and he shrugged. "It's about a photographer."

"It's about a voyeur!" Laughter burst from Brynn, and Sebastian couldn't help but chuckle with her.

"And a murderer," Sebastian added. "Let's not forget it's about a murderer."

"You're both wrong!" Orly smiled, good-natured as always. "Well . . . maybe you're not *wrong.* But it wasn't really about a voyeur or a murderer to me. It was about a voyeur who used his camera to catch a murderer. And that sparked something in me. There is tremendous power to be found in the lens of a camera. It all just comes down to whether you use the power for good or evil."

Sebastian put the Bronco into Park and then glanced again at the rearview mirror and was surprised to see Brynn smiling at him. He couldn't quite decipher it, but he suspected that if he pulled his gaze away from hers and looked into the mirror at his own eyes, he'd find the same . . . what? What was it, exactly? Reverence, maybe? Awe and wonder at the medium they loved, and maybe even a little bit of unspoken, unexpected gratitude to be caught up in an uncommon moment in which everyone shared that reverence?

Maybe.

Or maybe her smile was the result of images of George Clooney still flitting through her head.

"Hey, Brynn?" Orly was leaning forward in his seat, turning his head to the left and then the right and then back again as he watched the citizens of Adelaide Springs mill about.

Brynn exhaled and diverted her eyes to Orly as she unbuckled her seat belt. "Yeah?"

"I appreciate that heads-up you gave me on the plane. You

know, the one about how I'd probably be the only Catholic in town. City folk. All of that." He expanded his view by turning around to face Brynn and, by extension, the sidewalk on the other side of Main Street. "But I think you neglected to mention this is a town made up entirely of white folks."

A sheepish expression overtook her face, while Sebastian laughed and elbowed Orly. "Not entirely. *Mostly*," he conceded. "But not entirely."

Brynn leaned in and rested her elbows on each of the front seat backs. "It's just that the town was founded by a bunch of white settlers in the 1800s, and no one else exactly flocked here in the years since the silver mining dried up." She turned to Sebastian. "I mean, I guess. Any big influx I don't know about in the last twenty years?"

Sebastian turned to her and was surprised to discover her face so close to him. He was even more surprised when she didn't budge upon the discovery of their proximity to each other.

"Nope. I'm pretty sure I am the sum and substance of the twenty-first-century Adelaide Springs population boom."

It was her scent that surprised him most. If he'd been asked to make a wager, he would have put his money on her smelling like some high-priced perfume with an enticingly distant and unreachable celebrity in its ads. The kind where Rachel Weisz or David Beckham or someone is the mysterious "It" girl or guy at a party and then disappears before sunrise. But she just smelled like lilacs. Freesia, maybe. Something soft and comfortable that dared to whisper the word *spring* over and over while the cold wind of winter blew all around it.

Orly cackled. "Okay, well, as long as I'm not *completely* on my own . . ." He placed his palm on the handle, threatening to open the door, and Sebastian felt desperation boil up inside of him.

Open it. Get some fresh air in here.

Sebastian could have just opened his own door, of course, but that didn't seem to occur to him just then.

Brynn turned her head to face Orly, and Sebastian felt the reprieve for a single moment, before he got a whiff of her long brown hair as it passed by his nose. It matched the scent of her body. Not the same flower, exactly, but it all worked together to create a breathtaking bouquet.

He quickly swallowed down the lump that formed in the back of his throat as he began to panic. Just for a second. Just long enough for him to begin wishing Murrow was there to sense his anxiety, as he always did. But then Orly opened his door. And it wasn't just that the fresh air reminded him it wasn't quite yet spring after all. It wasn't even that Brynn turned away from him at the sound of the creaky door, phone tightly in hand, and began scooting over to Orly's side of the vehicle, preparing to climb out, giving him room to breathe.

It was that the moment the door opened, he heard talk radio blaring from Ken Lindell's insurance agency. He smelled fresh coffee brewing at the Bean Franklin. And he heard the new accessible pedestrian traffic signal at the corner audibly informing everyone it was safe to cross Main Street and continue on Elm. The surprisingly modern, not-in-the-budget traffic signal that even Bill Kimball had voted in support of as Helen Souza's eyesight deteriorated but she refused to quit volunteering at the library every day.

Sebastian loved this town, and Brynn Cornell had attacked it. That was the air he needed to keep breathing.

So maybe she smelled good. So what? And maybe there were moments when she seemed so human that compassion threatened to morph into some unwelcome desire to protect her from . . . something. Maybe, in the last few minutes, she'd even made him acutely aware of something he hadn't thought of in a very long time.

He was a man.

Well, it wasn't that he hadn't thought about being a man. He knew he was a man. He never quite forgot that. He was a *single* man who lived alone and rarely had to lower the toilet seat, after all.

But he was a man who, once upon a time, had really loved women. And not just in the way he loved them now. Now, he loved innocently flirting with the ladies at the senior center and seeing their faces light up in girlish delight when he oohed and aahed over Maxine's latest cross-stitch masterpiece. He loved watching Laila focus all her kindness and warmth on whomever she talked with, making them feel like the most important person in the room. He loved sparring with Jo, knowing that she would ultimately best him in wit and wisdom every single time. And he loved the way Andi didn't take any crap from people but would go out of her way to help anyone at any time.

In his life before, he'd loved Erin too much. His love for her had been toxic—at least that's what Erin, her lawyers, and every marriage counselor they ever conferred with said. His love hadn't allowed her to just be Erin, in addition to Sebastian and Erin. He saw that now, and he regretted it. She was remarkable and fascinating all on her own, and his love for her should have amplified that rather than even subconsciously attempting to diminish it. And he still believed he might have been capable of that sort of love if, at the exact same time he was loving her too much, he hadn't also been making the mistake of not loving her enough. If he had loved her enough to realize *hers* was the love worth fighting for, and that it was his responsibility to make sure no other women stood in the way of that.

It had been six years since his divorce was finalized. Six years since he'd moved to Adelaide Springs. Six years that he'd been too damaged, too disinterested, or too fond of any woman he knew to think of being anything other than a friend. A listener. A helper.

Occasionally a teacher but more often a student. A confidant. An advocate. And sure, a bit of a flirt under the right circumstances.

After six years, he knew he was still damaged. But was it possible he was no longer *too* damaged? He was not fond of Brynn Cornell, that was for sure, but suddenly he couldn't say with absolute certainty that he was disinterested. So whatever was happening, he would have to be careful. Otherwise he was afraid he might accidentally remember other things about being a man.

CHAPTER 13

BRYNN

MONDAY, MARCH 21
8:49 a.m. Mountain Daylight Time

I'd been squeezing my phone in my hands since I ended the call with Colton, but as I climbed out of the Bronco behind Orly, I shoved it into my pocket. I reached back in and grabbed the camera equipment from the back seat, handed it to Orly, and then shut the door.

"You ready for this?" I asked him.

"Are *you*?"

"I'll be fine."

And I meant it. The last few minutes had done more for my confidence than thirty minutes in hair and makeup at *Sunup*—and that was really saying something. You could walk in there feeling like Miracle Max's wife, Valerie, and before you knew it, Pierce, Greta, and Deb made you feel like Princess Buttercup after a Dirty Martini blowout at Drybar. But even Pierce's skills with dry shampoo and sea-salt spray had nothing on the feeling that came from winning over Sebastian Sudworth.

Okay . . . slow down, Brynn. I hadn't won him over. Not yet.

Not entirely. But we'd connected during those last few minutes. I was sure of it.

Connected? Now you're really getting carried away. At the very least, I suspected he wasn't quite as unwavering and resolute in his disdain for me as he had been just a few minutes prior.

I'd take it.

I leaned up against the vehicle and held one of Orly's camera bags while he adjusted a lens, and quickly looked over my left shoulder to make sure Sebastian wasn't within earshot. No worries there. He had wandered off without us and was easily twenty feet away, up on the sidewalk chatting with some guy who, at first glance, reminded me of Kevin Costner. Like, Kevin Costner now. On *Yellowstone*, maybe, but without all the murder and branding and stuff—I hoped. Too old for me to think of in terms of attraction, but definitely sort of hunky in that Kevin-Costner-will-never-not-be-hunky sort of way.

I pulled my eyes away, eager to catch a few seconds alone with Orly. Leaning in, I spoke quietly. "I think it's going really well, don't you?"

"How do you mean?"

I shrugged. "You know. With Mr. Nightly News over there. It's better. Don't you think it's better?"

"I guess so." Orly's eyes darted upward to verify we were still alone. "You don't think Colton was serious, do you? About you needing to turn Sebastian into your biggest fan, I mean."

"It couldn't hurt. It's better than the alternative."

He opened the bag I was holding and pulled out a battery. "What's the alternative?"

"The alternative is him hating me, writing a story for his little newspaper about how much he hates me, and then doing an interview with Anderson Cooper, who *also* hates me, about said hatred."

Orly chuckled. "Anderson Cooper hates you?"

I rolled my eyes. "It's a whole thing." A whole thing going back to that *Sunup3* feature I did on the legacy of his late mother, Gloria Vanderbilt, in which I gave him the nickname Andy Vandy. I thought it was charming, and based on how quickly it was trending and the way it caught on among Anderson's friends and foes, I'd say most of the world agreed with me. Andy Vandy was not amused.

"You didn't seem too worried about the prospect of him writing about you in that newspaper before you knew who he was."

"Orly!" My voice was a little louder than I had meant it to be, so I glanced over my shoulder again. He was still standing there with Costner, but also had his neck hunched over and was busily typing into his phone. "Of course I wasn't worried. I didn't know he was a real journalist who may actually know Anderson Cooper!"

He sighed. "Here's the thing, Brynn. I meant what I said to Colton. I think Sebastian's a really good guy. I know Colton said he was a news snob or whatever, but he always seemed nice and down to earth to me."

"Okay, okay. I know. Sure. Maybe he's a decent human being." I was still skeptical, but whatever. "Maybe he won't write anything bad. But if I can get him to write something *good . . .*"

"So what if he does? Sure . . . great. But we'll be back in New York, and you'll probably be back on the couch before that story hits the local papers, I'm thinking. At least that's the plan, if we focus on what we came here to do, right? Let's get some good footage. Go in there and win these people over. Don't make it all about Sebastian. I really feel like that would be a mistake."

"But people listen to this guy, Orly. That was obvious this morning, before I even had a clue who he was. So don't you think it's still worthwhile to make nice? To really treat him like he's somebody? Like he matters?"

He raised his eyebrow and studied me intently. "I do. Maybe even just because that's how we should treat *all* people."

"You know what I mean."

I looked in the other direction at the coffeehouse. The Bean Franklin. Cute. Very on brand—you know, for Adelaide Springs, if not for any other towns west of the Appalachian Mountains. When I was young, I'd known it as Marietta's, a tiny little homestyle diner owned and operated by Wes's mom until she died our senior year. Countless hours—enough hours to add up to months, probably—had been spent at those tables, drinking root beer floats and eating green chile stew.

I peered through the glass windows that covered most of the storefront. It didn't look all that different inside, apart from the fact that Marietta's had always been packed. As often as my friends and I sat at the tables, we probably sat on the floor in the kitchen more often, when paying customers took up all the other seats. The Bean Franklin was practically empty. I could see a grand total of three shadowy figures inside, two sitting near the far wall and one standing behind the counter.

"There's no one here. I don't have time to win over one person at a time!" Orly followed my gaze and I groaned. "Still think your buddy's not trying to sabotage anything?"

"Look . . . I don't know Sebastian well. I'm not claiming that I do. Back when I was working on the nightly news, he stepped in as substitute anchor three, maybe four times. That's the only time I ever met him. I'm nobody on a set, Brynn. You know that. I was *really* a nobody on *that* set. And yet seven years later, the guy recognized me on a prop plane in Colorado. I can't help but feel a little protective of a guy like that. That's a salt-of-the-earth kinda guy right there, and I just think that maybe you could . . ." He stopped, took the bag from me, zipped it up, and put the strap over his shoulder. "Never mind."

"No, what?"

He took a deep breath and then spoke more quietly but also

more authoritatively. "It probably isn't my place to say anything, but I figure you and I are in this together. And I hope you know I'm rooting for you."

I crossed my arms across my chest. "Say it, Orly."

"Maybe rather than trying to figure out how you can best recover your image after what happened last week, you could try to learn from it." He leaned in and spoke discreetly. "Maybe rather than trying to make it seem like you're a good person, you could just . . . *be* one."

CHAPTER 14

SEBASTIAN

MONDAY, MARCH 21

8:49 a.m. Mountain Daylight Time

"You weren't trying to take off, were you?" Sebastian asked Doc with a grin as he stepped up onto the sidewalk in front of the Bean. He offered his hand, and Doc accepted it, responding with a handshake Sebastian had always thought was a perfect representation of the man himself: firm, forthcoming, but not overbearing.

Also, Sebastian was always surprised by how soft Doc's hands were. To look at him, you'd expect them to be rough and calloused. He was the leader of a generation that had worked hard to keep Adelaide Springs a place that earned its laid-back lifestyle and never took it for granted. He wore boots and Wranglers and looked like he not only belonged in the small rural town but actually set the tone for its reputation. And he probably did. But in a community that valued working the land and living a simpler life than most people desired or understood, Doc Atwater was a bit of a Renaissance man.

"Are you kidding?" Doc answered Sebastian's good-humored chide with one of his own. "Do you think I'd miss an opportunity to see you trying to handle all of this? The circus doesn't come within a hundred miles of here. We have to get our entertainment where we can."

Shortly after Sebastian arrived in Adelaide Springs, he'd written a letter to his mother in which he tried to describe some of the locals. He and his mother shared a love of literature—in fact, he'd only ever started reading fiction, as a teenager, in order to try to connect with her, and it had worked. His true passion and path in life had been set by the little bit he had in common with his dad. But the hobby he shared with his mom had brought them closer through the years, while his father just slipped farther and farther out of reach, no matter how hard he tried to connect.

So, in that letter, he'd found a literary counterpart for all the notable personalities he'd come across in Adelaide Springs. There were a few classifications he still stood by, even after getting to know them better—Jo Stoddard as Professor McGonagall and Laila Olivet as Jane Bennet were chief among them—and he'd thought back on that letter many times through the years, amused and proud of his ability to read people. But it hadn't taken long to realize he'd only scratched the surface with his first impression of Doc Atwater.

He'd compared him to Matthew Cuthbert from *Anne of Green Gables*, and when it came to his kindness and generosity, maybe he hadn't been too far off. But what Sebastian had initially interpreted as shyness, Doc had soon revealed to be a belief that unnecessary words could be just as damaging as the wrong ones. What he'd dismissed as simplemindedness was actually an inspiring mix of humanity and humility.

Doc and Sebastian were, as far as he knew, the two most highly educated people in town. Truth be told, Sebastian lost that contest, but Doc insisted that since they both held doctorates, it was a tie. To truly understand how Doc Atwater surpassed him—in practically every way—Sebastian had only to look at the fact that he himself had arrived in Adelaide Springs six years prior compelled to narcissistically make sure everyone knew how smart he was. No, he hadn't talked to them about his achievements and awards, and he'd done all he could to conceal anything that would encourage them to rush to YouTube and pull up footage of him reporting from the West Bank. (In addition to wanting to keep certain aspects of his past private, he also knew that thanks to the town's antiquated connectivity, that sort of rush would, in Adelaide Springs, literally break the internet.) But he'd undoubtedly been a snot-nosed know-it-all who chimed in on every conversation with a firm belief his opinion was the correct one.

Doc, meanwhile, listened. To everything. To everybody. He'd give his honest thoughts when you asked for them, or if he truly believed he had something worth saying. But then he didn't expect anyone to attribute any more weight to his words than anyone else's. In spite of that, and probably because of it, everyone in town knew that every word out of Doc's mouth was worthy of a little extra attention.

As the handshake ran its course, Doc raised his eyes in Brynn's direction. "How's she doin'?"

Sebastian glanced over his shoulder and surveyed her as she leaned against the Bronco and chatted with Orly, who was preparing his equipment. "Fine, I think. Weird."

"She's doin' weird?"

He turned back to Doc and chuckled. "Yeah. That about sums it up." He took a deep breath and tried to process the events of the morning. He wasn't sure how much he was prepared to share with Doc—mostly because he still hadn't determined what had been real and what had been an art project, generously funded by the Brynn Cornell / *Sunup* Foundation for a Better Tomorrow. "The only reunion so far has been with Jo."

Doc nodded. "I heard. Wasn't exactly heartwarming, from the sound of it."

"I don't think 'heartwarming' was expected by anyone. They mostly pulled off 'cordial.'" A cheeky grin overtook Sebastian's face. "I was able to reap one interesting nugget out of their time together."

"Yeah? What's that?"

He kicked his leg out and rested the heel of his Vans on the cement as he crossed his arms, and then he leaned over and lowered his voice. "Brynn Cornell's real name is *Brenda*?"

With a chuckle, Doc raised his hand and dismissed any potential juiciness to the story. "Yes, but she never went by Brenda. Even as a kid. We've always called her Brynn." His eyes and his chin both rose as he thought about what he had just said. "Well, technically, I guess we called her Bren. As in *B-R-E-N*."

Hmm. Well, admittedly it wasn't going to be nearly as much fun to tease her about being fake and creating an image when she'd done no more than modify the spelling to make it resemble a real name. Bummer.

"Oh. Well, Jo called her Brenda."

Doc sharply took in some air through pursed lips. "That wasn't nice."

"What do you mean?"

"I'm pretty sure Elaine, Brynn's mother, was the only person who ever called her Brenda. Which I'd imagine is why she's gotten as far away from it as she has." He shook his head disapprovingly. "Jo knows better."

Dang it, Doc.

He had a way of making Sebastian feel like a horrible person just by being a really good one.

With a sigh he pulled out his phone and fired off a frantic text to Andi.

Forget what I said. Don't let anyone call her Brenda. I
didn't know that was a traumatic thing. I was just being
a jerk.

A funny jerk, he had thought, but in hindsight . . . just a jerk.

He looked back up at Doc, who had become completely pre-
occupied by the shingles hanging above Ken's insurance agency,
but Sebastian knew he hadn't missed a thing. Doc *never* missed
a thing.

Sebastian peeked over his left shoulder again and was once
again taken aback by what appeared to be actual human emotion
on Brynn's face. Orly was leaning in, speaking emphatically. And
though she was giving Orly her full attention, the way she was dig-
ging her fingers into her arm gave the impression she was having to
work pretty hard to stay present.

"There are moments when she reminds me of everything I hate
about the life I left behind." He turned back to face the man who'd
finally lost interest in pretending to show interest in shingles. "And
there are moments when she sort of makes me miss it."

"Journalism, you mean?"

Yeah, journalism. *Mostly* journalism.

"I thought she was superficial. And don't get me wrong—she
is. Like, ninety-five percent of the time. But every so often . . ."

"Every so often, I suspect you get a glimpse of the girl we
knew." Doc cleared his throat gently. "I'm glad to know she's still
in there somewhere. That's the girl I was hoping to see today."

"Well, I'd keep those hopes in check, if I were you. Like I
said . . ."

Doc laughed. "Only five percent. I know." His eyes softened,
and the laugh lines began blending in with the rest of his weathered
face. "Funny. Humans and chimpanzees are identical in their DNA
except for . . . what? One percent?" He chuckled. "One percent is

all the humanity it took to create the *Mona Lisa* and the steam engine. Beethoven's Ninth and the Declaration of Independence. Seems to me like there's been a whole lot of good to come from a whole lot less than the best five percent of someone." He nudged Sebastian with his elbow. "Give her best five percent a chance to grow into more. That's how it happens. That's how you bring out the best in people. Not by focusing on the ninety-five, that's for sure."

Doc released a heavy sigh then, and it became clear he was shifting gears from the philosophical to the practical. "Bill's preparing to make a bit of a scene."

"What do you mean?"

"He sent everyone home and decided the council needs a personal apology before Brynn can do any filming around town."

Sebastian stepped away from the wall enough to get a better look through the window. He'd been so focused on Doc as he approached, he hadn't even noticed how empty the Bean was. Bill and Jo sat alone at a table in the back, and Andi's face was scrunched up and she appeared to be grumbling to herself as she sorted cream and sugar packets.

"Are you kidding me? He can't do that. We voted. She has the right to—"

"I know." Doc nodded and spoke calmly and slowly, no doubt hoping to bring Sebastian's escalating temper alongside.

"She doesn't owe us an apology. I mean, maybe she does, but not in any sort of official—"

"I know, Seb. I'm with you. And so is Jo. But you know what a stink Bill can cause—"

"Because we let him!" Sebastian seethed. "She's going to think we . . ." He rolled his eyes as he saw it all playing out in his mind. Great. "She's going to think *I* set this up. Set *her* up."

Doc shook his head. "Don't worry about that."

Sebastian scoffed. "Easy for you to say. She and I haven't exactly been making progress on our Camp David peace accords as it is."

As Doc's eyebrows rose in amusement, Sebastian figured the older man was probably thinking at least one of the same two things he was at that moment. Either "Camp David peace accords? Why do you always have to be such a dork?" or "Why do you care what Brynn Cornell thinks?"

Doc was a lot nicer to him than he was to himself, so he was probably just thinking the second thing. They were both excellent questions, but the dork one would be waiting for him later, as it was *always* waiting. The caring one probably deserved some attention he didn't have time to give just then.

"I'll talk to her," Doc offered. "Let her know it's not your fault."

"Oh, whatever. I mean, only if you want. It's not that I really care."

"Of course."

Sebastian felt like he should backpedal some more, but deep down he knew it wouldn't do any good. Not when he didn't have a clue what he was pedaling away from or toward. Really, he was just spinning his wheels.

"I'll, um . . . I guess I'll go tell her you want to talk to her, then." He tapped Doc twice on the arm with the side of his balled-up hand and began walking back to Orly and Brynn.

"Isn't it funny?" Doc called out, just as Sebastian turned away. "It's just that tiny little percentage of difference between us and the monkeys that keeps us from slinging our poop at one another."

Hard to believe he'd never seen *that* cross-stitched nugget of wisdom hanging on Maxine's wall.

CHAPTER 15

BRYNN

MONDAY, MARCH 21
8:56 a.m. Mountain Daylight Time

I tried to maintain eye contact with Orly, but my eyes felt too heavy. Too strained. A like-poled magnet was coming straight at me from Orly's intent gaze, repelling my eyes and my senses. And the opposite pole of the magnet was anywhere—*everywhere*—else, attracting my focus and scattering my defenses, which were panicked, searching for a place to grab hold.

"Hey, Sebastian." Orly said it in a loud, intentional way that made it clear the subject of our discussion was approaching. Or at least he *had* been the subject of our discussion, until it somehow became about me.

"Hey. So . . ." Sebastian released a gust of air as he stepped closer. "This may have been a bit of a bust. I thought there would be more people here."

I sniffed and feverishly blinked a few times before facing him. "Oh, really?"

He took in my snide tone—one I hadn't even intended to use—and an impatient expression overtook his face. "Yes, really."

He crossed his arms and his closed-off body language mirrored mine.

The magnets in my eyes suddenly seemed to affect my brain too. When had my mind opened for business as a hands-on magnetic polarity exhibit at a children's museum? Pushing and pulling, attracting and repelling. It was too much. I couldn't remember what role I was supposed to be playing.

"Maybe rather than trying to make it seem like you're a good person, you could just . . . be one."

When I looked at Sebastian, I saw his annoyance with me, and that made me want to both spar and apologize. I didn't know which to pick. Just under his layer of annoyance was so much sincerity. Even as his body was closed off to me and his eyes fumed, I could detect the apology and humility with which he had approached us. But the fight came so easily. For both of us, it seemed.

It was this place. It had to be. No, the fact that my words had gone out to a live audience on Friday hadn't been my fault, but it was easy enough to believe the subject matter of my hometown had thrown me off my game, just enough. And if even discussing it had that sort of impact, was it any wonder I couldn't get my bearings now that I was back here? Adelaide Springs was my Bermuda Triangle, sending my compass and gauges spinning.

I'd spent twenty years trying to rid myself of what remained of *B-R-E-N.* Brenda Cornell wasn't bad or weak, but her life and her mind were chaos. She was full of regret and sadness. She was lonely. She was a fighter, but not the right kind of fighter to survive in the world I had chosen to inhabit. Brenda fought for survival, and I was grateful that will to survive had lasted long enough to get me out. But those survival instincts weren't the same ones you needed to get ahead. To keep climbing. To find the confidence and determination to convince the world you weren't just a scared, broken little girl begging for someone to throw you a life rope.

B-R-Y-N-N didn't belong in Adelaide Springs, Colorado, any more than *B-R-E-N* belonged in studio 2-A in midtown Manhattan.

I took a deep breath and implored my body to at least give off the appearance of letting down its guard. That guard had been built up over an entire lifetime, and it wasn't going to crumble easily. But if I had any hope at all of sailing out of here with so much as a life raft intact, I had to start somewhere.

"Thank you, Sebastian. It will be nice to visit with whoever *is* here."

Sebastian stared at me, his shoulders relaxing as every other muscle in his body seemed to bristle at the same time. I almost felt for him. Truthfully, I'd never had an easy time making sense of what was going on in my own head. I could only imagine how disturbing it must have been to witness from the outside.

"Yeah, well . . ." He cleared his throat and took another step toward me. "You may not feel that way here in a second."

My stomach dropped. "Why?"

He stepped around the front of the vehicle and joined us. "I guess the city council sort of wants to have a chat with you."

"The city council? Aren't *you* the city council?" Nervous, absurd laughter spilled out of me. "Do I have some unpaid speeding tickets from twenty years ago or something?"

"I really don't know much more than you do. The mayor just told me one of the other council members was insistent on some time with you. I guess he sort of chased everyone else off." He shrugged, and for the first time I sensed his anger wasn't just directed toward me. This time. "Honestly, Brynn, I didn't know anything about this. This really is where all the locals hang out in the morning. The owner's a good friend of mine, and I checked with her before we came. There was a good crowd. I . . ." He raised his hands in the air, and words seemed to fail him.

"It's okay," I said softly.

"They probably just want to unload a little about last Friday."

I smiled at Sebastian—*for* Sebastian, maybe?—and shook my head. "Depending on who we've got in there, I'm willing to bet they've been carrying around some things for longer than three days." One corner of my mouth managed to maintain the smile formation, but the other slipped down as I thought about the reality of that statement.

On the scale of hatred the citizens of Adelaide Springs felt for me, just for leaving without saying goodbye—and not even factoring in the *Sunup* stuff yet—I didn't have to think very hard to determine who was probably at the top of the list. And I knew the people who had the most reason to hate me were also the ones who never would have needed me to explain why I left. They would have packed my bags and cheered me on. Which, I suppose, made it all the more unforgivable that I hadn't told them. That I hadn't said goodbye. That I spent the next twenty years doing all I could to forget they were still out in the world, probably wondering what they'd done wrong. I hadn't even had the decency to tell them that the only thing they'd done wrong was love me more than I could accept if I was to have any chance of making it without them.

Tears sprang to my eyes. *Pull yourself together, Brynn. You don't have time for this.* I'd had so many different types of armor through the years. Desperation. Immaturity. Ambition. The swapping of a *Y* for an *E* and the addition of another *N*. In twenty years I couldn't remember ever truly regretting what I did or how I did it. And I didn't have time for the Bermuda Triangle of the Rocky Mountains to make my internal compass go haywire right now.

"Are you okay?" Orly asked.

"Yeah. Of course." I was grateful for the always reliable gusts of cold March wind sweeping through. Everyone's eyes watered when the air hit. I quickly flicked away the moisture in the corners of my eyes and looked at Sebastian. His head was lowered, but I caught him discreetly raising his eyes to look at me. "So who's on the council, apart from you?"

"Jo. And Bill Kimball—"

My eyes flew open. "Old Man Kimball's still alive?"

Sebastian chuckled. "Are you kidding? I'm pretty sure he's going to outlive us all."

"Is he still a curmudgeonly old—"

"Oh, most definitely. And for the record, I'm pretty sure he hates me."

I laughed. "I'm pretty sure he hates everyone." Sheesh. Old Man Kimball. Talk about someone I never thought I'd see again. And it certainly wasn't that I was looking forward to the reunion. But it was funny . . . the fear was gone in an instant. My former teacher and the grandfather of one of my best friends. They were each terrifying in their own ways, but deep down they had both loved me once, and I had loved them.

Well, maybe Old Man Kimball hadn't loved me, exactly, but he'd had plenty of opportunities to make good on his threat to run and get his shotgun when we'd all snuck into the bar late at night with Cole, and he never had. If years of not shooting someone when you have the chance isn't love, I don't know what is.

"Orly, are you ready? Film it all. For better or worse." I lowered my voice and added, "Although there's a very good chance only half of what Bill Kimball says will be appropriate to air."

I stepped between them and began walking toward the Main Street storefront, but Sebastian's hand on my elbow stopped me.

"Before you go in . . ."

There was something about the tiniest bit of human touch right there in that moment, when I was feeling the vulnerability that came with a long-postponed day of reckoning, that made me want to turn around and get a hug. To let one of them hug me. I didn't even care who—although, let's face it, my only slim chance for a hug was from Orly. But to just let someone . . . *beg* someone to wrap their arms around me. To make the chill go away. To make, just for a second, the whole blasted thing go away.

Needless to say, Sebastian Sudworth hadn't stopped me in hopes of giving me a hug.

"The mayor would like to talk to you for a minute."

I bit my lip and turned back to him. "Okay. Sure." I looked up at the man he had been speaking with on the sidewalk, just as Sebastian pointed to him. I would inquire as to the ousting of Lady Xanadu another time.

"I'm pretty sure you know Griffin Atwater. Doc."

What in the name of *Dances with Wolves* was happening?

Mouth agape and with eyes as big as the whole wide *Waterworld*, I studied the man with the denim shirt tucked into his jeans that led down to cowboy boots and then snapped my eyes back to Sebastian. No . . . he was messing with me. First of all, Doc's name was Griffin? I was this many days old when I learned that. But that couldn't be him. Could it? I couldn't quite come up with a logical explanation as to why Sebastian Sudworth would think to play that particular practical joke on me, but there was no way that was Doc Atwater. I'd been shocked by Mrs. Stoddard, but *this*?

Except . . . I was looking right into his eyes. And even with all Costner references aside, the man in front of me raising one hand in greeting and smiling was suddenly as familiar to me as every single note of *The Bodyguard* soundtrack, which Addie, Laila, and I had listened to on constant loop for about two years, pretending we could sing like Whitney. I saw the only doctor I'd ever had in the first half of my life. I saw my best friend's dad. I saw the person who'd paid for my bus fare to California—though he probably hadn't known that's how I would put my graduation gift to use. I saw the man who used to set a place for me at his table every night, just in case my mother forgot to buy groceries or pay the electric bill. Just in case she didn't bother coming home.

I saw the only adult man my little-girl self had ever felt completely comfortable with.

The emotion bubbled up in me, and heaves overtook my breathing as I tried to swallow it all down, but the longer I stared into his heartbreakingly familiar eyes, the more hopeless it became. I grabbed on to Sebastian's arm, because he was there, and begged my knees not to give out. It was too late for my eyes. Tears were falling freely, and Doc saw it. Doc saw *me* and came rushing over, and within seconds I was safe and secure and wrapped in his arms, and the compass in my head was finally pointing north.

"Welcome home, kid."

CHAPTER 16

SEBASTIAN

MONDAY, MARCH 21
9:05 a.m. Mountain Daylight Time

Jo looked up from her coffee and Bill looked up from his newspaper in response to the jingle of the bell above the door.

"What are you doing, Bill?" Sebastian asked as soon as he entered. He pulled off his jacket and hung it by the door before walking up to their table, pulling out an empty chair, and swinging it around, slinging his leg over and sitting in it backward like he was Mario Lopez, circa 1991. He couldn't remember ever sitting in a chair that way, but in the moment it just felt right. Like invoking the power of youth and Bayside High would help him win the day. "What can you possibly hope to accomplish with this little coup d'état?"

Bill returned his eyes to his paper. "As I see it, you and Doc are the ones staging the coup. You forced this whole thing on us—"

"We voted!"

"—and come to that, I think we need to revisit the bylaws. Why should the mayor have the deciding vote?"

Jo sighed. "Then like I said, Bill, we can discuss that. Bring it up at a town meeting. Maybe we need to have a fifth person on council. Whatever. But the vote was fair—"

Old Man Kimball lowered his paper in a huff. "The *vote*, if you recall, Josephine, was supposed to be about Township Days. That's what was on the agenda. I'm not even sure the vote about the Cornell girl has any legal standing."

Sebastian's eyes grew wide as they locked with Jo's, and she rolled hers and shook her head. *Legal standing.* Bill was one to be a stickler about legal standing, considering the number of times Jo had had to record into the minutes things like, *The quorum proceeded with the vote after Mr. Kimball dozed off.*

"Where is she, anyway?" Jo asked. "Did she get scared away?"

No, she hadn't gotten scared away. She'd probably had every right to refuse to go along with whatever this was, but she hadn't fought it.

"She's out talking to Doc."

The sight of her—tough, obstinate, often rude, usually infuriating Brynn Cornell—wrapped in Doc Atwater's arms had taken him off guard. Her face buried in his chest and her shoulders bouncing up and down. Heaving. With every heave resulting in Doc holding her tighter.

He just hadn't been prepared for that.

Bill harumphed under his breath. "Always the nice guy."

"And what's so wrong with being the nice guy, Bill?" Jo asked. She pushed up and adjusted in the wooden chair. "I'm as put out with her as anyone. She made her choices, and she has to deal with the consequences of them. But I'm guessing she's dealing with a lot tougher stuff than you wanting to scold her and try to make her feel guilty, or whatever you're doing. So if Doc's choice is to be nice to her, good for him. Someone needs to be."

The bell over the door jingled again, and all three of them looked up. Doc's arm had guided Brynn in, but he stepped back slightly as they crossed over the threshold. Orly trailed close behind, camera on his shoulder, but as soon as they all got inside, he crossed to the other side of the room and became nearly invisible in plain sight. Sebastian met Brynn's eyes, red and swollen from the tears and the wind, and offered her a smile.

Someone needed to.

She smiled back and then stepped toward them. Her focus wandered away from Sebastian, and he felt relieved as he let the grin dissipate. It wasn't that he didn't want to smile at her, it was just that the expression didn't match the way he was feeling inside. For the first time, he realized he probably understood how she was feeling more than anyone else could.

She deserved to be yanked off the air. She absolutely deserved it. Just like he had deserved it. She deserved to be suspended. Maybe even to be fired. They'd made the same mistake—each in their separate ways. They'd allowed the personal to encroach the ground of the professional, and in doing so they'd broken one of the sacred rules of journalism. Even *entertainment* journalism. Sebastian had long ago accepted the consequences he'd had to face, and like Jo said, Brynn would have to come to terms with hers too.

But she didn't deserve to be bullied. She didn't deserve to be sent on a wild-goose chase toward redemption that, if he knew Bill Kimball, would always be out of reach. He'd keep dangling the carrot, just because he was a miserable old man who insisted on company in his misery.

"Good morning, Mr. Kimball. It's good to see you again."

Brynn stepped up to the table and placed her hand on the top corner of Sebastian's chairback, which his arms were crossed on top of. He looked down at her slender, perfectly manicured fingers as they mindlessly traced the ornate etched pattern of the wood, just an inch away from his arm.

"And, Mrs. Stoddard, I want to apologize again for how awkward I made things this morning. Thank you for your hospitality. It's amazing what you've done with that house. It's like it was always meant to be what you've made it."

Sebastian was afraid to move. Afraid to breathe. Brynn had probably just grabbed on to the first tactile thing she could find. She was probably trying to avoid fidgeting. She just needed something to do with her hands. She probably didn't even realize his arm was so close. And he didn't want to move and unnecessarily jar her into awareness.

Then again, what if—in an absurd, messed-up turn of events—she felt like *he*, of all people, was the closest thing she had to an ally at the table. What if there was nothing mindless about the proximity between their skin at all? Was it insane to believe that maybe he was providing her some small amount of comfort?

The small likelihood of that made him simultaneously hesitant and desperate to put some space between them.

"You might want to take a seat," Bill ordered her under a thin veil of suggestion.

There were only the three chairs at the table, and Sebastian literally jumped at his opportunity to gracefully step away from the possibility her finger would accidentally brush against his forearm.

"Here, take this one," he whispered to her as he stood and with his right hand whipped his chair around to face the table properly. It was a deft, smooth, seamless escape under the guise of chivalry and politeness. He nailed it. Or, rather, he would have nailed it if, as his left hand offered her the chair, his right hand hadn't landed on her lower back to guide her to the seat.

She was wearing a big puffy coat. Maybe she hadn't noticed.

Yeah . . . maybe she hadn't noticed his hand, which was still lingering weightlessly, his fingertips barely brushing against the slick outer shell of her coat. But their sudden proximity to each other was pretty difficult to miss.

"Thank you," she said softly as she tilted her chin up and met his eyes. It was all so quick, just a matter of seconds, and he really would have had to be paying attention to notice the way the tip of her tongue darted out and wet her lips before a subdued smile overtook them. The way her right canine tooth held on to the tiniest pinch of mauve lips just long enough to then cause her to carefully maneuver her tongue to that tooth, just in case some lipstick had rubbed off. The pink flush that rose from the bottom of her jaw to just under her eyes when she realized he was still looking down at her, not saying a word.

He would have had to be paying an absurd amount of attention to catch any of that, and he hadn't missed a thing.

"And thank you for not making me sit like I was A.C. Slater trying to avoid detention with Mr. Belding," she added.

Her left eye fluttered closed in a nearly imperceptible wink, and then she sat down and scooted her chair forward to the table.

"No, it's fine." Doc nudged Sebastian aside good-naturedly as he came between him and Brynn with a chair from the two-top across the way. "I'll get my own chair."

Sebastian was so startled by the sound of Doc's voice—and a million other tiny things—that he stumbled backward a couple steps. Only Doc seemed to notice, and he quirked his eyebrow.

"Um . . . sorry." Sebastian cleared his throat. "I'll be right back. Feel free to start without me." He rounded the table and headed toward the kitchen. Or the walk-in freezer behind the building. Maybe Montana.

He swung around the dividing wall and spotted Andi in the back corner, stirring a big pot of soup on her industrial oven. She turned and faced him, and their eyes met just before Sebastian's flew open in alarm. He spun on his heel and hurried back around the dividing wall, and his gaze locked with Brynn's instantly. "Not that I know what is starting. And not that I even want to be part of it. I don't. For the record. Whatever this is."

She tilted her head and nodded. "Okay." She was looking at him like he'd lost his mind. She was probably right. She raised two thumbs-up into the air toward him. "Got it."

Sebastian nodded his head once and tried to determine how to make a graceful exit, but of course that ship had long ago sailed. "Cool. Cool, cool, cool." He mirrored her thumbs-up. "Be right back."

"What was that?" Andi was barely containing her laughter when he finally made his way back into the kitchen.

Sebastian shook his head and leaned against the far wall, then slid down until he was sitting on the cold black-and-white-checkered linoleum. He couldn't sink any farther, but he would have liked it very much if the Bean Franklin's floor could have mystically opened up, revealed a portal to, oh . . . just *anywhere* else, and swallowed him whole.

"I have no idea," he muttered as he crossed his arms over his propped-up knees and lowered his forehead onto them. "One minute I was completely annoyed by her, and the next we were bonding over our common interest in *Saved by the Bell.*"

Andi slid down and sat in the space between Sebastian and the upright glass-door refrigerator she mostly filled with homemade pies.

"You bonded with Brynn Cornell?" She adjusted slightly so she was partially facing him. "Over *Saved by the Bell*?"

Sebastian nodded into his arms. "She's not aware of the fact, thank goodness."

He knew it was about more than *Saved by the Bell*, of course. That had been low-hanging fruit. They were of the same generation and he'd been sitting in a trademark A.C. Slater way. What *other* reference could she have possibly made? No, the bonding had happened before that. Something had changed. Maybe it had happened in the moment when he realized she didn't look around to see if anyone was watching or if Orly was filming her emotional reunion with Doc. Maybe it came from that little bit of empathy that had slipped in regarding her on-air failure or the way she had grabbed his arm to stabilize herself and he had involuntarily tensed in response to her touch. Or maybe he had just chosen her as the lesser of two evils in a head-to-head battle with Bill Kimball. Whatever had caused it, he needed to get himself in check.

"She sure is pretty," Andi said in a low voice.

Okay. There it was. That got him in check.

His head snapped up. "That has nothing to do with anything."

She shrugged. "Didn't say it did." A smirk spread across her face.

Sebastian sighed and rolled his eyes as he pushed off the floor with his fingers and rose to his feet. Once he had brushed off the back of his pants—as if the meticulously tidy Andi Franklin would ever allow dirt or crumbs on her kitchen floor—he offered his hand to his cheeky friend and pulled her up.

"I think you know me well enough by now to know a pretty face is not going to turn my head." Even if, admittedly, Brynn's beauty was worthy of a full one-eighty. But Andi was pretty. Laila was pretty. He was not a man who was weakened by a woman's appearance. He hadn't been for a long time.

"Well, sure, but when you combine her looks with her kindness. Golly . . . that girl-next-door sweetness . . . not to mention loyalty and integrity. And brains!" She was trying to keep a serious expression on her face and failing. "I can see why you, of all people, would bond with someone whose job it is to sit on a couch and show off her shoes."

"You're being mean."

"Yeah, and you're being a man."

"What's that supposed to mean?"

"Oh, come on, Seb. You were being a self-proclaimed jerk to her literally minutes ago. Do you really want to stand there and tell me you're back here hiding for any reason other than she worked the same magic on you she's worked on most of the world?"

She patted him on the arm and crossed back to the stove to stir her soup. "That's fine. It is. Just relax and indulge your little crush. But don't forget that three days ago she pretty much spat on a whole town of people who have done nothing to deserve it. A bunch of people who had every right to turn on her twenty years ago but instead insist that television out there is tuned to *Sunup* every weekday because it's not in their nature to do anything other than cheer her on. That's all I'm saying."

She was right, of course. But she couldn't have been more off base in her insinuations that he'd forgotten or stopped caring about any of that. He cared more than ever. Like he'd said to Doc, he both hated and missed the life he had left behind. Brynn embodied a lot of the bad and a bit of the good, but some of the *best* was the feeling that there was a lead worth following. That you didn't judge a book by its cover, you didn't take a source at their word, and you could never be satisfied with someone else's version of a story.

It had been so long since he'd felt the rush of unearthing a lead, so he was rusty, but he knew in his gut that somewhere behind all the defenses, Brynn Cornell was a story worth pursuing.

"I'd better get back out there."

Andi grabbed a clean spoon from the drawer next to the oven, dipped the tip into the pot, and handed it to Sebastian to taste. "Yeah, you'd better. I don't care what she's done or who she is. She doesn't deserve to be torn apart by Old Man Kimball."

————⌒

Laughter. He really hadn't expected to walk back in to the sound of laughter. But so it was. It was all so jarring that it took Sebastian a moment to figure out from where and whom exactly it was coming, and then the discovery sent his discombobulation over the edge.

"Hey, Seb," Doc greeted him. Doc—who was not laughing.

Jo scooted her chair back and stood, grabbing her jacket from the back of her seat as she did. "I think we're about finished here." No laughter there either.

"It's good to have you back," Bill said as he stood, laughter . . . having recently subsided? Could that be right?

A somewhat creeped-out grin spread across Sebastian's face. "What did I miss?" An old Buster Keaton film? A George and Gracie radio show? A roomful of wedgies and purple nurples? He really had no idea what made Bill Kimball laugh.

His ear tuned to the lilting, higher-octaved accompaniment, and then he turned his head to look at Brynn. Sure enough, she was the other laugher. Their eyes met and hers grew wide, as if to communicate, "Who'd have thunk it?"

"We were just catching up," Brynn answered as she became the final one to stand. "Old times, good memories . . . stuff like that. It's been really great."

Jo came around the table and stood by Sebastian and Brynn. "You should tell Sebastian about the offer you just made. I think he'll be interested to hear."

"Oh, I don't know that he would—"

"Well," Jo interrupted, "whether he's interested or not, he's the fourth member of council. So he needs to be filled in before the vote." She slapped Sebastian on the back and squeezed through the gap between them to head to the door.

"What vote?" Sebastian looked from Jo back to Brynn. "What is she talking about?"

The smile on Brynn's face was appearing less genuine by the second—bright, toothy, and camera ready. "I'm going to do what I can to help support the return of Township Days. Isn't that great?"

Oh no.

"You mean . . ."

"She said if the date is set before the end of the week, she'll announce it on *Sunbeam*."

"*Sunup*, Bill," Doc corrected. "The show is called *Sunup*."

Sebastian grimaced. "Well, that's just fine and dandy." He plastered on a smile that he hoped came across every bit as authentic as hers. "But we don't have a council meeting scheduled this week."

"According to the bylaws, as long as all members of the council are notified no more than . . ."

Sebastian stopped listening once Bill started quoting specific guidelines and resolutions. When the rules were Bill's friend, they were sacred, inexorable mandates. *What is she doing?* Never mind. Scratch that. He knew exactly what she was doing. Brynn Cornell was a master at making people like her. That's all that mattered, right? It didn't matter how fake she had to be, or what sort of mess she left in her wake for others to clean up. She'd promised what she had to in order to win over the grumpiest man west of the Mississippi.

Bill was still prattling on about articles and sections and quorums, but that didn't even matter. Sebastian had known that Brynn's last-minute visit was nothing more than a stay of execution on the vote, but he'd thought it would buy him more than a few hours. Whatever. It really didn't matter. Things were going to play out regardless. But he couldn't help but be disappointed in her.

"You're pushing for the return of Township Days?"

She squared her shoulders and kept the smile intact. "Well,

sure! It was always such a special event for this town, and I think it will be really great to—"

"Don't you know any other words?!" Apart from switching it up and going with "great" instead of "precious," nothing had changed from the day before. *Wow.* He was out of practice. His journalistic gut instinct had died, apparently. At the very least, it was enjoying its retirement somewhere on a beach, drinking frozen beverages with little umbrellas in them.

Well, he might have been mistaken about something inside himself having been awakened, but something had sure come to life in her all of a sudden. The Morning TV Host Barbie smile fell away as her fists slammed onto her hips.

"Why can't you let me have this? Why do you care? You didn't bother staying in here while we were talking, so I don't think you have any right not to like the way the conversation went. If you'd been here, you could have—"

"If I'd been here, Brynn, I would have called you on your crap. You realize that, right?"

"*Excuse me?* Why, because you think you know me or something?"

"No, because it was only about seventy-five hours ago when the whole world heard you make fun of this town's interest in 'colonial times.' Isn't that how you said it? 'Obsessed with colonial times'? Even allowing for our collective 'twelve brain cells,' how stupid do you think we are, to think you came around"—he snapped his fingers—"just like that?"

She opened her mouth to reply, but he was done. And not just with the conversation.

He looked around at his fellow city councilors and then focused in on Doc. "I'm sorry, but I'm out. Someone else can babysit from this point on."

CHAPTER 17

BRYNN

TUESDAY, MARCH 22
8:04 a.m. Mountain Daylight Time

I couldn't remember the last time I had slept past 5:00 a.m.—and
that lazy, leisurely time was just reserved for the odd weekend. Getting up while it was still dark had begun in high school, actually.
Long before it became a requirement of the job. Long before I'd
taken to spending an hour in hair and makeup so that a bunch of
people home in their pajamas, working on their first cup of coffee,
would welcome me as one of them.

I'd started running sophomore year. Well, that's when I started
the literal running. The figurative running had been going on a
lot longer than that. But in tenth grade I discovered the beauty of
getting out of the house before my mother woke up. Sometimes
before she got home. I don't know that I was ever more relaxed
than when my feet were pounding against the packed gravel. I don't
know how many times I thought about what it would be like to
just keep running.

In LA I learned to run like someone who belonged in
Hollywood. Griffith Park. Runyon Canyon. I'd race the sun and

win every time. I'd also race a bunch of those professional fitness trainer types in their sports bras and tight little spandex shorts, their long blond ponytails reaching all the way down their backs, swaying back and forth at a bouncy, consistent tempo. I may not have looked as good as they did when I ran, but my lungs had been trained nine thousand feet higher. I could outrun them *and* not spill my Jamba Juice.

When I first got to New York I loved the novelty of running in Central Park, but that hadn't lasted long. Soon I was recognizable. And as much as I loved the validation that came with that, I did start to miss the freedom of running. And then, at some point, I guess I didn't seek the freedom anymore. I sought staying in shape. I sought the perfect amount of muscle definition. And that was what those trainers with the sleek, perfect ponytails were for.

My trainer's name was Rasmus. He didn't have a ponytail, but the shorts were pretty accurate.

I pulled my pillow from under my head and used it to shield my eyes from the sun streaming through the window. It was a strange sensation, having nowhere to be. After Sebastian stormed out of the Bean Franklin the morning before, we hadn't had a lot of luck finding a new "babysitter." Doc had patients to see, and Mrs. Stoddard managed to get away before we could inquire as to her availability. Old Man Kimball made the generous offer to drive us around for a bit, but after getting me to run into the pharmacy to pick up his blood pressure medication for him, he insisted he had to head home so he didn't get stuck driving after dark.

That was at about 11:00 a.m.

Orly managed to get some beautiful exterior footage on our walk back—we had been dropped off at the end of the county road—and he filmed me talking through some mildly entertaining memories from my childhood. And then we were at the inn, all alone and effectively stranded. Apart from sneaking down to the kitchen for food as needed, I hadn't left my room for the rest of the day.

Orly had texted me at about 9:00 p.m. to inform me Mrs. Stoddard had offered to drive us around the next morning and that he thought the goal should be to conduct as many B-roll interviews with the citizens of Adelaide Springs as possible. Even I could see the writing on the wall about how well that might go if I was standing there staring at people as they were asked to share honest reflections and recollections about me. I told him to have fun without me and then jokingly encouraged him to just get people to talk about anything so that we could piece something together later. Like the critic quotes in a movie trailer. "'Mind-blowing!' says so-and-so of the *Chicago Tribune*," and you can't help but wonder if the actual quote was something like, "It's mind-blowing that anyone would pay twelve dollars to see this junk!" With any luck, we could at least salvage "Brynn Cornell might not . . . actually be . . . the devil" out of the week.

I'd spent the rest of my evening attempting to research Sebastian Sudworth. And since the internet in Adelaide Springs was only about two infrastructure advancement steps ahead of the old AOL floppy disks we used to get in the mail, it had taken a while to dive deep. Not that he was difficult to find on the World Wide Web, of course. It was just like Orly and Colton had said. Emmys, Peabodys, Pulitzers, war zones, anchor desks, presidents, kings, dictators, and then . . . nothing.

It was the six years of nothing that fascinated me most, but sometime around 3:00 a.m. I gave up.

Truthfully, I'd been hoping to pull up some of *his* crap that I could call *him* on. Colton and Orly had referenced NDAs and buyouts, but those could be the results of so many different things. I wondered if he'd had some sort of breakdown, but even then I had more questions than answers. Had he suffered a complete mental breakdown? A breakdown from sheer exhaustion? And who among us hadn't broken down in tears of joy and relief whenever Jennifer Aniston found love, and even more so when Jen reminded us all that she is her own true love and soulmate?

No matter what Colton and Orly thought of me, I would never judge anyone for any of those types of breakdowns. We were all just human, after all.

My phone buzzed—again—on the bed beside me, and I groaned as I turned over to grab it. It had been buzzing all morning, and each time I had ignored it and fallen back asleep. But now I was awake, and I couldn't live in denial any longer. I had to face reality. A reality that had already been active for five hours or so on the East Coast.

> **Colton Passik, 4:54 a.m. MDT**
> Update?
>
> **Robyn Morgenstern, 5:09 a.m. MDT**
> Are you watching? What time is it there? Elena's with Mark today. Please tell me things are going well. She and Mark aren't awful together.
>
> **Robyn Morgenstern, 5:11 a.m. MDT**
> I take that back. But it's not Elena's fault. She's reaching for the brass ring.
>
> **Colton Passik, 5:31 a.m. MDT**
> Bob wants you in live segments Friday, all 3 hours. Footage of you making nice with the city council people was good stuff. Running promos starting tomorrow. Tell Orly to send me whatever he can today.
>
> **Colton Passik, 5:36 a.m. MDT**
> Seriously, Brynn, I need an update.

Orly Hill, 6:29 a.m. MDT

Good morning, Brynn. This is Orly. Jo made
homemade scores. I managed to leave you one at
great personal sacrifice. LOL

Orly Hill, 6:30 a.m. MDT

Scones. Not scores.

Hayley Oswell, 6:41 a.m. MDT

We sure miss you around here! Cheering you on!
Xoxo -H

Unknown Number, 8:07 a.m. MDT

Hey, it's Sebastian. Sorry about (some of) what I said
yesterday. This is my number, in case you need a ride
or something.

I smiled at the last four messages and chose to continue ignor-
ing the first five for as long as I could. And the best way to do that
wasn't by taking a ride but by taking a run. Well, first a shower,
then a run.

No, scratch that. First: one of those homemade scores.

CHAPTER 18

SEBASTIAN

TUESDAY, MARCH 22
8:08 a.m. Mountain Daylight Time

He'd been prepared to feel text regret the moment he sent it, but so far he was okay. Truthfully, he did regret (some of) what he'd said. Not because he didn't stand behind every last word of it, but because it wasn't Brynn's fault he had dared to believe she was more or better than she proclaimed to be.

Sebastian sat outside Cassidy's in the parked Bronco, glancing back and forth between his phone and the front door. He wasn't scheduled to work until that evening, when the adventures and misadventures of the PTA group would await him, but he needed to stay busy. Cole's Wrangler was parked in the back, and if Sebastian joined him inside, he would inevitably be given inventory to stock or vegetables to prep or glasses to clean. That all sounded great. Mindless work that would require focus but not intense concentration.

On the other hand, he owed his mother a phone call. If he didn't return her call soon, she would contact the Bureau of Land

Management or the National Park Service or ski patrol—she really had no concept of his life in Colorado—and have them begin searching the peaks and canyons for him.

His choice was clear.

"Sebastian?" She squealed his name in her unique I-love-you-and-I-want-to-kill-you high-pitched mom voice. "I was beginning to worry. Are you okay? Why haven't you called me?"

He smiled in spite of himself. "Hi, Mom. I'm fine. I texted you on Saturday—"

"Oh." The word was long and drawn out and filled with impatience and disapproval. "You know I don't look at my texts. What's wrong with a good old-fashioned phone call every now and then?"

"You mean like we had last Wednesday?" Her end of the call went silent for a little too long, and he found himself hoping his dad wasn't listening. If so, a lecture about respect would be imminent. *Dial it back. We're clearly not in a teasing mood.* "Sorry, Mom. It's been busy."

"Tell me again, what is it they have you doing out there?"

It had been six years. *Six years.* And still, no one in his family understood what he was doing in Adelaide Springs. They didn't understand what had taken him there, and they certainly didn't understand what had kept him there. At least his mother *tried* to understand. The woman was brilliant. High performing. A Rhodes scholar who had spent a few years clerking for Sandra Day O'Connor. Clearly she didn't put too much effort into understanding—otherwise she would have understood. But she pretended to try. She pretended to care. That was more than he could say about his father and brothers.

"What is it that *who* has me doing out here, Mom?"

"The newspaper you're working for."

Sure. No problem. We can go through this again.

"I'm not really working for a newspaper. I *bought* the newspaper."

"Which one?"

"The one here in Adelaide Springs. It's just a little local paper that had sort of fizzled out, and I'm trying to give it some new life. That's all. I probably won't even launch the first issue for several months still, and then my readership will max out at about two hundred people." He was being generous. "It's really just a passion project more than anything else."

He held his breath and anticipated her next question. At least she'd led up to it. It was always the one his dad started with.

"Well, that can't pay very much, surely. What are you doing for money?"

Sebastian switched his phone to his right ear and used his left hand to grab the lever and recline his seat. He might as well settle in. "I'm fine, Mom. I work odd jobs. Remember? I told you about the bartending job and the driver job?" And, technically, his local government job, though the $150-a-month stipend and up to two free movie rentals a week from Video Palace probably wouldn't ease the worried mind of Dr. Elizabeth Haney-Sudworth, JD, MBA.

"Do you work for Uber? I don't feel comfortable having you work for Uber. There was a woman in McLean last year who reserved an Uber driver to take her to an event in Arlington, and they found her two days later in Silver Spring, disheveled and unsure as to her whereabouts."

"It's DC, Mom. People show up disheveled and unsure of their whereabouts all the time."

Again, silence.

"Look, I don't work for Uber. This is a really small town, and everything is privately owned. We don't even have an app, okay? You have to pick up the phone and talk to a person in order to get a ride."

"Well, that's something."

Besides, don't you remember? I got a huge payout from the network when I went off the deep end and they wanted out of my contract. And Erin only got about half of that. I could have a high six-figure deal tomorrow if I would agree to write my memoir, yet I choose to borrow a 1974 Ford Bronco, I live essentially in a yurt, and on PTA Night I make a killing in tips. I'm good.

Of course they didn't know any of that. Or who knows? Maybe they did. Sebastian always figured his dad would have had to go out of his way not to learn the truth with the circles he ran in. And there was a very real possibility that he had done *exactly* that. It wasn't difficult to imagine he continually went out of his way to avoid learning something about his son he would consider humiliating. Regardless, the Sudworths were experts at being a loving, caring family who stayed in regular contact with each other and never actually talked about anything.

"How are you? How's Dad? You guys staying put for a bit?"

She sighed so melodramatically that it wouldn't have been surprising to hear her say the word *sigh* in a very onomatopoeia sort of way. "You know your father."

Sure. He supposed he did. As much as anyone could. "So where is he now?"

"Turkey. He wants me to join him there next week, but Betsy Marsh has her annual fundraiser for the Bethesda animal shelter, and she's counting on me being there."

"Well, you certainly wouldn't want to miss that."

"Seb, are you sassing me?"

No, actually. That time he wasn't.

"No, ma'am. I wouldn't dream of it."

Okay . . . *that* time he was.

It had to have been difficult for her, being married to a man who claimed he needed only his copy of the US Constitution and his passport in order to be fulfilled in life, plus raising three sons who had spent so much time trying to become who they believed their dad wanted them to be that they tended to overlook the strong, brilliant, accomplished woman who folded their laundry and cooked their meals.

Or who at least had daily household meetings to determine what meals the housekeeper would cook for them.

"Oh!" Her voice had risen about three octaves. "I almost forgot the reason I called."

"*I* called *you*."

"You called me *back*. Finally. And the reason I called was to tell you I ran into Paul and Becky at the Mediterranean Way."

"What were they doing there?"

"It's the only place you can find decent grocer's goose liver pâté, Sebastian. You know that. They also have a truffle oil that—"

"Mom!" He squeezed the bridge of his nose between his thumb and forefinger. "I meant what were they doing in Dupont Circle?"

"That's what I called to tell you. They aren't in Chicago anymore. Becky started teaching foreign policy at Georgetown this semester, which makes no sense to your father and me. She was head of the department and had tenure at Northwestern, but of course Paul can be a surgeon anywhere."

Paul and Becky Whitford. Adventurous, hilarious intellectuals who didn't come across as intellectuals. Becky had been his favorite poli-sci professor at Northwestern, and when one of her student research assistant positions opened up sophomore year, he'd jumped at it. Within six months he'd fallen in love with her daughter. While he and Erin were together, Paul and Becky had been his mentors, his friends, and the parents he'd secretly wished he had. And when Erin left him, Paul and Becky were added to the very long list of important people in his life who no longer seemed to care if he was dead or alive.

He couldn't blame them. Not really. They may have claimed to love him like a son, but she was their actual daughter. And, as it all became clear in the end, he hadn't been a very good husband to her. Besides, Sebastian got to keep the London apartment in the divorce. He couldn't have expected to get to keep his in-laws too.

He raised his seat back to a sitting position. "So how was that? Seeing them, I mean. Was it awkward?"

"Why would it be awkward? Paul and Becky and I weren't the ones who made a mess of things."

He exhaled. "Thanks for that, Mom."

She gasped softly. "I'm sorry, Seb. I don't know why I said that. Truly."

Because that's probably what Dad's been saying, verbatim. Because it's how you secretly feel. Because it's true.

"It's fine. Well, look, Mom . . . I need to—"

"Erin's pregnant, Sebastian. That's why they moved to DC."

The floor dropped out from under him, and he grabbed on to the steering wheel to stabilize himself. He took a deep breath and let it out. And then again. His eyes began to sting, and he raised them up to focus on the visor and began chewing on his lip. "I see," he muttered through his nearly closed mouth.

"Her husband is investigative counsel for the Office of Congressional Ethics, or something pretentious like that. I mean, seriously, Sebastian. Have you ever heard anything so pretentious in your life?"

No. No, I haven't. At least not since the uttering of the words "decent grocer's goose liver pâté."

"I didn't even know she was married." He did say that, right? Had the words actually made their way out of his mouth, or had they gotten caught up in his teeth, which were clamping down tighter and tighter by the moment?

"Mom, I really have to go. Tell Dad hi for me. I love you."

"I love you, too, dear—"

He hit the End button on his phone before she could ask if he had messages to pass along to Darius or Xavier or their wives or his nieces and nephews or, most likely, her pet cockatiel, Edna.

He pulled the keys out of the ignition as quickly as he could— which wasn't nearly quick enough, with the way his hands were shaking—and opened the door. He slammed it behind him and then ignored the instant guilt he felt for treating Andi's classic Bronco with so little regard, stomped the ten yards to the forest of pines that surrounded the perimeter of Cassidy's, and screamed as loud and as long as his lungs would allow.

CHAPTER 19

BRYNN

TUESDAY, MARCH 22
9:18 a.m. Mountain Daylight Time

Nineteen feet. Pathetic.

The exhilaration of my brisk morning mountain run had awakened something in me, and when I found myself just on the other side of the fence from the 152-foot-tall Ponderosa pine tree that had bested me a lifetime ago, I'd been confident my foe was finally going to meet its match. I would claim victory over the failures of my past as I scaled the tree's mighty branches and surveyed the majestic landscape. Adelaide Springs and all the challenges awaiting me would appear smaller and smaller beneath me the higher I climbed. And if that wasn't darn near poetic, nothing was.

Frost and Keats would have been quick to abandon poetry in favor of self-preservation if a squirrel had skittered past on a branch right by their faces too.

Now here I was, nineteen feet in the air, practically paralyzed by an unexpected wave of fear that this climbing attempt wasn't going to turn out any better than the last. I weighed my options, and I really didn't care for either one of them. I could call Orly, of course, but he was with Mrs. Stoddard. I could still remember the way she'd fussed at me the last time I had tried climbing this tree.

And the only other phone number I had was sure to lead to a lecture, too, but I really didn't see what choice I had. At least Sebastian wouldn't have state-of-the-art film equipment on him.

Although I wouldn't put it past him to track some down, just for the occasion.

After wrapping my right arm around the tree, clenching a thick branch with my hand, and stabilizing my running shoes between the trunk and some burl, I lifted my left wrist to my mouth and ordered Siri to call Sebastian Sudworth.

Except I hadn't saved him in my contacts.

"Do you mean Sebastian Stan?"

I rolled my eyes and then briefly contemplated letting that call go through. An Avenger would surely pull off a better high-stakes rescue than a guy who'd lost more Pulitzer Prizes than he'd won, right?

I sighed. Ultimately, it was all about proximity.

At first, as the squirrel grew more courageous and began freely staring at me from four feet away, I couldn't think of how to make the call work. But once I remembered my most recent text had been from non-Avenger Sebastian, I knew I could at least get Siri to reply.

Thanks for your text. Would love to discuss more. Have some time now?

I waited a few seconds for a reply, but when one didn't come, I realized I would have to go ahead and be honest. Better for it to be a marathon rather than a sprint toward total mortification.

I'm stuck in a tree at the Fielding farm. Is it still the Fielding farm? The big pine on County Loop 42. If you can help get me down, I promise to sit quietly for three whole minutes and allow you to make fun of me however you see fit. Please?

His response came almost immediately.

Make it five minutes and you've got a deal. Be right there.

Not even a minute later I heard a motor start up with a rumble, interrupting the deep-throated *craw-craw* of the two ravens flying overhead. They seemed to share the curiosity of my squirrel friend, who was stuffing his cheeks with his eyes glued to me, like I was the horror film he couldn't tear himself away from. I turned my head as much as I dared, and though I couldn't see through the surrounding trees, I was able to gather that the vehicle was getting closer. Just another minute or so later, I saw the orange-and-white Ford Bronco turning onto the farm's property.

I braced myself. Yes, for the quickly approaching moment when I would have to release my death grip on the tree, but mostly for the inevitable period of humbling myself to simultaneously accept both his help and ridicule.

"Whatcha doin' up there?" he asked from the ground.

I wasn't scared of heights. That wasn't the problem, so I didn't have any trouble looking down at him. "Oh, nothing. Just hanging out."

He laughed softly and created a visor over his eyes with his hand. "You've actually got some decent footing for the first six or seven feet. It's more stable than it probably looks from your vantage point."

"And after the first six or seven feet?"

He squinted up at me. "Yeah, after that you're going to have to jump."

My eyes flew open. "I won't be able to jump!"

"Oh, come on." He unzipped his jacket and pulled it off, then threw it onto the ground behind him, where the direct sunlight had melted away the snow and revealed brown patches of mostly dead grass. "It will only be about ten or twelve feet at that point. Not enough to kill you. I'll even move my coat over to cushion the fall."

He wasn't wearing his glasses today, and I was able to see the mischievous twinkle in his squinting eyes, even from that distance. "Okay . . . you were joking."

"Of course I was joking, Brynn. You'll be fine. You're just going to have to trust me a little."

Huh. Well, if I didn't want the squirrel to win, I was going to have to try.

With footwork so deft I would have made an Edward Cullen "spider monkey" reference if not for my hesitance to open myself up to more ridicule, Sebastian jumped up and grabbed on to a branch three feet over his head. Then he pulled himself up like he was doing chin-ups on the branch, revealing surprisingly impressive biceps for a man wearing a Weezer T-shirt, ascended a few more feet as easily as if he had found a marble staircase I hadn't been able to see, and then his face was at my knee. His hand was on my hip.

"Okay, you're going to need to rotate around and face the tree." He tapped on my left hip to indicate the direction.

"But I won't be able to see where I'm going."

"That's what I'm for."

"But you can't see either."

He groaned and let his forehead fall against my knee for just a second. He was probably wishing it was a wall he could bang against. "Yes, you're right, but I'm not the one who's stuck."

"I'm not stuck, exactly . . ."

"Oh, you're not?" His hand left my hip and grabbed on to a branch. "Then I'll just be going—"

"Wait!" Dang it. "Fine. I'm a little stuck. Not because I'm scared, though. I want you to know I'm not scared. I think I just got in my head a little too much, and—"

"Hey, Dr. Phil, this is fascinating stuff, but do you think we could possibly climb down from the 150-year-old state-protected tree before we dive too deep into psychoanalysis?"

"Fine," I said again, but this time I grumbled it. "But that little Dr. Phil jab counts against your five minutes."

"Worth it." He smiled at me and placed the palm of his right hand on my left hip again.

It was so warm out that I had left the inn in only my high-rise lululemon running tights and my adidas by Stella McCartney cropped hoodie, and when I was running, with the sun getting higher and higher in the sky, that had been plenty. But I'd been in the tree for a while now, and no sunlight was getting through the thick, piney branches. As I turned against his fingers, it took everything in me to focus on the task at hand rather than how nice the warmth of his touch felt through the thin material. And how self-conscious that made me.

Soon my abdomen was pressed up against the tree, and I was having to put equal effort into holding on to the bark as my fingers got colder and not thinking about the view Sebastian had as he looked up from just below.

"Good. Okay, now I'm going to guide your foot to the next knob." He grabbed my ankle, bare between the tights and my no-show socks, and I responded to the pressure he placed, first on one foot and then the other. "Good job. We're going to do that same thing a few more times."

And we did. It was easy, and he never once led me astray, and by the time his right hand rested on the cold, exposed strip of skin at my waist, my squirrel friend had scampered off above, and the warmth of Sebastian's chest was against my back, and his breath was dancing against my ear.

"I'm sorry you had to come help me," I breathed. "This . . . Well, this is pretty humiliating."

His breath against me stopped, as did the heaving of his chest, and if not for the pounding of his heartbeat against my shoulder blade and the slight twitching of his fingertips against my skin, I might have wondered if he had abandoned me.

"There's no reason to feel humiliated," he finally whispered. "I'm pretty impressed, to be honest."

I scoffed, still humiliated, whether he thought there was reason to be or not. "Impressed? That I can get stuck in a tree?"

"That you tried to climb it at all." His rhythmic breathing resumed as he moved into action again. "Now the next part's going to be a little trickier. The branches and knobs are plenty big, but we'll have to step down together. Just try to stay in step with me and you'll be fine."

I didn't know why he thought that part would be trickier. It was the easiest thing in the world, like staying in step with a shoe once you had strapped it onto your foot. His hand pulled away from my abdomen for a moment. Just long enough for him to ask, "Is this okay?" as he wrapped his left arm completely around my waist, and I nodded. And then my knee bent as his bent. My foot stepped as his stepped. My hips pivoted as his pivoted. My lungs breathed as his did.

"I fell out of this tree about twenty-five years ago," I confessed as we continued our descent.

"You fell? How high up were you?"

I turned my chin to the right to try to get some perspective, but I hadn't realized his face would be right there. A perfectly scruffy five o'clock shadow at ten in the morning, unruly tufts of brown hair poking out from under a Real Madrid Club de Fútbol cap, and dazzling green eyes reflecting back at me the sun and the shadows bouncing off the pine needles.

So much for perspective.

I cleared my throat and faced the bark again. "A little lower than this. Of course I was a lot smaller than I am now. It sure seemed higher then." And yet then I'd been fearless, just chasing the freedom.

"Were you hurt?"

"I was, actually. My stylist complains every single time about the scar on the back of my head and how it makes my hair grow in weird there."

I could feel the warmth of his breath lingering at the back of my head, and I knew he was wondering if he could see the scar, or at least the cowlick.

That could have been the end of the story. We kept descending, a few inches at a time, and Sebastian didn't pry. Maybe he wasn't interested. Maybe he was busy focusing so neither of us obtained any new scars that would mess with our hairlines. And maybe I was just too aware of how much I was enjoying the feel of his body against mine to be comfortable in the silence. For whatever reason, I decided to tell a story I had never shared with anyone.

"Laila, Addie, and I climbed together, but I was the only one who fell. I hit my head pretty good, as evidenced by the scar, and for two days I convinced them both to pretend we were playing a round-the-clock game of Soap Opera to explain the bandage we'd wrapped around my head."

Sebastian stopped mid-step. "Soap Opera?"

I chuckled. "Yeah. My character, Jessica LaFontaine"—I adopted Jessica's deep southern drawl, which I had probably picked up from *Steel Magnolias*, as I said her name for the first time in decades—"had just come out of a coma and had amnesia. After a brain transplant, of course."

"Of course." He began descending again, and my body went where his did.

"Wes was my twin brother, from whom I'd been separated at birth, and Cole was my husband I had no memory of—not that either of the boys were aware of any of it. We were just so scared of getting in trouble."

My toes slipped on a loose piece of bark, and I gasped. Sebastian's arm tightened around my waist. "I've got you. We're almost there."

My breath was shallow after that, for a whole bunch of reasons, and without saying a word about it, I could tell his lack of motion was for my benefit, to give me a moment to regulate my breathing. As if that was going to happen the longer we stood there, molded together.

"So why would you have gotten in trouble for falling out of a tree?" he asked against my hair.

"There was a No Trespassing sign," I whispered. Again, that could have been the end of it. But the truth was that the No Trespassing sign was behind my friends' fear. Addie and Laila had parents they respected, who set rules and boundaries, and they loved their parents enough to not want to disappoint them. My fear looked a bit different. "And besides, I knew a visit to the doctor would have meant a doctor's bill, which probably would have meant my mom would have to work more hours. And I'd have been paying for that for a long time." I choked out a humorless laugh. "The key to my best possible life with Elaine Cornell was to lay low and hope she forgot I was there. But when my head started bleeding at school and my vision got blurry, we couldn't blame it on my brain transplant anymore."

I felt Sebastian's pulse accelerating against me, and I wanted to make a joke. Blow it off. Maybe climb back up and settle into my new life as a tree person. That was what I had always done, right? (Minus the tree-person part.) And that was even among my friends. The people who loved me. Why was I telling any of this to the mysterious reporter who hated me?

Because he's broken too.

The response came from deep within me, and I had to fight to swallow down the wave of emotion the answer had brought with it.

"I remember crying and asking Doc if I could do chores around the clinic to pay the bill. I remember him having to shave a spot on my head and sewing me up with ten stitches. I remember him telling me I had a concussion, and that it was really dangerous to not have known sooner. He told me there would always be consequences for my actions, but the sooner I owned up to them, the sooner I could start healing. And I remember him telling my mom that he needed to keep me at his house for a couple weeks for observation. I was a lot older before I realized how unnecessary that had been." A sob bubbled out of me but I forced it back down. "Before I realized how wrong it was that my mother never questioned it. She was just glad someone else was footing the bill and taking me off her hands for a while."

He breathed against me, slow and steady, and then we were making our way down the tree again, just as slow and just as steady. And before either of us said another word, I heard his feet crunch against the snow. His right arm joined his left around my waist and lifted me the last foot to the ground. His grip on me loosened and he began to pull away, but I crossed my arms across my abdomen and gripped his forearms with my fingertips.

"Thank you."

I felt his fingers flinch, but he didn't constrict me within his grasp again. He didn't pull away either.

"No problem."

We stood there like that, in silence, for a few more seconds, until a voice shouted at us from farther back on the property.

"What do you kids think you're doing?"

I jumped away from him and turned to the angry-sounding elderly man. "I'm so sorry. We were just . . ." I shielded my eyes from the sun with my hand, as Sebastian had earlier, as I looked at another blast from the past. "Mr. Fielding? Oh my goodness. I'm not sure if you remember me—"

"Of course I do."

Unexpected nostalgia and tenderness for a man I had never known very well washed over me. The sentiment didn't last long.

"How many times do I have to tell you and your friends to stay away from my tree? Seb, is that you? You should know better. You both should. Didn't you see the No Trespassing sign? D'you think I just put that up as decoration? Go. Get. I have the right to call the authorities, you know. Do you know that this tree is protected by the land conservancy and the state and—"

"Yes, sir. I'm so sorry, Mr. Fielding. I assure you we didn't do any damage to the tree. She's a beaut, alright." Sebastian had such an earnest expression on his face, and that was ultimately what made the giggle burst through my tightly clenched lips.

I began backing toward his vehicle as the laughter became more uncontrollable, and I tugged the back of Sebastian's T-shirt to get him to move along too. "Yes. A beaut." It was hopeless, my attempt to keep a straight face, and made more so by the fact that Sebastian was fighting his own losing battle.

"If I ever see you near my tree again . . ."

I hurried around to the passenger-side door before he could finish his threat, but I jumped out again just as Sebastian climbed in without his jacket. "Shoot!" I ran over and picked it up from the ground as the vehicle rumbled to life. "Good to see you again, Mr. Fielding!" I hopped back into the Bronco, and we were peeling down the driveway, laughing all the way, before I'd even shut my door.

CHAPTER 20

SEBASTIAN

TUESDAY, MARCH 22
10:11 a.m. Mountain Daylight Time

They weren't saying anything as Sebastian drove them back into town, but every now and then a quiet laugh would escape from one of them or the other. He was grateful for the laughter. He didn't know what he was going to do when their frantic escape from the Fielding farm was forgotten and the focus was once again on everything before it.

When she texted, he'd just wandered out from the pines after his lather-rinse-repeat regimen of screaming at the sky until his voice gave out, running along the trails until he got winded, and then skipping stones across the partially frozen pond until the frustration boiled up in him again.

He and Erin had stopped talking by the end. Long before the end. It had taken a lot of therapy to sort through a lot of things, but there was no big mystery as to why his marriage hadn't worked out. It failed because he'd taken for granted that it would succeed. He'd worked hard at everything else, but he treated his relationship with his wife like it was the one thing he shouldn't have to work at.

He couldn't have gotten it more wrong.

Sebastian may not have had any romantic interests since moving to Adelaide Springs, but he'd tried to apply that hard-won lesson to all his relationships. He'd have been so much more comfortable, most of the time, if he could have just become a miserable, antisocial recluse. He knew from experience that it was much easier to worry only about himself. But the first time he'd found himself in Doc's clinic, a shaking, numb, unable-to-breathe victim of a severe panic attack—when he was supposed to be in the off-the-beaten-path little town to relax—he made a promise to the kind doctor he'd just met. He promised not to take the easy way out.

He took a deep breath and pulled over to the side of the road, just a few yards away from the start of downtown. He put the Bronco in Park, turned off the motor, and unbuckled his seat belt before turning to face Brynn.

"Would you mind telling me what you were thinking when you told Bill Kimball it was a good idea to bring back Township Days?"

The smile dropped from her lips. *Well, that was nice while it lasted.* It would have been so much easier to take the easy way out rather than start another fight with her.

She considered the question and then shrugged her shoulders. "I just walked through the door that opened."

"Because I don't think you realize—" *Hang on.* "Oh. I sort of thought you'd make up some excuse."

She smiled, but only with her mouth. Her eyes looked sad. "It's always easier to use someone to get what you want if they want to use you too." Her shoulders rose and fell again. "Old Man Kimball got some new fuel for what he wants, and I got him to step aside so I can do what I need to do."

The honesty was disarming, but he still wasn't satisfied. "But you're going to leave. In three days you'll go back to New York, and the people of this town will be left putting on an archaic, expensive, *ridiculous* festival—"

"Oh." The short word was long and drawn out as she raised her hand and dismissively brushed away his words lingering in the air. "It's not that bad."

"If it's not that bad, why was it the thing you pointed out to Mark Irvine? The evidence you used to convict and sentence your hometown—"

"Because it's weird!" She undid her seat belt and mirrored his position, her knee up on the seat. "I'm not denying it's weird. How many kids outside of Colonial Williamsburg or, I don't know, 1776 have to grow up learning musket safety and how to churn butter? That was our life growing up in this town, until that stupid festival died off. And we didn't even have the Bean Franklin and Valet Forge back then. There was a George Wash-and-Go laundromat."

He was staring at her, irritated, until the smile finally made its way to her eyes, and he couldn't help but respond in kind.

"Seriously?"

Brynn nodded. "Oh yeah. And back then my friend Wes's mom ran the diner, where the Bean Franklin is now, and she always had these punny specials of the day. Eggs Benedict Arnold, Bunker Hill of Bean Soup, Lexington Biscuits and Concord Grape Jam, Boston Massa-curried Chicken Salad . . . stuff like that."

Sebastian laughed. "It's ridiculous. I mean . . . Bean Franklin would be clever anywhere, I think, when a coffee place is owned by someone with the last name Franklin. But the rest . . ."

She nodded. "I know. So stupid." Her face grew contemplative and she sighed. "But . . ."

"But what?"

"I don't know. It was kind of wonderful, too, I guess. We'd all get dressed up in these colonial outfits that Mrs. Kimball made—"

"Bill's wife?" Sebastian had never heard anyone speak of her, and he'd never thought to ask.

"Yes. She was a sweet lady. They actually met at one of the first Township Days, in the seventies or whenever. Did you know that?"

Sebastian tried to do the math. "That wouldn't make sense, would it? When was Cole's mom born?"

"She was Mrs. Kimball's daughter from her first marriage. But they came out here, touring the West—Grand Canyon and such—and stumbled across Township Days. The rest is history."

Well, no wonder the stupid thing meant so much to Bill. Not that he ever would have been so human or vulnerable as to say any of that to Sebastian.

Sebastian leaned his head back against the headrest and exhaled. "We don't have the people to manage it, Brynn. The people who want it back are too old to do the work. We don't have anyplace to stay apart from the inn. The Bean and Cassidy's are the only restaurants . . ." He let his voice fade away. Even he was tired of hearing himself make all the same arguments over and over.

"So why don't you work with some of the nearby towns? Team up. Create a whole Colonial Colorado Tour?"

"People won't want to have to go to a different town just to—"

She dismissed his words again. "Are you kidding? We used to have to go to different towns just to get to school. Hospitals, movie theaters . . . Don't people drive to another town for those things all the time? People spend all day in traffic to get from one side of LA to the other, and all you have to look at there are the bumper stickers on other people's cars. Here, the time on the road will be spent in the clouds, not the smog. The journey from town to town is as much a reason to take the trip as anything else."

A lump formed in Sebastian's throat as he watched her talk

and brainstorm without an iota of self-awareness. As he heard her unironically and maybe unknowingly confess her appreciation for the town she claimed to hate so much.

He coughed and cleared away the emotion as subtly as he could so as not to break the spell. "But it's still a really stupid idea for a festival, isn't it?"

"About five hours from here, in Fruita, they have the Mike the Headless Chicken Festival every year to honor this chicken that lived without a head for eighteen months in the 1940s. In Nederland, up near Denver, it's Frozen Dead Guy Days, all because there's been some dead guy on ice in a shed in someone's backyard since the nineties." She tapped her knuckles against his knee on the seat. "The stupider the better."

Sebastian smiled at her. "I'm not convinced, but I'm intrigued. I'll give you that."

She smiled back and then turned her head and faced out the front windshield. "Me, too, actually."

He watched her, trying to make sense of her, until Brynn's eyes flew open and she leaned forward in her seat. Sebastian turned to follow her gaze and saw Laila loading pies for Cassidy's Bar & Grill—courtesy of Andi, of course—into the back of her Subaru Crosstrek.

"You should go talk to her."

Brynn's head snapped around to Sebastian, just for a second. Just long enough for him to see the moisture pooling in her eyes. Then she faced forward again. "It *is* Laila, isn't it?"

"Yeah. And I think she'd be really happy to see you."

She sniffed and laughed and then swiped at her eyes. "Oh, I don't know about that. I figure she's at the top of the list—"

"Of people who love you?"

A sob broke free, and she didn't even seem to try to control it. "Sure. Once. But now . . ."

"What did Doc say? When you had the concussion? That there would always be consequences for your actions . . ."

But the sooner you owned up to them, the sooner you could start healing.

Neither of them needed to say the rest of the words aloud. The message had been received.

Laila closed the gate of her vehicle and began walking into the street, around to the driver's side, waving to Ken Lindell who was out sweeping the sidewalk. In one fluid motion, Brynn pushed up on her left knee and held on to the steering wheel as she leaned over to Sebastian's seat and kissed him on the cheek. She pulled back and whispered, "Thank you," and then twisted around, opened the door, and hopped down onto Main Street.

Brynn yelled Laila's name before closing the door, and then Sebastian watched as Laila turned back and recognition dawned. By the time Brynn got to her, running all the way, Laila was rushing toward her, arms open wide.

Sebastian fired up the Bronco again, made a U-turn to head back to Cassidy's, and wiped from his cheek a tear that he thought belonged to Brynn, though he couldn't say for sure.

"Hey, Seb." Cole greeted him as he stepped onto the porch at Cassidy's. "I saw the Bronco here earlier, and then you vanished. Everything alright?"

What a crazy amount of humanity had been experienced since he'd thought about passing the time by helping out with inventory.

"Yeah, fine. I was going to see if you needed some help, but some things came up. Sorry about that."

Cole resumed sweeping the porch. "Nothing to be sorry about. I figured either you had other things to do, or the PTA ladies kidnapped you. Either way, I knew you'd come back to us eventually."

Sebastian laughed. "I don't get it. You're younger . . . better looking . . . you can cook . . ." He unzipped his jacket. He'd put it back on as he drove away from Brynn and Laila, but with the sun beating down on him, it was another of those strange, wonderful Colorado postcard sorts of days. Sunshine and snowcapped mountains. "So why do they like me so much? You're much more of a catch than I am."

"That's the problem with small-town life. Those ladies either grew up with me, in which case they saw me with zits and braces, or they were older than me, in which case they remember me as the obnoxious kid who used to prank call everyone in town pretending to be from the Publishers Clearing House Sweepstakes. A lot of people in this town had a fortune dangled in front of them, only to have it cruelly stolen away, my friend. *A lot* of people."

He smiled as he leaned the broom up against the screen door and then walked over to the thick wood railing of the porch and hoisted himself up onto it. "Laila ran into town to get the pies from Andi. PTA Night is such a strange cacophony of appetites."

"I saw her. I think she may be a while."

"Yeah?"

"Yeah. She and Brynn bumped into each other."

Cole looked down at his feet and released a deep breath. "Good. She's been looking forward to it and dreading it, all at the same time. At least it will be out of the way now, no matter how it goes."

"I can't imagine how weird it must be for you guys." Sebastian pushed himself up onto the railing a few feet down from Cole and leaned his back against the massive log column so he could face him. "Are you going to try to see her?"

"I don't know. Lai and I talked about it a lot this morning. I still don't know where I stand." Cole seemed to keep considering it for several moments, and then after all that consideration, added a shrug. "Yeah . . . it's just . . ." He copied Sebastian's position, leaning back against the other column and pulling his knee to him. "I've never really watched her on TV. Ever. I hear things from others—the good and the bad, I guess—but I've never wanted to see her that way."

"'That way'?"

"Just . . . however she is now. You know? Anything other than how I remember her." He stared off into the direction of the forest Sebastian had burdened with his unleashed frustration a couple hours earlier.

"I think . . . ," Sebastian began and then thought better of it. But he had Cole's complete attention, so he blurted it out, figuring Cole was probably the most objective person to share his thoughts with. "I think being back here is good for her."

Cole reached over and scratched at a rough patch in the wood beneath his foot. "So what happens when she leaves again?"

The unanswerable question.

Sebastian rested the back of his head against the log column and stared up at a sky so blue and clouds so white that they had always reminded him of the way a kid would draw them. "It's crazy for me to try to imagine what it must have been like for you all, growing up together. Like, the way you all knew each other and were part of each other's lives. I just can't wrap my head around it."

"I know our town is smaller than most, but it's not *that* weird, is it? How many kids did you go to school with?"

Laughter burst from him. "Well, that depends on which school." He lowered his head and met Cole's eyes. "The high school I graduated from, in DC, was the fourteenth school I was enrolled in. Military schools, private, public, arts, math and science . . . Went to a Quaker school for a few months." He smiled in response to Cole's laughter. "I graduated with a class of 742. And there were probably eight or nine kids who knew my name and I knew theirs. Not even one I would have counted as a friend."

"Okay, that is a little different from what we had here." Cole stepped down onto the planks of the porch. "I heard you yelling at a bighorn sheep or something earlier. Want to talk about it?"

He appreciated the offer. But his state of mind was so far removed from where it had been after that phone call with his mother, he really didn't see the point in going back there.

He followed Cole's lead and hopped off the railing. "Why would we waste time talking about my deep-seated emotional defects when we have the place to ourselves?"

Cole groaned and began walking toward the door. "Oh no."

"Oh yes, my friend. Oh yes." Sebastian stepped in front of him and grabbed the broom, then opened the door for them both. "The ladies won't be here for another"—he looked at his watch—"six hours or so, and there is a perfectly good karaoke machine through these very doors."

Cole's groan morphed into laughter, but the eye rolls didn't go away. "You are the only person I have ever known who is perfectly content singing karaoke in a room by himself, one hundred percent sober. That's so messed up."

"It's great therapy! You have no choice but to relax and let go and think about nothing except the melody and the lyrics—"

"And what a dork you are?"

Sebastian pulled the door shut behind them. "Just for that, I'm pulling it out tonight."

"No! You can't. Not on PTA Night."

"Are you kidding? PTA Night is the perfect time. You think those ladies love me now?" He tipped his ball cap as if it were a Stetson. "Just wait until they get a load of me sharing the gift that is the musical stylings of one Mr. Glen Campbell."

CHAPTER 21

BRYNN

TUESDAY, MARCH 22
10:29 a.m. Mountain Daylight Time

I had been the one to leave. *Right?* I had been the one to hitchhike to Denver in the back of a PT Cruiser, alongside an extremely *non*-hypoallergenic pug named Gypsy Rose Lee, before spending twenty-three hours on a bus to Los Angeles, during which time sleeping was impossible for a multitude of reasons—the Neil Diamond impersonator we'd picked up in Cheyenne, Wyoming, and Reno passenger "Ed the Egg Salad Sandwich Guy," as I'd dubbed him, just to name a couple. Those were pretty vivid memories, but the way Laila kept apologizing to me, I couldn't help but be a little confused. Confused enough that I spent a quick nanosecond wondering if I'd been brainwashed or incepted. (Incepted? Is that what it's called when Leonardo DiCaprio makes his way into your dreams? If so, I had been incepted *a lot* through the years.)

As we settled in at the Bean Franklin—where Andi Franklin née Gardner, back when she babysat us, greeted me with a "Hey," as if we'd seen each other every day for the last twenty years—I finally got a chance to make my big confession and explain why Laila had *nothing* to apologize for.

"It wasn't that you guys couldn't track me down. Or that you didn't try hard enough." I took a deep breath. "A couple months after I left, mail from Addie found its way to me. Right into my hands. And I was so desperate to avoid coming back to this place, I changed my name." Laila tilted her head in confusion. "Well, I changed the spelling of my name."

All because I felt the need to escape. All because I was too scared to trust anyone. After all, if I couldn't trust my own mother, how was I supposed to trust anyone else? Wasn't she supposed to be the one person who would do whatever it took to keep me safe? And wasn't she the one person who had continually put me in harm's way? How was a little girl ever supposed to trust anyone when she grew up with that as her reality?

But when I slept over at Addie's house, or Laila's, I didn't have nightmares.

When I was at school with Mrs. Stoddard, I wasn't so afraid to say or do the wrong thing that I didn't allow myself to say or do anything.

When Andi was in charge of us, I didn't flinch at every loud noise or sudden movement.

Even when I was working in the stockroom at Cassidy's with Old Man Kimball, I wasn't afraid to turn my back.

Wasn't that trust? Wasn't that love? Wasn't that maybe even what family was supposed to be like? Somehow that little girl had been fortunate enough to be loved by an entire town of people she could trust, and in the name of self-preservation, she'd written them off alongside the evil she shared a name and home with.

"I'm sorry, Laila."

I didn't know how many more apologies were going to be necessary before the week was through, but if the way my tense muscles were abruptly relaxing was any indication—not really in a relaxing way at all but more like when you crack the Belgian chocolate at the top of a tub of Magnum ice cream into jagged little pieces to reveal the creaminess that awaits you—this one was a good place to start.

Lester Holt had once told me I used too many metaphors in my reporting. I clearly needed to work on that. Regardless, tears were streaming down my cheeks and my spoon was ready to dig deep into the creamy goodness.

"I'm so sorry, Laila," I repeated and buried my face in my hands and propped my elbows on my knees.

Within seconds her arms were around me again. She crouched beside me and rested her head on my shoulder and rubbed my back soothingly as she whispered, "Shh . . . It's okay. Let it out."

She didn't have to tell me twice. The dam holding back my tears collapsed. Or the ice cream melted. Whatever.

Suck it, Lester Holt.

A few minutes later, once that round of tears had dried, she sat back down across from me and said, "That envelope? It was probably a wedding announcement."

I had been as impenetrable as Teflon for twenty years, but now guilt was forming an increasingly grimy layer on my heart, and I wasn't sure if I'd ever be able to scour it away. My hands covered my mouth and then crossed over my heart. "Where did she and Wes end up? Are they still here?"

She began chewing on her bottom lip, and my stomach dropped. What had I missed? "Laila?"

"Wes skipped town. The morning of their wedding. His dad showed up, after his mom died—"

"As in the dad he'd never met?"

She nodded. "Yeah. That morning, he and his dad were just . . . gone."

I'd already encountered several things I had not seen coming. I never would have believed Doc Atwater and Mrs. Stoddard would seem younger than they had twenty years ago. Never ever in a million years would I have believed that Old Man Kimball would sit in my presence without bringing up the $6.42 I owed him for whiskey glasses I had broken in 2001. But those were just surprises. I never could have been prepared for the shock of Addie Atwater and Wes Hobbes not living happily ever after together.

"I should have been here," I muttered.

"What's that?" she asked.

"I should have been here, Laila. I should have . . ." What? What could I have done? "I should have been here for her."

"No. You shouldn't have been."

"But—"

"You shouldn't have been here, Brynn." She lowered her head to meet my eyes. "Yes . . . you should have let us know where you were. You should have trusted us enough to know Elaine would *never* get any information out of us. Never. Not from anyone in this town. It makes me really sad that you didn't know that." Her chin tightened. "But you had to go. You had to figure things out and figure out a life away from this place. That's nothing to be ashamed of." She got up and grabbed a box of tissues from behind the counter and then sat back down in the seat next to me. We each grabbed a tissue and blew our noses. Laila grabbed my hands. "You know, Wes lost his mom senior year, and then within months, we lost you. Then we lost Wes." She sniffed and, never letting go of my hands, raised her forearm and brushed it across her eyes. "Then, for a while, Addie lost herself . . . and then *she* left. So, yeah . . . it was a rough few years. And it just felt wrong—it *was* wrong—that you weren't part of our lives anymore. But you're back now—"

"Laila, I'm not staying here."

"Oh, I know. I don't mean in Adelaide Springs. I just mean . . .

you're *back*." Her front teeth dug into her bottom lip and she pulled her eyes away from mine. "You are back. Aren't you?"

What did that even mean? I would be leaving on Friday. Returning to New York. Returning, I had to believe, to *Sunup*. Working a schedule that was unrelenting and unforgiving. I'd go back to reading cue cards. And though the spelling distinction was small, who I had been as *B-R-E-N* and who I had become as *B-R-Y-N-N* weren't compatible.

As if sensing my uneasiness, Laila changed the subject, and I couldn't have asked for a more effective distraction.

"Addie's in the CIA."

"What?!" My jaw dropped. "Addie? Addie Atwater? *Our* Addie?"

She raised her hands in the air and then did the "cross my heart, hope to die" gesture in front of her chest. "And that was after the air force. She's like a full-on monster, in the best way."

"*Wow.*" Addie Atwater. What in the world was happening?

"Her husband is apparently even higher up than she is." She looked around to make sure Andi wasn't within earshot, and then she leaned in and whispered, "We don't talk to Wes anymore, of course, but he's a senator in Connecticut or somewhere and married to Wray Gardner."

The jaw drops just kept on coming. "Andi's little sister?" I mouthed, and Laila nodded slowly with her lips sealed shut.

We sat in silence a few more seconds, and I played all of that over in my mind until she stood from her chair and walked over to the counter. "Want something to drink?"

I jumped up and joined her. "Just some water would be great." I took the glass of ice she handed me and looked around the storage area and then in the refrigerator.

"What do you need?"

"Water?"

Laila rolled her eyes. "The tap, Brynn. Water comes out of the tap."

Oh. Yeah. I'd forgotten what it was like to be somewhere where the water from the tap was safe to drink and didn't feature that coppery flavor enhancement we New Yorkers paid extra for.

I helped myself to water from the sink and took a sip. The cold, clear liquid trickled down my throat, slowly at first, and then faster as I guzzled it. By the time I pulled my lips away, my glass was empty and I was winded from the rapid swallowing.

"Heavenly days, I'd forgotten how good that is." I refilled my cup.

"So tell me what I've missed with you," Laila said as we sat back down.

I shrugged. "Not much, really. I think I inadvertently committed to nationally televised coverage of Township Days, and I tried climbing the Fieldings' Ponderosa pine again." *Nothing much other than that. Basically, I'm just doing a horrible job with what I came here to do and staying busy avoiding texts and calls from my agent and my executive producer. Oh, and Sebastian Sudworth's been a bit of a distraction . . .*

"Yeah, heard about all that."

"Even the tree? It *just* happened."

"You *have* been gone a while if you've forgotten how fast news travels. But I mean what have I missed in your life?"

"Since when?"

She looked at me like I'd lost my mind. "Since you left, obviously."

I chortled. "Since I left here? You mean, since I left twenty years ago?"

"Yes. Do you want me to go first?"

I sat back in the chair and crossed my arms, smirking all the while. "Sure."

"Okay, let's see. My cat died, like, two weeks after graduation."

If that delicious water from the tap had been in my mouth right then, it would have spewed all over her. "Laila! We cannot go through every detail of our lives from the last twenty years!" My smile faded, and I sat up straight again. "Hang on. Edward Scissorhands?"

She shook her head. "Oh goodness, no. Edward lived another eight years or so. That cat had, like, fourteen or fifteen lives, easy. It was to the point that I was wondering if I needed to leave him to someone in my will. No, Jerry Maguire died."

Laila had always named her pets after movie title names. In addition to Edward and Jerry, I'd known of Mrs. Winterbourne, Ace Ventura, and Private Ryan. And then there had been the time in high school when Annie Hall, a stray calico she'd taken in, had given birth to a litter. Her parents only let her keep one of the kittens, and she had promptly named her Hannah. The rest of the litter she had to find homes for were affectionately known as Her Sisters, of course. (Even with the world not as sensitive and aware then as it is now, we tried to caution her that naming pets in homage to Woody Allen was problematic. She could not be deterred.)

I listened as Laila proceeded to tell me some of the insignificant details of the last two decades. More cat deaths, the various jobs she'd worked around town, and what a whole bunch of other people in town had been up to. Mrs. Stoddard's husband had died seven years ago, leaving her all his money—some of which she hadn't even known he had. Cole, who had been adopted by his mom the day he was born, had spent some time a decade ago looking for his birth parents, without any luck. Roland Cross had married and had a bunch of kids with Paula Peet. She finally got around to telling me her parents had divorced fifteen years prior, but not until after she had filled me in on every detail of the weekend four years ago when Chris Pratt and some friends stopped at Cassidy's for dinner, on their way through for a hunting trip. And it all led us to the exciting culmination of the feline adoptions throughout the course of the last twenty years of, among others, Larry Crowne, Captain Phillips, and Florence Foster Jenkins.

Her version of twenty years of catch-up had taken approximately three minutes.

I shook my head and laughed. "Glad to see you haven't changed. Mostly. *Less* glad to see you're still naming cats after Woody Allen movies."

She shrugged. "His moral character does not make the name Vicky Cristina Barcelona any less suitable for an orange tabby."

There were so many more things I wanted to know. She was smart, beautiful, had a huge heart, and had always been really good at whatever she set her mind to. I had to have missed more over the past twenty years than just cats and waitressing jobs, right here in Adelaide Springs. But I was afraid to ask, because what if I hadn't?

"Your turn. Get me caught up."

No way. Not yet. I couldn't possibly follow up the version of her adult life she had just shared with me. At least not honestly. I'd lived more lives than Edward Scissorhands. How would that make her feel?

But then I thought of something I honestly couldn't wait to share with her.

"I dated John Mayer for a while."

Laila had launched a well-organized and extremely earnest campaign to get "Your Body Is a Wonderland" chosen as our senior class song. When Mrs. Stoddard refused to allow it and threatened detention if she didn't drop her crusade, Laila had settled for "No Such Thing" from the same John Mayer debut album. That actually ended up being a pretty great choice—certainly better than the pick Addie and I had advocated for ("Independent Women, Pt. 1" by Destiny's Child, which had caused Wes and Cole to threaten to boycott graduation), and the boys' choice ("Ride Wit Me" by Nelly).

"You what? When? How? You . . . You *what*? Tell me everything!"

Total nonchalance. Cool and collected as only *B-R-Y-N-N* could be. "It was no big deal. We went to a couple parties together. He made me dinner once. Portobello burgers because, for some reason, I was pretending to be a vegetarian for a while there. I think I was sort of his Katy Perry rebound, so it was never going to last. But he wrote a song for me."

All the color left her face. "Shut up! Shut up, shut up, shut up." I tittered as she pulled her iPhone out of her pocket and attempted to pull up a music service. "Stupid Wi-Fi!" She let her phone drop to the table with a *thud*, and her eyes looked up toward the sky and darted from side to side as she began calculating in a way that reminded me of Russell Crowe doing math in *A Beautiful Mind*. "Which song? 'Slow Dancing in a Burning Room'? No, that's too early. Couldn't be 'Shadow Days.' That was about Jennifer Aniston. 'Love on the Weekend'? Oh my gosh, it's 'Love on the Weekend,' isn't it?"

I shook my head. "No, actually. It's called 'Brynn Don't Like No Mayo on Her Burger' and it's sung to the tune of 'Grandma Got Run Over by a Reindeer.' I never understood why it didn't get more radio play."

She wadded up her napkin and threw it at me, and we erupted into giggles, just as we always had. I was cool and collected as I regaled her with the tale of my three dates with John Mayer, but the giggling? That was all *B-R-E-N*.

A few hours later, after I'd finally convinced Laila to walk with me to the inn so I could put on some real clothes and then walk back to the Bean Franklin, where the door was left unlocked for us though Andi had long ago gone home, we made brownies and ate half of them before Laila's eyes flew open in a panic.

"What's wrong?" I asked as I picked up stray brownie crumbs from the table and shamelessly licked them from my fingers.

"I have to go to work."

"Oh. Okay." I was sad the time was coming to an end. Undeniably sad.

Her excitement about John Mayer had spurred me on to tell her some more fabulous stories. And as I told all those fabulous stories about places I had been and people I had met, I'd accidentally begun sharing the story of my life since she had seen me last. The real story. The crappy college boyfriends. My struggles to find friends as good as the ones I had left behind, and how I had eventually stopped trying. The career opportunities I had lost out on because I wouldn't go out with a certain local news producer or go up to a hotel room with some guy who was a member of the same gym as some network honcho. My feud with Andy Vandy.

I told her about how I only learned my mom had died because I had set a Google alert on my phone for that very occasion. How I pulled up her obituary while I was at dinner with Colton Passik, interviewing for a spot on *Sunup3*, and when I got the job, I put away the fleeting thought I'd had about potentially attending her funeral.

But now, Laila had to go to work.

"You should come," she said, standing from her chair and stretching her arms over her head.

"Oh . . . I don't know."

What, Brynn? What do you have to do that's more important than spending more time with Laila?

I scrunched up my nose. "To Cassidy's?" She nodded. "I don't know, Lai. Who will be there?" I followed her lead and grabbed my jacket after she had turned off all the lights.

"Cole, for one. Sebastian, for another."

"Ooh, boy. I'm not sure how either one of them will feel about me showing up."

"Sebastian is the nicest guy on the planet. You know that, right?" Of course most people are wonderful in the eyes of the nicest girl on the planet. "And Cole will be excited to see you."

"Will he?"

"He will be once I tell him he should be."

We stepped out onto the sidewalk, and she locked the door behind us. She motioned for me to follow her to her vehicle, and I did. Apparently I was going to work with her.

"Do you want to go by the inn and pick up . . . what's his name again?"

"Orly?" I climbed in and buckled my seat belt. "Nah. He texted a little bit ago to tell me Mrs. Stoddard wore him out today and he's in for the night."

His response when I asked him if he'd found anyone who had anything nice to say about me had been, "Colton only wants three minutes of B-roll. I'm sure we'll be able to piece something together." Knowing that after an entire day out and about with the people of Adelaide Springs, it was still going to take some effort to cobble together three minutes of nicety, I was relieved Orly wouldn't be accompanying us to Cassidy's. As confident as Laila was that Cole would be happy to see me, I just wasn't so sure. And it wasn't that I wanted to keep that from getting on air, it was just that I didn't want to be distracted or looking for open doors, as I apparently had with Cole's grandfather.

In our little group, Cole had always been the defender and protector. It was Cole who insisted on waiting until any of the three of us girls got inside before leaving when he dropped us off, and it was Cole who tried to be there for us whenever we received bad news. In second grade, he'd written a poignant, beautiful eulogy for a hamster named Miss Daisy. At eleven years old, he had been nervous to the point of nausea whenever he had to leave Addie's side at her mom's funeral. On the rare occasions Addie and Wes fought, he was their mediator, reminding them of all the things they treasured in each other. At sixteen he had flown into a rage and punched my mom's boyfriend when he held on to my arm and wouldn't let me leave.

He'd loved us. And he loved Laila most of all. So it wasn't difficult to imagine that he might not be as ready to forgive the pain I had caused. He might not be ready to forgive the pain I had caused *her*.

The short drive was over almost before it began, and she pulled into the parking lot of the old log-cabin bar. At least I was pretty sure we were at Cassidy's. That's what the lit-up sign a few feet from the road said. But it looked less drab and dull than I remembered it.

I glanced at the sign again. "Bar and Grill?" I asked her as we unbuckled and prepared to open our doors. "When did the Grill part happen?"

"A few years back. His grandfather wanted Cole to stick around and run the place, and he said he'd only agree if he was allowed to make a few changes." We stepped out into the rapidly cooling early evening. "Cole's quite the chef."

I tilted my head in surprise. "Really?"

"Yep." She shut her door and talked to me across the hood as I made my way around. "He went to culinary school and everything."

We walked up the stairs of the porch but stopped short of the door. "Was *Magic Mike* Night one of the changes he wanted to make?" I asked with a laugh. "What in the world is happening in there?"

From the sound of it, Channing Tatum was in there doing his thing. Women were hooting and hollering and yelling out things that were skating right on the edge of obscene. The laughter from inside was riotous and rowdy, and it made its way through the transom windows, cracked open slightly, and bounced off the edge of the forest.

"Oh, goodie. I'd forgotten." Laila wagged her eyebrows and opened the door. "It's PTA Night."

CHAPTER 22

SEBASTIAN

Sebastian couldn't stop thinking about how it was simultaneously a blessing and a big-time shame that his mother couldn't see him right then. Sure, she'd be humiliated, and yes, by the time his father caught wind of the scene, he'd be disowned. But if she could get a load of all the tips he was pulling in, her concerns about his financial sustainability would go the way of yesterday's leftover goose liver pâté.

He caught Cole's eye as his friend served more baskets of fries and plates of buffalo wings to the hysterical ladies and winked at him in the cheesiest, lounge lizardy-est way he knew how. Cole laughed and then cupped his hands around his mouth and made a big show of hooting and hollering with the patrons as he returned to the kitchen.

"Well, ladies, I'm going to need to take a break." Boos of displeasure filled the air. "Only long enough to refill your drinks. Don't worry." The cheers and catcalls resumed. "But I think we've got time for one more song before I go."

It had been two years since he'd convinced Cole to recommission the relic they'd found in Old Man Kimball's basement. It was a seventies-era Cassette/8-Track Singing Machine 3000 that, until Sebastian played Dr. Frankenstein with it, ran on ten D batteries and a prayer. All the lyrics were still on paper, but Sebastian had laminated the originals and cataloged the entire library. The library that consisted of only seventies and eighties country classics and far too many accompaniment renditions of "Delta Dawn."

Most nights, no one touched it unless tourists wanted to explore the novelty of it or Fenton Norris had a few too many beers. But on this night, Sebastian Sudworth was the karaoke king.

"What do you think? Should I do one more?"

"No!" Cole yelled from the kitchen.

"You know what his problem is?" Sebastian grabbed his stool from the back corner of the stage he had talked Cole into letting him construct after the first-ever Cassidy's Bar & Grill / Adelaide Springs Parent Teacher Association Karaoke Extravaganza pulled in the highest-ever single-night revenue since Cole took over from his grandfather. "He doesn't feel the music like we do. Does he, ladies?" They shook their heads in emphatic agreement. Sebastian sat down and propped the heels of his Vans on the footrest. "No, that's right. He may make a mean spinach artichoke dip—"

As predictable as clockwork, two of the ladies ran to the bar and shouted into the kitchen that they'd like an order of spinach artichoke dip.

"—but his soul isn't one with the music like ours are. He doesn't understand the pull and the sway and the hustle."

At this point, even Sebastian didn't have a clue what he was saying. But it didn't matter. He'd found his rhythm and a roomful of small-town, middle-aged soccer moms were gleefully dancing to it with him.

"Sing 'Rhinestone Cowboy'!" three of them shouted in unison

in the sort of orchestrated way that made it obvious they had con-
spired together to make sure they were heard.

The 8-track was already in his hand—this was his greatest hit,
after all—and he flipped it in the air with a flourish before pushing
the cartridge into the slot with his index finger. Everyone began
cheering so loudly he had to lean in closer to the speaker to make
sure he could hear his musical cues. Not that it would matter. They
couldn't hear any more than he could. But he wanted to *earn*
those tips.

It was about the time he got to the second chorus, just as he
was tossing the microphone from one hand to the other with the
aplomb of Elvis performing in Vegas in 1969, that in his peripheral
vision he saw two more patrons enter. That wasn't unusual. The
PTA ladies came and went throughout the night, depending on
how wild they were feeling, and of course they were open for dinner as usual. He turned to greet the new audience members with a
welcoming smile, but the smile—and, briefly, the showmanship—
faded when he spotted Brynn Cornell staring at him with eyes the
size of Graceland, lashes blinking at a furious rate, and her mouth
twitching in amusement.

Well, great.

Any other night. Any other night he would stop the music,
step aside, and return to his spot behind the bar. He'd offer her a
drink and charge her double the price. (She was used to Manhattan
prices. She wouldn't even flinch.) Then he'd stay busy and never
give her the opportunity to make any of the snide remarks she
would undoubtedly want to make. But this was PTA Night. And
PTA Night wasn't just about food, drinks, and fun. Oh no. PTA
Night was an experience, and he wouldn't allow these ladies to be
robbed of that.

Sebastian doubled down and hopped from his stool, eyebrow cocked in Brynn's direction. He walked to the edge of the

stage—which was only about two feet off the ground—and stepped down to walk among his adoring fans. They were respectful—but just barely—as they grabbed the waist of his jeans and pulled on his T-shirt. He looped the twenty-five-foot microphone cord around his arm and made his way toward Laila, who had jumped right into work. Good thing, too, since Sebastian and Cole had been covering her since five o'clock, when she was supposed to be there. Okay, *Cole* was covering her. Sebastian was, well . . . doing this.

And doing it darn well, if he did say so himself.

Laila kept her head down, picking up empty dishes, but peered up at him and shook her head in a way that clearly said, "Stay away from me. I'm busy, and I will not be part of this ridiculous thing you're doing." *Yeah. Good luck with that, Laila Olivet.*

The grin spread across her face and color rose in her cheeks as he put his scruffy cheek against her smooth one and held the microphone in front of them, just in time for her to join him on the final chorus—which of course she did. Laila could always be counted on to keep the good times rolling.

The song ended, and he returned his microphone to its stand and headed back behind the bar after promising to take requests later—as long as those requests were songs by Glen Campbell or John Denver, since those were pretty much the only ones they had. Or, of course, he always had "Delta Dawn" at the ready.

Brynn didn't join him at the bar as he had expected her to but instead sat at a two-top on the far side of the stage.

"What's that about?" Sebastian asked as Laila sidled up to the bar with drink orders.

She turned her head to follow his eyes. "We had the best day, Seb. It was . . ." She closed her eyes and clutched her tray to her chest as she breathed in through her teeth. "It was so good. Such a long time coming. She was honest and real and humble and—"

"Seems to be a lot of that going around."

"What do you mean?"

He finished shaking the martini and poured it into a glass. "I don't know if you heard about—"

"The tree?" She nodded. "Of course I did."

"Honest, real, humble." He paused and considered the words. He also couldn't help but spend a moment considering the way Brynn had held on to his arms at the end there, after the danger was behind them, as if he were still her only hope for rescue. "Yeah. That's kind of what I saw too. But be careful, Laila. She's still working an angle."

"You're just determined to see the worst in her, aren't you?"

"No, I'm really not." Or maybe he was. But even he would have to admit it was getting increasingly difficult, no matter how determined he may have been. "It's just that for all the good I've seen today, I've also seen her turn on the 'Brynn Cornell, live from the *Sunup* couch' persona when it will help her get ahead. All I'm saying is it probably wouldn't be that difficult for her to manipulate the emotions of someone who is really wanting to see the best in her."

Laila set down her tray and put her hands on her hips. "Sometimes when you look for the best in people, you actually find it."

He knew he would never win this argument with her. All he was going to do was make her angry with him, and that was the last thing he wanted. "Forget I said anything." He loaded up her tray and smiled at her. "I wish I was as trusting as you. I do. I mean that."

Her icy demeanor—at least icy by Laila's standards—melted in a flash, and the smile returned to her face. "I know you and Cole think I'm naive—"

"I don't think you're naive. I don't."

"I know her, Seb."

"You *knew* her."

Laila shrugged. "Okay, sure. I *knew* her. But you didn't. So maybe, just for a minute, trust that I have a little bit of expertise here that you don't." She squeezed his hand and winked. "I know that's hard to imagine."

She sauntered away, expertly balancing her tray and greeting each person along the way. Sebastian's eyes followed her until she stopped at one of the wilder of the PTA tables, and all the women there began tittering and blowing kisses in his direction, as if it had been them he'd been eyeing with affection and admiration. He smiled and waved indulgently and then pulled his focus to Brynn's table. She was sipping the water Laila had dropped off for her and perusing the menu, and every now and then raising her eyes to look around and examine every corner of the room.

"Only one way to find out," he muttered to himself, then threw the dish towel over his shoulder and hurried over to her. Around the perimeter, of course. If he tried to walk through the throng, he might never get there. He came up behind her and said, "Hi."

She jumped in her seat a bit and looked over her shoulder. "Oh. It's you."

"Sorry to disappoint." He circled the table to the empty seat across from her. "May I?"

She gestured to the chair with an open hand. "Sorry. I'm just . . . Well, I haven't seen Cole yet."

"No Orly tonight?"

She shook her head and laughed softly. "I'm not doing a very good job, am I? I mean, if the goal is to get a lot of great footage of me reuniting with people . . . I sort of suck at this."

Sebastian had just sat down, but as the silence permeated—he knew it was his turn to talk, but for the life of him he couldn't think of what to say—he pushed his chair back away from the table and began to stand. He couldn't help but notice how red and puffy her eyes were from all the tears, and how beautiful it was that, though she had clearly taken the time to change out of her running gear, she hadn't made any attempts with makeup to cover the humanity etched all over her face. What was he supposed to say to that? "Well, I should get back—"

"No way. Not yet." She pointed her left index finger down toward the chair, signaling him to sit. He wasn't quite sure why he did it, but he did. "You don't get to leave until we talk about your little stint as the Wichita Lineman."

"Rhinestone Cowboy."

"Whatever."

She stared at him, amusement written across her face, and he stared back. "What can I say? I try to give the people what they want."

Her head bobbed up and down and she laughed softly. "Seems like you do it well. There's no denying you have a very satisfied clientele."

"Well . . ." He pulled his eyes away as the sensation of heat spreading up his neck took him by surprise. He was going to say something about how he hadn't gotten any complaints, but the good-natured feel of their banter suddenly felt a little too flirty. And sure, he knew that was rich after having to remind himself more than once, when they were in a tree together, to stay focused on the task at hand rather than the task his hands *wanted* to focus on. But he'd meant what he'd said to Andi. Maybe his self-control was getting a workout for the first time in a while, but he could resist Brynn Cornell, no matter how beautiful she was.

It was the conversations that were going to get him in trouble.

He stood up and pushed the chair back to the table. "Need anything else to drink, or are you good with just water?"

The humor left her eyes. "Water's fine, thanks." She seemed to be biting the inside of her cheek, and her eyes focused on the table, her phone, out the window—suddenly anywhere but on him.

"Um . . ." She cleared away the frog in her throat and still refused to look at him. "Thanks again for earlier."

"Like I said, no problem."

"I don't just mean the tree, Sebastian. I mean, obviously the tree. But . . . yeah . . . thanks."

He swallowed the forming lump and leaned one hand on the table as he said quietly, "Don't forget I still have about four minutes and forty seconds on my tab."

She tilted her chin and met his eyes. "I think you earned the right to make fun of me however you want."

He'd been going for lighthearted, but in an instant, his heart was broken by her. *For* her. "I won't," he whispered and then swallowed hard. "Hold back on the 'Rhinestone Cowboy' jokes, and we'll consider that debt paid in full."

"Deal."

Their eyes stayed in lockstep with each other until she abruptly declared, "I'm going to go get a little fresh air." She turned her head and downed what was left of her water and then set the glass down a little too hard, which made her chuckle to herself. As if Sebastian was owed an explanation, she looked up at him and said, "I need to be careful. I already have a glassware tab at this place."

In response, Sebastian smiled at her. Why did he smile at her? What in the world was she even talking about?

He watched her walk away and tried to piece together as many context clues about her—about who she really was—as he could. Nothing about what he'd seen from her today matched with her *Sunup* persona. *This* Brynn Cornell looked and talked nothing like the network-crafted America's Sweetheart or Girl Next Door or Heidi the Happy Helium Balloon or whatever her nickname was. This girl *almost* seemed like she belonged in Adelaide Springs. He'd climb trees with this woman any day—at least he would if she wrangled up some clothes appropriate for the occasion. Her socks were probably from the Louis Vuitton As-Casual-As-We're-Willing-to-Go winter line. But even that wasn't seeming like enough of a deterrent right then, as an image of her with her hair pulled up in a ponytail and wearing his baggy purple Northwestern Wildcats hoodie barged into his brain and began assaulting his senses.

"Do you mind if I go with you?" he asked, but thankfully she was already gone. How long had she been gone? One second he'd been looking at her, and then for the next however many he'd been staring at that unwelcome fantasy version of her in his head. It was *that* version he'd asked to accompany outside. And that version didn't exist.

He shook it off and headed back behind the bar. Six different PTA ladies were waiting on him when he got there. Two of them wanted margaritas, three wanted wine, and if he'd understood the drunken slurs properly, the sixth wanted him to join her in Tampa for the annual homeschool parent conference.

He had learned how to tend a mean bar. He would even pull out a little "One Way or Another" and do his best *Coyote Ugly* on the bar if it pleased the crowd. *Two notes to self, Sebastian: (1) We don't have "One Way or Another" on 8-track. (2) Cole must never know that you even mentally, to yourself, referenced* Coyote Ugly. But he absolutely drew the line at whatever sort of *American Gigolo* insanity happened at homeschool conferences.

Laila came out of the kitchen carrying a tray full of entrees, and Cole stepped out right behind her. He untied the strings from around his waist and slung his apron over Sebastian's shoulder.

"Where do you think you're going?" Sebastian asked. "I've got to get back onstage in a minute. There's a cassette of 'Sunshine on My Shoulders' over there calling my name."

"I need to go talk to Brynn." He looked around the room and

landed on the now empty table with a menu and water glass on it in the corner. "Where'd she go?"

"She wanted some air." Sebastian motioned toward the front door. Cole began walking that way. "Is everything okay?"

Cole turned back to him, and there was emotion in his eyes that Sebastian was pretty sure he'd never seen there before in the six years he'd known him. "Laila says she's back."

He'd always considered himself a proficient and reliable judge of character. He'd known when military generals were lying to him. He'd known when presidents and dictators were keeping something from him. What was it about a beautiful, complicated, intelligent woman that clouded his judgment and made him question what was real and what wasn't?

"Look, Cole, I just don't want to see you guys get hurt. She's not *back* . . . you know? At the end of the week she's going to go back to her life and—"

Cole held up his hand to stop him. "Thanks for your concern, Seb. Really. I understand where you're coming from, and I appreciate it. But . . ." He looked down at his feet and then back at Sebastian, and the emotion had only compounded. "Brynn's our family. You don't refuse to take a chance on the people you love just because there might be some pain involved."

Whatever words or arguments Sebastian may have attempted to bring forth got caught in his throat. He nodded once and slugged Cole on the arm as he walked past toward the door. Then he took a few steps to the right and angled himself so he could see outside. The lights on the porch caught Brynn's silhouette as she turned to the sound of the screen door opening. She had her arms wrapped around herself, and Sebastian quickly darted his eyes to the back table, where her puffy, white three-quarter-length coat was folded over the back of her chair. He contemplated grabbing it and running it out to her—or asking Laila to, since she would certainly be a much more welcome intruder—but as soon as the gesture entered his mind, it was deemed unnecessary.

The shadows flickered, pulling back his gaze just in time to see Cole wrap his arms around Brynn's shoulders and pull her against his chest. Her arms encircled his torso, and the tears streaming down her cheeks glinted in the harsh yellow light shining down on them. Cole kissed the top of her head and seemed to say something into her hair that made her laugh. She pulled back and looked up at him, and with their faces just inches from each other, they laughed in a way that was far too intimate and comfortable considering they were, by all accounts, strangers now.

Laila walked behind the bar and followed his gaze. Sebastian knew he should pull away now that he'd been caught spying—ideally he would have pulled away just before that point—but he couldn't. And as Laila joined him, linking her arms with his, which were folded across his chest, and resting her head on his bicep, he felt like maybe it was okay to keep spying. Good thing.

"They dated, you know."

Well, okay. *That* got him to tear his eyes away. He looked down at the blond locks against his arm, but she kept watching the patio. "Cole and Brynn?" She nodded—not that she could have possibly been talking about anyone else. "No, I didn't know that."

"I think they actually would have been perfect together, if they didn't love each other so much."

Sebastian chuckled and let his eyes return to the patio. They were still standing with their arms wrapped around each other, chatting, laughing, and crying. Something about the intimacy of the scene made him feel cold and isolated. He uncrossed his arms and threw his right arm around Laila's shoulder. She effortlessly slipped against his side, generously sharing her warmth with him. It felt like as good a time as any to ask the question that, in six years, he'd never been brave enough to ask—although it was always right there. Front of mind and on the tip of his tongue.

"Why didn't you and Cole ever get together? You love each other too much?"

She didn't look at him in surprise or pull back, or even take in a deep breath. Nothing changed. She just calmly replied, "Nah. We love each other just the right amount."

He wasn't sure what that meant, exactly, but he knew he didn't need to. Laila seemed to understand it perfectly.

Her left hand squeezed against his belt, and then she pulled away and picked up her tray from the bar. "I think you're due for another song."

He suddenly felt so tired. He was no longer interested in distracting himself from the things he didn't want to think about, and the adrenaline that had been fueling the distraction had all been spent anyway. But as the food on their tables ran out, and with the chef MIA, he knew he only had two options to appease the ladies of the Adelaide Springs Parent Teacher Association. He could slip a little melatonin into their drinks and drive them all safely home, or he could once again cover the figurative eyes of his Pulitzers so they wouldn't think less of him and pour his heart into his next performance.

With a sacrificial sigh he yelled out over his shoulder, "Are we ready for more?" His call to action was met by the return of thunderous hoots and hollers as well as amused smiles from the porch as Cole and Brynn turned and caught his eye through the door. Cole seemed to be filling Brynn in on what *that* was all about, and with each word her smile grew bigger. And the longer Sebastian stood looking at her, and her back at him, the more he questioned his usually astute instincts. He had no idea what to make of her. All he knew right then was that his instincts were telling him to try to look cool by hopping over the bar like Patrick Swayze in *Road House* or something. Proof positive that his instincts misled him on occasion.

Thankfully his forty-year-old body kept his mind in check. Instead of attempting a move that inevitably would have resulted in broken dishes and quite likely a broken tailbone, he walked around, crossed to the stage through the throng of usually strait-laced women, grabbed his microphone, and sang "Rocky Mountain High" like the sensible adult he was.

CHAPTER 23

BRYNN

WEDNESDAY, MARCH 23
7:38 a.m. Mountain Daylight Time

I picked up my phone and reread the text I had received from Sebastian at six thirty.

> I'm back on chauffeur duty, but only because you've
> proven you can't be trusted on your own. See you at
> eight.

I hadn't brought any of the right clothes. Not a single thing I'd packed was suitable. I groaned in frustration as I picked through the silk blouses and chenille sweaters strung across the pink roses on the bedsheets. My boots would work. (It would break my heart a little if I got them muddy, but only a little. A little bit of heartbreak was good for the ego.) Everything else? Useless.

I pulled my knee-length coat on and zipped it up over the towel I had wrapped around me and expertly tucked at my chest. My hair was still loose and wet from my shower, hanging down over my shoulders in stringy ribbons. I could not be late today. I wouldn't give Sebastian the satisfaction. But I also couldn't climb a mountain in Gucci.

I opened my door a crack and peeked down the hall and back. Nothing. I tiptoed out onto the old wooden slats with the maroon runner and followed the path it laid out like Dorothy heading to Oz. Hurrying to the staircase, I tilted my head down in every direction to make sure no one was hanging out on the second floor either. Orly was probably already in the kitchen, eating breakfast with Mrs. Stoddard. The scent of raspberry wafted to me, filling my head with images of muffins and scones. I wasn't sure *what* she had baked, but I would be pleased as punch with any of it.

"Orly?" I knocked on his door and stage whispered his name. "Are you still in here?" I put my ear up to the varnished wood and heard the bed creaking. I looked at my wrist to double-check the time, but I hadn't put my watch on yet. Regardless, I knew it wasn't very long until Sebastian would be there to pick us up. "Orly?" I knocked again, a little louder. "You're not still asleep, are you?"

Shuffling footsteps from inside approached, and I stepped back in anticipation of the door opening. But I sure didn't anticipate what I would see when it did.

"Hey, Brynn," Orly said. Well, he sort of said it. It was barely above a croak and mixed together with some truly hideous coughing. The kind that made you want to step back in case a lung was deposited at your feet.

"Oh my gosh, Orly. What happened to you?"

I had checked in with him when I got to Cassidy's last night and offered to take him dinner, but he'd told me Mrs. Stoddard had made pozole rojo, which is this really amazing stew with pork and hominy, and that I was the one missing out. I texted him again when Cole and Laila dropped me off, just to let him know I'd gotten back okay, and he hadn't responded. It had been after midnight, so I hadn't given that a second thought—even if I briefly wanted to be hurt that he hadn't been sitting up waiting for me like an overprotective father.

He had in no way prepared me for the ashen complexion he was now sporting—the color you only expected to see where a campfire used to be after you let it burn all night.

"You're sick," I stated, quite unnecessarily.

He coughed into his elbow and shook his head. "No, I'm fine. What time is it? I'll get ready." He turned to head back into his room, but he swayed and staggered to the point that I had zero confidence in his ability to make it the four feet to his bed.

I rushed to him and climbed under his arm so he could lean on me. "Absolutely not. You're getting back in bed."

Orly is not a small man, so while I tried to help him sit down gently, I'm afraid I more just sort of let go of him, allowing him to collapse back onto his pillow. "I'll be fine. You need to film—"

"I know how to run a camera." I did not, but I still shrugged like I didn't have a care in the world.

"No offense, Brynn, but you're not touching my equipment."

"Hey! I've helped you . . . you know . . . put in batteries and stuff. It will be a good learning experience."

He covered his mouth to cough, but he kept eyeing me warily and shaking his head.

"Actually, though," I amended, "maybe I should stay with you." I placed the back of my hand on his forehead. Not nearly as hot as I assumed he would be based on the way he looked, but far from normal. "Yep. Let's just settle in and . . ." I had begun to unzip my coat, but thankfully about the time the zipper got to my collarbone, I remembered I was wearing only a towel underneath. "Um . . . did you bring plenty of clothes?"

He tried to make sense of the words. Poor guy. "Huh?"

"I was just wondering if you had a sweatshirt or something I could borrow. I don't have any of the right clothes."

He lifted an arm and motioned over toward the chest of drawers in the corner. "I'm so sorry about this. I think if I can just get up and moving . . ." He tried to sit up, and I gently pushed him back down and adjusted his pillows.

"Don't you even worry about it. Do you have stuff to drink?" I shook him softly when his eyes closed, and he didn't respond. Soon a hearty snore filled the room, so at least I knew he wasn't dead.

I crossed the room and opened the top drawer, then promptly closed it while diverting my eyes. I had really expected to go my entire life without laying eyes on Orly Hill's tighty-whities, but some aspirations were not to be. Squinting, I slid open the second drawer, then opened it fully with a relieved breath. The first long-sleeved T-shirt I pulled out would have been perfect—big, baggy, and cozy. But if I accidentally did anything to his *Proud Florida A&M Dad* shirt, I'd never forgive myself. I folded it back up and replaced it, then pulled out a *Sunup* hoodie. Did everyone have these except for me, or had he bought it in the gift shop? Regardless, if I spilled anything on that one, I was fairly certain I could track down another one.

I threw it over my shoulder and closed the drawer, then looked back at him again. He was still in the awkward position I had dropped him in, and though his heavy, regulated breathing gave me the impression he wasn't at all bothered by that, I knew he deserved better.

I bent over his bed and attempted to straighten him out. I ended up having to go to the foot of the bed and grab one of his legs under each of my arms to pull him down a bit, and unfortunately that's exactly the position I was in when Sebastian appeared at the door.

"Please tell me you didn't murder Orly."

I was roasting in my down coat, and as a single bead of sweat trickled down from my neck, my hand fluttered to the top of my chest to absorb it into my coat and stop the tickle. It was like swatting at a fly in your face. You don't think about it before you do it, and you certainly don't consider the consequences. Consequences that, in most cases, would include little things like accidentally thumping the person next to you on the shoulder or causing a distraction in a serious meeting. *My* consequences were more along the lines of dropping Orly's leg onto the sweatshirt, which had fallen off my shoulder onto the bed, and loosening the towel from around my chest and feeling it fall down in a hoop around my ankles.

Sebastian caught it all, of course, and even though he could technically see less of my skin than he could have before—since the coat was still zipped and in place, and the towel was covering my bare feet—I felt completely exposed under the interrogation of his eyes.

I cleared my throat and tried to keep an expression on my face that communicated everything was completely normal and as it should be. (And that I had not murdered Orly dressed as a Burberry streaker.) "Orly's sick. I was . . ." It would have been so much easier to explain if he hadn't been looking so amused by it all. I lowered Orly's other leg and yanked the sweatshirt out from underneath, stumbling backward a bit as it flew to me.

If you fall down, it's all over, Brynn. Whatever dignity you have left . . . gone. I caught myself just as Sebastian rushed forward to catch me if needed. Thankfully, it wasn't needed. Unfortunately, his arm was looped around my waist, and my hand was on his chest before that became completely evident.

"I like your shirt," I said, my hand absorbing the feel of the soft, worn-in cotton and the unyielding muscle beneath it. Today he was sporting a relic from Janet Jackson's 1990 Rhythm Nation World Tour.

"Thanks. And I like your . . ." He surveyed the length of me, from hood to bare legs to towel-buried feet. "Dress? Sorry. Fashion is beyond me. But whatever this is, it works."

I laughed and pulled my hand away. He followed my lead

and took a step back. "I just came down to see if I could borrow something from Orly and found him in pretty rough shape. Flu or something, I guess."

Sebastian stepped to the side of Orly's bed and straightened him out with much more ease than I had exhibited. Then he pulled the blanket up over him. "The fresh air gets people sometimes. Not to mention the elevation."

"Yeah. I'm sorry you came out for nothing."

"Oh." He nodded and stepped toward the door. "You going out with Laila or something? I'm happy to still drive if you want me to. Both of you, I mean."

"Well, that's nice of you, but I actually meant I should hang out here with Orly. Take care of him. You know?"

"No offense, but can you afford to give up a full day of filming?"

I had stuck around Cassidy's until they closed down—long enough to watch middle-aged woman after middle-aged woman throw themselves at Sebastian. I'd honestly never heard John Denver sing as many John Denver songs as I'd now heard Sebastian Sudworth perform, but I'd enjoyed every moment of it. He was actually really good. I mean, not Radio City Music Hall or Lincoln Center good but definitely better than half the people performing at bars in the East Village on any given Friday night.

It was fascinating to see him so relaxed. And mind-boggling that *that* was relaxing to him. He flirted effortlessly and harmlessly, making every woman in the room feel like he was genuinely happy to spend time with her. I'd been dying to ask him how much he made in tips on nights like that, but that felt rude. So I'd asked Cole. He refused to say, but Laila raised her eyebrows and silently mouthed, "A lot."

Then Cole and Laila and I had visited a few of our old haunts. The school, the meadow, the natural amphitheater in the wall of the canyon where we used to camp. Mostly we laughed and got caught up.

As little sleep as I had gotten, I probably should have felt relieved to have been given the day off, but I didn't.

I puffed my cheeks full of air and released it through pursed lips. "Probably not, but I can't just leave him."

He tilted his head and his lips parted, but no sound came out at first. He then turned, walked out of the room, and hurried down the staircase.

Well, okay, then. At least someone *is happy about the unexpected sick day.*

But within seconds he was back, and Mrs. Stoddard was following him. She looked disapprovingly at what I was wearing—certainly not for the first time—and then shifted her attention to Orly.

"You go. I'll keep an eye on him."

I shook my head. "Thank you, but he's my responsibility—"

"That's funny." Her eyes met mine. "I thought your responsibility was saving your career. I can handle this. Go."

I raised my arms in the air in exasperation, and then quickly realized I shouldn't be doing anything that would hike up my coat. "Thank you. Truly. But Orly is very protective of his equipment. I already asked, but he simply will not allow anyone else to use his camera."

Sebastian walked back over to Orly's bedside and nudged his arm. "Hey, Orly . . . Sorry you're sick, man."

"Seb?" Orly mumbled.

"Yeah. So, hey, do you mind if I use your gear to film for Brynn today?"

I crossed my arms and rolled my eyes. "I've already told you, he—"

"Yeah, that's fine, man. Thanks." And then the traitor rolled over and fell back asleep.

I huffed and looked at Sebastian, who motioned his head toward the door. "Go get dressed." A mischievous smirk spread across his lips. "Unless you're planning to wear that."

"She most certainly is not wearing that," Mrs. Stoddard said, causing his smirk to deepen.

Then it softened into something . . . different. Sweet. Confusing. "Seriously. Go."

Burberry needed to launch a new marketing campaign for these coats. They weren't designed for fashion. They were designed for survival. On bare skin, they could keep scientists in Antarctica toasty if they got locked out of the biodome. Although even my ankles were flushed right then, so maybe it wasn't just the coat.

"Well, okay . . ." I looked down at all the bags and equipment. "I'll be back in a minute to help you carry stuff down."

Sebastian bent down and opened the biggest of the bags. He pulled out a camera, a lapel mic, a receiver pack, and a couple of batteries. When he looked up, he was level with my knees, causing him to get up as quickly as he could and me to hold my coat down so he didn't get a glimpse of anything more than he already had.

"This is all we need," he said, holding up the equipment.

"Well, are you sure we don't—"

"Good grief, *yes*! Some of us know how to do more than show up and look pretty."

His eyes caught mine, and my brain told me to be insulted. I was an accomplished woman who had managed to survive and thrive in a patriarchal society and, specifically, a male-dominated industry. My brain told me not to take that from him. But instead I huffed, "Fine," picked up the towel from the floor, and hurried to my room. Because my brain may have wanted to be offended, but everything else in me was fairly content.

Sebastian Sudworth thought I was pretty.

CHAPTER 24

SEBASTIAN

WEDNESDAY, MARCH 23
7:57 a.m. Mountain Daylight Time

"Thanks for doing this, Jo." Sebastian had accompanied her down to the kitchen, where she was gathering some essentials onto a tray for Orly.

"Happy to," she responded. "I'd be lying, though, if I didn't admit I'm a little surprised."

"Why? You can't blame her for still needing to get out there. The clock is ticking." He snatched one of the saltines from the pack she had just set down and took a bite.

"Not her, Seb. You." Jo slapped his hand as he reached to steal more of Orly's crackers. "You were as good as off the hook. You're the fish that reeled the fisherman back in."

Oh. That. Yeah, he'd been sort of surprised by that himself. Not just that he was willing to make a little extra effort to help her not lose the day, but that he'd been disappointed to be let off the hook. *Disappointed?* Yes. Disappointed. Not because he wanted to spend the day with her. It wasn't that. Well, it *was* that, but only

248

because he still had a few too many unanswered questions bouncing around in his head.

He'd watched the three old friends all evening. The way they'd snuck over to each other for hugs at random moments, and the way their smiles were bigger and their laughs were louder, and their happy tears always seemed to be just under the surface, ready to appear. The way Brynn had no longer appeared conflicted or tortured or whatever you wanted to call it. From the time she was with Cole on the patio to the time the three of them drove off in Cole's Wrangler together after Sebastian offered to close up, she seemed like the weight of the world was off her shoulders.

He needed the time with her today. And as sorry as he was that Orly was sick, maybe it was for the best that he wouldn't be there. He'd gotten politicians to acknowledge affairs and dictators to acknowledge missile tests they'd spent months denying. If Brynn Cornell's change of heart was a ruse, he'd get it out of her.

"The sooner she can get her footage, the sooner she'll head back to New York and we can move on with our lives," he finally said in response to Jo.

Jo helped herself to the package of crackers Sebastian's hand had just been slapped away from and began nibbling on the corner of a saltine. "Pretty sure Steve said the plane is taking off Friday morning regardless of how much footage she's shot, but you tell yourself what you need to."

"What's that supposed to—"

"Sorry I took so long."

Sebastian turned his head at Brynn's voice and the sound of her bounding down the steps and then had to swallow hard at the sight of her. Her hair was in a neat—but not slick or perfect—braid down her back, and it bounced behind her as she hurried toward them. She was still wearing those impractical boots—the ones clearly not meant to ever get wet—but today they covered leggings or yoga pants or whatever they were called. And she wore a long gray sweatshirt. About the same length as the sweater she had worn yesterday, but so much more casual and flattering. Well, it was flattering on *her* in that it wasn't designed to be flattering at all. It was formless and bulky, with the yellow *Sunup* logo embroidered on the front. Her hands were stuffed into pockets that appeared to have tears in the stitching.

"It's . . . That's . . . Yeah, it's no big thing." His ears were ringing. Why were his ears ringing? "We're cool."

"Lord, have mercy," Jo muttered under her breath as she turned away and pulled the orange juice from the refrigerator.

Brynn reached the bottom of the steps and quirked an inquisitive eyebrow at him. "Cool."

In fairness, never once—not a single time—had Omar al-Bashir or Raul Castro or even Justin Trudeau shown up for an interview looking almost exactly as he had fantasized about them just twelve or so hours earlier. He just needed a moment to recalibrate.

"Thanks again for keeping an eye on Orly, Mrs. Stoddard." Brynn reached for the memo pad and a pen on the counter and wrote down some numbers. "This is my cell. Would you please call me if he gets worse or anything?"

"I'm sure he'll just sleep."

Brynn nodded and then looked up at Sebastian. "Shall we?"

He grabbed the little bit of Orly's equipment he had decided they needed and headed to the door, scurrying to get past Brynn so he could open it for her. She was almost there when she spun on her heel, ran to the kitchen, and grabbed two of the raspberry scones. She flashed her pearly whites at Jo.

"Thank you, Mrs. Stoddard!" She hurried back to the door and gave Sebastian one of the scones before shuffling through.

"Lord, have mercy," Jo repeated, causing Sebastian to shush her before he took a bite of the scone and shut the door behind him.

CHAPTER 25

BRYNN

We ate our scones, stopped by the Bean Franklin to get a cup of coffee to go, talked to Laila while we waited, and then climbed back in Sebastian's vehicle. And we had yet to actually say a word to each other since we'd left the inn. Finally we spoke out of necessity.

"So where do you want to go today?" He put the gear into Reverse and backed out onto Main Street. "Are there more reunions on tap?"

I'd given the plan for the day a lot of thought. "I don't think so. I was sort of thinking maybe we could go up into the mountains, if you don't mind. I'd love to just show the beauty of the place."

"Okay."

I watched him as he checked his mirrors and U-turned. His Janet Jackson shirt was paired with an MIT ball cap, creating much the same look he'd sported all three days I'd been in his presence—but a very different one than featured in most of his photos on the internet. I still hadn't gotten to watch very many video clips—I kept dozing off while they buffered—but I felt like I had been able to get a fairly comprehensive overview of his career's fashion timeline. He looked most natural in the field, when he was wearing khakis and a dress shirt open at the collar. During his time as a Washington correspondent, he'd relied on a buttoned-up dress shirt and a tie, but he still usually had the cuffs rolled up on his forearms. When he sat behind an anchor desk, he wore immaculate tailored suits.

It was strange how jarring the images were. How unlike his current persona he appeared in photos where his face was clean-shaven and his hair was tamed. But from what I'd seen, he didn't look any more out of place then, *that* way, than he did now, *this* way. That life had suited him just as this suited him. It was the man inside the image who had changed, I was guessing.

We were going to be spending a lot of time together today. Might as well get the tension and discomfort rolling. "Why did you come to Adelaide Springs, Sebastian?"

I saw and sensed every muscle in his body tighten and he tilted away from me slightly. He turned off Main Street and onto the first of many side roads for the day.

"I'm not trying to pry, but you've got to admit you haven't followed a very predictable career trajectory."

He grinned. "That's true."

"It seems like everyone likes you, so you must have made a better first impression on them than you did on me."

He glanced my direction, and I smiled. He shook his head and returned his eyes to the road. Then he shifted in his seat and reached for the radio. "Want to listen to some music?"

"Not really."

His fingers dropped and returned to the wheel.

We drove up the winding path of Banyon in silence, and I looked out the window down into the canyon. Of all of us, Addie had always been the one afraid to drive on these roads, which made it even more baffling to think of her as an air force pilot. Cole drove with caution, taking very seriously his responsibility for his passengers. Laila just wasn't a big fan of driving in general. The youngest of us and the last to get her license, she'd been content just letting us all keep doing the driving, even after she joined our licensed ranks. But Wes and I were the adrenaline junkies who loved the freedom that we found behind the wheel. In California, I'd never quite adjusted to freeway driving. By the time I moved to Manhattan, I preferred to take the subway or a cab—or, eventually, a car service—so that I could get work done while I traveled.

But there was nothing like mountain driving. It felt danger-ous and exhilarating to follow the hairpin curves mandated by the mountains rather than go straight on a path that was built by plow-ing over whatever got in its way.

"So why did you leave the news business?"

He groaned in frustration. "Are you expecting me to just open up and tell you all my deep, dark secrets here, Brynn? Like you're interviewing some twenty-two-year-old kid with a number one album to promote? Sorry. That's not me."

"Fine." I crossed my arms and turned to face out my window again.

"Fine," he repeated in a huffy, elevated voice that was clearly intended to mimic my own.

We rode in silence, each stewing in our discontent, for several minutes, but it continued to eat at me. Not what he had said, neces-sarily, and not just that Larry David and Kristen Stewart combined hadn't been as difficult to get to know as Sebastian, but that I really was just trying to get to know him, and he'd questioned my motives. Again.

"I know you don't like me, and that's fine." I dug my finger-nails into the seat. "I know you don't trust me, and why should you? I get it. I can't make you trust me, and I can't make you believe me, and I certainly can't make you like me. But I woke up this morning thinking I would try. To make you like me, I mean." Even that probably sounded artificial to him. "Not because I *need* you to like me. Just because . . . Well, you were really nice to me yesterday. I don't know why I told you the stuff I did, and if I could take it back I probably would." Especially since I was beginning to suspect he would rather career off the mountain than so much as tell me his favorite color. "But you were nice. *Kind*. And I appreciated it." I took a deep breath. "I just wanted you to know I'm trying." I extended my left hand and pushed on the old AM/FM radio knob.

A few bars of some modern country song played, but before I could even hope to identify the song or singer—I pretty much only knew Maren Morris, anyway, and it wasn't her—the truck went silent again, except for the sound of the noisy engine working hard as it climbed in elevation. I turned in Sebastian's direction just as he began speaking.

"While you were getting stuck in a tree yesterday, I was learning that my ex-wife is remarried and pregnant with her first child. So that's fun."

I took a sharp intake of breath and grimaced. "No, that sucks."

He shrugged, eyes still focused on the road. "We've been divorced six years."

"And how many years were you married?"

"Eleven. And it's not like I didn't know this would happen eventually. I'm happy for her."

"Are you?" I asked.

He nodded. "Yeah. I really am. I want her to have a better life than what I gave her." I believed him. "It just hit me harder than I expected."

"How did you find out?"

"My mom . . ." He started laughing over the words. "My mom ran into Erin's parents. Erin. My ex. My mother ran into her parents, and she tells me every insignificant detail before getting around to the fact that Erin's pregnant." His laughter dropped off, and his voice went quiet. "I didn't even know she was married, and all of a sudden she's not only married, she's having a kid and her parents are shopping for truffle oil."

"I don't know what that means, exactly, but I do know good truffle oil's hard to find."

He chuckled and glanced at me. "Now *you* my mother would like."

I didn't understand what was happening, but I didn't want to move or speak out of turn for fear that I would mess it up. I was filled with curiosity, but I knew enough to know Sebastian was used to being the one asking the questions. I felt honored that he had told me as much as he had, and I figured if I hoped to learn more, I needed to show a little sacrifice and reciprocity.

It was like the time on *Sunup3* that I thought it would be cool to go to Comic-Con with Keanu Reeves, and he only agreed to an interview if I committed to talking about nothing but climate change. I was strictly prohibited from talking about any of his movies, even when the cameras weren't rolling. Awkward? Sure. Disappointing not to be able to tell him I had watched *The Lake House* fourteen times? You bet. But I still got to be the only person walking around Comic-Con with Neo.

"I left Adelaide Springs to get away from my mother. Well, my mother and the various men she seemed to attract from every dark corner of the world." If nothing else, we could commiserate over our mothers. Although I was pretty sure my mother's best day could beat truffle oil. "That may not be much of a revelation, after what I told you yesterday, but there it is."

It was a strange thing, though. It was what I'd begun to realize the day before. There was a different sort of hesitancy I felt in talking to Sebastian as opposed to anyone else. Not because I didn't think he could handle my stories, but because I was afraid he could.

"I'm sorry I called you Brenda."

I laughed. "It's okay. I was just always Bren. I never really felt like 'Brenda Cornell' was my name. My mother used to say, 'If I'd wanted your name to be "Bren," that's what it would be.' And of course I was all about not giving her what she wanted, every chance I got." I nudged him with my elbow, trying to break up the heaviness that had settled between us. "Besides, you know as well as I do 'Brenda Cornell' never would have made it to the network level. Someone would have changed it, somewhere along the way."

Sebastian scoffed. "What are you talking about? With that name you would have done great in Albuquerque. Reno, maybe."

I laughed harder than I meant to. "'Reporting live from the county fair—'"

"Oh no, no, no." He placed his hand on my forearm, just for a second. "'Brenda Cornell' is not a reporter. No way. Brenda Cornell is an anchor, baby." He took on his network nightly news voice, which was sort of magical and perfect. "'I'm Sebastian Sudworth.'"

"'And I'm Brenda Cornell,'" I completed seamlessly. We laughed and then I added, "It's sort of shocking to me that you made it as far as you did with a name like *yours*."

His eyebrows rose, and he feigned offense. "What's wrong with my name?"

"Nothing. Nothing at all. It's just . . . Well, it doesn't exactly roll off the tongue, does it? Of course I'm just assuming Sudworth is your real name. It's not actually Parker or Jones or something, is it?"

He chuckled and shook his head. "Afraid not."

I waited until the laughter had dissipated, and then I glanced at him to make sure he still appeared at ease. There was a chance it was still too soon, but with that professional delivery of three simple words—two of which were his name—he'd made it bla-tantly obvious he belonged in a newsroom. It was too good an opportunity to pass up.

"Sebastian?"

"Hmm?"

"Why *did* you give it up?"

The good humor was gone again. Instantly. I watched as his hands clenched tighter around the wheel, and I listened as silence moved in where laughter had been. I turned away and began look-ing out the window again, half expecting the radio to turn back on in a moment.

And then, "Don't take this the wrong way, but can I count on you not to talk to anyone about anything I say?"

Something about the vulnerability in his voice made me cer-tain we were embarking on a confidence I would never dare to betray.

But it was still more fun to tease.

"Don't take this the wrong way, but what makes you think I could ever find anything about you interesting enough to share?"

I turned back to him in time to see him bite at the inside of his cheek, causing the corner of his mouth to tighten as it rose and some rather appealing crinkles to appear around his eyes. Teasing him had been the right play.

We had stopped climbing in elevation, and I opened my mouth in the beginning of a yawn to pop my ears, just as he did the same. It was quiet for thirty seconds more, but I knew he would start talking when he was ready. And I knew not to pressure him. I didn't have any idea what he was about to tell me. My internet searches hadn't pulled up anything more than rumors and speculation and a lot of headlines that included the words "mysterious circumstances." So I didn't know how to prepare myself, or even if preparation was necessary. I just knew that he was at least contemplating talking to me about something he didn't usually talk about. I was honored even by the contemplation.

"I was in Maungdaw Township." He darted his eyes to the right and said, "That's an area in—"

"Rakhine State in Myanmar. Yeah. You were there reporting on the Rohingya genocide, presumably?"

"I didn't expect you to know that." He took a deep breath as he looked into the rearview mirror and then pulled off to the right at the old abandoned Adelaide Gulch ski pass. "I'm sorry that I didn't expect you to know that."

I shrugged. "I'm used to being underestimated. The first time I met Mark Irvine, he told me that his first rule of journalism was to never trust anyone with dimples."

Sebastian exclaimed, "Ouch!" and laughed, though somewhat painfully, and I joined him. He shifted the vehicle into Park and then turned to face me.

"I have no doubt it was a sexist insult coming from Irvine, but in fairness, I adopted the same rule after meeting Morley Safer the first time."

Laughter erupted from deep within me, and he watched me and chortled softly to himself. Then he pointed behind my head. "This an okay spot, you think?"

I nodded. I didn't have to look behind me to know where we were or exactly what we would find when we got out and explored on foot. When I was a kid, Adelaide Gulch had still been a thriving tourist location. Maybe even the primary attraction, apart from those four revolutionary days in September. Adelaide Gulch, though not technically within city limits, made the town of Adelaide Springs a traveler's destination rather than just a place to rest for the night and grab a quick meal before continuing on in the journey to somewhere a little more worth planning a trip around.

"The Inn Between . . . ," I muttered and then laughed softly. We were each getting out of our respective sides of the vehicle, so thankfully Sebastian hadn't overheard the moment, right then, when the cleverness of the name of Mrs. Stoddard's bed-and-breakfast finally clicked in my brain. I would have hated to admit I'd slept there three nights without catching it. I'd have certainly negated at least some of those "Don't underestimate Brynn Cornell's intelligence!" points I had just won.

"Hope you don't mind getting those boots wet," he called out over the top of the vehicle and then reached in and grabbed his own much more rugged and broken-in boots from the back seat. He bent over and quickly pulled off his Vans and slipped into the boots.

"It'll be good for them," I called back.

It wouldn't be. Walking up the rough, rocky, and muddy path that still had up to a couple feet of snow in certain places would destroy them. But I was still itching to get them on the trail and see what they could do.

Sebastian came around to where I stood and stared up with me at the ski lift that hadn't been used in twenty-five years. "I would have loved to see this place in its prime."

I nodded, wishing there was a way to invite him into the memories that had been stored in the deep recesses of my mind and yet had sprung to the surface in a flash. "It really was something." I began walking up the trail, and he followed me. We climbed at a forty-five-degree angle for a full minute before I pointed to the right, up about thirty more feet in elevation. "Just on the other side of that ridge there—"

"Stop talking!"

I whipped around to see what was behind the urgent instruction—my first guess was a bear; my second was he was enjoying the view, and the sound of my voice ruined it. But I hadn't expected to see him running back down the rocky, snow-covered yards we had traveled, back to the vehicle.

"What are you doing?" I shouted at him. I wanted to be insulted that he had cut off my nostalgia in such a rude way, but as I watched him expertly jump from rock to rock—the faster way, but certainly the more perilous—I was just amused. "If you think abandoning me here would be a good way to kill me, you're wrong! I could Donner Party it up in these mountains for years. *Years*, I tell you!"

He didn't respond, not that I would have heard him if he had. He was facing away from me, down the mountain, and with that much distance between us, the wind would have carried everything away.

Ah. The wind. There it was. If I remembered correctly, we were right around eleven thousand feet now and climbing. It probably hadn't been my smartest move to leave my coat at the inn, but smart didn't matter right then. What mattered was the way I suddenly felt more alive than I had in twenty years.

I stepped out from the shadows of the giant snow-covered pines and aspens and into a patch of sun, and that exact feeling— near-frozen, wind-chafed skin responding to the sun's rays by spreading joy and thankfulness through every nerve center in my body—felt like home. The best parts of it, and none of the bad.

Nothing I'd held on to and allowed to fester for twenty years, and everything I'd pretended had never existed.

"Brynn?" His voice only inches away didn't startle me, even though at some point my eyes had closed.

"Hmm?" I asked. My arms were spread out and my face was tilted toward the sun, and my wind-stung eyes were releasing gentle tears from the corners. They almost made it to my ears, but the wind and the sun worked together to dry them before they got that far.

The wind and the sun and Sebastian's thumb.

His voice hadn't startled me, but his touch sent shock waves.

I tilted my head down slowly, instinctively afraid to move too fast for fear I would ruin something. Even if I had no idea what that something was. My eyes opened and caught him studying me, his right hand still on my cheek. His thumb still toying with the tears as their trajectory adjusted with the direction of gravity.

"The mountains suit you." His voice was still only inches away, but it was no longer his voice I was focused on. The moisture had stopped streaming from the corners of my eyes, but his hand hadn't budged, apart from the meticulous trail his thumb was tracing across my jawline.

"You too." I'd never spoken a truer statement. My internet research had proven Sebastian Sudworth was a man who looked equally at ease in war-torn strongholds, chasing down militant combatants and demanding answers, and in the Oval Office, asking the questions no one else dared ask. But he belonged *here*. The wind whipping the wisps of hair that couldn't be contained by his cap, his black-rimmed glasses fogging up a little bit from the warmth of his breath, his lips parted as his lungs worked overtime after the run back up the rocks at more than two miles in elevation.

All too often in books and movies, kisses seem to be these uncontrollable things with lives of their own. Someone just can't help but close that gap between themselves and someone else, throwing caution and consequences to the wind. That's nice and all, but all too often, once the impetuous kiss is over, they have to say they're sorry and talk about how they don't know what came over them.

That wasn't the case with me. I knew I was going to kiss him. I knew we were both going to like it very much. And I knew I wasn't going to be sorry.

I also knew that if I was wrong about any of those things, it was going to be a very long trip back down the mountain, but that was a chance I very intentionally chose to take.

I leaned into his hand, just as the pressure from it eased and it seemed as if he might be preparing to pull away. His green puffer jacket was only closed to his collarbone, and I gripped each of my hands around the unzipped material. I hesitated just a second as our eyes locked, giving him an opportunity to protest before it was too late. Because, seriously . . . if I misread the cues, I might have to put my wilderness survival money where my big-time Donner Party–talking mouth was.

But I hadn't misread a thing.

He leaned forward and whispered, softer than the wind, as his thumb made one last sweep over my cheekbone and his fingers fanned through my hair to the back of my head. "We might regret this when we're no longer caught up in the romance of the mountain."

"Then let's never come down."

I rose on my toes, and we pulled each other closer simultaneously. I'd expected urgency, but his lips met mine with tenderness and careful, gentle exploration. I gave in without hesitation and let him set the tone. I wasn't wearing glasses, but the warmth of his breath had the same effect on me that it had on his lenses. I felt the steam spread throughout my head, creating a fog in my brain and over my eyes.

With my fists clenched around his jacket at his chest, tightly squeezed between his body and mine, I could feel our intermingling pulses, but the material was doing an admirable job keeping his body temperature all to him. And as his lips continued their tantalizing exploration of mine, I felt the need to be closer to him. I needed more. I was jealous for his warmth and desperate for that feeling. The one that I knew would signal I was no longer alone. That I wasn't the only one invested in my survival.

I began unzipping his jacket but began to panic when his lips stilled on mine. There it was. I'd known I would eventually ruin things by moving at the wrong time or speaking when I shouldn't, and it had finally happened. He probably thought I was trying to undress him. I was the girl who had made out with one of the One Direction guys in a dark NYC club on New Year's Eve, after all. (I honestly only knew Harry and Niall, and it wasn't either of them. Not my proudest moment, even in a lifetime of questionable choices.) What would make him think I was above trying to seduce him right there on the mountain, in calf-deep snow?

He doesn't know about that, I reminded myself. *He doesn't know anything about you. And he* already *doesn't like you.*

His fingers were no longer in my hair. My eyes fluttered open, and I wanted nothing more than to go back and implore my hands to stay right where they were, so that his would stay right where it had been. So his lips would never leave mine. But it was too late. The spell had been broken.

But his eyes didn't seem to know that yet. They were only two inches from mine, full of questions and answers, it seemed. He leaned in and brushed his lips against mine, lingering for just a moment on my bottom lip. Then he pulled back again, our eyes locked into intimacy I wanted to run from and to, and placed his hand over mine and finished lowering the zipper of his jacket. Tears pooled in my eyes as he held it open and smiled. My lip trembled as I responded to the invitation in his eyes and wrapped my arms around his abdomen and spread my hands out across his back, between the warmth of his down jacket and his T-shirt. I rested my cheek against his chest, and he kissed the top of my head and wrapped his arm around my shoulders as my tears let loose all over Janet Jackson.

CHAPTER 26

SEBASTIAN

WEDNESDAY, MARCH 23
9:19 a.m. Mountain Daylight Time

He had *not* seen that coming.

He'd only run back to the Bronco to grab Orly's equipment. He'd completely forgotten about it, and then he'd had a hunch Brynn was about to say something beautifully human. He'd already discovered that was when she was the most irresistible. And that's when he remembered he was pulling double duty for the day. The world needed to see her *that* way. Endearingly fragile and freakishly strong, all at once. The more likable and human he began to view her as, the more he truly wanted to share that side of her with the world.

And, apparently, the more he wanted to keep her all to himself.

He hadn't been prepared for the sight of her, up on the rocks above him, with her braid blowing in the breeze and the bluest of clear blue skies as her backdrop as she ignored the bitter wind and soaked in the rays of the sun. The surrender in her raised hands and the vulnerability and trust in her closed-eyes expression. Complete abandon. The entire scene was as beautiful as anything he had ever seen.

Brynn Cornell was as beautiful as anything he had ever seen, and he just hadn't seen that coming.

He still held Orly's equipment in his left hand, and he wanted nothing more than to set it down and wrap both of his arms tighter around her. To let her know she was safe from whatever it was she feared. But he was pretty sure Orly would murder him if he came down from the mountain without the camera in particular. If he was like other cameramen and -women he'd known, he'd probably prefer Sebastian came down the mountain without Brynn if forced to choose.

Sebastian felt the first of her tears beginning to soak through to his skin, and he juggled the best he could to embrace her around the shoulder with his left arm, camera and all, and stroked her hair with his right hand.

"It's okay," he whispered against her bobbing head as the cries began robbing her of the thin oxygen that surrounded them. He shushed her, not to try to get her to stop or be quieter—no, she clearly had been in dire need of the freedom she now seemed to be experiencing, and he wouldn't have taken that from her for anything. But he did feel it was his duty to keep her from hyperventilating.

"I'm sorry," she choked out.

"Don't be."

His lips rose in a smile against her hair that smelled like a rose garden. *The* Rose Garden, actually.

In 1991 his dad had taken him to the White House for the first time. That was the only time his dad accompanied him there, though he'd been there countless times on his own as an adult. But in 1991, he wasn't there as a journalist. He was just a boy excited to meet Michael Jordan and the rest of the NBA Champion Chicago Bulls. He wasn't particularly a basketball fan—he and his brothers had been brought up to support baseball, the most patriotic of all team sports, in his dad's estimation, and particularly the Yankees, the most patriotic of all teams—but there wasn't a boy his age in the entire universe who wouldn't have jumped at the opportunity to meet Jordan in 1991. Even a Sudworth boy wasn't above the appeal of that.

The only thing more appealing had been a day alone with his dad. Darius and Xavier had gotten to accompany their dad to the White House on various occasions, but until that day Sebastian had never been deemed mature enough. Though Sebastian didn't fully understand the political particulars until later, the day had really been about Rose Garden strategy—a technique in which the president makes use of events happening on White House grounds to hold important meetings somewhat under the radar. Sebastian had hardly spent any time at all with his dad. But while Martin Sudworth met with the president and who knows who else in the Oval Office, Sebastian had wandered around the Rose Garden, smelling every single flower and cementing the names of them to memory to distract himself from the day's disappointment.

His dad was nowhere to be found when the Bulls were chatting with people in the receiving line, and Sebastian had been too shy to meet them on his own.

He still remembered the names and scents of every rose he studied that day. So the last time he made the Costco run to Colorado Springs for Jo and Andi and Cole, and all the other business owners who stocked up on supplies to last them several months, he'd brought back pretty much a lifetime supply of shampoo and conditioner for the inn, because the scent reminded him of the dark red Pat Nixon Rose. Jo had hated it and said it was far too potent, but Sebastian had told her if she didn't like his choices, next time she could make the eight-hour round trip. She'd never complained again.

And now, against his cheek, Brynn Cornell's hair smelled like a Pat Nixon Rose. The most beautiful, poignant, perfect scent that had been the highlight of his loneliest day.

Sebastian kept trying to juggle the equipment, desperate to comfort her without knocking her in the head with the edge of the heavy plastic. And just the idea that she was trusting him with not only her vulnerability but not to knock her unconscious after all the horrible things he had said to her was enough to make him reevaluate the order of his priorities.

"Hang on." He released her from his arms and pulled away, and his heart broke as her eyes darted around, seemingly looking for explanation. Escape, maybe? She expected to have to fend for herself, just as much as he always had. "Just . . ." He raised his hand, and she looked at it, then up into his eyes. "I'm not going anywhere. Don't move."

He shucked his right arm out of the jacket and then switched all of Orly's equipment to his right arm so he could repeat the shucking motion with his left. "Yowza!" The bracing wind assaulted his bare arms, causing him to dance around and her to laugh at him.

"What are you doing? And who says, 'Yowza,' you dork?"

Sebastian threw his jacket down onto the snow and then leaned over to spread it out as much as he could before gingerly setting the expensive equipment down on it, freeing his hands completely. When he rose and looked at Brynn again, the humor had faded from her face.

"Hang on. Are you . . . ?" The tremble began in her tightly clenched chin and then traveled up to her bottom lip, clenched between her teeth. "Just so I . . ." She looked down at his jacket and then back at his bare arms. "You're insane."

He chuckled and wrapped his arms around himself, just as the hopping began. "Well, perhaps. But in my defense, there was a lot more body heat being shared when that started." He looked up at the sun—getting close to its midday position directly overhead, but currently hidden behind a family of puffy white clouds. "There was also more sunlight. I'm not sure we have much control over that, but . . ." His arms opened to her again, but she didn't move. Fantastic. Nothing like ruining a moment and acquiring hypothermia all in one fell swoop.

"I hate my job." As soon as the words escaped, she gasped and covered her mouth with her hands. "Oh my gosh." Her muffled voice spoke through her fingers and nearly closed mouth, but her eyes were wide open. More than just literally, it appeared. "I've never said that before." Her hands left her mouth and slid to her cheeks. "I'm not sure I've even thought that before. I'm not sure I knew that." She glided her palms up to her forehead. "I don't actually hate my job. Right?"

Sebastian lowered his arms and wrapped them around himself again, still hopping. "Well, I suppose—"

"I have the best job in the world, Sebastian. Everyone wants my job. People do horrible things to land a job like this." She dropped her hands and quickly pointed at him. "Before you wonder, no . . . I didn't do horrible things. Not to get the job, I mean. Not to get *this* job, specifically. Sure, I skipped my own mother's funeral, but that really had nothing to do with the job. How could I hate this job? I don't. I love this job. Right? How could I not love it?" Her voice was carried away with the wind.

He knew Brynn was in the middle of a major breakthrough. A real catharsis, from the looks of it. He couldn't help but contemplate the consequences of asking her to continue said catharsis in the car. He eyed his jacket. Thirty more seconds, then it was going back on.

"Mark Irvine is so dull. Have you met him?" He nodded, and she kept going. "I mean, apart from abandoning me last Friday, he's been nice enough. But yeah. I really can't stand him. He's so fake." She scoffed. "Who am I kidding? *I'm* so fake. I'm the worst!"

Seb remembered telling Cole and Laila that. Exactly that. And he began growing warm again at the realization of just how wrong he'd been.

"The stuff they write for us to say?" A loud, painful guffaw erupted from her. "You almost forget how you really talk. You just know that *no one* talks like that. And yet *you* sort of do. I don't know. That probably doesn't make any sense. Or maybe it does. To you, I mean. Is it possible that I just like being famous? It's got to be more than that, right? If not, how shallow am I? Or maybe it's not about being famous, exactly. I just kept moving up and moving up, and I don't think there's anything wrong with that. I mean, why bother doing something if you aren't going to try to be the best at it? And yeah, sometimes, eventually, being the best makes you famous. So I like being famous. But I also sort of hate it. Right now, I mostly feel like I'm stuck between the top seat on that couch and the fetal position."

His teeth were chattering, but he managed to ask, "What about 'Good night, and good luck'? The power of words? The power of television? All of that?"

Her face contorted into a pained expression. "Okay, don't hate me, but I made that up. I'm sorry. It was just another open door that I walked through. I mean, I guess there's some truth to it." She thought for a moment and then doubled down. "There definitely is. But that's not why I got into television. You want to know why I got into television?"

He nodded. Not that she was paying any attention to him right then. She was in an escape room of her own creation, all by herself, determined to track down the rest of the clues if it killed her.

"I got into television because some guy I was serving coffee to at a coffeehouse thought I was attractive, so he asked me if I wanted to be an intern at *Good Day LA*, and I thought, 'Hey, that sounds better than spending those few extra hours in my crappy apartment every morning with my psycho roommate and her weird lampshade collection.'" A sort of unhinged cackle escaped from her and got carried away by a gust of freezing air. "Sebastian, no matter how fake I am, and no matter how screwed up everything about me may be, there is one thing I want you to know for sure. One thing that will never change. I have *never* gone to a George Clooney movie for any reason other than to forget about the world and stare into his deep, dark, soulful eyes. I never have, and I never will. I promise you that."

She bit her bottom lip again, and his body temperature continued rising as he watched her manipulate it between her teeth. Brynn Cornell was a mess, and he was crazy about her.

She shrugged and laughed again. "Who knew that all it would take for me to completely question every choice I've ever made in my life was a trip home? Do you know how much money I wasted on therapy?"

Probably about as much as he had. And though he didn't view his as a waste, he understood what she meant. Brynn had run from Adelaide Springs for the same reason Sebastian had run to it—to avoid getting hurt. Ultimately, for both of them, healing didn't seem to be found in any particular thing they were seeking but in the willingness to stop running.

She'd stopped crying, but the reminder was still all over her face in the form of black smudges under her eyes and streaks down her cheeks. Her cheeks were red and glowing—wind, sun, and he was guessing exhilaration-tinged adrenaline all working together to breathe more life into her system than she'd likely experienced in years. With a self-satisfied grin he acknowledged to himself that he may have even played a small role in the emotional rebirth of Brynn Cornell.

"Brynn?" He said her name over his shoulder as he bent down to pick up the equipment and began brushing off his jacket and slipping back into it. He'd interrupted her cathartic soliloquy, but then again, it had been a day full of interruptions. There were a lot of things he hoped they would get back to later.

"Hmm?" She ceased her pacing across the rocks and patches of ice and turned to face him. "Oh, I'm sorry. I got kind of caught up in—"

"No, it's fine." He zipped up his jacket and relaxed into its warmth. "It's great, actually. I'm just wondering if you still want to film? You know . . . since you hate your job and everything."

Sebastian stood there holding Orly's equipment, silently imploring her to say no. But it had to be her choice. If she'd had half the breakthrough it appeared she'd had—or that she was in the midst of, anyway—this was going to be a tough decision. It was one thing to realize you weren't fulfilled by the choices you had made in your life. It was another thing entirely to make one more decision and do something about it. He knew that as well as anyone. As much as he wanted her to leap, he knew that if he were in her shoes, he would probably still hedge his bets until he figured out what came next.

"That depends on you," she finally said after seeming to give it a lot of thought.

"Me? Why does it depend on me?"

Joyous mischief spread across her face as she took slow steps toward him. "Earlier, before you told me to stop talking, I was about to tell you that just on the other side of that ridge right there"—she pointed behind her—"is an old shed with leftover equipment from the ski lift. Years ago, Laila, Addie, Cole, Wes, and I came up here and buried a bunch of sleds underneath it."

"And you think they're still there?"

She looked around. "It doesn't look like anything has changed, so I'm guessing so. We buried them pretty deep." She reached him and helped herself to the pockets of his jacket. His left hand joined her right, and their fingers looped together inside the pocket. "But I'm finding something to ride down this mountain on, regardless."

"Well, Ms. Cornell, as fun as that sounds, I'm not sure it's safe. Warmer weather . . . melting snow . . . avalanches . . . all of that."

"Oh, good grief, newbie." She rolled her eyes. "See those gray clouds, way off in the distance? When they get here, we won't go sledding. But for now . . ." She raised her left hand and ticked her safety tips off on her fingers, one at a time, starting with her thumb. "Avoid thirty- to forty-five-degree slopes. Stay windward. Watch for missing trees below the tree line. Guard against terrain traps. Stick to broad ridgelines . . ." She waved her fingers in the air. "Need me to go on? These are my mountains. Stick with me, baby. I'll take care of you."

Sebastian laughed. "Says the woman who got stuck in a tree."

"Hey! You said you weren't going to make fun."

"Not making fun. Just pointing out the obvious." He tilted his head and leaned toward her and spoke against her lips. "And anyway, what, exactly, does any of that have to do with me and filming?"

She pulled him closer by the pockets and her lips fluttered against his ear. Sebastian, meanwhile, showed the greatest restraint of his life and didn't throw the film equipment into the air, allowing it to land where it would, devil may care.

"I just think you'd probably only be able to get good shots if you stood to the side or took your own sled." Her lips left a trail across his jawbone before landing back on his, and she took as much liberty with his mouth as she had with his pockets. "I thought it would be more fun to share."

Alright. Enough messing around.

Sebastian hooked his arm around her neck and kissed her thoroughly for as long as he could, until he felt her weight redistribute as her knees seemed to lose the ability to support her. Then he broke the kiss but not the embrace—for fear they would both collapse to the ground if they didn't have each other to hold on to for support.

"Yowza," she moaned against his lips with halting breaths.

Through jagged breaths of his own, he whispered, "You're such a dork."

Then it was another five minutes or so before he finally had the strength to leave her and return the equipment to the Bronco.

She was right. It would be a lot more fun to share.

CHAPTER 27

BRYNN

I'd never been so cold and exhausted and sunburnt and windburnt and happy in all my life. And hungry. So unbelievably hungry.

I hadn't eaten anything all day long but the scone from the inn and a bag of beef jerky from Sebastian's vehicle. That hadn't seemed to matter at all when the only choice, if I wanted to eat, was to interrupt the bliss of being with Sebastian on the mountain. I'd have gleefully wasted away to nothing if it meant being able to soar down the path, over and over, with his arms and legs wrapped around me, forever. When our frozen extremities needed a break from playing in the snow, we drove higher. I led him to overlooks he hadn't yet discovered, and he introduced me to some nature conservancy areas that had still been privately owned when I lived here. Finding food would have meant going back into town, where reality was waiting.

But now the sun was almost completely down, and even our newly discovered method for staying warm wouldn't keep us from frostbite overnight. Or so Sebastian insisted. I sort of wanted to test it out and see.

274

"You hungry?" he asked me as we made the last few loops down to the elevation of the town.

"Hardy-har-har." I squeezed his arm as he teased me. Since I couldn't kiss him while he was driving, I'd had very little to distract me from how famished I was—so I'd talked about very little else for the last thirty minutes.

"I have to run by my house and let Murrow out, and then we can swing by Cassidy's and get some dinner, if you want."

Silence fell over the space as we both grew stone-faced and stared straight ahead. I assumed that he had been as jolted by his seemingly routine suggestion as I had. It carried with it a sense of reality crashing down. It was, maybe, a first date . . . but maybe not. If we had a first date, would there be a second?

It had been an entire day of joy and happiness and truth and contentment. Freedom. It had been an entire day of me loving Adelaide Springs and its breathtaking scenery more than anyplace else in the world. A day of memories and stories and so much laughter. And we hadn't filmed a single moment of any of it. Had that been me making a decision about my future, or had I just been caught up in Sebastian?

I may have begun accepting a renewed love for my hometown, but what could a future here look like? I couldn't go from a national platform—the commitments and contracts and obligations tied up in that—to . . . what? Working at a newspaper in Adelaide Springs, Colorado? It just wasn't possible.

And yet . . . I wouldn't be the first.

My left hand had been resting on his arm as he drove—I just hadn't been willing to stop touching him completely—and I ran my fingers down the length of the arm of his jacket until I reached his hand. I wrapped my fingers around his, and he peeked at me briefly and smiled.

"I'm sorry I said that whole dinner thing so casually. I just meant we're hungry and should get food. I didn't mean to act like there aren't still a ton of things to talk about."

"Sebastian?"

"Hmm?"

I cleared my throat and shifted in my seat so I could watch him. "What happened in Myanmar?"

He kept his eyes focused on the road as he turned off Banyon and, rather than turn toward Main Street, turned down the county road toward his house. "I guess we had to come back to that eventually."

I cared so much more than I had when the subject was broached that morning. I was so much more invested. I was beginning to know who he was now. Whoever he had been, and how he changed from who he had been to who he was—from the anchor desk to the *Adelaide Gazette*—all traced back to Myanmar, I suspected.

"I'm sorry," I whispered. I wished I hadn't brought it up. I was pretty sure he didn't hate me anymore—at the very least, his lips and mine had become very good friends—but I had no idea if I was someone he wanted to discuss this with. Whatever it was. Whoever I was to him. "If you don't want to talk about it . . ."

He shook his head. "No. Let's talk about it." He squeezed my hand and flashed me a comforting smile. "But can we wait until we get to my house?" He swallowed hard. "I haven't talked about it much—"

"Of course. Whatever you need."

"It's just that . . . Well, it's probably best that Murrow's there when I do."

Huh. "Oh. Okay." I looked away from him, through the front windshield toward his strange little house at the end of the gravel road. I was trying not to be judgmental. I really was. And I was increasingly confident I was still going to like him, no matter what he told me. But what was with him and this dog?

"So, um . . . Murrow's a psychiatric service dog. I don't know if anyone in town knows that, except for Doc. It's not like Adelaide Springs is the type of place to make me dress him up in those harnesses or carry a certificate around. And most of the time he's just my dog now. But . . . yeah. If I'm going to talk about this . . ."

"You almost talked about it at the Gulch. Was that dangerous?"

He ran his thumb across my knuckles. "I wouldn't have talked to you about it this morning like I will now." He pulled into his driveway, put the car in Park, and shut off the ignition. "If that's okay."

"Of course it's okay."

"No, Brynn, listen—" He took off his seat belt and shifted to face me. "This is . . ." He sighed. "This is most definitely something that could change your opinion of me. It's the biggest regret in my life and the biggest pain, and I know you're leaving in"—he raised his wrist and checked the time, then looked back at me—"forty hours or so. Maybe it doesn't make sense to—"

In one fluid motion my right hand unbuckled my seat belt and I scooted as close to him as I could. My palm was on his cheek, and I was savoring the feel of his scratchy beard against my tender skin.

"Nothing about this day has made sense." My voice was soft and shaky. "This week. Yesterday I was convinced you hated me."

He tilted his head and kissed the inside of my wrist. "Yesterday I may have."

I smiled. "See? Making sense is clearly not our top priority."

Five minutes later, after I had walked into his house and out again, and then repeated that about three more times to make sure I really wasn't allergic to Murrow, and after Sebastian had taken him outside and then brought him back in and put food in his bowl—and after I raided his kitchen cabinets and found a box of melba toast to munch on—I sat on the couch waiting for Sebastian. I was petting Murrow, who was much more interested in the attention I was giving him than the awful-smelling gravy stuff in his bowl. He was a cute little guy, truth be told. Murrow, I mean. My analysis of Sebastian's appearance had far surpassed cute. No one that brilliant and fun was supposed to be as hot as he was, I was pretty sure. And I was quite certain that no one wearing an MIT cap and a Janet Jackson shirt at the same time (or separately, for that matter) was supposed to kiss as expertly as he did.

"Who was the last person you kissed? Before me, I mean. Obviously." It was such an awkward and personal question, but it didn't feel weird to ask it. Well, it didn't until I began thinking about the women in Adelaide Springs who might have had the opportunity to go out with Sebastian. And it didn't take long to realize who the most eligible bachelorette in town was and that Sebastian was most definitely one of the two most eligible bachelors. "Oh no. If it was Laila, don't tell me. Just . . . I don't know. Lie to me. Tell me it was someone I don't know." Laila and I had never fought over a boy, and I didn't want to start now.

He rounded the corner from his kitchen and set the dish towel he'd been using to dry his hands down on the counter. "It was someone you don't know."

Well, shoot. "Oh. Okay. Um . . . cool."

He smirked at me as he sat down on the opposite side of the couch, Murrow between us. "Not Laila."

Thank goodness. I'd been mentally preparing to give her John Mayer's phone number if that's what it took for her to let me have Sebastian, but that would have been a disaster. She would have been too nice for him, and John definitely didn't possess the maturity to handle someone as wonderful as her. He no doubt would have fallen in love with her and written a song about her after he broke her heart, of course, and then she would have gone back to being a crazed fan and ultimately a restraining order would have been necessary for one or the other of them.

"In that case, tell me everything."

"Wish I could. It was a woman I met at a bar in Dhaka."

"Bangladesh!" Golly, I was eager to prove to him I was smart. "Sorry. Don't know why you make me want to win *Jeopardy!*"

"I *always* feel the need to prove I could win *Jeopardy!* No judgment here. But yeah . . . Dhaka. About two weeks before my wife left me." The corner of his mouth tightened. "I bet it's difficult to imagine why my marriage didn't work out."

He seemed to be watching to see how I would react, so I did all I could to prevent any reaction at all from appearing on my face. He had been divorced for six years and hadn't kissed anyone in all that time. Whatever had happened in those years, he clearly wasn't the same guy who had been unfaithful to his wife.

He kept watching me, so I repeated his words. "No judgment here."

"Thankfully it didn't go any further than a kiss in a bar. That was bad enough, of course, but . . . yeah. I didn't know anything about her. It's mortifying to have to tell you that I don't even know the name of the last person I kissed, but that's the truth."

"Yeah." I grimaced. "Same."

He tilted his head and smiled. "You don't know the name of the last person you kissed?"

I sighed. "I know it definitely wasn't Harry Styles. Or . . ." Well, shoot. I'd forgotten the name of the other one I knew it wasn't. "Yeah. Wasn't Harry Styles. Beyond that . . ." I shrugged.

He laughed. "Wow. There are a lot of possibilities in the world who aren't Harry Styles."

My eyes flew open. "No! It was definitely a member of One Direction. I just can't remember—"

"Louis?"

"You don't seriously know the members of One Direction."

"Liam? Niall? Zayn?"

"Zayn! I think it was Zayn! Is he the one with all the tattoos?" I gestured toward my neck and shoulders and chest.

"They all have lots of tattoos, except for Niall."

"I can't believe you know that."

"I can't believe you don't!"

I shook my head and smiled. "I know he had really great facial hair."

"And dark, dreamy eyes?"

A snort escaped. "Yes."

"That's Zayn. The 'bad boy' of 1D. Did you know his name actually means 'beauty' in Arabic? Oh, it's true. Yep, every man dreams of being the follow-up to Zayn. Now if you'll excuse me, I'm going to go hide in my closet and cry."

I howled with laughter and stomped my feet at the entire thing—air quotes around "bad boy" and all.

Murrow stood from his curled-up position on the couch cushion, and I felt bad for scaring the little guy with my outburst. Except I didn't seem to scare him at all. Rather than jump off the couch as I expected him to, he stepped up onto my lap, even as my chest still shook from laughter and my legs were still bouncing up and down. He rested his head against my stomach and settled in. I looked up at Sebastian in adoring surprise.

"He likes you." He slid over to the middle cushion and overtook Murrow's abandoned spot. "He's not the only one." He leaned in to kiss me, but before he could I reached out and removed his baseball cap.

And then I whimpered. I full-on whimpered like an adolescent girl losing it over her crush. Quite possibly Zayn. But my crush was there on the couch with me, and the removal of his MIT cap had revealed thick, loose, gorgeous, unruly curls that my fingers *needed* to touch.

Sebastian was trying to slip his hat back on, but I would have none of it. "I was afraid you were going bald." That had been my most common experience with men who wore a cap all the time, but Sebastian had broken the mold. I grabbed the cap from his hands and threw it across the room, and then dove in with both hands. "Why would you ever cover up this hair?" I asked as my fingers explored and delighted in the soft, curly wonder of him.

His cheeks were red. "I've always hated it, and I'm way past due for a haircut."

"How can you hate it? I *love* it."

He chuckled and leaned into my hand. "Well, admittedly, you're making me hate it a little less."

I clenched my fists in the curls and pulled him to me. Instantly Murrow jumped down and ran into the kitchen. Apparently loud noises and abrupt movements were of no concern to him, but he wouldn't tolerate the kissy-kissy stuff.

CHAPTER 28

SEBASTIAN

WEDNESDAY, MARCH 23
7:19 p.m. Mountain Daylight Time

"So I was in Maungdaw Township in 2016. The Rohingya were being slaughtered by the thousands. Villages being burned, women raped, senseless murders . . . It was awful and endless." He hadn't intended to just dive in like that. Especially after a few moments that had been so carefree and passionate. But Brynn was in his arms and he wanted nothing more than to share with her the part of himself he shared with no one. "I was so frustrated—so many people were—because the diplomacy agencies seemed to be spending all their time collecting data and studying the situation, trying to determine if what was happening could be constituted as genocide. *Of course* it was genocide. Ethnic cleansing, plain and simple."

She settled her head against his chest and wrapped her arms around him. "Why did the definition matter? To them, I mean."

"Because they could get more funding for genocide. In the crudest of ways, to the philanthropists who thrive not only on what their money can accomplish in the world but what their impact in the world can do for their name and notoriety, genocide is the flashiest of all atrocities." Sebastian's chest rose and fell, and Brynn's head accompanied it, her pulse calibrated to his. "While the data was calculated, endless lives were destroyed. Generations and bloodlines were depleted, and anyone with power to make a difference sat by and waited for permission to act."

"And you were there, seeing it happen?" She shook her head gently. "I can't imagine."

"I was one of the few on the ground, but I hardly had any access. I traveled with contacts from Bangladesh, and if I'd been found out . . . Yeah, the Burmese government wouldn't have taken well to a Western journalist sneaking in. It was just me and a camera. Whatever I was able to film didn't get shown back home, because of fears I would have been found out. Of course I didn't care about that."

"You didn't?"

He shook his head. "Not really. The job came first. The story came first. And if I died following something that mattered, I thought at least I would die doing something important. It was never about making it home." He stared at Murrow across the room in his little bed and thought about everything he'd had wrong in his head for so long. "And again I ask: Is it any wonder my marriage failed? So no, I really wasn't worried about my safety. But they wouldn't have shown much of what I got anyway. Until they agreed upon the terminology, it was just in-fighting and squabbles in a part of the world few Americans had ever heard of." He kissed the top of her head. "Not everyone is as smart as you."

She chuckled softly. "I'm glad you realize that." She sat up so she could look at him but grabbed his hands to keep the link between them. "So what happened?"

What happened was the part of the story he thought about every single day. The part of the story that he'd sought God's forgiveness for and that he'd never stop seeking absolution for, even though he believed he'd been forgiven. Even by himself. But he would still see the images in his head, every day, for as long as he lived.

"I was in a village that was attacked. All around me, homes burned and people screamed for the loved ones they couldn't save. Fire literally rained down from the sky as helicopters flew overhead. And I watched. I made sure the camera was rolling, and I ducked out of view, and I watched, Brynn. Finally I got the story. Finally I had the evidence of what was happening over there. I was angry, but I was also so excited. Finally they'd see."

She raised her arm and wiped her eyes on her sweatshirt, but she never let go of his hands. "That's what you were there to do."

He nodded as Murrow jumped up onto the couch, climbed over Brynn to get to him, and squeezed in between the crook of his arm. Murrow was there to do a job, just as Sebastian had been. Brynn watched what was happening, the way the tiny, fluffy Havanese didn't let anything come between him and his human, and Sebastian saw realization dawn in her eyes. Most of the time Murrow was just his dog. But first and foremost, he was there to do a job. To help regulate Sebastian's pulse when he sensed an oncoming attack. When the PTSD threatened to overtake him. In those early, awful days, to give him something to live for.

Sebastian pulled one hand away from Brynn and rubbed Murrow's head. "I'm okay, boy," he whispered. He raised his eyes back up and met Brynn's. "Yeah, that's what I was there to do. The story came first. But I had a first-aid kit in my backpack that was more sophisticated than any hospital in the vicinity—not that they could have gotten to a hospital. Not that they would have been allowed to go. Not that they would have been treated if they somehow found a way. But rather than pull out a tube of cheap, dime-a-dozen Neosporin and possibly save a kid's leg or tie a tourniquet and keep his mother from bleeding out, I pulled out my camera." He ran his fingers through Murrow's silky coat. "But none of that occurred to me—the first-aid kit, the lives I might have saved, my obligation not as a journalist but as a human being—until I stopped rolling. Lives were on the line, and *I* was the one with power to make a difference. And when the moment came, I just sat by and waited for permission to act. By the time that dawned on me, it was so much quieter than it had been. The screams had turned to tears or death, and I was a shoo-in for another Pulitzer."

Brynn squeezed his hand, the tears flowing freely down her cheeks. "But that's not why you were doing it. People needed to know. People needed to see the reality of the situation."

"Maybe. Or maybe there were just some mothers who didn't need to lose their children that day." He smiled sadly at her. "Maybe there was a way to do both."

She leaned in and rubbed Murrow's paw and then planted a soft kiss on Sebastian's lips. "Maybe."

"I escaped from Myanmar with my sanity hanging on by a thread—and the final thread of my marriage having already snapped. The network was in a sticky situation." Sebastian met Brynn's eyes and answered her unspoken question. "I was clearly unhinged and too much of a liability, but if the whole story came out, that would include memos and emails from the powers-that-be that said things like, 'Say "bloodbath" instead of "massacre"—it trends better,' and 'When Clooney or Jolie steps in, okay. Otherwise it's dead air. Pull out.' So they bought me out, including the footage, and sent me on my way. I just . . ." He ran his hands through his hair and scratched ferociously, the frustration still present after all this time, causing even more chaos in his curls. "I wish I hadn't signed. I wish I hadn't given up the film. At the time I thought I never wanted anyone to know. I just wanted out. I thought I could move on and put aside the shame I felt, as long as no one else knew.

But now the only shame I feel most days is that I allowed them to silence me."

"What choice did you really have?"

"I was brought up to be an observer. You know? An unbiased contributor to society. And I still believe in that. I do. I still believe in the importance of presenting a story—the good, the bad, and the ugly—not for the sake of arguing on behalf of one side or the other but for the sake of informing and educating, so that each person can then apply their own moral code to the facts. That's what I loved about being a reporter. *Reporting.* Being the eyes and ears for the people who couldn't see it and hear it themselves. Sometimes their brain, even. But never their heart. The problem is that I was so diligent about not being *their* heart that somewhere along the line I forgot how to access mine."

"And then somewhere along the line, you remembered. I think that's remarkable, and it doesn't seem like you give yourself enough credit for that."

He shook his head. "If anyone deserves credit for that, it's the people of this town. I didn't expect that. I certainly wasn't looking for it."

Murrow seemed satisfied that Sebastian was doing okay. He hopped down from the couch and returned to his bed. Brynn took his place again, against Sebastian's chest. His arm wrapped around her, and he pulled her closer.

"Can I ask you something?"

She nodded against him. "Sure."

Here it was. Here they were. The moment of truth. He'd shared with her what so few people knew in its entirety, and he wasn't sure he understood why he'd felt it was safe to tell her. But he hadn't doubted it. Even knowing she would leave the day after tomorrow. Knowing that no matter how authentic and true the side of her that Adelaide Springs had resurrected was, the other side hadn't gone away. Not completely. Not yet. And he knew better than anyone how good this town was at helping you to believe that everything outside of it didn't matter quite so much.

"Have you seen *Somewhere in Time*?"

She chuckled against him and leaned her head back to look at him. "That's what you wanted to ask me?"

The corners of his lips curled up. "I'm going somewhere with this. I promise."

The smile still on her face, she rested on his shoulder. "That's the depressing time-travel one with Superman and Dr. Quinn, right?"

"Yes."

"Yeah, I've seen it. I don't like it, but I've seen it."

He gasped and cupped his hands around her shoulders and pushed her up. "How can you not like *Somewhere in Time*?"

Brynn's shoulders drooped. "Oh, seriously? Sebastian, why would you do that to yourself? It's supposed to be this epic love story—"

"Which it is."

"But it's so creepy. She's old and from forever ago—"

"That *is* sort of the point."

"And don't they both die? Like, the happy, romantic ending is that they're dead together?" She stuck her tongue out and wrapped her hands around her throat to act like she was choking herself. "Just kill me now."

He sighed. "Your heart is made of stone, Brynn Cornell." She laughed and pulled away enough to grab her melba toast and start munching. "Regardless, the reason I asked is I'm sort of wondering if Adelaide Springs is the penny."

She had just stuffed an entire piece of the crunchy snack into her mouth, so she covered it with her hand to prevent crumbs from flying out as she asked, "What penny?"

"Remember? Richard pulled the 1979 penny from his pocket—"

"Oh my gosh, you know his name?"

Sebastian continued, undeterred. "He pulled the 1979 penny from his pocket and the spell was broken—"

"Because *that's* how time travel works."

"—and he went back to 1980 . . . or whatever—"

"Oh, it's too late to act like you're not sure."

"—and Elise"—Brynn raised her eyebrow and he indulged her—"Dr. Quinn was left in the past. Remember?"

She scrunched up her face. "Yeah."

Sebastian shifted in his seat and then shrugged. "The spell's going to be broken, you know. You're going to pull the penny out of your pocket, and you're going to remember you don't live in 1912. You're going to go back to 1980 where you actually belong."

Brynn stared at him and nibbled with her front teeth. "Okay . . . that's sort of a valid comparison. Except Superman—sorry, Richard—*didn't* belong in 1980. Not really. I mean, after he stepped out of the DeLorean in 1980, didn't he sort of just wander around for a while until he starved to death and got to reunite with Dr. Quinn and Jack and Rose on the *Titanic* version of heaven, where long-lost loves wait decades for their soulmates to die?"

He groaned and jumped up from his seat. "Brynn!"

"What?" She laughed and stood to join him. "I thought we were doing a funny little banter bit."

"But I'm being serious now."

"Oh. Sorry. I didn't realize." She set the box on the couch, cleared her throat, and straightened up to look at him face-to-face. A comically serious expression overtook her features. "How about this? I will only use my debit card from here on out. No cash. Definitely no coins."

He rolled his eyes and turned his back to her. "Forget it." He grabbed his jacket from the counter. "Still want to grab some dinner, or are the crackers enough for you?"

"Hang on." She walked up behind him, grabbed his arm, and forced him to turn around. "You're actually worried about this."

"No. I'm not. I'm not worried."

Brynn knocked the jacket from his arms and then jumped into them and kissed him.

"You are. Because you like me. You don't just like me. You *like* me like me." Her lips brushed softly against his, daring him not to kiss her back. "You like me!" She sang the words more than said them, and he rolled his eyes in response to her childishness—even as he lost her dare time and time again.

It was his turn to feign solemnity. "I haven't even decided if I like you yet, much less *like* you like you."

"Oh really?" she whispered against his lips before calling his bluff.

"I mean . . . you're okay, at times," he finally muttered in surrender against her jawline. "There are certainly aspects of you that—"

"Hang on." He was perfectly content retracing his steps along a trail of kisses he had left on her neck until she clasped his face between her hands and raised his eyes to meet hers. "We should talk about this."

"About what?" he managed to ask through squeezed lips and cheeks.

"About what happens now."

"No, see, I wanted to talk about it, and you made fun. Now I'm not interested in talking anymore." He smiled and pushed against her hands in an attempt to get back to her lips, but she was resolute.

"What do you think this is to me?"

"What? *This*?"

"Yeah. You and me."

He exhaled. "I don't have any idea. And that's okay. I know that you think less of me now, in light of the *Somewhere in Time* conversation, but I don't mean to come across as needy or clingy." He pulled away and leaned against the wall. If they were really going to talk, he needed a little distance. "I'm not those things. I am fully aware that what happens in Adelaide Springs tends to stay in Adelaide Springs—"

"Ah." She nodded and stepped back, gaining a little additional space of her own. "I see."

"What do you see?"

"You think *we* are a thing that could only happen in Adelaide Springs."

He tilted his head. "Don't *you?*"

Brynn shrugged. "I really don't know."

"And that's okay. It really is. I get it. I guess . . ." His fingers attempted to run through his hair but got caught in the curls. He groaned and looked around for his cap, which he found on the floor and returned to his head. "I guess I just need you to know . . ." What? What did he need her to know? "I don't talk about Myanmar. I don't let people know that Murrow used to have to go into town with me every single time, not because I was training him to be around people as I pretended. Are you kidding? He's better trained than I am. I had to take him with me everywhere because if a helicopter flew overhead, there was a pretty good chance I would black out or forget how to get home. And I really don't go from not trusting someone to telling them all of this in a day or two."

She kept her distance, physically, but the warmth in her eyes brought them closer. "Well, for the record, I don't go around kissing random guys I hardly know who aren't even members of 1D." He chuckled, but she rolled her eyes. "I *do* go around making jokes to actively avoid genuine emotion, though. Sorry about that."

"I think it's safe to say we're both damaged goods. Emotionally, you know?" She nodded. "And I need you to know I'm not scared off by that if you're not."

"I'm not." Her wet eyes locked with his. "I'm really not."

"Good. Now, here's what I *really* need you to know. I'm not convinced you hate your job. You hate aspects of your job, sure, but I'm pretty confident what you actually hate is not being able to be who you really are." Brynn opened her mouth to protest, and he raised his hand. "Just let me say this, if that's okay. And then you can feel free to tell me how wrong I am." She closed her mouth and nodded slowly. "I think you feel this need to be respected, and that makes all the sense in the world. We *all* need that, but *you*? After growing up the way you did? Of course that matters to you. But I think you're walking this tightrope between feeling like you have to earn your keep—lay low and stay out of trouble—and just wishing that for once in your life you could feel like your value didn't have as much to do with what you do as who you are."

He took a hesitant step toward her. There was more to say before he could reach out and dry those tears. Once he touched her, it was anyone's guess as to whether or not he'd remember how to speak.

"See, here's the thing, Brynn. I have a hunch—a pretty strong one, actually—that if you go back to New York or LA or wherever you want to be and combine the strength and ambition and talent that got you to *Sunup* with the brave, tenderhearted, hilarious woman I spent the day with today—the Brynn Cornell who's sharp as a tack and doesn't need anyone writing her lines for her; the Brynn Cornell who blows that stuffed-shirt Mark Irvine out of the water and *never* should have been number two to him; the Brynn Cornell who isn't ashamed of where she came from, because every wonderful thing about her is either because of or in spite of what she's been through—well, let's just say you need to be figuring out what you want to do next, because it's yours for the taking." He took a deep breath and let it out, hoping he hadn't overstepped but knowing she shouldn't have to wait any longer for someone to tell her how remarkable she was. "Okay. I'm done now. Let the arguing commence."

She laughed self-consciously through her escalating tears, then lifted her arms and rushed toward him. And Sebastian welcomed her in. He'd said what he needed to say. The rest was up to her.

CHAPTER 29

BRYNN

"Shoot, shoot, shoot," I muttered as I attempted to yank a hairbrush through my tangles and ultimately lost the battle. And possibly the hairbrush. Surely it was still in there somewhere, in the mess of kinks and knots.

I'd overslept—of course I'd overslept—and therefore skipped washing my hair in the shower to save time. No big deal, usually, except it had been so late when Sebastian dropped me off the night before, and I'd been so tired, that I'd skipped brushing it before bed. And, unfortunately, I'd skipped putting it up in the messy bun I usually slept in. I'd made it as far as pulling out the braid, and then I'd fallen asleep with it loose and wild. Throw in the hot, humid air of a shower in which you try not to get it wet, and the result was the lion's mane I was currently staring at in the mirror.

Sebastian had pushed our start time back by an hour because he had some things to do, but maybe I could catch him. I unplugged my phone from the charger and began texting.

> If you haven't left your house yet, do you have a baseball
> cap I could borrow? My hair is hopeless.

I stared down at the message thread, determined not to reck-
lessly abuse my new access to him. I'd only texted him about thirteen
times since I woke up, so I was off to a good start. When no texting
bubbles appeared, I threw my phone on the bed, dug the brush out
from deep inside the honeycomb that was my head of hair, and gave
it one more go. I finally got it straightened out enough for a puffy
ponytail. That was going to have to do for today.

The wardrobe had already been picked out, so that came
together pretty easily. Before we'd left Sebastian's house, I'd asked
him if he had a shirt I could borrow for the next day so I didn't have
to take a chance on seeing Orly's underwear again. He got strangely
excited when I asked, ran to his bedroom, grabbed a sweatshirt, and
threw it at me. There in my bedroom at the Inn Between, I pulled
it up to my face and inhaled the scent, as I had already done many
more times than I had texted him. He probably thought he would
get it back from me before I left, but there was no way I wasn't
sneaking that thing into my suitcase.

Finally satisfied with what I saw in the mirror—and by satisfied I mean there was nothing more I could do to save myself—I
grabbed my coat and phone and bounded down the stairs, so
excited to spend another day with him.

The excitement reached the end of its shelf life before I reached
the end of the hallway on the second floor.

> I'm going to be tied up for a while. Emergency city council
> meeting to vote on Township Days. (Thanks a lot.) So it's
> your own fault that you'll have to live with hopeless hair
> for a while.

When I got downstairs, Orly was sitting alone at the kitchen island, eating scrambled eggs covered in Mrs. Stoddard's home-made green chile sauce. "Is there more?" I asked him in greeting as the delicious scent overtook me.

He pointed to the oven but never stopped chewing. I opened the oven door and found a plate warming for me. *Well, that was nice.*

"How are you feeling?" I sat down across from him and took my first bite. *Oh, heavenly green chile, where have you been the last twenty years of my life?*

"Great. Jo's quite the nurse."

A little bit of guilt made itself known in the pit of my stomach. "I'm sorry I didn't stick around, Orly."

"Stop it," he insisted between bites. "I just felt bad I wasn't there to keep you and Sebastian from killing each other." His fork hovered in front of him as he added, "You didn't kill him, did you?"

I shrugged. "He's actually not so bad once you get to know him."

"Wow. I did only miss the one day, right?" He laughed and resumed eating. "Did you manage to get any good stuff?"

I felt the prickles of heat spread up my neck and to my cheeks. *You have no idea.* I bit my bottom lip and looked at him sheepishly. "We didn't actually film anything."

"Nothing?"

"Nothing."

I pulled my gaze away from his and took another bite of eggs, but I could still feel him watching me. I grew more embarrassed with each passing second. I wasn't entirely convinced every thought about Sebastian and every memory of his lips on mine and his arms around me wasn't being spelled out via a scrolling marquee across my forehead.

"Okay." The word was quiet and abrupt once it finally came, and then he returned to his eggs.

"I'll make sure Colton knows it isn't your fault—"

"So what's the plan? From what I can tell you've stopped even communicating with Colton. He's been nagging me for updates nonstop. I've sent him the stuff I filmed on Tuesday, of course, but he really wants to know what to expect tomorrow morning."

I set my fork down. "What have you told him?"

"That you know what you're doing. That he just needs to trust you."

"Thanks, Orly."

He leaned over toward me with his elbows on the counter. "You do know what you're doing, don't you?"

I raised my eyes to focus on him. "What do you mean?"

He leaned back and grabbed his napkin from his lap, then wiped off his hands and set the napkin down beside his plate. "Are you going to be okay leaving?"

"Why wouldn't I be?" I lifted my plate and stood from the stool, my appetite suddenly gone. I walked over to the sink and fed the rest of my breakfast down the garbage disposal—a travesty I was certain to regret later.

"It's nothing. Maybe it's none of my business, so feel free to tell me to butt out, but it just seems to me like something changed this week. I know I haven't been around you much, but it doesn't take more than two seconds to see that being here's been good for you. And that's great. But what's gonna happen . . ." He sighed and then it morphed into a forced laugh. "Don't mind me. Like I told the boss, I'm sure you know what you're doing. Forget I said anything."

I watched the water run down my plate and let the water and the disposal continue running for the length of two deep breaths in and out, then turned everything off, set my plate and fork in the sink, and turned around.

"Thanks, Orly." I hurried around the counter and threw my

arms around his shoulders and rested my cheek against the back of his head. "I don't know if I know what I'm doing or not. But it's really nice that you believe in me."

"Are you kidding me?" He patted my arm under his chin. "Whatever the plan, you're going to come out on top, kid. I've never doubted that for a minute."

"Jo said we can use her car," Orly said a few minutes later as I washed our breakfast dishes, only half seriously considering licking the green chile off his plate.

I set down the dish towel and turned around. "Oh." I glanced at my Apple Watch. No texts for me.

"Key's on the hook by the door." Orly held up his phone and continued reading. "She said the city council meeting is at Cassidy's. If we want to swing by, she said Cole will make us breakfast." He looked up from his phone and met my eyes. "But I guess since we've already had breakfast—"

"I could eat."

I hurried over to the couch and grabbed my coat and Orly's. We were definitely going to Cassidy's. It was my last full day with Sebastian, and there was no way I was going to let anything get in the way of that. Not even a city council meeting that was, in fact, entirely my fault.

Ten minutes later, after Orly finally admitted he didn't know how to drive a stick shift and we pulled over and switched seats— mercifully ending the Gear Grind of Horrors carnival ride—we parked at Cassidy's. There were a lot of cars there, and that made me a little nervous. The entire town was clearly invested in the whole Township Days debate, and I really hoped I hadn't made things worse.

"Are you going to wait for me?" Orly called out as I hurried across the gravel parking lot to the door.

I looked back over my shoulder. *Wasn't planning on it.* "Oh . . . sorry. Do you need help with . . ." He was grabbing his camera out of the back seat. "Honestly, I'm not sure there's much point in filming any of this." Orly didn't know about my "I hate my job" epiphany, of course, but he was certainly insightful enough to realize I hadn't been rushing toward Cassidy's because I just couldn't wait to get to work.

He shut the car door, finished attaching the camera lens, and smiled as he began walking toward me. "Just think of me as the guy on the ground at Tiananmen Square and the Berlin Wall who now films your vacation home movies."

"Seriously, Orly." I stepped in front of him as he approached. "Thank you for being here this week. I know it's the job, but I can't think of anyone else I would have rather had as my traveling buddy." I hooked my arm in his and we resumed walking.

"I've loved every minute. You know . . . except for the flight. And feeling like I was going to die yesterday. Wasn't crazy about you and Sebastian fighting."

I smiled. "But other than that . . ."

"Jenni's always wanted to travel, and I'm plain ashamed of myself that I've gotten to go to all these amazing places and never taken her to a higher elevation than Las Vegas." He looked around him at the pine forest and the mountainy, snow-covered backdrop. "Look at this place. I need to show her places like this before we get too old to enjoy it."

We turned and headed up the steps, and as we got closer to the screen door I heard "Annie's Song" wafting through the air.

"You might want to hurry up and push the Record button." He looked at me questioningly and I laughed as I held the door open for him. "I bet Brokaw isn't half the singer Sebastian Sudworth is."

He propped his camera onto his shoulder as I followed him through the door and nearly jumped out of my skin when we were greeted by a roomful of cheering and smiling citizens of Adelaide Springs. Fentón Norris was the one on the stage singing John Denver this time, so my eyes immediately began searching for Sebastian. That's when I noticed the "Welcome Home" sign over the bar and balloons spread throughout the space, mostly tied to chairs except for a few helium escapees bouncing against the ceiling.

"What in the world?" I asked aloud.

Laila was the first to run over to me. Bounce, more like. Laila just tended to bounce everywhere she went. Just as she got to me she noticed Orly, who had turned his camera toward us. She smiled awkwardly for the camera and offered a wave, at which point Orly muttered, "Don't mind me," and began expertly blending into the crowd.

"Are you surprised?" Laila asked once the camera was no longer *right there*.

Words failed at first as I looked around at everyone. "Shocked, more like. What is this?"

"It's your welcome-home party, silly." She laughed and hugged me.

"I really . . ." I had begun speaking to Laila, but I quickly realized there were about fifty people leaning in, trying to hear what I was saying. I cleared my throat and spoke to the room. "I really didn't expect this. And . . . I don't deserve it." A few people watched me cautiously, mistrust in their eyes, but most of them were smiling at me. "Thank you for this. And for everything. Thank you for welcoming me back. I really am so sorry . . ." I sniffed, determined to at least get through a simple little speech without crying. "I'm so sorry I said what I said, and even more than that, I'm sorry I felt that way. I think I created something in my head to make it easier to be away from you all. But all you ever did was love and support me." My eyes landed on Mrs. Stoddard. "That's all you ever did. And you deserved better. I really am so sorry."

The expression on her face remained as stoic as ever, but her arms opened, and I ran into them. I'd gotten through my little speech. Mission accomplished. Now my tears were free to do as they saw fit.

"I thought you hated me." I sniffed against Mrs. Stoddard's shoulder. "I thought *everyone* hated me."

"Nah. We love you too much to hate you." She placed her hands on my shoulders and pushed me back so she could look me in the eyes. "But if you ever talk that way about us again, I'm gonna march out there to New York and personally make you wish you'd thought better of it. You understand me?" The corner of her mouth tilted upward, but her eyes meant business.

"Yes, ma'am. Understood." I nodded and sniffed again. "I'd expect nothing less."

"Alright, alright. That's enough of all that, now." Old Man Kimball's voice came up behind us, and Mrs. Stoddard and I turned to face him. "I only agreed to be part of all this hullabaloo because Sercastian told me we'd vote first and I could be on my way."

I mouthed, "Sercastian?" to Mrs. Stoddard as I pulled away from her, and she rolled her eyes in exasperated fashion.

"Yes, yes, Bill. We can always count on you to stand in the way of a good time. Thank you for the reminder. Doc!" she yelled right by my ear and then wandered off toward Doc. "Let's do this so the killjoy can get home for his first nap of the day."

"Are you causing problems, Grandpa?" Cole came up behind me and wrapped his arm around my shoulder. "You're not going to want to hurry off too quickly. There's cake . . ."

"You know I prefer pie," he grumbled.

"And pie."

Old Man Kimball cleared his throat. "Don't mind if I do." He walked over to the round table in the front of the room and sat down.

I looked up at Cole and smiled, and he leaned down and kissed me on the cheek. "Love you," he whispered as he pulled away.

"Love you," I responded.

"Hey, hey . . . watch it," Sebastian said from behind Cole as he walked out of the kitchen.

Cole laughed as he moved toward the kitchen himself, and I was pretty sure I heard him say, "Never forget, she was my girlfriend first."

"You're not jealous, are you, Sercastian?" I asked.

He approached me but kept his distance. We'd talked about a lot of things the evening before, but if and when we would tell the people of Adelaide Springs about the romantic turn our relationship had taken hadn't been among the topics. But I sure loved that he'd apparently been unable to resist talking to Cole about me.

I had a text thread with Laila approximately the length of Fenton Norris's bar tab to prove I'd been every bit as chatty.

"Sure I am. I'm jealous of anyone who gets to kiss you in the middle of a room like that."

"Hey, kid." Doc came up beside me just then and kissed the top of my head as he wrapped his arm around me. Sebastian's eyes grew wide and then narrowed in a comical fit of jealousy. I leaned into Doc's shoulder and tried not to giggle. "Seb, we should do this thing. You ready?"

"Ready as I'll ever be." He grimaced and followed Doc to the table, where Old Man Kimball was diving in to the pie Cole had just brought him, and Jo was just getting settled with her notebook.

It took everything in me not to reach out and grab Sebastian's hand as he passed, but instead I said softly, where only he could hear, "Let's hear it for Township Days!"

He narrowed his eyes again and pointed his index finger at me as he sat, and my giggles finally escaped.

CHAPTER 30

SEBASTIAN

THURSDAY, MARCH 24
9:29 a.m. Mountain Daylight Time

"In the matter of bringing back the four-day festival known as Township Days, we have a motion from Mr. William Kimball and a second from Mrs. Josephine Stoddard. We'll now open the floor to discussion, prior to holding a vote of the council."

While it was true they weren't used to an audience, Sebastian still didn't understand why everyone was being so formal. From Jo narrating the proceedings like a David Attenborough wildlife documentary to Bill using words Sebastian assumed he'd picked up from a little light reading of the *Harvard Law Review*, it was a total farce. And he wanted nothing more than to be in the back of the room where Brynn, Laila, and Cole were whispering and laughing and no doubt offering gripping analysis worthy of C-SPAN. Andi sat nearby, laughing at occasional things they said. But no. He had to be at the table with the Adelaide Springs Repertory Players.

And Doc. Doc was normal, of course. But Doc also hadn't said a word the entire time. And now that the floor was open to discussion, he still wasn't saying anything. Thirty of the fifty or so people in the room made general statements in support of bringing back the festival. Things like, "We need to do something to bring this town back to life," and "Remember how much the kids used to love churning the butter?" (It was at that point that Brynn and Laila both shot their hands into the air, no doubt to issue opinions of dissent, but Cole pulled their arms down and the giggles erupted again.)

"If there is no more discussion from the floor," Jo said once the comments had slowed to a trickle, "we'll turn it to a vote."

Doc may not have been saying anything, but he was sure looking at Sebastian like he thought *he* should.

"I think I've said all there is to say, Doc," he leaned over and whispered.

"You sure about that?"

Sebastian stared at Doc a moment, then furrowed his brow and leaned in farther. "I'm clearly in the minority—"

"All in favor of bringing back—"

"Sorry, Jo." Sebastian raised his head to look at her. "Can you give me just a second?"

Jo nodded and Bill grumbled, and hushed speculation filled the restaurant as if Sebastian were Atticus Finch about to deliver his closing statements.

Sebastian turned back to Doc. "What are you suggesting I do?" he asked quietly. "You've made it pretty clear you think we should bring it back too."

Doc shrugged. "Eh."

"I'm sorry . . . 'Eh'? Not once have you indicated you would vote no. And if I'm the one holdout now—"

"So what if you are? As I recall, you were the one holdout in favor of letting Brynn come back to town, and the one holdout against you taking responsibility for her time here. I'd say that's all turned out pretty well, wouldn't you?"

Sebastian closed his eyes and shook his head slowly. Doc had gotten him there, and he knew it. The one time he thought he might just let the inevitable play out without putting up a roadblock. Without exhausting himself standing up for principles no one else shared. Without being the reason everyone had to wait longer for cake.

He opened his eyes and immediately saw that every other eye in the room was on him, but it was the two really stunning chestnut ones in the back that he sought out.

Her ideas were good. He'd turned them over in his mind and looked into their potential more than he cared to admit since Tuesday, and he knew they could work. There were so many little towns within an easy drive that were every bit as close to dying as Adelaide Springs. And just like Adelaide Springs, they were *refusing* to die because they were *home* for everyone who lived there. A restaurant here and a hotel there. Some food trucks could be brought in and, like Brynn said, the journey could be the best part of choosing Township Days as a destination.

They hadn't made any commitments to each other, but he knew he couldn't get this train rolling unless he made a commitment to Adelaide Springs. He would have to see it through. And it wasn't like he'd planned on following her back to New York, but if he made this happen, the option was gone. The decision was made.

She smiled at him and tilted her head, no doubt attempting to interpret what was causing him to concentrate so hard. *This really is all your fault.* He smiled back at her and then pushed his chair back from the table.

"I make a motion that we postpone—" The chatter and indignation began at the mere word. Cole jumped up from his seat and looked ready to step in as Sebastian's security detail if necessary as the noise level grew.

"We've postponed this vote enough, Sudworth!" Bill shouted at him, and Sebastian did a double take. He'd actually said his name properly.

Sebastian raised his hand and let out an exasperated groan. He raised his voice in an attempt to be heard over the disgruntled herd. "Can I finish what I was trying to say?"

"Listen up!" Doc's voice carried throughout the room, and every person fell silent in an instant. Even if just from shock. "Sebastian has the right to speak just as much as any of you do. More than most of you. Most of you are happy to sit on the sidelines and blame someone else for what you don't like and take credit for what you do, and he's given more to this town in a few years than some of you lazy butts have given in your entire life. So we're all gonna shut up now and let him say his piece, ya hear? And then we'll vote. Go ahead, Seb."

Sebastian was as much in shock as anyone, but he was too experienced to let the dead air last for long.

"I make a motion we postpone Township Days until next year. And here's why."

He spent the next twenty minutes laying out the collaborative vision for the event. He'd already placed a few phone calls to other towns, just to put out feelers, and he reported on the excitement that had been communicated without exception. He gave a brief rundown of some estimated costs and how they could pay for them. And he made sure they knew how much it would stay true to and build upon the original 1975 absurdity. When he finally sat back down, the silence continued, and he wondered if he'd lost them somewhere along the way.

Finally, it was Orly who broke the silence. "I know I'm not a citizen of this town, but I think that's brilliant, man."

The affirmative murmurings began bouncing throughout the

room, but it was the proud and silent tearful beaming at the back of the room that mattered most.

"Of course it is." Sebastian grinned. "It was Brynn's idea."

"Aren't you going to get out there?" Cole asked Sebastian.

"Yeah, in a minute."

It was an hour until sundown, and the party was still going strong. Brunch preparations had morphed into dinner preparations, and between making up for lost time with Brynn and the council's unanimous vote to bring back Township Days in eighteen short months, everyone seemed to believe they had plenty to celebrate and discuss. Cole and Sebastian were in the kitchen, arranging platters of food, as they had been most of the day.

"I can finish this up, Seb. Go spend time with her."

There was truly nothing he wanted more. But then what? They'd landed on a casual, noncommittal approach to a potential relationship, and now he was committed to Adelaide Springs for at least another year and a half. And who was he kidding? Apart from knowing he was going to miss her like crazy, he had no desire to be anywhere else. Long distance was hard, even under the best of circumstances. And the lack of accessibility to Adelaide Springs was not even close to the best of circumstances. Major airport to major airport? Sure. If that was their reality, they would have been able to see each other every weekend. But major airport to connections at a couple more major airports before finally landing in a field outside of town, courtesy of a very expensive private service? Yeah . . . not so easy.

They'd stay friends. He knew that. He'd meant what he said about not taking the intimacy they'd shared lightly. And it wasn't like he was interested in a romantic relationship with anyone else, so staying connected to her wouldn't stand in the way of connecting with another woman. But for her? There were probably one or two or a thousand or a million eligible men in the world who would love a chance to date Brynn Cornell. She wasn't a young girl just heading off to college determined to stay true to her boyfriend back home. That wasn't realistic. No matter how much either of them wanted to pretend otherwise, they were destined to eventually pull the penny out of their pocket.

"Yeah. Okay." He popped a blackberry into his mouth before heading over to the sink and washing his hands.

"Hey, Seb?" Cole's voice stopped him at the door from the kitchen to the dining room.

"Yeah?"

"She's not gone yet, you know. And if you spend today acting like she is, I'm pretty sure you'll regret it tomorrow."

He was probably right about that. Not that Sebastian was going to acknowledge the wisdom. "Did you get that from a fortune cookie?"

Cole shook his head and smiled. "Nah. It was on one of Maxine's cross-stitched pillows."

Sebastian laughed and turned back toward the door, but stopped again when he heard the familiar, unrelenting, pounding repetition of the same note played on a piano thirteen times and then joined by the musical accompaniment of a typewriter clacking as it repeated.

"Is that '9 to 5'?" Cole asked, hurrying to join Sebastian at the door to see what was happening as people in the restaurant began cheering.

They inched around the door together just in time to witness Brynn and Laila on the stage, sharing a microphone, singing the opening notes of the Dolly Parton classic. Laila couldn't stop laughing and mostly dropped out before they got to the first chorus, but Brynn performed as unabashedly as if she were entertaining the masses at the Grand Ole Opry.

She wasn't very good—Sebastian was pretty sure she hadn't hit a single note, and she missed half the words as the speed of the lyrics got away from her. Her smile lit up the entire room, though, and every time she messed up she beamed bigger and bigger as her friends laughed with her. Orly sat on the edge of the stage holding the laminated sheet of lyrics for her—his camera had been abandoned long ago—and she studied the words diligently, but she knew the chorus by heart. And by the time she got to the second verse, she seemed as surprised as anyone to realize she knew the words to that too.

The hoots and hollers of support spurred her on, and she plucked the lyrics sheet from Orly's hands and dropped it to the ground and strutted and shook her hips and line danced through the rest of the song. By the end, everyone was singing along with her, but she was still the center of attention, exactly where she deserved to be. There was no denying she was a star, even if her voice didn't exactly give Dolly Parton a run for her money.

"I just remembered another quote I saw at Maxine's," Cole said from over Sebastian's shoulder. "It went something like, 'If a classic country karaoke dork is lucky enough to find a woman who can look that cute and be that irresistible while singing that badly, he'd be a fool to let her get away.'"

Maxine's cross-stitching was very wise.

Sebastian stepped into the dining room, and Brynn's attention snapped to him. The smile was still on her face, though it softened as they stared at each other. She was surrounded by her adoring public, but she was completely focused on him. He raised his hand in greeting and she mouthed, "Hi," in response.

"Hey, Sebastian? Did you hear—"

"Sorry, Fenton." He addressed his friend sitting at the bar, but he didn't take his eyes off Brynn. "Can we talk later?"

"I was just wondering if you'd heard about the avalanche up at the Gulch?"

Well, okay . . . *that* got his attention away from her. "What? No. How bad is it?"

Fenton pointed up at the television. And it was telling him pretty much nothing. It was tuned to a national news channel, and the ticker across the bottom was reporting nothing except that a group of high school students up from Phoenix on a ski trip hadn't been heard from in two hours. All the images were stock photos of various mountain passes and avalanches—not even the correct mountain range.

"They don't have anyone there?" Sebastian asked just as Brynn came up behind him.

"What's going on?"

"Alpine Rescue Team's on the way, but they aren't exactly sure where they're heading, from the sound of it." Fenton turned on his stool to face the gathering spectators. "And if they're coming from Denver, no one's going to get there too quickly with all that construction on I-25."

"They'll copter someone in," Doc contributed. "It won't be too long until rescue is on the ground."

"But what about media?" Sebastian asked, turning to face Brynn.

She nibbled on an apple slice. "If they're coming from Denver, they can just hop on . . . what is it? Highway 285?"

Fenton shook his head. "Sections are still closed from the mudslides. They're rerouting through US-50."

Jo whistled through her teeth. "That won't be speedy."

Sebastian watched Brynn for another few seconds as she kept her eyes on the television, reading the ticker, taking a bite out of her apple slice. Then he looked over the crowd and found Orly in the back, his camera rolling again. Of course it was. Orly had felt the change in the air as much as Sebastian had. And though the camera was most likely focused on Brynn, the cameraman's eyes were on Sebastian. Orly nodded at him, and Sebastian jumped into action.

"Grab your coat."

Brynn looked up at him. "Where am I going?"

"You're going to Adelaide Gulch, obviously."

"I'm not sure if you've heard, but right now's not the best time to go sledding." She took another bite of apple and smiled at him, confused. "You know all those precautions I was teaching you to watch for? Yeah, well, I know I didn't mention it, but whenever there has just been an avalanche . . ."

"Wow, you let that ambition of yours off the hook pretty easily, didn't you?"

She chewed and thought, and then her eyes flew open. *There it is.* Her eyes flashed to the television and then back to him. "You mean . . ."

He grabbed her elbows and leaned down to meet her eye to eye. "Listen to me, Brynn. There's not a national-caliber reporter any- where in the world closer to this story than you are right now. You can be live on the air in forty-five minutes, and every news network across the country will pick up your feed so they can finally stop airing stock photos from five years ago."

Sebastian moved his hands up to cup her face, fully aware that the story for the people there at Cassidy's Bar & Grill in Adelaide Springs was suddenly all about that. About them. Avalanche? What avalanche? Are Brynn and Sebastian together? Yep. He knew that he'd just singlehandedly fueled the rumor mill for the next couple of news cycles.

Well . . . as long as they were going to be talking anyway . . .

He leaned in and brushed his lips against hers and then whispered, "Opportunities like this don't come along very often. Trust me on that. This is an opportunity to be *the* reporter on *the* story. If you do this, it won't matter what footage you and Orly have captured this week. *This* will be the footage that runs on *Sunup* tomorrow morning. I promise you. The story will no longer be about a mistake, and it won't be about the scripted lines. The story will be about the *story*, and the way you choose to tell it. You just have to decide if that's what you want."

Her eyes remained locked with his. "Will you go with me?"

What a loaded question that was. He didn't see a way to go with her where her career was about to take her, but he suspected she knew that. Right now, she just needed to know if he would go with her to Adelaide Gulch. To the center of the action—a place he hadn't dared to go since smuggling himself onto a long-tail boat out of Kawthaung. He'd found sanctuary from all of that in this peaceful, ridiculous little town that he loved with his whole heart, and now this woman he'd hated at the beginning of the week was asking him to accompany her back to the center of the action— where lives would potentially be lost and helicopters would circle overhead, dropping rope ladders rather than bombs.

There wasn't even a question in his mind.

"Of course I'll go with you."

CHAPTER 31

BRYNN

THURSDAY, MARCH 24
7:12 p.m. Mountain Daylight Time

Not having any idea what the situation would be when we got up there, Andi sent us on our way with a promise to check on Murrow and the keys to her Dodge super-duper-heavy-duty-mega-max-dually-something-or-other pickup truck, which, thankfully, only Sebastian had her permission to drive. Sure, I knew how to drive a stick, and I'd taken my driving test in the mountains. I wasn't even scared of snow. But back when I was driving out here, I was pretty sure they didn't even make trucks that big that didn't require a CDL.

After a quick detour to the inn so Orly could pick up the rest of his packs of equipment, followed by a few minutes in which Sebastian and Orly nerded out together about advancements in satellite broadcasting (*"Remember when we couldn't broadcast without a giant dish on top of a truck the size of a small house?"*), we were climbing in elevation and carefully inching closer to the disaster zone. Above eleven thousand feet had gotten about a foot of new accumulation overnight, but Sebastian was expertly managing the treacherous roads while also using the drive time to coach me.

"The head of Alpine Rescue is a man named Larsen Perry. Good guy, but very matter-of-fact. He probably won't want to talk, but get him to go on the record with something. *Anything.* If he says, "Today is Thursday," ask him if you can quote him on that, and you'll have more than CNN's got right now."

"Got it."

"Chances are it was a cornice avalanche."

Sure, I'd been schooling Sebastian on avalanche safety just the day before, but this was different. He'd kicked into a different gear, and I'd shifted out of one. This wasn't life. This was news.

I typed into the Notes app on my phone. "And cornices are the ones where the overhang snow breaks off?"

"Yeah." He spun the wheel in precisely the right way to prevent a skid that had threatened to carry us away. "I'm willing to bet that the kids got too close to the edge. They should still be alive, if that's what happened and they didn't get buried. The problem is that a cornice avalanche can trigger other avalanches—"

"Right."

"So if anyone else was below . . ."

"Are we almost there?" Orly whimpered from the back seat. I turned around to face him and found him clinging for dear life to the grab handle above his window. He had started out sitting behind me but at some point had moved behind Sebastian. Presumably because the window on my side featured the best view of the "steep, plunging canyon of death," as he had referred to it.

"Just about five more miles." I patted him on the knee.

"Which means it's probably time for you to make a call." Sebastian glanced at me briefly and then got his eyes back on the road as he reached into the inside pocket of his coat and pulled out the satellite telephone Orly had handed him while they were nerding out. He set it on the seat next to me.

I closed my eyes and exhaled and faced front again. It wasn't that I was scared to make the call. It wasn't even that I doubted whether or not Sebastian was correct about all of this. I was pretty sure he was. I'd grown up in these mountains and knew them like the back of my hand. There were avalanches every single year, but never at Adelaide Gulch. I mean, Sebastian and I had been there yesterday, for goodness' sake. And rarely if ever were the avalanches in this area human caused. It was news, without a doubt. You throw in a busload of teenagers, it was big news. We wouldn't know just how big until we got there.

So, yeah. It would be foolish to pass up the opportunity. This was my way back into the hearts and homes of television viewers. I had a chance to gain respect as an actual journalist. That was what I wanted, right?

Did I?

Or did I just like feeling smart? Was it like Sebastian had said? Was I just seeking the next thing and the next thing and the next thing that would get me farther away from the woman who had told me that the best part of her day was when she went to sleep and dreamed I had never been born? Was I still trying to prove to her that she had been wrong when she told me I was just like her but not as pretty and without as many people who loved me?

"She's dead, Brynn."

I hadn't meant to say it aloud. I hadn't really even meant to think it. But it was out there, as evidenced by Sebastian and Orly asking me, "Who's dead?" in unison.

"Sorry, I just . . ." I shook my head. "My mother. I think I just realized . . ." I cleared my throat. "I mean, I knew she was dead, obviously, but . . ."

Orly wasn't sure how to respond, but Sebastian got right to the heart of it. "You don't have to prove anything to her or anyone else. You know that, right?"

I nodded. I did know that. For the first time in my life, I knew that.

"You know what?" I laughed. Laughter just bubbled out of me. "I hated asking Recep Tayyip Erdogan challenging questions about the Turkish debt crisis. I don't *care* about the Turkish debt crisis. I mean, I'm sure it's important, but I really don't care. Does that make me a horrible person?" I didn't wait for an answer. "But I *loved* talking to Chiwetel Ejiofor about *Doctor Strange*. Loved it. Loved every single minute of it." I turned to Sebastian and grabbed on to his arm urgently, which made Orly gasp, but Sebastian was still in complete control of the truck. "What does that say about me? Seriously. Do I sound less smart? Do you think less of me because I don't care about the Turkish debt crisis?" I once again didn't wait for a response, but the affectionate grin on his lips made it pretty clear what it would have been. "It doesn't matter if you think less of me. You know why? I *am* smart. And I deserve to be with someone who knows that!"

He chuckled. "Okay, I'm all for letting you work this out on your own, but I've got to step in here because it sounds like you're escape-rooming me right out of the picture. For the record, I know you're *very* smart, and I think it's fantastic that you care more about Chiwetel Ejiofor. Most people outside of Europe and Asia should."

I released his arm and pointed my finger in his face, making Orly gasp again. "But you don't. Do you?"

Sebastian sighed. "No, not really. But I'm not normal. I think that if more people understood the impact of Erdogan's authoritarianism—"

It was my turn to gasp, which made Orly gasp louder and cover his eyes. But my gasp had nothing to do with the fear of impending doom or death. The sky was getting progressively grayer as the snow began to fall again, but everything had just become clear from where I was sitting.

"What's wrong?" Sebastian asked as he began slowing down, just as flashing lights appeared in the distance, reflecting eerily off the mountain and the low-set clouds.

Sheriff's deputies had the road blocked off, so we were going to have to go the rest of the way on foot. And to be allowed through, I'd need media credentials, which I had. But if I wanted to broadcast, it was time to call Bob Oswell. I picked up Orly's satellite phone and turned it over and over in my hands. My mind raced as the truck came to a stop. Bob would get me on the air. Of course he would. Regardless of my current status in the hearts and minds of the American public. Like Sebastian had said, there wasn't a national-caliber reporter anywhere in the world closer to this story than I was.

Except for one.

"You should do it."

He did a double take as he turned off the ignition.

"What are you talking about?"

"This isn't what I do, Sebastian."

"It can be. You've covered breaking news before."

I placed my hand on his arm. "Let me rephrase that. This isn't what I *want* to do."

He studied me, and I studied him right back, watching confusion morph into resistance on his face. "No. Why would I do it? No way. That's all so far behind me now—"

"But it doesn't have to be."

He shook his head. "No way, Brynn. That's seriously a different lifetime." He chuckled nervously. "I've been in a lot of therapy to make sure that's the case."

I unbuckled my seat belt and scooted closer to him as a sheriff's deputy began walking toward us. "If you can tell me that there isn't a part of you—maybe even the biggest part—that wants to do it . . . that there isn't already a part of you building the story and delivering the report in your mind . . . then I'll drop it, and I'll do it. No hard feelings. No further questions. But if even the tiniest bit of your hesitation is wrapped up in thinking this is *my* shot?" I shook my head. "Don't hold back for me. I'll be fine. And you can be *the* reporter with *the* story. This cagey old news veteran I know told me these opportunities don't come along very often."

We stared at each other, and the longer the silence continued, the more I hoped against hope that I was right. I was pretty sure I was, but I was also scared that if I was wrong, I'd have to buy him an additional dog. Murrow would never forgive me if I accidentally caused him to go through all that again.

"There's no guarantee they'll put me on the air."

I scoffed. "Whatever! Every argument you used against me applies to you as well. Except even more. Viewers don't hate you like they do me. They just think you were abducted by aliens or something."

The corners of his mouth rose, and I could swear I could see actual fire behind his eyes. Just then the deputy reached the truck and tapped on Sebastian's window. The fire was still in his eyes as he rolled down the window and faced him.

"This road is closed. You're going to have to circle back."

Sebastian took a deep breath and glanced at me one more time before turning back and saying, "I'm a journalist, here to report on the avalanche."

I held up my media credentials for the officer to see. He blinked furiously, looking from my media pass to my face and back again. Admittedly my clearance went a little bit higher than the *Adelaide Gazette*.

"Hang on. You're . . ." He pointed at me, and then recognition registered on his face as he looked back at Sebastian. "And you're . . ." He looked in the back seat, and Orly leaned forward with his hand out for the deputy to shake.

"I'm Orly. You don't know me. But yes. She's Brynn Cornell and he's Sebastian Sudworth."

The officer was still gobsmacked. "What in the world are you doing here?"

"We live in Adelaide Springs." I had said it. I actually said, "We live in Adelaide Springs," though I clearly hadn't been thinking when I said it. I certainly didn't know what I meant by it. I saw Sebastian's eyes dart briefly my way, but otherwise he let it pass.

"You're going to have to go the rest of the way on foot."

Sebastian nodded. "That's fine." We all began stepping out of the truck. Sebastian kept talking with the officer, asking questions, getting details . . . and he didn't record any of it in his Notes app. He was just absorbing it all for later use in his report. And I knew there wasn't anything wrong with the fact that I had to take notes, but I did think it was very cool and sexy that he didn't.

I gestured to Orly that I would be right there, and then I dialed and lifted the satellite phone to my ear.

"Bob Oswell's office. May I help you?"

"Yes, this is Brynn Cornell. I need to speak to Bob."

There was a long pause, and then, "I'm sorry, Ms. Cornell. He's not avail—"

"Okay, listen. I'm standing a hundred yards from an avalanche in Colorado where a group of teenagers is trapped. I know for a fact that Bob's news division is currently showing photos from a 2017 avalanche in Rigopiano, Italy, so they clearly have nothing. If Bob doesn't want to talk to me, that's fine. Will you please just let him know that Sebastian Sudworth, Brynn Cornell, and Orly Hill are about to jerry-rig together a live broadcast, and it's going to the first network to answer my call. He may want to go ahead and reach out to CNN or ABC or CBS to see if he can simulcast their coverage—"

"Brynn! This is Bob. So good to hear from you. Tell me what you need, my darling."

_____ℯ

Over the course of the next ten hours, a total of thirteen teenagers and two adults were pulled to safety, one by one. And based on what Orly was hearing in his earpiece, the entire country was tuning in as, for ten hours, Sebastian Sudworth was the authority on all that was happening.

It was about three hours into the saga when the Adelaide Springs cavalry arrived.

There had been so many lights and sirens and voices that they all blended together, but there was no mistaking the voice of Mrs. Stoddard.

"Set up the tables over there. Cole, you and Laila set up the coffee and soup over near Roland's truck. He's got the generator. Jake, do me a favor and unload the blankets. Who's got the handwarmers? Larry, check in with Larsen and see if his guys need anything."

I was too cold and busy to cry, but I came pretty close when I saw Cole disregard Jo's instructions long enough to army crawl through a couple feet of snow to Sebastian, making sure he was out of Orly's shot, and stuff handwarmers into Sebastian's boots. Never missing a beat, Sebastian reached his hand that wasn't holding the microphone down and patted Cole's head. It was a small gesture that said everything.

We were four hours in when the first of the boys made their way to us. They'd been thoroughly checked out by medical authorities, and hot food was served to them while they waited for their families.

It was around six hours in when the families began arriving, and in addition to hot food and coffee and blankets, each one of them was able to find a shoulder to cry on or a friend to pray with or a hug from Doc Atwater, who I knew from experience gave the best hugs in the world.

I took the chair I was offered, and I jumped up so Orly could sit in it each time he had a moment to breathe, but Sebastian didn't sit down the entire time. When he wasn't live on the air, he was getting quotes from rescuers and the survivors of an avalanche that, by all accounts, should have been deadly. In the end, it was a dramatic, suspenseful, feel-good story of overcoming the odds, and Sebastian had been the constant voice uniting everyone together in their fear and relief.

"Repeating the headlines from the last few minutes here, all thirteen students and their two adult chaperones have been rescued. There are broken bones and cases of hypothermia and frostbite at varying levels, and an immeasurable emotional toll on these young people and their families, but as we reach the end of a night that, as it progressed, seemed to carry with it the dread and promise of fatality, there is a sense of relief and gratitude that also cannot be measured. Wrapping up our live coverage of the Adelaide Gulch avalanche, this has been Sebastian Sudworth, with Orly Hill and Brynn Cornell. Stay tuned for further updates throughout the day."

"We're out." Orly's voice sounded as tired as I felt.

I stood up, letting the blanket little Jake Morissey had brought me during hour three fall into the chair, and began walking toward him. He hadn't moved since Orly said the camera was no longer rolling. He stood there, frozen. Maybe because after ten hours he could no longer feel anything. Maybe because after ten hours he wasn't sure what he was supposed to do next.

"Hey." I unclipped the lapel mic from the collar of his jacket and disconnected it from the receiver clipped onto the waistband of his jeans. I passed it behind me to Orly, who grabbed the equipment from my hand. "You were so good. You were . . . amazing. I just can't get over how good you were."

And I meant it. I had never been prouder to be part of anything in my entire life. I had never been prouder of anyone, or more blown away by the talent a person possessed.

I placed my hands on his cheeks. My hands were cold, but in comparison his face felt like dry ice. So cold it burned. I ran over to my chair and grabbed the blanket, then hurried back and wrapped it around him. I held his hands and rubbed them between mine.

"Are you okay? What do you need? What can I do for you?"

Those were the magic words to bring him back to reality, apparently. His eyes slowly focused on mine, but once they did, they were locked in.

"You could kiss me."

"To warm you up?"

He smirked. "Sure." He looped his arm around my neck and pulled me to him with all the pent-up urgency of the night.

"You included my name at the end," I whispered against him. "That was nice."

He kept his arm around me as we began walking. He pointed past my shoulder. "Ginger Zee from *Good Morning America* is over there."

I pointed behind him. "Dylan Dreyer and Al Roker are over that way."

"It was good of them to finally show up."

Sebastian began helping Orly put his equipment away as the satellite phone rang in my pocket. I pulled it out and then held it up for them to see.

"Hi, Colton." I put him on speaker so they could hear.

"*Now* she answers my call."

"You caught me in a moment of boredom."

He laughed. "Good job tonight."

"Thanks, but I didn't do anything. That was all Sebastian and Orly. You're on speaker, by the way."

"Good. I needed Orly too. We still want you to go live on *Sunup*."

Orly's head fell back. I didn't know how much more the poor guy had in him. No matter how seasoned he was, it had been a while since he'd spent this much time out of a studio. Truthfully, I didn't know how much I had in me either. Sebastian, on the other hand, seemed to have gotten a second wind—it would take a while to extinguish all that adrenaline—but while I had no doubt it had been the right decision to hand off my last assignment to him, this one had to be all me.

"When?" I looked at my watch. Four forty-nine. *Sunup* went live on the East Coast in eleven minutes.

"Top of the hour. Just give a quick rundown of Sebastian's report—"

"I'm not going to do that, Colton. There's plenty of footage from the night."

"Brynn, viewers need to see your face in front of that mountain . . ."

I looked out over the slopes Sebastian and I had sledded down yesterday. The slopes I had spent countless hours on, sledding and skiing and throwing snowballs and building snowmen. At the base of the slopes, about twenty of the most kindhearted people in the world, who had given up the warmth of their homes all night in order to care for strangers—and a couple of their own—were packing up. No one had called them up and thanked them. None of them were going to turn the night into a career opportunity. There weren't millions of viewers gathering around their televisions in anticipation of seeing their faces in front of the mountain.

"I'll be in front of the mountain, but we're not focusing on the avalanche. The plan was for me to apologize, and that's what I'm going to do." Sebastian grabbed my hand that wasn't holding the phone, and I squeezed it as tightly as my frozen fingers would allow.

Colton was quiet for a moment as he no doubt moved the chess pieces around in his mind. "Okay. And then I want you back on the couch with Mark on Monday."

Sebastian smiled at me. Proudly. Sadly.

Orly gestured with his thumb that he was heading back over to reconnect everything he had just disconnected. Sebastian quietly asked if he could do anything to help him, but not quietly enough.

"Is that Sebastian I hear in the background?" Colton asked.

Sebastian grimaced. "Hey, Colton."

"I hope you know every news division in the country is going to be blowing up your phone . . . once anyone finds your number. Broadcast journalism is better when you're a part of it. That's all there is to it. I'm not in a position right now to offer you anything specific, but if you have time for lunch in the next—"

"Colton, I'm going to have to stop you there. I'm flattered, and I appreciate you guys letting me on your airwaves today. I had no idea how much I'd missed it." I looked up—proudly and sadly—and studied him as the next words came out of his mouth. "But I'm not going anywhere. Keep on being one of the good guys, and you'll be the first one I call if that changes."

"I can't ask for more than that. Thanks. And again, good work. Brynn, are you still on the line?"

"I'm here, Colton."

"I don't suppose you have a monitor for the feed, do you?"

Sebastian rolled his eyes for my benefit, and I perfectly understood what was going through his mind. Thoughts about how nice it would have been to have a monitor as he chatted with broadcasters and authorities from all over the world all night.

"Nope. No monitor. Just an in-ear audio feed."

"That works about half the time," Sebastian muttered.

"Okay. Well, we'll make do. We'll have Mark and Elena on the feed, and we'll be broadcasting whatever Orly can get to us."

"Got it."

"Then call me after."

I took a deep breath. "Colton, I need a nap. I'll call you Monday."

He spoke hesitantly. "Monday you'll be here. Back on the couch."

Here it was. The moment of truth. *Another* moment of truth among more moments of truth than I could keep track of. A career that I'd be a fool to walk away from. A man who would never forgive me if I walked away *for* him, but whom I couldn't imagine walking on without. And an entire town of people who, I finally understood, would love me no matter what I chose to do.

"I need a little more time, Colton. A little more time to figure some things out. I'll call you Monday."

Sebastian's eyes were hidden from me as he looked down and began studying the snow under his boots, but I saw the grin that spread across his lips, and that was all I needed.

Colton sighed. "You're going to be the death of me, Cornell. Just go get on the air."

As soon as Colton was off the line, Sebastian kicked back into on-the-ground action-news reporter mode. "Here." He reached under his coat and disconnected the receiver that was still looped onto him. "Orly, do you have the—" Orly handed him a handful of cords and the mic and receiver I had removed from Sebastian's belt and lapel just a few minutes earlier. "Thanks." He took a moment to straighten and unloop and connect, and then he was two inches in front of me, asking, "May I?"

I had no idea what he was asking permission to do, but the answer was an easy yes.

Sebastian crouched down, and his left hand was suddenly at my midthigh level, skating up my leg under my coat. When his fingers got to my hip, he stood back up, my coat rising with him. The assault of the freezing wind against my legs had little effect as his left wrist rested gently on my waist. He reached his right hand down the back collar of my coat, pressing me against him in the process, and never once pulled his eyes—still only two inches away—from mine as he gently lowered the receiver by its cord, from his right hand to his waiting left, like a bucket in a well. My breath caught as he pulled the waistband of my jeans away from my skin, just enough to slip on the receiver. He then removed his left hand from under my coat, leaving my leg colder with the coverage from the down than it had been while he was touching me, and his left hand joined his right behind my neck to clip the cord onto my collar. Finally, while his left hand slipped the earpiece into my right ear, his right hand cupped my face and he brushed his lips against mine.

"Done," he whispered.

"So that's how the pros do it," I muttered against his lips and tried to remember how to breathe.

"Old trick I picked up from David Muir when we were covering the earthquake in Haiti." He winked and kissed me one more time, then pulled away and shouted over my head. "How much time does she have, Orly?"

"Fifty seconds," he called back.

Sebastian lowered his eyes to meet mine. "You ready?"

I nodded. "I am."

Suddenly his eyes flew open and his hands were a flurry of activity, unzipping his coat and reaching inside. "I totally forgot. You asked me to bring you a hat to borrow." He pulled the curled-up ball cap out of his inner pocket and handed it to me. I stared at him in disbelief as he worked on straightening it out. He held it up and showed me the purple Northwestern logo on the front. "See? To match the hoodie." I kept staring at him until he asked, "What?"

"Are you kidding me, Sudworth? Are you freaking kidding me?"

"Thirty seconds, Brynn," Orly called out.

"We have literally been sitting at the base of an avalanche all night, freezing half to death, and I'm a few seconds away from going live on national television with a frizzy mess that I'm sure Christiane Amanpour and Ronan Farrow are going to be making fun of at CNN poker night—"

"Andy Vandy's going to have a field day."

My eyes flew open. "You call him that too?" My eyes narrowed as his grin widened. "You're making fun of me."

"Do you want the hat or not?"

I stared at him until Orly yelled, a bit more urgently, "Brynn! Ten seconds."

"Fine." I yanked it out of his hands, slipped it on, and pulled my ponytail out the back as I ran over and took my spot. "And to think . . . I was going to say nice things about you."

He laughed and then called out, "Hey, Brynn?" from just behind Orly. I looked up at him as Orly began counting down. "I really do like you. A lot."

"We're live in five, four . . ." Orly's fingers took over the count.

A camera-ready smile took over my face as I reunited with the *Sunup* fam, and for the first time, I wasn't faking a thing.

BRYNN

MONDAY, MARCH 25
Two years later
8:55 a.m. Eastern Daylight Time

"Coming in the third hour of *Sunup*, Hayley will be telling you where you can get your hands on pocketbook-friendly versions of the fashions that took Madison Avenue by storm at last year's Fashion Week."

"That's right, Mark. And Lance is going to be cooking up some delicious delicacies with Chef Xavier Stone, who I hear may be willing to spill a couple of details about the upcoming season of *America's Fiercest Chef.*"

"Ooh, I hope so, Elena," Mark chimed in. "That's one of my favorites. By the end of each episode, I just about have Bunny convinced she should let me back into the kitchen."

Elena laughed and imploringly gazed into the camera. "Don't do it, Bunny!" Mark elbowed her gently as she comically rubbed her jaw. "My teeth haven't recovered from those last bricks he brought to work."

"Those were pralines, thank you very much."

I chuckled at their banter as I stood next to camera one in the *Sunup3* studio and watched them on the monitor. It was sickening, of course, but Mark and Elena actually made a decent team. Besides, even the stiff, scripted dialogue of yesteryear couldn't burst my bubble today.

"And, of course, you'll want to stick around for Brynn's exclusive *Sunup3* interview with legendary international reporter Sebastian Sudworth."

"'Legendary.'" Chills ran down my spine as I felt his breath against my ear. "Do you hear that, Ms. Cornell? I'm legendary. Are you sure you're up for the task? It's not every day one interviews a legend."

I spun around and faced him and even managed to keep my hands to myself like the professional broadcaster I was.

"Eh. Last week was Disney Channel reunion week, and I interviewed the casts of *That's So Raven* and *Lizzie McGuire*. I'm pretty used to it."

He was smiling at me, but he was also fidgeting with his tie and looking around for a mirror. "Is this thing even straight? I'd pretty much forgotten how to tie a tie."

I fiddled with the knot and straightened it. Or at least I pretended to. It was already perfect, but who was I to pass up an opportunity to indulge in a little workplace-appropriate PDA?

"You're not nervous, are you?"

"Of course not." He looked over my head at the monitor. "Why is Mark Irvine holding up a framed picture of me?"

"He brought it from home." His eyes flashed to me, unamused, and I winked. "Why do you think? They've been promoting this for weeks. It's sort of a big deal that we got the exclusive with you. Ratings are going to be through the roof."

Truth be told, for the past twenty-two months, we hadn't even been able to figure out where the roof was. We just kept climbing. After a couple more weeks in Adelaide Springs, I'd ended up back in New York, but only after all parties had agreed that Elena would stay teamed up with Mark on the *Sunup* couch, and I'd move back to *Sunup3* in the top position. Robyn had actually been the most skeptical. But once I was able to convince her that I wasn't incinerating my career—and her flawless reputation by extension—with a Molotov cocktail of panic, homesickness, and infatuation, she had handled all the negotiations for me like the superstar agent she was. As it turned out, Hayley Oswell and I were a match made in morning-television heaven. Even Lance seemed to like us, most of the time. Things only got better from there. I'd told the whole ugly truth about my upbringing and my convoluted path to contentment in my memoir, *Not All Sunshine, After All*, and for whatever reason, people seemed to like me more after that. Maybe it was like that cross-stitched pillow at Maxine's house said, "The only thing people appreciate more than honesty is someone mowing their lawn for them."

Or so Cole claimed. I'd yet to see that one for myself.

"Are you actually straightening my tie or just looking for an excuse to manhandle me?"

I looked up at him and batted my eyelashes. "Can't a girl multitask?"

He smirked and shook his head, then pulled away as my hands released him.

"Hey, Sebastian," Hayley greeted him as she passed on her way to the stage. "Sure you're up for this? Brynn made Meryl Streep cry last week, you know."

I shrugged dismissively. "Meryl was just showing off. You'll be fine."

He was still fidgeting. Once I'd gotten back to the land of decent internet, I'd watched the man escape crumbling buildings in Beirut and dodge drug cartel gunfire in Mexico without batting an eye. Apparently sitting on a couch wearing a Hugo Boss tie was going to be his undoing.

"You're actually freaked out about this, aren't you?" I crossed my arms and cocked my hip against a column. "Maybe you should have brought Murrow."

"He's with a production assistant in the greenroom."

I stood up straight and grabbed his arm. "I was joking! I didn't know you were actually worried. Seb, seriously . . . are you okay?"

He studied me and then started laughing. "I just didn't want to leave him alone at the hotel. I'm fine."

I released the breath I'd begun holding just as Sheila, our executive producer, called my name. "Brynn, we're on you and Hayley in sixty seconds."

I nodded my acknowledgment and then looked back to Sebastian. "You look fantastic, by the way." It was my first time seeing him in a suit, live and in person, and it had pretty much the exact same effect on me as seeing him in a Foo Fighters tee. There was no ball cap today, of course, and while he'd been sure to get a haircut, there was only so much he could do to tame those delicious curls. "Hayley and I've got about four minutes of chat, and then I'll see you over there after the first break."

I spun on my Louboutin heel and began walking away, but spun back when he said, "Brynn?"

"Yeah?"

"Don't forget, we agreed . . ."

I nodded. "I know. Hardball."

"I mean it. No question is off-limits. Don't feel like you have to take it easy on me."

I quirked an eyebrow and smiled. "Sebastian Sudworth, when have I *ever* taken it easy on you?"

—————— e

"Now, joining us in a *Sunup3* exclusive, celebrated international journalist Sebastian Sudworth. His revelatory coverage of the genocide in Myanmar was aired for the first time three months ago, but until now he's not spoken publicly about the atrocities he witnessed. We're going to touch on that and more, and of course you can read the entire story for yourself in his firsthand account of what he saw and what he learned—in Myanmar and throughout the world. *Conscience: Fair Reporting in an Unfair World* debuted last week as an instant *New York Times* bestseller, and his groundbreaking podcast of the same name is currently topping all current-affairs podcast charts. Sebastian, welcome."

"Thanks for having me, Brynn."

"From the sound of things, you've been very busy lately."

"You could say that."

"And on top of all of that, I understand congratulations are in order. Rumor has it you recently got engaged."

He shifted on the couch as the crew began laughing behind the cameras. "Yes, that's true."

"Tell us a little about your fiancée, if you would."

He took a deep breath and rolled his eyes so subtly I knew no one else could see. Then he glanced at the prompter, but of course nothing was there. It was a new day at *Sunup3*. "Well, she's wonderful, of course, and we're very happy."

"And we're all so happy for you." I folded my legs as Kate Middleton had taught me and leaned forward, resting my forearms on my thighs. "You love her a lot?"

His lips twitched and he said, "Of course I do. In fact, until about thirty seconds ago, I was convinced she was the best thing that ever happened to me."

"When's the wedding?"

He chuckled nervously and looked offstage to Hayley, probably hoping she would step in and give him the interview he had expected. She just grinned and shrugged. *Good girl.*

"Well, um . . ." He started fidgeting with his tie again. "Are you sure you don't want to talk about the book?"

"Oh, we'll get to that."

"Okay . . . um . . . Well, we haven't set a date yet . . ."

"And where will the wedding be held?"

"I . . . um . . . I guess we haven't decided that yet either."

"You should have it right here on *Sunup3*!" I turned emphatically to the camera. "Wouldn't that be amazing, fam?"

Sebastian shook his head. "No way. We're not doing that."

I pouted a little, causing the crew to laugh again. "It was just an idea. It doesn't sound like you've given it much thought yet, so—"

"Are you kidding? There aren't many minutes of the day when I'm not thinking about marrying her."

I sat up straight. "Really?"

He rolled his eyes again, and this time everyone in America was probably able to see it. "Yes, Brynn. Really. It's going to be in her hometown, of course, because that's where we met, and we plan to keep a house there so we can visit all the time. Besides, she's told me at least thirty times now that she wants to get married in early September in the mountains, just as the trees are changing color. Of course we're going to have to plan around Township Days, because her freakish creativity combined with my freakish ability to make things happen turned this stupid little festival into a cultural phenomenon. But we'll figure it out. We always manage to. Now, considering my ring is on your finger and our engagement photos were in *People* magazine, can we please stop acting like we're fooling anyone and just talk about the book?" He pulled down on his suit jacket as a simultaneously annoyed and enamored smirk overtook his lips. "For the record, this isn't what I meant by hardball."

"Well, you did say no questions were off-limits. And we at *Sunup3* are the people who gave up-to-the-minute election results from the deck of Rihanna's yacht. I don't know what you expected here . . ."

He nodded. "That is true. I have only myself to blame."

A giggle escaped, then I adjusted my position to look at camera three, where the red light was definitely on.

"If you're just joining us, I'm Brynn Cornell, and I'm madly in love with my guest today, Sebastian Sudworth. Much, *much* more to come, after this."

ACKNOWLEDGMENTS

Kelly Turner, thanks for still being my favorite after all these years. And thanks for letting me steal "Andy Vandy." You get all the credit on that one. Sorry "Throwback Thursday" was stolen from you. Ethan and Noah, I'm so glad I'm your mom. Mom and Dad, I'm really glad you're my parents. Missy, I really wish you'd read my books. (And I guess I'm glad we're sisters. Whatever. I'd probably be gladder if you read my books.)

I am so blessed to get to work with some of the best humans in publishing—Amanda Bostic, Kimberly Carlton, Leslie Peterson, Kerri Potts, Savannah Summers, and Margaret Kercher, just to name a few. I'm grateful for the geniuses I get to work with now, as well as those who had so much impact along the way. Thank you, Kelsey Bowen, Jocelyn Bailey, and Jessica Kirkland!

Laura Wheeler, I adore you. I will forever cling to the reminder you sent me when I was in the throes of deadline panic and struggling with this book and suggesting a new title (I HATE BRYNN AND SEBASTIAN AND THEY HATE ME, SO WHO CARES IF THEY HATE EACH OTHER OR NOT?!) and threatening to run away from home. You reminded me that I'd felt much the same panic as I rewrote *The Do-Over*, and that was exactly what I needed. (Well, that and all of your brilliant edits and suggestions.) Thank you for wrangling the insanity and believing in me when I can't see any reason why you should.

A special thank you to my future bestie, Jenna Bush Hager. I just know that the only thing standing between where we are now and the deep, meaningful, lifelong friendship we could have is the fact that we haven't met yet.

Same goes for you, Colin Firth, but you are, admittedly, a handsome dude, and I'm a happily married woman, so maybe our friendship should be more of a pen pal sort of thing. Just to keep it all on the up and up.

If there is any wisdom at all to be found in the pages of this book, it probably stems from a lesson I learned from you, David Ramsey. In a few cases, I stole lines directly from you. No one outside of my editorial team helped me unpack and develop Brynn and Seb more than you did.

There are a few people who, honestly, didn't particularly contribute to the writing or publishing of this book. (Okay, truth be told, there are *a lot* of people who didn't. Like, oh . . . I don't know . . . Sarah Jessica Parker. You didn't do squat. What's up with that?) But there are people who are represented in every word I ever write, because their friendship makes me who I am. Thank you, LeeAnn, Jenny, Tonya, Anne, Caitlyn, Sharon, and Laura. You do immeasurably more for me than that deadbeat SJP.

Thank you, Jesus, my Lord and Savior, for loving me so much that you willingly accepted the punishment I deserved. And thank you for not letting death be the end of the story.

Readers . . . I love you. Thank you for the messages you send and the reviews you post and the gorgeous pictures you share and for giving me a reason to write. Text me sometime at (970) 387-7811. I look forward to getting to know you better!

And just in case superstardom strikes and my dad gets to keep the dedication in the front of the book, I need to go ahead and thank Paul Rudd. Particularly Paul Rudd with unruly hair and glasses, holding a little dog. And in case the book's a flop, I'm still glad you pushed for a dog, Dad. You were right, and I'm grateful. But consider this the end of it. I seriously don't ever want to hear about it again.

DISCUSSION QUESTIONS

1. Though Brynn's foot-in-mouth moment was more public than most, many of us have been there. Was there a time you got caught saying or doing something you'd meant to keep private?
2. Brynn is known as America's Ray of Sunshine, until she reveals just how snarky she can be. Can you name some celebrities who you perceive to be genuinely nice people?
3. Brynn, Laila, Cole, Addie, and Wes were extremely close all through school. Did you have a group of friends like that? If so, have you stayed in touch?
4. Brynn, Sebastian, and Orly discuss movies as inspiration for their respective careers. What led you to take the career path you chose?
5. Who was your favorite resident of Adelaide Springs? Why? Who was your least favorite? Why?
6. Parental relationships play a big role in the story. What negative traits do Brynn and Sebastian each carry into adulthood as a result of their respective parents' influence?
7. In spite of the trauma of those parental relationships, can

you see ways in which Brynn and Sebastian eventually turned the pain into something positive?

8. Sebastian is most attracted to Brynn when he senses she's being authentic. What is it about Sebastian that Brynn ultimately finds attractive?

9. Laila tells Sebastian that she and Cole love each other "just the right amount." Do you think they'll ever leave the Platonic Principality?

10. Do you have a go-to karaoke song? If not, why not?!

DON'T MISS THESE CLEVER AND SWEET ROMANCES BY BETHANY TURNER!

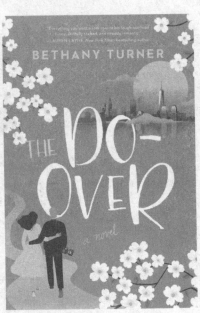

AVAILABLE IN PRINT, E-BOOK, AND DOWNLOADABLE AUDIO

ABOUT THE AUTHOR

Bethany Turner has been writing since the second grade, when she won her first writing award for explaining why, if she could have lunch with any person throughout history, she would choose John Stamos. She stands by this decision. Bethany now writes pop culture–infused rom-coms for a new generation of readers who crave fiction that tackles the thorny issues of life with humor and insight. She lives in Southwest Colorado with her husband, whom she met in the nineties in a chat room called Disco Inferno. As sketchy as it sounds, it worked out pretty well in this case, and they are now the proud parents of two sons. Connect with Bethany at bethanyturnerbooks. com or across social media @seebethanywrite, where she clings to the eternal dream that John Stamos will someday send her a friend request. You can also text her at +1 (970) 387-7811. Texting with readers is her favorite.

———— e

bethanyturnerbooks.com
Instagram: @seebethanywrite
Facebook: @seebethanywrite